RELENTLESS
PURSUIT

RELENTLESS PURSUIT

PETER BORCHARD

iUniverse, Inc.
Bloomington

RELENTLESS PURSUIT

iUniverse books may be ordered through booksellers or by contacting:

iUniverse
1663 Liberty Drive
Bloomington, IN 47403
www.iuniverse.com
1-800-Authors (1-800-288-4677)

ISBN: 978-1-4620-3445-1 (sc)
ISBN: 978-1-4620-3446-8 (ebk)

Printed in the United States of America

iUniverse rev. date: 07/15/2011

DEDICATION

This book is dedicated to my wife Elaine, and to my Editor, Jenny Crickmore-Thompson. Without their support, this novel would have remained a dream.

I would also like to give special thanks to my Agent, Ronald Payne, and Brenda Wise-Consulting Agent.

CHAPTER ONE

The young officer leaned back against the doorjamb of the bridge, bracing himself against the continuous motion as the ship thrust her bow into the southwesterly swells. The storm had dissipated during the early hours of the morning, and now it was nearly dead calm. The only movement of air was the slight breeze he felt on his face generated by the ship's forward motion. Each incoming wave heralded a brief tremor through the steel deck plates underfoot, accompanied by a magnified throb of the ship's engine as she strained to lift her bow over the top of each huge wave and slide into the following trough.

Black coal smoke boiled from the tall yellow funnel painted with bands of black, white, and red, the national colours of Imperial Germany. Below the rings a huge insignia emblazoned on the funnel proudly proclaimed her lineage – she was a ship of the German East Africa Line, built primarily to serve the recently annexed colonies—Cameroon, Togoland, German South West Africa, and Tanganyika. Imperial Germany had scrambled to acquire colonies; she too was now a member of the European empire club.

The *SS Tanga* slipped into the first clammy wisps of a seemingly endless fog bank that stretched across the ocean, a legacy of the previous night's storm. Visibility had been reduced to a few yards, and the captain was forced to order a reduction in speed.

The foghorn blast startled the young officer out of his reverie, its low rumbling sound reverberating through the ship as its warning boomed out into the mist. Soon, cold damp tendrils of water vapour enveloped him, and the bridge railings and deck dripped with condensation. He strained to catch the sound of breaking waves, the distant boom of surf that was the first warning that the ship veered too close to the treacherous shore

"*Herr Leutnant,*" the captain said to the young man, who had been his companion for the past four weeks on the long sea voyage, "I'm afraid this damn pea soup will delay us. This coast is dangerous and more so in this fog. We are only hours away from Swakopmund, but if this doesn't lift, well . . . we'll have to heave to and wait it out. I'm sorry, I know you are looking forward to stepping ashore today."

The lieutenant chuckled softly, more in despair than amusement.

"We'll wait, *Herr Käpitan,* what else can I do? A few more days won't make any difference," he said. "God, I feel like the Flying Dutchman, cursed to stay on this ship forever."

Oberleutnant Werner von Dewitz was a career officer. Born in 1874 in Kiel, Germany, the son of a general in the Imperial German army, there had never been a choice for him. He came from a long line of military men, and family tradition set the rules; he would assume his father's role. As attaché to the Imperial Consular Services, his father's postings had taken the family to England and Portugal, and Werner spoke both English and Portuguese fluently.

Two months ago, he had been transferred to the *Abwehr Abteilung*, the German military intelligence, and from there sent to join the *Schutztruppe*, a marine division assigned the task of protecting the German colonies. On his arrival in the colony, he was to report to a Major Zietzmann, the officer who headed up the *Abwehr Abteilung* in German South West Africa. He now wore his new blue-grey *Schutztruppe* uniform, but his shoulder boards, the black base with the four silver cords and the star signifying his rank, were still from his previous regiment, immediately revealing his actual military origins. Not that it mattered; transfers were not unusual.

Still in his late twenties, he was tall, six foot two, his light brown hair cut short in typical Prussian fashion, his chiselled facial features pale from too little sun. Although hidden in a bulky winter uniform, it was evident that his body was lean and hard. He had shaved early that morning, but his cheeks and chin still revealed a faint shadow. Most officers sported moustaches, trying to emulate the Kaiser, some taking this to ludicrous extremes and sporting waxed, twirled and pointed ends. Werner was an exception, preferring his upper lip bare. Piercing steel grey eyes flecked with tiny specks of silver indicated a stubborn masculine strength; women found him attractive.

At the ring of the ship's telegraph, he turned to look at the huge dial atop a polished brass pedestal bolted to the bridge deck. The needle now pointed nearly straight down, reading "Dead Slow". The ship was beginning to wallow in the swells, barely making headway.

"I was going to skip breakfast but now that we seem to be wallowing in the doldrums," he said, bored. "I think I'll get myself something to eat. I'll be back later." He flicked a half-smoked cigarette over the bridge wing railing.

The captain nodded and resumed his vigil.

Werner entered the small dining saloon. Most of the other passengers had yet to make an appearance, but a young woman stood at the sideboard. He frowned. Miss Eggers confused him. She was exceptionally beautiful, and he had hoped for a brief romantic interlude over the four week voyage. However, she had kept to herself and except for the occasional polite greeting; they had said little to one another. Clearly, she was not one drawn easily into conversation. While it could not be said that she rebuffed him, it was clear that she chose not to mix, meting out the same treatment to all twenty passengers aboard.

She was seated at the captain's table every evening. To Werner's chagrin, the captain insisted that he, as an officer, should host another table. While his fellow diners were pleasant, none was a beautiful single young woman!

However, the captain willingly volunteered such snippets of information as he had garnered. Were he the lieutenant, well . . . he too would have had more than a casual interest.

Dorothea Eggers was returning home, after having recently qualified in Germany. She was a doctor, which was a surprise; in the face of overwhelming male prejudice, very few women chose to be medical doctors in this male-dominated profession; truly, a resilient woman, Werner thought. The ship's captain had once remarked that you could count the total female medical doctor population of Germany on two hands!

She stood now, helping herself to a roll and cold meats. The breakfast served was typically continental—croissants and rolls, cold meats, pickled herring and cheese.

He looked at her in the mirror above the buffet. Her auburn hair, which cascaded to her shoulders, surrounded her face, emphasizing her high cheekbones and full mouth. It was her eyes though which he thought her most attractive feature – these were a startling light blue, and when she looked at him, he invariably felt a twinge of unease; it was though she saw right through him. She too was tall. Although she wore a long skirt and a blouse buttoned to the neck, there was no mistaking her narrow waist and well-proportioned body.

"Good morning," he said, giving her a friendly smile, lowering his head in the customary bow.

She acknowledged his greeting but then ignored him.

"Well, Fraulein Eggers," he said still smiling, attempting to draw her into conversation, "We're nearly there."

"Yes," she replied, not turning around to look at him, her voice devoid of any encouragement for further conversation.

"Are there people waiting for you in Swakopmund?" he persevered.

"No. I'm leaving for Windhuk by train."

"Ah, then maybe we'll be travelling together again."

"Really, how interesting." She indicated that she had heard him, but ventured no further information.

Impossible woman, he thought, realizing that if he persisted he would make a fool of himself.

They took their places at separate tables, and ate in silence.

The engine revolutions increased slightly; the ship was underway again. Through the saloon windows, Werner saw the mist was clearing, shafts of bright sunlight already stabbing through the fog.

"It would seem that we are lucky to-day."

She smiled slightly.

He returned to the bridge.

Swakopmund was no more than a small cluster of buildings interrupting the flat, bare coastal desert expanse and dominated by a high lighthouse and watch-tower. These structures stood stark against the forlorn pale background and the scattering of high-roofed two storey buildings that made up the town. A huge half-constructed jetty penetrated a half mile into the incoming waves, its seaward end a hive of activity, pile-driving machinery and cranes precariously perched on a lattice work of girders, steam engines belching smoke.

South of the town, he spotted the mouth of the Swakop River; this, he knew, silted up, creating a barrier to the sea. In the riverbed he could see the first signs of vegetation, interspersed with swathes of tall reeds. Beyond the river was a sea of sand dunes. The river formed a barrier against the encroaching sand: from the riverbank, the dunes stretched southwards as far as the eye could see, their advance ending abruptly at the water's edge.

Swakopmund was a typical colonial boomtown. Of its few hotels, the two-storey Bismarck Hotel was the most prominent, built on a bluff overlooking the coast. The beaches were pristine, shimmering white in the sun that had broken through the mist, assaulted by the huge waves that continuously crested and tumbled into a cauldron of white foam. There seemed to be no trees at all.

As ordered, he reported to the officer in command of the transit barracks, receiving his orders and a rail ticket for the train leaving that evening for Windhuk, the capital and hub of the colony, about three hundred miles east. The building was complete with a typical barracks gateway, an arched entrance with boom and guardhouse, manned by two marines with bayoneted rifles. The outermost walls of the buildings even had ornamental medieval embattlements, not for the purposes of war but rather as décor. Here in the desert, he thought it resembled a fort plucked from a Beau Geste novel.

It would be a slow journey, the coaches swaying from side to side, the fine dust of the Namib Desert penetrating everywhere. The narrow-gauge train contained only three passenger coaches, the remainder of its length being taken up by box and flat bed rail cars loaded with imported supplies and war material.

The local Imperial forces were waging a civil war against the Namas and the Ovahereros, indigenous tribes refusing to submit to German rule. Farmers had been forced to abandon their cattle ranches and seek shelter in the local towns where detachments of imperial troops were garrisoned, so creating safe havens. Despite this precaution, more than a hundred German farmers and their families had perished already in the conflict, murdered by marauding tribesmen using guerrilla hit-and-run tactics and armed with modern rifles and the knowledge to use them.

The train departed Swakopmund during the late afternoon; most of the passengers were imperial marines with only a few civilians. Werner saw Dorothea Eggers on the station platform and waved. She acknowledged his greeting stiffly.

At the station cafeteria, he purchased two large bread rolls, sliced down the middle and stuffed with ample portions of sliced smoked sausage and pickle. A hawker sold beer. The packaging was ingenious, packed in bags with wet straw to both protect and cool the contents. He bought a bag. These bags were hanging in all the compartments, and once the train departed, they swayed violently with the train's motion, the movement through the air assisting evaporation, keeping the beer surprisingly cold.

He retired to his compartment for the evening, hanging his own bag of beer from a coat hook. Once the train left the coast, its speed matched the speed of the sea breeze, there little movement of air. It became stifling hot. The locomotive initially struggled, no faster than a fast run, straining to pull the coaches and wagons up the slight incline that led to the hinterland. Soon, however, belching smoke and steam, the train chugged its way through a flat desert landscape, the ground bare, completely devoid of any vegetation. A thin film of dust now covered everything. In the distance he could see the odd outcrop of rock, while far on the eastern horizon, a small range of mountains jutted into the sky, its peaked slopes now tinged orange by the setting sun. To the south, the ground slowly sloped down towards the dry Swakop River, a few miles away. It flowed east to west, parallel to the railway line. Only during exceptionally wet years did the river flood, the water breaking through to the desert, a raging quarter-mile wide torrent that occasionally overflowed its banks, discharging silt, bloated animal carcasses, and uprooted trees into the sea.

Werner never left his compartment, other than to relieve himself. He ate the rolls, washing these down with the refreshing cold beer. A black bedding boy appeared to prepare his bunk and at about ten that evening, he retired. He removed his tunic and boots, undid his shirt and sprawled out on top of the bedding; it was far too hot for blankets. He sighed; thankful he had the compartment to himself. The soldiers and NCOs who made up the bulk of the other passengers were not so lucky. They shared, four men to a compartment.

One moment he was asleep, the next violently flung from his bunk, crashing into the opposite wall. Fortunately, the opposite middle bunk had not been raised, and its padded backrest absorbed his momentum. As his head hit the wall a stunning blow, there was an enormous crash followed by ear-splitting grinding and shattering sounds. The carriage was no longer on its rails. It vibrated violently as its wheels cut through the sleepers, still borne forward by its own momentum. With a screech of tearing metal and a splintering of wood, the carriage eventually stopped, leaning over precariously.

Stunned and blinded by the enveloping dust, Werner lay on the floor for a few seconds. Most of the light-bulbs had been shattered by the impact: the dark left him disorientated. He gingerly felt his forehead. An enormous swelling threatened, but little skin seemed to be broken and there was only a touch of wetness, he thought.

Then amid the shouts and cries for help, he suddenly heard rifle shots.

Christ, he thought, it's an ambush!

He groped in the dark for his tunic and boots and struggled into these, the riding boots requiring enormous effort in the darkness and confined space.

The sliding door of the compartment refused to open, the distortion to the frame jamming it shut. He kicked out the jagged pieces of the shattered windows, climbed over the sill, and cautiously lowered himself to the ground. Pandemonium reigned. Shots were ringing out in the darkness, bullets ricocheting off the coach.

A sergeant stood next to the wrecked train, bellowing at his men climbing and crawling from the wreckage. He marvelled at the sergeant's tenacity; even in this initial atmosphere of chaos, the NCO still would not overlook a shocked and disorientated soldier who clambered from the wreckage without his rifle.

"Get back and find it!" he bellowed.

"Help!" Werner heard a muffled female voice call.

Miss Eggers! He fought his way towards the front of the shattered coaches, peering into the broken windows, calling her name. The half-toppled coach towered over him, and he expected that at any moment it would crash down on him. It was pitch dark inside.

Faintly he heard movement from within a compartment.

"Miss Eggers? Are you all right?" he asked loudly.

"I think so, but I can't get up. Ugh! There's something heavy on top of me."

Using the butt of his automatic, he smashed the remaining shards of glass and heaved himself carefully over the sill, still afraid that the coach could topple over. She too had been catapulted from her bunk, but the force of the violent impact had broken the bunk from the wall, and it was now lying across her, pinning her to the floor. He grabbed hold of the bunk and with a Herculean effort lifted it slightly. She wormed her way from under it.

"You're not injured, are you?"

"No, I don't think so . . . just shocked and bruised."

"You're going to have to climb through the window. I'll help you down," he said, grabbing her arm, assisting her to her feet amid the shambles of the partially destroyed compartment.

"No, wait! I need my gown and bag; I'm still in my night clothes."

He could see her vaguely in the dark, rummaging in the wreckage of the compartment.

"I can't find my bag!" she said exasperatedly, pulling her gown over her head.

"What bag is this? For God's sake, leave it! We'll look for it later."

"It's my medical bag!" she insisted.

Of course, she was a doctor. She would need her bag.

He joined her on all fours to scrabble for both her shoes and medical bag.

Out of the window with her beside him, he looked around, trying to get his bearings. The NCO had taken command of the situation, and the hapless soldiers were now organized, with those uninjured establishing a defence perimeter around the wrecked train. He could hear only sporadic shooting now.

"*Sanitär!*"

"I'm going to help," she said, alerted by the call for medical attention. In the faint light of the approaching dawn, he saw that she had sustained a few scratches and a nasty cut to her forehead, which she kept dabbing. It was pointless trying to stop her; she was resolute. She grabbed her bag and rushed off to where the shout for medical help had come, her gown trailing in the dust.

Werner scrambled down an embankment to where the soldiers lay prone on the ground, their rifles at the ready. The shooting had subsided.

A *Feldwebel* who stood behind the prone soldiers threw him a salute.

"*Herr Leutnant*, I think they are withdrawing. If they intended to wreck the train, well . . . they've managed that, the damned thing is completely wrecked!" the sergeant said, gesturing towards the train. Most of the coaches had toppled over.

"Sergeant, how are your men?" Werner enquired.

"Fortunately, only two are in a bad way. The others have only minor injuries. I regret to tell you that one civilian was killed and another wounded by enemy fire. The engineer and fireman are OK. They jumped when they saw the destroyed rail track, realizing they could not stop the train. The engineer either broke or sprained his foot, I'm not sure which," the *Feldwebel* replied.

"Where is your captain?"

"On the other side of the train, *Herr Leutnant*," the sergeant indicated with an outstretched arm.

As happens only in the tropics, the faint pre-dawn light rapidly brightened, and the vast expanse of the surrounding landscape was soon visible. He realized they were still in the desert, but this was no longer barren, it was now interspersed with scrub and patches of thin desert grass. The sergeant remarked that they were near Usakos, a small town on the fringes of the desert, which served as a rail junction.

"No more than a settlement, sir," the sergeant added. The mountains, which encircled the town, were visible in the distance.

Dry gullies and small wadis criss-crossed the surrounding area and on the banks, small flat-topped thorn trees grew, none taller than a man. The rare rains on the fringe of the desert were just sufficient to enable these hardy trees and bushes to survive the arid climate. Obviously the guerrillas had taken cover in these dried gullies and concentrated their fire on the train from these. A small band of men, he thought—their objective appeared to be not to engage the troopers, but to destroy the train. They obviously harboured a deep respect for imperial tactics and firepower. Before the *Schutztruppe* could undertake any retaliatory action, they had melted into the desert again, a classic guerrilla warfare manoeuvre.

Werner and the sergeant picked their way through the wreckage to the front of the train. The forward section of the train had jumped the narrow track, which was buckled and distorted from the explosion. A number of shattered boxcars and flatbed rail trucks lay on their sides, their cargo scattered over the ground. The locomotive also lay on its side, severely damaged; probably irreparably, Werner thought. The boiler appeared to be still intact, hissing steam into the dawn morning sky.

He found the Captain and the train engineer inspecting the wreckage.

"What a mess," the captain said. "We've attached a portable telegraph to the overhead lines alongside the rail track, but it seems the rebels have cut the lines. We're not able to contact either Swakopmund or Usakos. But it's not too bad. When we don't arrive and they don't hear from us—you know, no telegraph contact—they'll send the *Draisine* from Usakos."

"What are those?" Werner asked.

"Hand-operated trolleys; they're slow so it will take a while."

The *Feldwebel* seemed to have a better grasp of the situation than his optimistic Captain, and politely interjected.

"Sir, I better get the men started on finding the train's water bottles and anything edible. We might be here for a day or two. They'll have to send coaches from either Windhuk or Swakopmund."

"Excellent idea, do that," the captain responded heartily.

"You'll appreciate that I've only just arrived from Germany, but should you require my assistance, I'm here at your command," Werner said politely.

The train guard pushed over to join them, not in the least intimidated by the officers.

"I've had this happen before. I have cable to repair the telegraph lines. These swine are always cutting the telegraph lines. You'll probably find that these were cut only a few miles from here. If we only had horses . . ." the guard ventured.

By ten o'clock, no help had arrived. The blistering heat of the mid-morning sun forced all to seek shade. The soldiers kept a constant vigil for the guerrillas, but they had vanished.

Suddenly, over a small rise from the direction of Usakos, a column of about twenty horsemen appeared; Imperial *Schutztruppe*, their light-grey uniforms and African campaign hats recognizable even from this distance.

The cavalry column halted, the commander saluting before he dismounted and introduced himself.

"*Rittmeister* von Brandt," he said, bowing his head and clicking his heels. The other officers responded similarly.

"*Herr Hauptmann*," the *Rittmeister* said, addressing the Captain, "We've just come from Usakos. During the night, the guerrillas cut the telegraph lines, and at daybreak we were despatched to repair these. We found the cut about three miles from here and have repaired this. While the two linesmen were up the telegraph poles, they reported smoke in the distance, we decided to investigate and here we find you." He stared at the wrecked train. "As I said, the lines are repaired; you should be able to contact Usakos."

"Thank you, sir."

The train guard scurried off to the rear of the train to set up his equipment and make contact with Usakos.

"I'm Jurgen," The *Rittmeister* said, offering Werner a cigarette, which he gratefully accepted.

"Werner von Dewitz, but by all means, please address me as Werner," he responded, pleased to note the turn from the usual rigid form of address common amongst officers in the Imperial army.

By noon, Werner could see the approaching *Draisines;* four or five trolleys loaded with men, rails, and sleepers, they slowly moved along the track towards the wrecked train. When they got to the break in the line, they stopped and the men immediately started to off-load their equipment, readying themselves for work, taking instructions from the supervisor. Only once he was satisfied that his men knew what to do did the supervisor leave his men and approach the waiting officers.

"Not the first time the guerrillas have mined the track in this region, sir," the supervisor said. "We'll have the line repaired in no time, but the train is a different matter; a salvage crew will need to come from Windhuk. Meanwhile, a locomotive and coaches should have left Usakos by now. You'll soon be on your way."

The train finally got underway in the early hours of the next morning, the *Draisines* coupled to the rear of it, hitching a free ride. The cavalry detachment under the command of *Rittmeister* von Brandt had left the scene of the accident as soon as the replacement train had arrived, in pursuit of the guerrillas they had sworn to track down.

The sun's heat was unrelenting. Fortunately, it was a dry desert heat. Werner remained in his compartment, removing his uniform tunic, only venturing out for short periods. The train was slow but its motion was enough to disturb the dust, which billowed up from beneath the coaches' wheels penetrating everything and adding to the discomfort.

The train eventually left the desert behind, travelling through rolling savannahs occasionally interspersed with thorn trees. As it wound its way further into the hinterland, the savannahs gave way to dense African bush, granting the passengers an occasional glimpse of antelope, baboons, and guinea fowl.

At each stop, hawkers offered a variety of items, including the bags of beer. These were extremely popular, the only cold refreshment available other than fresh water kept in canvas bags. These were not quick stops: the train usually stood for an hour or more, the engineer and his fireman refilling the boiler tanks with water. And, if necessary, taking a meal break. Clearly, the train ran to no fixed timetable: it was on colonial time.

Dorothea Eggers' initial aversion to any form of social interaction with him seemed to have eased, and they exchanged small talk during some of the stops.

"I'm to take up a position with the Finnish Lutheran Mission in the north, close to the Angolan border," she said. She hinted that because the mission desperately needed professional medical assistance in the clinics they had established, the Finns were not opposed to female doctors. It required dedication and above all, an overwhelming desire to help your fellow man in order to serve in these remote outposts. Obviously, she was an altruistic and unusual woman!

Windhuk lay sprawled across the valley, surrounded on all sides by high mountains and hills. The bush and the grass were drab and scorched, the ground burnt to dust by the harsh sun.

The architecture was similar to towns in Germany, and most buildings had familiar steeped roofs. They were widely separated from one another, with large tracts of vacant land in between; no trees, just flat expanses of gravel and sand. The roads were mere gravel strips, and any movement over these resulted in clouds of dust, the mica flakes contained in the soil glittering in the sunlight. Apparently, the rainy season would only start in the next few weeks. Meanwhile everyone had to put up with the choking dust.

The main road, aptly named Kaiserstrasse, had shops fronted by cemented boardwalks and overhead canopies. A horse-drawn tramway plied the gravel street from the Ausspanplatz at the end of town to its opposite terminus close to the railway station. The Ausspanplatz was a specially designated area where all wagons out spanned their oxen, as ox-wagons not allowed in the town. Only horse-drawn carriages were permitted.

Overlooking the town, a previous administrator had built an imposing stucco plastered building resembling a fort. This now housed the German High Command, and military and civilians alike referred to it as the *Alte Feste* – the Old Fort. A strange name to give a fort, Werner thought, this implied the existence of new fort, but where this was, he had no idea.

Werner took his seat opposite Major Zietzmann. The major, resplendent in his tropical marine uniform, was a typical high-ranking German officer; formal, not given to small talk, with a somewhat overbearing attitude towards junior officers.

A huge portrait of Kaiser Wilhelm II stared down from a wall, the emperor in full uniform complete with pickle helmet and tall riding boots. The German Imperial crest, the black eagle with spread wings, adorned the opposite wall.

"Lieutenant," began Zietzmann stiffly, "the Ovahereros are well armed. Mauser rifles; to be precise, K88's, the most common weapon in southern Africa. It was and still is the Boers' favourite rifle. Ask the British, they'll tell you of its accuracy during the Boer War a few years ago. Now large supplies of these weapons, plus explosives and other armaments, are being smuggled in to the Hereros and Namas, and we believe that these emanate from Angola, from the Kunahama tribe."

The major paused, twirling one end of his moustache and contemplating Werner, his face expressionless. The young officer possessed extraordinary qualifications, he thought. But was he about to send him on a suicide mission?

"This is actually a sub-tribe of the Ovahereros that lives in southern Angola, and they often cross our border to get medical attention from the Finnish missions situated up north."

"I've heard of the missions," Werner volunteered.

"Right. Well, Angola seems to be the source of most of these illegal weapons. The Portuguese have very little control," the major said.

"Sir, why do we not ask the British to intervene?" Werner asked.

"The British intervene? You must be joking!" The major gave a dismissive wave of his hand. "The British don't like us. Our emerging German empire concerns them. They proclaimed Bechuanaland a protectorate in order to create a buffer zone between the Boer republics and ourselves, concerned that we would support the Boers during the Boer War. I'm sure you'll recall that at the time, Germany was extremely sympathetic towards the Boers and assisted by exporting arms to the port of Lorenco Marques in Mozambique. These went directly by rail to Pretoria, the capital of the Transvaal Boer Republic. The British have not forgotten." The major paused for a moment, taking a sip from his coffee cup before continuing.

"So, as to your assignment. We want you to infiltrate the gunrunners' operation."

"Good Lord, *Herr Major*, that would be spying!" For a moment, Werner visualized himself facing a Portuguese firing squad or worse still, the noose.

"I know, but we are not at war with Portugal. Even if they found out who you were, the worst that could occur is deportation."

Werner frowned.

"How am I supposed to go about this?"

"You will pretend to be a Portuguese trader from Lorenco Marques, an agent for two German firearm manufacturers. This has already been arranged with these manufacturers and they will verify your bona fides should that ever be necessary."

"How do I get there?"

The major did not immediately reply. He offered Werner a cigar from a humidor. The young officer declined. Meticulously the major prepared his cigar, clipping the end. Only after it was alight, did he continue.

"A German steamer has rounded the Cape of Good Hope en route to Germany from Tanganyika. Fake documents will state that you boarded the vessel in Mozambique. On its return voyage, it docks at both Swakopmund and Benguela. One of our Askaris, who also speaks Portuguese and some German, will accompany you. He is already in Swakopmund, where he will join you aboard."

"Why Benguela and not the Angolan capital, Luanda?"

"Most of the illegal weapons finding their way into Herero hands appear to come through the ports of Benguela and Namibe; these towns are on the southern Angolan coast. Namibe is not really a town; it's a fishing village – just a few huts. Intelligence has established that a Mr. Antonio dos Santos, a local trader and entrepreneur, is the kingpin, the big *commanchero*, if you like. We believe that as a legitimate agent for the *Mauser Waffenfabrik*, you may be able to get close to him."

"*Commanchero*, what's that?" Werner asked.

"Ah yes. The Americans gave that name to gunrunners in their wars against the Red Indians. I believe it's actually Spanish."

Werner realized that intensive planning had already gone into this undercover operation and all options carefully considered. That the relationship between Germany and Portugal was cordial, he knew. The major was right; there seemed to be little danger in what he was about to undertake. He had no doubt that he could play the part well, as his knowledge of the language and Portugal were excellent. In fact, he had a few influential friends in Portugal. The military had probably also considered that aspect. He would be able to drop a few names that would stand him in good stead, should the need arise.

The major handed him a thick red-ribbon-tied folder.

"These are the companies you represent as an agent. Study this in detail and return it to me once you have memorized the information. My aide will assist in providing you with all the civilian kit you will require. The paymaster's office will ensure that you have sufficient funds, and a letter of credit from the Banco Nacionale Ultramarino."

"How do I contact you?"

"Difficult. However, in the file is an address you can use to send a telegram. It will have to go a roundabout route, but that's the best we can do. As I said, you're on your own here."

Werner was aghast at what he read; this was a lucrative business, involving vast sums of money. It was evident that the army had not been able to penetrate the close-knit band of men involved; the only way to proceed was to get to the operation from within. He also realized that if the gunrunners ever blew his cover, his life wouldn't be worth a damn! Good God, he had never volunteered for this! Just because he had the background and language skills, the army believed he could masquerade as a Portuguese trader. Did they not realize that he would continuously be under scrutiny?

He was a firm believer of the old adage; you can bluff some of them some of the time, but not all of them all the time. How long would he be able to get away with this?

CHAPTER TWO

Three days later the ship dropped anchor in Lobito Bay, a natural harbour situated about six miles north of Benguela. The usual barges congregated around the ship to take on the cargo that the ship's derricks swung out over the water and slowly lowered. These also brought cargo from the shore: timber, coffee, sisal, salt, hides, and boxed ivory. The same barges took the two men ashore, the only passengers to disembark.

Werner knew that the town of Benguela had been founded in 1617. It was a typical colonial town, with the distinctive Portuguese architecture similar to that found in Brazil, dominated by the Catholic cathedral. The buildings were set well apart, the streets beautiful, lined with crimson-blossomed acacia trees.

Angola had been engaged in a low-grade civil war for years, with the Portuguese exercising full control only in the towns. A full company of colonial troops was garrisoned in Benguela, commanded by white Portuguese officers and NCOs, and the remainder of the garrison made up of indigenous blacks.

Although slavery had long been abolished and the Portuguese government a signatory to the anti-slavery manifesto, the inhuman practice was still rife; Brazil, which before independence was Portugal's largest and most prosperous colony, still demanded slaves. Tribal headmen selected prime candidates from their own people and handed these over to the slave-traders, using them as human trade goods. Of course, this took place in the utmost secrecy, as the penalty for slave trading was severe.

Philippe soon found a small horse-drawn carriage, which Werner hired on a semi-permanent basis. With Philippe playing the part of the *cavalerico*, the horse boy and servant who trotted alongside on Werner's left, any passer-by would have thought a well-to-do *cavalheiro* had arrived in town, precisely the impression he wished to create.

The hotel was an imposing building with a large balcony on the first floor overlooking the street. The balcony housed an extension to the dining room, its sides open to the outside with green canvas roll-down awnings to protect the interior should it rain. It overlooked the sea, and in the evenings would be a good vantage point to observe the splendour of the setting sun disappearing over the horizon. A slight breeze blew from in the sea, the cool air a refreshing

13

welcome after the hot summer day. The hotel must surely draw a fair clientele during the evenings; a good place to start, Werner decided, especially with a glass of wine or beer.

"Good day, your best room please, and accommodation for my *cavalerico*," he demanded from the Portuguese woman behind the reception counter, assuming the pompous attitude expected from a prosperous businessman from Portugal.

"What time is dinner served?"

"Dinner starts at eight, Senhor. However, maybe Senhor could be a little early and have an *aperitivo* with the other guests? I could introduce Senhor to the others. We also have a few locals coming to dinner. Some are important people."

She bent over the hotel register to read his entry, her low-necked dress displaying her ample cleavage.

"Thank you. That is kind of you. My *cavelherico* . . . ?" Werner prompted.

"Be assured, we will look after him, Senhor. Please ask him to report to the outside kitchen door at the back of the building."

His room was on the top floor. It was full of light, with a high ceiling and large windows, the bed linen snow-white. A servant brought the luggage, which he neatly stacked on the floor. "Would you bathe, Senhor?" he enquired.

Soon a troop of three hotel servants entered carrying large buckets of hot water, who proceeded to fill a large copper bath in an adjoining room. Werner disrobed and stepped into the hot water and lay back, a stein of beer in his hand, feeling rather pleased with himself.

He dressed for dinner with care, so as not to appear too ostentatious. Although his dress was purposely subdued, he exuded the air of a prosperous merchant.

A thunderstorm had passed over during the late afternoon, resulting in a light rain, just sufficient to further cool the air and dampen the dust, releasing that wonderful smell of rain and wet dust experienced only in Africa. He walked down the stairs to the large lounge and adjoining dining room, both flooded with the orange glow of the setting sun. A number of residents and guests were enjoying the customary *aperitivo*.

The hotelkeeper took him by the arm.

"Senhor de Almeida, people tend to be less formal in the colonies. May I introduce you to a few of the guests?" she asked.

She had also changed, and her black gown had an attractive low neckline. In her mid to late thirties, her thick shining black hair tumbled to her shoulders and her fair skin revealed a slight olive tint. Way back in the past her ancestors had crossed the colour line, and she was probably a third or fourth generation *mestiço*. In all probability, her grandfather had been a *degregado*, a criminal from Portugal sent to Angola instead of jail. Often illiterate peasants transported and dumped in the colonies; these men frequently took up with African peasant women. This was the norm, there being ten white men for every white woman in Angola.

She steered him towards two men and a woman, the younger man dressed in the uniform of a captain of the Portuguese colonial forces.

"Excuse me," she said smiling, "I would like to introduce you to our new guest."

The captain's wife, a pretty young woman, softly acknowledged his greeting. Captain de Sousa was a young man in his early thirties. He flashed Werner a friendly grin and shook his hand. The other man was elderly, his hair and goatee beard grey. That he was a man of stature was evident, his bearing and mannerism a giveaway.

"This is his Lordship Senhor Alberto de Mello, the provincial *juiz* for the Benguela district," the hotelier announced with affected deference.

The men exchanged pleasantries and as a bell tinkled, signalling that dinner was about to commence, the judge invited Werner to join them at their table.

Barefoot blacks, immaculate in white tunics and black trousers, the customary red sash from shoulder to waist, served the best of Portuguese cuisine: a fresh shellfish entrée followed by a choice of game or white fish or the finest steaks followed by dessert.

The subject of Lisbon dominated the conversation, as this was the judge's home city. Had Werner never lived in Lisbon, the judge would soon have recognized him for an impostor!

"So what do you hope to sell in this part of the world?" the judge finally enquired.

"Well, I represent several manufacturers and I understand you have a large Boer population here, those who fled from the Transvaal and Free State Boer republics when the British threatened invasion of these. Much of the merchandise I have to offer would stand them in good stead. For instance, I've ploughs and other farming equipment, steel tools and kitchenware, as well as rifles, pistols, ammunition and a host of other items."

"Are you aware that we have clashes with the indigenous tribes from time to time?" the captain interrupted.

"Yes, so I've heard. This seems to be usual in the colonies."

"Of course, I need to remind you that the selling of weapons to the indigenous people carries a severe penalty," Captain de Sousa said quietly.

"I'm well aware of this. You may rest assured that I have no such intentions," Werner replied, hoping he sounded sufficiently convincing. He certainly did not want to find himself under scrutiny by the local authorities.

The judge intervened.

"Take care. There are gunrunners around. Not that they are selling weapons to the locals, but rather they take these across the border, to the blacks who are fighting the Germans. There is a full-scale war in German South West Africa, you know. The Germans are extremely sensitive and believe we are not doing sufficient to halt these gunrunners. This is both mine and our captain's biggest headache."

Judge de Mello looked at both Werner and the captain, waiting for a response.

"His Lordship is right. Gunrunning is extremely lucrative and stopping it is difficult."

"Who are they?" asked Werner.

"Some Portuguese locals. I daresay you'll find out soon enough. Not comprised of the dregs of society, surprisingly: in fact, we believe some members of the elite are involved."

"Gentlemen, let me assure you, I don't deal with gunrunners," Werner assured them.

"Please Senhor de Almeida, if I have been misunderstood, I apologize. I would never have thought that of you. I merely mention it," the captain stated in an apologetic tone, careful not to offend Werner.

The judge did not comment. The table was silent for a while as they ate.

Captain de Sousa put down his knife and fork as if to indicate that he had an important announcement to make. He dabbed his moustache with his napkin and spoke.

"You may not have heard, but we are plagued by a troublesome tribe, the Kunahamas, who control the land in the vicinity of the Kunene River, the border with the German colony to the south. The Kunahamas are very sympathetic to the Hereros, the tribe that is at war with the Germans. In fact, they are really one tribe split by the border. We believe the Kunahamas are ready to start a more intensive campaign of insurrection in our country. Currently I'm awaiting reinforcements from Luanda. Under the circumstances, I would suggest you proceed with caution and should you go inland, avoid going south."

Werner was surprised at the captain's remarks: that the Portuguese proposed to deal with the Kunahamas was excellent news.

"I have no intention of getting embroiled in some uprising. I note your concerns," he replied.

The next day Werner went through the pretensions of being what he was supposed to be. He called on traders, showed them his catalogues and took what orders were forthcoming. He was surprised. The traders showed great interest in his wares, in particular, in the rifles and ammunition, the finest German weapon manufacturers could produce, and competitively priced to boot. He realized that he actually could make a fair living!

A few days later, a coastal steamer from Luanda docked and discharged a detachment of two hundred and fifty men to reinforce the local garrison. Predominantly black soldiers with about fifty professional white cavalrymen, this force was commanded by a Major Olazabal who now assumed command of the total military contingent in the district.

Werner soon realized that the man had never served in the colonies before. It was evident that he lacked experience in both the tropics and the terrain. Major Olazabal was all pomp, tailor-made uniforms, gold braid and feathers, with an attitude that did not permit local advice. Werner hoped the new major would at least take advice from his captain, a man of experience who knew both these parts and the ways of the local population well. Sadly, in all armies, rank often stifled experience and initiative, a flaw that at times results in disaster and defeat.

During the last few weeks, reports had filtered back that the Kunehamas planned attacks on homesteads and smaller settlements along the banks of the Kunene River. The river flowed south through the colony and then turned west, over the Ruacana Falls to the Atlantic Ocean, creating the border between German South West Africa and Angola.

Major Olazabal combined the force he had brought from Luanda with both the local militia and the garrison to form a mixed brigade. Some were mounted on tsetse-fly hardened horses, others riding oxen, while the remainder either marched on foot or rode on ox-wagons.

Amid some fanfare, the column departed Benguela towards the Kunene River, where Major Olazabal hoped to be reinforced by a further contingent of mounted Boer militia.

As Werner wanted to get nearer to the gunrunning, rumoured to be rife in that area, he and his *cavalerico* joined the column, riding horses purchased by Werner. Only Paulo, Captain de Sousa's footman come servant, also had the luxury of his own horse; all the other servants were on foot. Both black men were suitably armed with rifles.

Huambo is a large settlement in central Angola through which the railroad the British were building would pass. Although Olazabal's column would turn south well before the town, the Major proposed to send a detachment of mounted troops to Huambo in order to make his presence known. From Philippe, who had heard it from other servants, Werner garnered that Antonio dos Santos, the most important trader in that region and de facto administrator, ran his gunrunning operation from the Huambo area, in the heart of Kunehama territory. Werner requested permission from Major Olazabal to accompany the detachment.

At Bolambo, a village on the wagon-trail to Huambo, the main column turned south. The detachment, under the command of Captain de Sousa, broke away and continued eastwards, needing to cover about fifty miles before reaching Huambo. The major had retained the more seasoned troops in his column, leaving the captain with most of the recently trained black troopers and a few NCOs and militiamen. The NCOs were spread amongst the men, but the militiamen formed their own group, not mixing.

They were hard working colonists, comprised of some Portuguese but mostly Boers trying to protect their possessions. Most eked out a living as ranchers or were coffee and sisal plantation owners. The Portuguese government, keen to increase the white population, had granted these men large tracts of land, sufficient in size to ensure a viable livelihood. The government still received convicts, the *degregados* transported from Portugal and Brazil. They were set free here, virtually without restrictions, in the hope that they would integrate with the existing colonists. Most of them soon adapted, settling in well, usually taking black women as wives, retaining their rugged and rough lifestyles. They were certainly not the company a gentleman or officer would seek. Werner avoided them. He and Captain de Sousa had developed a comfortable rapport, and in the evenings, they sought each other's company, sharing a campfire.

After passing through numerous indigenous tribal villages where the locals maintained large herds of cattle and tilled the land primarily for their own use, the column eventually entered Huambo on the third day. Werner was surprised at the size of the tribal settlement, which sprawled over a large area from which most of the bush had been cleared. Huambo village was the seat of a local sub-tribal chief who, with his subjects, counted their wealth in cattle. The locals came from far and wide to barter their goods at the few trading stores established here, who carried everything from clothing and trinkets to cooking pots, rudimentary agricultural tools and just about anything else required. From the inhabitants, the traders received sisal, hides, raw rubber, corn, salt and ivory. However, the item every man desired was a rifle. This was never said aloud, but all knew it. A rifle was a prize.

Captain de Sousa decided that his unit should spend a few days at Huambo. The few resident traders had erected primitive dwellings for themselves, but none was a guesthouse, and there was no hotel or lodge. The village did not cater for modern-day travellers. They found a suitable camping site amongst the widely dispersed huts and the troops were directed to erect tents and build a large boma, a corral constructed from cut-down thorn-tree branches to provide protection for the horses and oxen overnight. Marauding lion and leopard were as much a danger as cattle theft, a lucrative pastime amongst the tribes and even more so during this period of simmering discord.

By the time the sun had crept close to the western horizon, the men had transformed the open area into an organized camp. The tents were in neat rows; in-between the aisles of canvas and forming a straight line down the centre, rifles had been stacked at exact intervals. It was clear that de Sousa was a stern disciplinarian. Werner's opinion of the man's military prowess improved day by day as he watched him exert his command over this motley band of men. They respected him.

The two officers shared a tent. A large canvas awning had been attached to the tent, creating some shade from the harsh sun. A folding table and chairs stood below this.

With a sigh of weariness, de Sousa collapsed into a chair, gesturing for Werner to do the same.

"It seems the locals consider our arrival quite an event. I'm hoping the traders invite us for a drink and possibly a meal. This lot is hungry for news," he said, taking a long drink from his water bottle.

"Where on earth would we eat? I've seen no proper buildings," Werner asked.

The captain laughed.

"You're right, there are no houses. They also live in huts, just like these tribesmen. But you'll be surprised how comfortable and well appointed these are. These traders make a good living and they live accordingly, with all necessary amenities, including women."

"Women?"

"Oh yes. Most have brought their own women with them." He lowered his voice. "Some even have one or two white men in their employ. Invariably, these are dubious characters and should be avoided . . . they are thugs, and some are ex-convicts."

Paulo, the captain's dark-skinned batman, appeared with two beers and a note, which he handed to the captain. Werner took a sip of the beer. He face lit up with surprise; the beer was cold.

"Good God, where did this come from?"

"I told you, the traders live in style."

The captain studied the note and looked up.

"Well, we've been invited by the kingpin Senhor Antonio dos Santos himself. This should be both pleasant and interesting."

He raised his beer in a toast, taking a generous drink and loudly smacking his lips. Straight from a cool-room, the beer was a welcome change from the lukewarm water they had been drinking.

Late that afternoon the two men, accompanied by a detachment of four soldiers, rode to dos Santos' store. The day was ferociously hot. Werner and de Sousa were both dressed in jodhpurs, high riding boots and white collarless blouses, as it was far too warm for any type of tunic or jacket. Werner wore a pith helmet, the captain, a Portuguese officer's cap adorned with a short black ostrich feather. Custom and etiquette had little place in this climate.

Their destination was a great deal more than a "store"; it was a huge compound, surrounded by an eight foot high wall of wooden stakes, made of poles as thick as a man's arm, and driven vertically into the ground, each so close as to touch the other. The entrance to the compound was a labyrinth designed to restrict the number of persons who could gain entrance simultaneously, a series of passageways so narrow as to allow not more than two men to pass, constructed of the same closely packed perpendicular stakes. Within this stockade, huts of various sizes had been built. Some were dwellings while others were clearly used as storerooms, stables and open-sided sheds.

A large thatched hut stood on a small knoll, dominating the centre of the stockade. A long, wide veranda surrounded the building. Windows had been cut into its thick walls. These contained no glass but shutters made of woven reeds, hinged at the top, so that they could be opened and closed from within. This was no rickety hut, but a properly built abode clearly capable of protecting the interior from the worst of thunderstorms.

Once inside the stockade, a swarthy white man accosted them. Without greeting them, he motioned for them to follow him. He had a livid scar from his left ear across his cheek to his mouth, this lending him a menacing appearance.

"One of those I spoke about," de Sousa said quietly to Werner.

"Scarface," muttered Werner.

"Captain! It's been a year since I last saw you!"

A voice boomed from the hut. Werner was unable to distinguish anything in the dark shadow of the porch. As Scarface waved them forward, both men climbed the few wooden stairs to the landing where a huge man confronted them.

He stood tall, his legs widespread on the planked floor, his hands on his hips, his forearms almost the size of an ordinary man's upper leg, his shoulders massively wide, his belly hanging over the belt of his jodhpurs. Although the man at first glance, might appear fat, there was no hiding his enormous strength. Werner likened him to a wrestler; not somebody he would care to physically confront.

"Dos Santos, you get bigger every time I see you," de Sousa joked, returning the greeting.

"And who is this with you?" the huge man indicated Werner. "A civilian? I'm surprised."

"I brought him along especially to meet you. He is in the same type of business as you. This is Senhor Joachim de Almeida from Portugal, recently from Mozambique."

The captain stepped aside to allow Werner to pass and take dos Santos' proffered hand. The man's hand was the size of a ham and he expected his fingers to be crushed. In fact, the handshake was quite normal as dos Santos greeted him with due deference.

"I need to know the latest news. Come, please sit."

He snapped his fingers; two servants immediately appeared and awaited his instructions.

"Bring beer and wine," he demanded, his tone brusque, "And bring lamps," he added as an afterthought.

Werner looked closely at the gigantic man. Perspiration bathed the man's face as he continuously wiped it with a large bandanna. Although seated a few feet away, he could actually smell dos Santos; no amount of cologne could disguise the rancid smell of the sweat which his body seemed to ooze continuously.

They exchanged the latest news, the trader extremely interested in the progress of the railway the British were building from Lobito into the hinterland. He, in turn, confirmed that the situation in and around Huambo was tense, with the locals influenced by the war raging in neighbouring South West Africa as the Kunahama tribe began to believe that they could take on their Portuguese masters in similar manner. Recently, there had been attacks against homesteads, easy targets, as by the time the military arrived the attackers were long gone. The insurrection was still sporadic but the Portuguese authorities feared that a proper revolt would encompass all the territory along the banks of the Kunene River, the home to many colonists.

"The situation continues to ferment, but fortunately, the locals view me as a necessity, supplying the items they need."

"Are they well armed?" the captain enquired.

"Indeed they are."

"I hear many have the latest rifles. Where do they acquire these?" the captain probed.

Dos Santos seemed to hesitate and then with a sweep of his arm, indicated the horizon.

"From all over—even from South West Africa, some from our own military deserters. Many rifles originate from the war in the North and from the Belgian Congo. These savages are fighting wars on all fronts in all colonies, be they British, Portuguese, Belgian, or German. There seems to be an endless supply of weapons. The same goes for ammunition; they have large caches of ammunition."

Werner said little, letting the two men talk, the information giving him insight into the customs and actions of the local population in the face of the storm clouds of war gathering in this part of Africa.

"Senhor de Almeida," the huge man addressed him. "What brings you to this outpost in wildest Africa?"

"Please, call me Joachim. To be brutally frank, business. I'm an agent for a number of German manufacturers. I was in Mozambique previously, and I was told that I could do quite well here."

The man laughed, his belly shaking.

"Of course, you have heard that I'm a trader. In fact, I pride myself as being the biggest in these parts. My purchases are enormous, from cloth, farming equipment, knives, rifles, ammunition, pot and pans: you name it, I buy it, in bulk, all directly from Europe. What do you have that I haven't already got?"

Dos Santos did not drink wine or beer, but rather a popular Portuguese brandy drunk by the locals. Werner had tried it before; it was rough on the palate and had a kick like a mule, certainly not for the faint-hearted! The huge man was not sipping his drink, but taking generous swigs from his glass. There was no doubt that the evening would develop; all it needed was time and copious quantities of brandy.

He needed to capture the man's attention.

"Well, I believe I could negotiate a handsome discount, were you to do business with me. In fact, my principals have instructed me to establish some sort of permanent trade relationship with the traders in this country, and in order to do so, have been quite generous. I'm sure you will be surprised at the terms and discounts offered."

He paused for a moment to allow the man to digest this information, then continued. "But let me not bore you with business this evening. I'm your guest and that would not be proper."

"Senhor de Almeida, my storerooms are full of valuable merchandise. I have large quantities of ivory and hides, bales of sisal and bags of coffee. Would you not prefer to barter with me? You would profit handsomely from such an arrangement. This would rid me of the task of having to transport these to the coast and arrange for export. I could make you a deal you could not refuse."

For a moment the man lapsed into silence, and then added, "Ah but I forget, we'll discuss business tomorrow."

The oppressive heat and the insistent buzzing of insects attracted by the lamps irritated Werner. He tried to limit his intake, but by the time they eventually sat down to dinner late in the evening, both he and the captain had drunk too much. Dinner was served by two servants, and overseen by dos Santos' mistress, an exquisite woman of mixed blood, with flashing green eyes, black hair, a thin waist and a voluptuous bosom. Werner tried not to stare at her breasts below her plunging neckline, bobbing with her every movement. Dos Santos noticed his furtive glances.

"I see you find Maria attractive," he remarked with a sly grin. The bastard, Werner thought, he was doing this on purpose. He made a mental note to take care; this man was dangerous.

"Yes, she certainly is beautiful," he said quietly.

She obviously heard him. She smiled at him, flashing her white teeth but refraining from any comment. Dos Santos merely smirked.

After the drab fare of the last few days, the excellent food was welcome. Fillet steak skewered on long sticks, grilled over an open fire, complemented with wild potatoes were washed down with copious quantities of wine and beer. Werner watched dos Santos: the man's appetite was astonishing and he devoured the equivalent of a two-man meal, accompanied by glass upon glass of cool red wine. As his alcohol consumption began to take its toll, what little decorum he had previously displayed evaporated. As Maria served him, he would stick out an arm and fondle her, winking at his table companions as if it were a joke, ignoring her obvious embarrassment. The ribald remarks accompanying these gestures merely added to the woman's discomfort.

The man's behaviour annoyed Werner, but he remained silent not wishing to initiate any confrontation. The man and his woman was a private affair.

While appearing not to do so, Werner continued to watch Maria. From her body language and demeanour, he soon realized that she was in fear of the man. How could such an attractive woman have allowed herself to be trapped in a situation where she had to co-habitat with such a repulsive man?

The rest of the evening degenerated into an alcohol-induced fog with dos Santos getting louder and louder, and de Sousa reduced to a state of euphoria, a weak, sick grin on his face. Periodically he would burst into song, to which a drunken Werner would add his off-key baritone voice. Finally, dos Santos succumbed, collapsing in his chair, his loud snores heard even above the raucous behaviour of the other two men. With the assistance of a servant, Maria got dos Santos to his feet and led him to their sleeping quarters.

When she returned, Maria emerged from her shell, smiling and laughing and encouraging the two young men in their merriment. She even had a few glasses of wine. She brought a gramophone out from the house and proceeded to play a fiery Portuguese dance.

"Come, dance," she insisted, "come, dance with me!"

Werner and de Sousa forgot the heat, and their exertions left their skin shiny with perspiration as they pirouetted and capered the length of the veranda. She never seemed to tire, her head thrown back, talking and smiling at her partner.

Finally the two thoroughly inebriated men rode back to their campsite, serenading the countryside, their escort keeping a diplomatic distance behind them.

Werner groaned. He had collapsed onto his cot the previous night, not closing the mosquito netting which hung from an attachment above his bed. His arms, upper torso and face were now covered in mosquito bites. To add to his discomfort, his head pounded, threatening to burst like an over-pressurized boiler.

He called for Philippe who stooped to enter the tent. The *cavalerico* took one look at Werner, shook his head and muttered to himself.

"If you wash your face, *Mestre*, you'll feel better," Philippe said.

Werner carefully swung his legs off the cot and hung his head in his lap, slowly massaging his temples. Staggering to the table, he held his head over a huge enamelled dish while Philippe slowly poured water over his head. Werner gagged, rubbing his hair and face with the cascading water.

"Good God! Never again," he mumbled, falling into a chair and dabbing at his face with a cloth the servant had handed him.

"Should I arrange to have breakfast brought to you?"

He pulled a face, a clear indication that food was the furthest thing from his mind.

"Christus! Have you no compassion? Just bring black coffee."

Philippe snickered and left, returning some minutes later with a large mug. Werner sipped the black coffee; it was strong and sweet.

"How is the captain? More to the point, where is he?" Werner asked, only now noticing that the captain's cot had been removed from the command tent.

Philippe rolled his eyes, a sympathetic look on his face.

"Not good, *Mestre*. We moved his cot out of the tent and erected a separate tent for him alongside."

"Why?"

"He's the commanding officer and others should not see him like that," said Philippe, pantomiming some wretch losing his supper.

"This came for you."

Philippe handed him a note. It was from dos Santos requesting that he please attend a meeting at his stockade.

Taking Philippe with him, Werner rode off before the captain woke. The two men left their horses in the care of a servant at the main entrance and entered the labyrinth of poles.

Maria was waiting to greet him with a warm smile.

"Senhor de Almeida. How do you feel this morning?"

He still had a pounding headache.

"I've felt better, but no doubt, it will improve as the day goes by."

She smiled knowingly.

"Follow me; I'll take you to Antonio."

Dos Santos was seated behind a large table on which was spread with an assortment of documents and catalogues. The man seemed totally unaffected by the previous night's proceedings. Werner was dumbfounded; the man had consumed enough liquor to fell a horse! Yet here he sat as if nothing had happened. He obviously has a cast-iron constitution, Werner thought, it took an exceptional man to survive last night unscathed.

"Good morning, Senhor de Almeida. Are you ready to discuss business?" the huge man asked.

"Morning to you, Sir. Yes, I'm ready to talk, but please, I must first thank you for your kind hospitality of yesterday." He turned to Maria, "The food was excellent."

"You may again dine with me this evening, that is, if you wish."

"Thank you, I'll speak to the captain, but I believe he is impatient to be on his way. We still need to meet up with the main column again."

Dos Santos stared at him for a moment and then spoke. The relaxed atmosphere of the previous evening was no longer evident – this was business.

"Let's get straight to the point. I have a warehouse full of goods. I have an inventory thereof here in front of me," he said, pushing a few sheets of paper across the table to Werner.

Werner took the pages and studied them. He was amazed. There were bags of coffee, bales of raw rubber, many bundles of salted dry cattle hides and at least a ton or more of ivory.

Werner looked up.

"This is worth quite a sum, a fortune in fact. I would have to do a calculation and will need some expert help to place a fair value on this. The bank in Benguela would assist me, as they mentioned that they were conversant with items traded in these parts. What do you wish to buy from me?"

"Most of the items you have. I studied your catalogues early this morning."

This surprised Werner. Last night this man was dead to the world before them, but he had still risen early enough to have studied his catalogues and prices. A lesser man would have had a touch of alcohol poisoning!

"I'll take from all your items, but what I'm really after are your rifles, both the Mauser and Steyr. I'll take two hundred and fifty of each."

"Two hundred and fifty of each!" Werner blurted, visibly astonished.

"Yes, that would be sufficient for a year. That's no more than a rifle or two a day. An easy sell or barter in this part of the world."

"Who would you sell these to?"

"I sell most of these in the British and Belgian territories. The local Boers will also buy."

Werner knew this to be a blatant lie, but dared not say so. He knew that the Belgians and British jealously guarded their own markets; they would not permit any intrusion by the Portuguese.

"The law states that I may not sell to the indigenous people in Portuguese territory. Well, I abide by that, but that's really none of your concern. This is a business transaction."

"No, you are right, it's not my concern. Time is more my concern. This could take a day or two to take care of, and Captain de Sousa is impatient to leave."

Dos Santos gave a dismissive wave and then said nonchalantly.

"Let him leave. You and your servant should stay a night or two here and then catch up with the column later. If you need an escort of a few men, I can provide such a detail. Maybe this deal is big enough to warrant you returning to Benguela without having to go south?"

He heard footsteps and turned. Maria entered the room bringing more coffee.

"Maria, Senhor de Almeida will be staying a night or two. Please make arrangements."

"Whoa! Not so fast. I need to speak to the captain."

"Don't worry, it will be fine. I'll vouch for your safety."

This is madness, he thought. Here was his biggest enemy and the man was vouching for his safety! If the man only knew who he really was – he would be as good as dead!

This new development placed him in a quandary. He desperately wanted to go south and find out how the weapons got over the border into *SudwesAfrika*. He could only do that if he travelled with Captain de Sousa. However, dos Santos' surprise proposal presented him with a unique opportunity.

Werner left the stockade and returned to the camp. As he thought, the captain insisted he stay behind and make the most of this lucrative business opportunity. He had said nothing of the guns involved in the transaction, leaving him to believe that a wide assortment of merchandise was involved.

"Did he offer to purchase rifles from you?"

The direct question surprised Werner, and he remained silent. Captain de Sousa took this as an affirmation.

"How many?"

Werner hesitated for a moment. He decided not to mention a figure.

"We haven't discussed numbers yet, merely prices."

"Well, if it's OK by you, I like to know how many he proposes to buy. In fact, Joachim, I must insist that you divulge this information. The military needs to know."

"Why?"

"It would not bode well for us if these fell into the wrong hands. We like to keep our eye on these things."

Were the Portuguese authorities suspicious of dos Santos? If they were, well, that was a new development. Werner considered it too soon to probe the captain's reasons for asking. May be at a later stage, he thought.

Early the next morning, in the cool before the sun rose, the two men bade each other farewell, expressing the hope that they would see each other soon.

"Be careful when dealing with dos Santos, my friend," the captain said. He refused to elaborate when pressed by Werner. "I am not happy that dos Santos supply an escort. I insist that an NCO with twenty men remain with you at Huambo, to escort you when you choose to rejoin the column."

Philippe remained behind at the military camp with the troopers while Werner rode to dos Santos' stockade. Maria welcomed him warmly and showed him to the guest room. It was part of the hut complex, but quite removed from what he thought was his host's section of the abode. A huge bed dominated the room, made up with spotlessly clean white linen. A mosquito net hung suspended from a beam in the roof. Reed mats, decorated to depict some sort of local flora, covered the floor. The usual washstand with toiletries stood in the corner and next to it a small cupboard and a chest of drawers for clothes.

Maria bubbled with excitement, happy to have him staying with them. She was a sultry beauty, but she was keen to chat, and Werner took the opportunity to do a little prying.

Once he had settled in, dos Santos took him on a guided tour of the trading complex, finally entering his main storeroom, a large warehouse. The warehouse was crammed with bundle upon bundle of raw rubber, bales of sisal, the floor littered with ivory tusks of all sizes, blocks and bags of salt, and dried and stacked wild animal and cattle rawhides.

"This is all yours," the man indicated with a sweep of his arm. "You should profit well. All you have to do is undertake to deliver my five hundred rifles and the other goods. These must be delivered to Namibe."

"Where on earth is Namibe?" Werner enquired.

"It's a small fishing port south of Benguela. Just a few huts, but it has a natural harbour."

"Do ships off-load cargo there?"

"No, not normally. Only if requested. The facilities are far too primitive. Everything is brought ashore in small boats. The recipient has to arrange these boats – there is no harbour authority, military establishment, or police force. I hire the boats from the local fishermen. I'll give you the details later."

Damn! This man was certainly well organized, he reflected. Was this how he got his rifles ashore and avoided customs?

"All right, let's do the sums. You need to tell me how am I to get this to Lobito. There's got to be a few wagon-loads here," Werner said with concern, not knowing how to arrange the transport.

"Don't worry, I'll arrange with local transporters to load this and take it to Lobito for you at an acceptable price. However, final packing will be your responsibility. I'll see to it that Maria's father assists you with crates – he owns a large carpentry shop in Benguela."

They returned to the room that served as dos Santos' office. It was already hot and Maria brought beers. The men haggled over their calculations and finally agreed to the exchange; five hundred and forty rifles plus ploughs and various other agricultural implements and some riding tack were traded for the total contents of the storeroom, the barter to be approved by Werner's bankers.

There was a smaller storeroom which dos Santos never included in the tour and that he pointedly ignored.

"Anything in there?" Werner asked as they walked passed.

"Unimportant, used agricultural and carpentry tools, nothing worth inspection," the man brushed the question aside. However, the manner in which the door was secured with two large locks that bolted down a large cross bar seemed to indicate otherwise and the offhand comment merely aroused Werner's curiosity.

After a large lunch, all retired to their rooms for the customary siesta. Werner lay on his bed, finding it difficult to sleep in the oppressive heat but eventually dozing off.

Suddenly, some inner sense awakened him. Without moving, he slowly opened his eyes. Maria was standing next to his bed, silhouetted against the light from the doorway.

"What are you doing here?" he asked, taken aback.

"Shhhh! He's asleep," she whispered a finger to her lips.

She moved nearer and placed her hand on his arm.

"I need help. Please, won't you help me?"

"What do you mean?"

"I need to leave here; I can no longer live with this man. Please!" she pleaded. "Take me with you when you leave."

"Good Lord, I can't do that, I'm his guest. He'll kill me! Really, this is none of my business," Werner hissed, his features taut. "Please go, leave the room before somebody sees us!"

She walked to the door and turned to face him.

"I'll speak to you tonight," she said quietly, and disappeared.

He was dumbstruck. This was serious; he could not get involved, it could upset his plans. At worst, dos Santos would be after him with a vengeance, all deals off, the military intelligence division's plans shattered. And he would probably be dishonoured in their eyes. God! They could cashier him, he thought. Nobody would believe she came to him, everyone would think he had made a play for her!

Late that afternoon he and dos Santos made final arrangements for the removal of the stored goods and the order and reception of the new shipments. If dos Santos opened the letters addressed apparently to Werner's principals, he would find nothing to arouse suspicion; all had the appearance of a normal business transaction. Werner thought the matter somewhat amusing, wondering how the German military would respond to this request to supply rifles.

As the sun set on the horizon, the two men relaxed on the veranda, the servants ever at the ready with cool beer, wine and brandy. His jowls glistening with perspiration, dos Santos knocked back quite a few brandies. Werner rationed his intake of cool beer, careful not to be obvious; a repetition of the previous night would not do.

They agreed that Werner would leave the next morning in order to catch up with Captain de Sousa's small column. The bartered goods would remain warehoused in Lobito until the arrival of the rifle shipment from Germany. Dos Santos did not appear concerned about customs: no custom or military officers were stationed in Namibe, a forlorn stretch of deserted beach on the coast of the Namib Desert, although the occasional patrols did pass through from time to time.

The trader had made no request for ammunition. This intrigued him.

"No, I've ample supplies, besides, ammunition is available from Portugal; it's suitable for these rifles and a damn sight cheaper," dos Santos said when asked.

What Werner and German intelligence did not realize was that large quantities of ammunition had been smuggled from South Africa. These stocks originated from hidden Boer arms caches, unearthed after the Boer War, and the ammunition found its way on ox wagons through Bechuanaland and Rhodesia into southern Angola and SudwesAfrika.

By nine o'clock that evening, dos Santos had again drunk himself into a near stupor, barely coherent. Apologizing to Werner, Maria finally persuaded him to retire and led him to their bedroom. Werner remained on the porch, too hot to contemplate sleeping. He lolled in the large woven cane chair, his shirt open to his navel, his legs spread out in front of him, a stein of cool beer at his elbow.

Maria returned and sat down in a similar chair opposite him, sipping a glass of wine, peering at him over the rim of the glass.

"He won't wake before morning," she assured him, removing any fear that the man could suddenly return to the porch unannounced. "I know him, he's dead to the world." He stared at her apprehensively. A faint sheen of perspiration glistened on her face and on the swell of her breasts, revealed by the plunging neckline of her blouse. She now wore a flared dark red skirt, and she hitched this up revealing her legs to the knees. Did she wish to cool herself or did she have some other ulterior intention? Deep inside he felt the stirring of a wanton need, which he tried to ignore. This woman was about to play him—a dangerous game.

"Are you going to help me?" she asked quietly.

He shook his head. She had to realize that this was not possible.

"Please!"

"How can I help you? I'm doing business with this man, that's important to me . . . and then to help you escape, well . . . I just can't do it, in fact, I don't want to hear any more about it." He rose to leave the veranda.

"No, no, I understand. Do what you have to do, but don't forget. Maybe one day you'll have a chance to help me. You'll come this way again."

He doubted whether he would ever come this way again, but that he could not tell her.

"I'll remember."

He took a chance.

"What's in that locked storeroom?" he asked, his voice so low she could hardly hear him.

"Why?"

He hesitated for a moment.

"Well, he says there's nothing of importance, yet it is the only store that is locked, more than that, it's virtually barricaded."

She looked down the length of the veranda before replying.

"Guns."

"Guns?" he hissed, repeating her.

"Yes, he will soon take the shipment south. So I've overheard. Of course, I'm not supposed to know that these are guns but it is difficult to keep a secret in this compound. I also speak the local language fluently; these people are my friends. I hear much from them."

His immediate thought was that she could be an asset, but as quickly dismissed the idea. He was not taking her with him.

"When will he leave?"

"Within the next two weeks. He awaits a message from one of the Kunahama tribal chiefs. He'll leave with two or three wagons and about twenty men. The two white men will also accompany him. They've done this before."

"That's a small army."

"That's right. And don't forget he has the protection of the Kunahamas, no-one would dare attack him."

"Hmmm, so that's how the cookie crumbles," he mused reflectively.

"What's that?"

"Nothing, I was just thinking."

"Do you want to see the storeroom? I can get the keys."

He was undecided. He was very keen to see where the guns came from. But the danger? If they were seen, he doubted whether either of them would see the light of day again.

"It's still early, he'll never wake up."

"What about the servants?"

"They hate him; he beats them and has even killed them. They will never say a word."

He hoped she was right. He nodded his head in affirmation.

He followed her down the steps into the faint moonlight. He could discern the surrounding huts, most showing no light, the huts of dos Santos men clustered in a far corner. Even these were dark, most occupants having retired.

"What about the white men?" he anxiously queried her.

"Don't worry; they're on the other side of the compound."

She quietly removed the locks, then indicated he should lift the wooden bar. He did so, placing it gently on the ground. As she opened one of the double doors, it gave a loud creak; they both froze, fearful it had been heard all over the compound. Nothing stirred except the continuous chirr and squeak of crickets and insects.

The strong smell of grease and gun oil accosted his nostrils as they entered the storeroom. In the faint moonlight that illuminated the interior, he could see crate upon crate stacked on top of each other. He stepped closer, trying to distinguish the stencilled writing on the wooden slats. It was too dark. Beside him, she produced box a matches. He took these and struck a large match, the sudden flare scaring him, afraid that it could be seen.

He studied the writing in the yellow light. It was German, the Gothic style immediately recognizable. Emblazoned on the crates were the words *Mauser Waffenfabrik*. Below this was recorded the type of rifle. Shit! These are German rifles, he thought. How did he get these? The match died. Reluctantly he struck another, still fearful that the light would be seen. Finally, he found the destination stencilled on the green painted wood. It read:

Zuid Afrikaansche Staats Artillerie

Hoofdmagazyn

Kerkstraat

PRETORIA

Zuid-Afrikaansche Republiek

Over

Lourenco Marques, MOZAMBIQUE

Boer weapons, originally consigned to Pretoria during the Boer War which ended in 1902. These rifles were probably part of the last weapons consignments, and had never reached their destination. The crate contained a dozen 8mm K88 German Mausers. He estimated there were about twenty-five crates in the room, three hundred rifles.

How dos Santos had got his hands on these was a mystery. The Portuguese or rather, associates of dos Santos, had probably misappropriated these in Lourenco Marçues at the close of the war, he thought. With the confusion which reigned during the latter part of the war, anything was possible.

"Ok, let's get out of here before we're discovered," he said, taking her the arm and guiding her out of the storeroom. They carefully replaced the bar and locks, and then slunk back to the porch. She did not let go of his hand.

It was only a few minutes past ten. The servants having already left, she poured them each a nightcap. They sat on the porch, and she neither raised her proposed desertion nor made any mention of their clandestine visit to the storeroom.

This was dangerous territory; he was convinced that dos Santos would not hesitate to resort to murder to retain his secret. That the man was ruthless and without conscience was evident. He could only speculate what he would do to this woman were she to desert him. He desperately wanted to assist her, but to do so would jeopardize the whole operation. It would have to wait.

"Well," he said finally into the silence, "I'm off to bed. Good night."

Once again he awoke with a start. The room was lighter, the moon now higher in the sky. The windows was open, the shutters not lowered, allowing the moonlight to stream in. The mosquito netting restricted his vision; he was not able to discern anything clearly beyond it.

Suddenly, the netting moved as it was lifted from below. He could clearly see the shape of her body through the translucent nightdress. Not saying a word, she let the netting fall behind her and lay down on the bed beside him, pressing her body to his.

She brought her lips close to his ear.

"I need you," she whispered.

"Christus! Are you mad? What are you doing?" He realized immediately what a stupid question it was. "We can't do this!"

He spoke as quietly as he could, certain that his voice travelled far, out through all the open windows and into the rooms without doors.

Softly, she began to kiss his face, her moist lips gliding across his skin, all the while slowly running her hands over his body. He smelt her sweet fragrance and felt the first stirrings his own of arousal. This was not lost on her. She kissed him passionately. His instinct was to push her from him, but he found himself succumbing to his desire, throwing caution to the wind and responding fiercely to her advances. He returned her kiss, both his hands sliding over her body beneath the nightshirt, finding her breasts, the nipples firm and erect. He pulled up her nightshirt and took a nipple into his mouth and rolled his tongue around it. She moaned softly.

Their breathing quickened.

Suddenly he thrust her from him.

"Please, be sensible, this is stupid!" he hissed, reluctantly holding her by the shoulders, at arms length from him. "Go back to your room – now!"

"Will you help me?"

This time he did not hesitate. If this was what it was going to take to get her to leave, he was prepared to concede to anything: he was terrified that dos Santos would make a sudden appearance.

"Yes! But only if you leave. I promise I will help when I am ready, but this could take a few weeks. You'll have to believe me."

She stared at him, silent.

"All right, I'll go, but remember we are accomplices now. You know about me as I know about you. And . . . I think I know what you are doing here. You're more than just a trader! Still, I'll keep your secret."

With that, she rolled off the bed. The flimsy nightshirt fell to her knees but not before, he glimpsed the dark triangle of her sex. Without a further word or glance backwards, she disappeared under the mosquito netting.

Lieber Gott! Werner thought to himself, falling back onto the bed. That was close. Still, he could not help being disappointed; he had not made the most of the opportunity.

CHAPTER THREE

Werner could see a few isolated thundershowers far off on the eastern horizon, but despite it being the height of the rainy season, still the rain eluded them. It was now March, the ground was parched and grazing was sparse. What little there was, was dry and without nourishment. Most of the game had migrated, the wildebeest, kudu and buffalo moving northeast to where good grazing was still to be found. Surprisingly, the thorn trees, always the last to suffer from a lack of rain, still carried a thick green canopy.

Every afternoon, the clear sky would magically transform, small puffs of floating cotton wool appearing, rapidly growing to large cumulus clouds. But before these could condense and rain fall, strong winds would blow in from the desert in the west, driving a dust storm that drove the clouds away, leaving the land as parched as before.

The heat was intolerable. The oxen moaned as they pulled the heavy wagons, the wagon-drivers either leading their animals or walking alongside the train of oxen and wagons, cracking huge rawhide whips to drive the oxen on. Near naked in their loin-cloths, their bodies coated with the dust raised by multitudes of hoofbeats, these men allowed no ox to shirk its duty.

Ahead of the ox-wagons marched a small troop of African soldiers—Askaris, led by an NCO on horseback. Only a few enjoyed the luxury of a horse, but the bulk of the troopers were on foot, single file, forming a straggling line which wound its way through the bush. Both Werner and Philippe were on horseback, immediately behind the ox-wagons.

"For God's sake, Philippe, when is it going to rain? God, we need water," Werner grumbled, finding the heat unbearable. He had stripped off his cotton jacket, and his collarless shirt was open to the waist.

The servant remained silent, lifting his eyes and searching the sky. After a while he spoke.

"Patience, *Mestre*. It will rain soon. All the signs are there. But we will have water this evening. The Kunene is near."

Philippe's tone was resigned, in typically African fashion, his voice flat and monotonous, as if he considered Werner's question an affront. One did not question nature—that was God's business. Would the white man never learn?

The NCO had been pushing the animals and troops for the past three days, and still their forward scouts had not made contact with Captain de Sousa's column. Werner was uneasy. It was rumoured that the Kunahamas had risen in revolt, deserting their villages. However, the NCO was a veteran and had already led many a troop into the hinterland. The men were disciplined, their sergeant ensuring that his scouts reconnoitred their proposed route well ahead of the small column. In addition, he also placed outriders on each side, about five hundred yards distant from the column to warn them of an ambush.

Suddenly, a horseman emerged from the bush on the side of the track. Startled, Werner drew his rifle from its scabbard, working the bolt action, pumping a round into the breech.

"*Mestre*, it's okay, that's a scout," Philippe said, holding out his arm.

The NCO immediately raised his hand, bringing the column to a halt. The scout spurred his horse forward and there was a quick whispered conversation with the NCO before he turned round and trotted back in the direction he had come. The NCO beckoned Werner forward, an expression of deep concern on his face

"Major Olazabal's column has been attacked by hordes of Kunahamas. They have been wiped out to a man, including the Boer militia that recently joined them. The rebels struck while the troops were encamped on the riverbanks, about thirty kilometres south of here. God help us! Olazabal's force made up more than half our total southern Angolan military contingency. Other than a few soldiers garrisoned at small towns, Captain de Sousa's men are all that's left. This is a disaster!"

"Christ! What about Captain de Sousa? Are he and his men safe?"

"He has dug in at a strategic spot on the river believing an attack on his force to be imminent. He is hoping we will attempt to join up with him. I propose we do that, immediately," the NCO said, clearly not asking for approval, merely informing Werner of his intentions.

"How far from here to the captain?"

"About fifteen miles."

"Will we still make it to him today?"

"We have to. The Kunahamas will not fight at night if they can avoid it. We must move on immediately. I want you and your *cavalerico* to move up and ride alongside me."

The NCO quickened the pace. Joining de Sousa's detachment would strengthen their numbers and increase their chances. He allowed no further stops for rest, and the troops ate on the march. By the time the sun disappeared behind the horizon, bottles were dry, and men and animals alike were dry and thirsty. The oxen bellowed. They had not drunk for two days, and water was now the rallying cry. Suddenly, the pace of the horses and oxen quickened, the use of a whip no longer necessary.

"They've picked up the scent of water," Philippe replied in answer to Werner's enquiry.

The bellowing increased as the heavy animals broke into a trot, straining at their yokes. As they burst forth from the bush that lined the river course, smelling the shallow river in front of them, there was no stopping them. They pulled the wagons into the knee-deep stream, and there they stopped, lowered their heads and drank their fill. The horses followed suit, all oblivious to the danger of crocodiles.

"Fucking stupid animals! Get them out of the water, now!" the NCO shouted.

With difficulty, the troops drove the horses and oxen out of the water. Once back on the riverbank, the men filled buckets with water and placed these before the oxen and horses, allowing all to quench their thirst before resuming the march.

Ahead of him, through the dense bush and thorn trees lining both sides of the riverbank, Werner discerned a flickering of light. Quite unexpectedly, the troop broke out into an open expanse bordered by bush on three sides and the river on the other. Other lights now became visible in the dark, the campfires set by Captain de Sousa's detachment. He wondered why the Captain had revealed his position by permitting his troops to light fires. Riding next to him, the NCO appeared to read his mind.

"Don't worry. The Kunahamas know exactly where he is encamped, although I don't think they expected us to arrive. They won't know we have broken from the main column. Anyway, they know he can't move and that he has chosen the best defensive position he can find. They'll attack at their leisure. Hell! Be sure, we'll not be going anywhere from here!"

"Shouldn't we rather take the fight to them instead of waiting for them to attack us?"

The NCO did not respond. Werner was about to repeat the question, when it crossed his mind that NCO probably considered military tactics beyond the comprehension of a civilian, not worth a reply. He did not pursue the matter.

As they entered the camp, soldiers ran forward and led the animals into a boma already full of oxen and horses. He dismounted and saw Captain de Sousa approaching. There was no welcoming smile on his face; he looked exhausted. The burden of responsibility his friend carried was more than most could be expected to shoulder. The news of Olzabal's end hung like a pall over the camp, and most felt they were about to share the same fate. De Sousa was haggard, unkempt and unshaven, his uniform coated with dust, his attitude one of near resignation.

"I'm certainly glad to see you again, even though I actually sent a runner to tell your NCO not to try to contact us. I must assume he was intercepted by these bastards," De Sousa said, and then shook his head resignedly. "I just can't believe it! It was a complete massacre; the good Major Olazabal didn't even have scouts out! The Kunehamas caught them completely in the open—totally unprepared! The bastards killed them all. Those that weren't killed outright, black and white, were horribly tortured and then bludgeoned to death. The sight was ghastly, bodies like broken dolls amongst the thorn trees. Christus! The vultures had already gathered; it was sickening!"

"How many were killed?" Werner asked, his face registering his shock.

"We counted three hundred and thirteen all in all."

"Did you bury them?"

"No, it was too dangerous to stay. The terrain afforded us no protection; we had to get out of there. The only thing to do was head for the river. At least, with the river at our backs, they can't surround us."

"What about help, you know, reinforcements?"

"Of course, I've sent out men on horseback, but I have no idea whether they made it or not."

Werner was silent; their position was precarious to say the least.

"How many men have you got?" he asked the captain.

"Merda! Not enough—about a hundred and thirty. A few more militiamen have joined us since the farmers heard the news. But I think we are up against about two thousand of these damn savages, most with rifles."

De Sousa paused, and then exclaimed furiously, "Fuckin' gunrunners! Rest assured, those that didn't have rifles before certainly have them now! Taken from the dead—and with ammunition to spare. How do I rate our chances? Well, to be honest, not good."

"Your defences?" Werner asked.

The captain gave a humourless chuckle.

"Not good either – certainly not up to an attack of a few thousand. I've done what I can: surrounded the camp with trenches. The ground is easy to work, no rocks. The troops have dug themselves in well. I don't believe the Kunehamas know how difficult it is to overcome troops hidden in trenches. Come, I'm about to do an inspection, see for yourself."

They walked the perimeter. Most of the men were eating their evening meal, hunkered down in the trenches, their rifles lying on the shallow parapets ready for immediate use. An atmosphere of fear pervaded the trenches. Most ate in silence. A grim silence hung over the men, the question of survival foremost on their minds.

The command post was little more than a depression dug in the bed of a dry stream, which, when in flood, emptied into the main river about a hundred yards behind them. This would afford them some protection from gunfire and from any attack from the rear.

The captain smiled wryly.

"I haven't any beer, but I can offer you wine."

"That's fine," Werner said.

"Were you ever a soldier?" the captain asked.

Werner was taken aback.

"No. Why do you ask?"

"Well, soldiers have a way about them. You've the same mannerisms. All I have to do is put you in uniform – you wouldn't be a soldier, but an officer. You are used to giving orders – you've done it before. You just have that way about you."

"Probably because of my father. He was an officer, in fact, quite a disciplinarian."

"You just stay close to me, OK?"

"Sure."

Werner opened his eyes to find Philippe shaking him.

"*Mestre*, wake up. The captain wants to speak to you."

He took the wet cloth the servant offered and wiped the sleep from his eyes. He was stiff, his joints reluctant to work properly in the early morning chill after a night on the ground on a blanket. The emerging dawn, an orange-pink streak on the eastern horizon, already lit the surrounding camp. He stumbled out and into the trench next to the captain. The trench was not that deep, only about chest high.

"Morning. Have you noticed? It's dead quiet. I can't even hear any birds. Usually they make quite a racket at daybreak. Something is going on out there."

"Somebody's coming!" whispered the trooper standing next to the captain.

Four men burst out of the bush and slid into the trench.

"They're coming!" the sergeant gasped. "Hundreds of them. No more than a kilometre away."

"Where do these men come from?" Werner asked, indicating the breathless quartet.

"Reconnaissance sortie. The moon was nearly full last night, providing sufficient light, certainly enough to be able to see."

Minutes after de Sousa had given the NCOs final instructions, the Kunahamas attacked the left flank, making a drive parallel to the river trying to avoid a frontal attack on the Portuguese forces. Sporadic firing broke out as the troopers saw the first signs of movement behind the trees and thorn bushes. A light breeze carried the smell of burnt cordite to those in the command post. As the conflict escalated, the sporadic rifle shots gave way to full barrages, and screams and shouts intermingled with the gunfire. It was quickly evident that the Portuguese forces faced an overwhelming onslaught. The Kunahamas charged en masse, breaking through the perimeter defences, driving the troopers out of their trenches and back towards the centre of the camp.

Making a supreme effort, the troops managed to counter this advance, driving the rebels back, but it was now vicious hand-to-hand combat and the dead and wounded were soon strewn on the ground, their blood seeping into the sand. Sanity no longer prevailed, rifles, bayonets, swords and machetes being used by men now driven by a madness only known to those fighting for their lives. The air was raucous with the shouting and screaming of men facing death. The Kunahama dead littered the approaches to the trenches, mown down by the hail of fire from the soldiers but still the casualties did not deter them. Seemingly endless reserves immediately replaced their dead and wounded, once again charging the trenches in full strength.

The battle had been raging for hours and still the troopers were managing to repel the assaults on the trenches. Werner had lost all sense of time, firing randomly at the enemy every time they presented a target. He believed he had shot dozens, his rifle so hot he could not touch the barrel. Dead and wounded lay all around him, the trenches offering the only cover from the continuous rifle volleys the enemy unleashed. But it was obvious they could not hold the enemy much longer.

Captain de Sousa looked at Werner.

"Joachim!" he shouted above the shooting, "You've got to get out of here!"

"Christ! I can't do that – what about you?"

"Don't fuckin' argue! I want you to cross the river, take your servant and my batman with you. We can't hold out much longer. I'll follow; you can give me covering fire from the other side. Take enough horses with you, as well as a horse for me—hurry!"

"A lot of the horses have been killed."

"Take any horses. Just hurry! There's no time left."

"The other men?" Werner asked, his conscience and his duty as an officer not accepting what the captain ordered.

"Christus! When it gets to hand-to-hand combat, it's everyone for himself. Most of them will just take off into the bush, strip off their uniforms and hide. Some of them have had to do this before! Just go – now!"

De Sousa's batman stripped off his uniform and donned a civilian shirt and trousers, removing his campaign hat and replacing it with a hat taken from a dead militiaman. Hunched over, the small group ran towards the boma, dust spurting around them as the enemy concentrated their fire on the movement. Once inside the boma they were hidden, but bullets still ripped through the stacked branches showering them with broken twigs and leaves. The stray bullets had found many animals, and dead and dying horses and oxen lay on the ground, blood seeping into the dust.

They rounded up four saddled horses, probably those from the reconnaissance group who had not had time to strip the saddles. Once in the saddle, Werner savagely drove his heels into the horse's flanks towards the river, forcing it into the flowing water. He had not realized how deep the water was until the horse sank below him, his weight driving it under. He slid from the saddle and with one hand grasping the pommel, swam with the horse to the other side. He was aware of the others doing the same around him. The river was swift, and the four horses were rapidly swept downstream, away from enemy fire. Reaching the opposite bank unscathed, they concealed themselves deep in the dense bush that thronged the riverbank. Here they waited, listening to the fight still raging.

Werner peered through the branches, watching the river.

The sounds of battle continued unabated, then suddenly escalated. There was an enormous volley of shots followed by wild cries, shouts, and screams.

De Sousa exploded from the bushes, sprinting for the river, a band of blacks in pursuit, some in loincloths, others dressed in trousers. Brandishing a mixture of rifles and machetes, yelling and screaming they tried to catch the captain. He leapt into the water, taking long high strides through the shallows, finally diving in and swimming frantically towards the opposite bank. Werner and Philippe immediately opened fire, and the surprised rebels hesitated long enough to give the de Sousa a chance. Swept downstream, the distance between him and his pursuers swiftly increased. Finally, he staggered through the shallows and scrambled up the riverbank, to be met by Werner's group and the horses. The exhausted man grabbed the proffered reins and swung into the saddle. They galloped into the bush away from the river, putting as much distance as possible between themselves and the rebels.

After about five miles, de Sousa reined in.

"I did not desert my men, so don't judge me!"

The captain looked at Werner, an anguished expression on his face. He spoke as if he wanted to make this statement before anybody questioned his actions.

"The command post was totally overrun, I'm lucky to have got away with my life. If there was anybody I could have assisted, I would have."

"Wait a minute, who am I to judge? I saw you fight, please, I understand what happened," Werner replied quietly.

"I'll never forget this. The bastards broke through our defences and simply overran us, shooting and hacking at my men. We held them off as long as we could and then when we could see there was no stopping them, we fled. Some of our blacks were clever and did as I told them to do, they stripped off their uniforms, picked up rifles and clothing from the dead rebels and made as if they were also rebels, just fusing in with that rebellious mass. It was absolute mayhem. I'm sure a few got away; I hope so," de Sousa said, his voice dull and emotionless.

"What do we do now?"

"We ride, and get away as far as we can. I think we should go southeast into the desert. That will give us our best chance of survival. The Kunahamas keep away from that area and the tribe that controls it; they are not involved in this rebellion. Or so I believe."

"Hell, we haven't got any water or food!"

"I know. But it's too dangerous to stay here. Do we have an option?"

De Sousa was silent for a moment, waiting for a reply. Receiving none, he continued.

"Well, that takes care of that then. Please, nobody is to shoot. We don't want to draw any attention."

They walked eastwards, trailing the exhausted horses behind them, the sun beating down relentlessly, the heat overpowering. Away from the river, the terrain changed, the bush less dense, so they could see a hundred yards or so ahead. The captain ordered his batman to reconnoitre ahead of them, telling Werner that Paulo was an experienced soldier and an excellent scout.

"That's why I chose him to be my batman in the first place," he said.

By the afternoon, the men were thirsty and hungry. The usual cloud build-up had started at midday, and by mid afternoon huge cumulus cloud concentrations dominated the sky, occasionally blocking out the sun. At least it gave the riders some relief from the heat.

Surely it was raining in the distance, Werner thought, as he saw distant lightning flashes and heard the low rumble of thunder. Gradually, the cloud mass above them darkened, and the lightning flashes neared. Suddenly, a lightning bolt struck the ground ahead of them, followed by a thunderclap seconds later. Soon the first intermittent large drops of rain dropped to the ground with loud plops, impacting into small clouds of powdered dust. In typical cloudburst fashion, the rain steadily increased in intensity. Soon they were drenched, water streaming from their hats, the horses' coats glistening wet. They cupped their hands to catch the rain, greedily drinking the water, smiling for the first time that day, the feeling of relief incredible. The deluge was so intense it was pointless trying to speak to one another, the drumming of water on man and horse drowning out all other sounds. The torrent soon weakened, but by then the ground was awash, small streams flowing everywhere. The cloudburst vanished as quickly as it arrived. The storm announced its departure with a few rumblings of thunder, these slowly receding in the distance, as did the lightning flashes. The rain had swept the heat away, and the light breeze which accompanied the rain was cool and refreshing.

The men allowed the horses to slake their thirst from the numerous streams which seemed to have materialized everywhere. After drinking as much as they could, the men filled their canteens, hoping this would see them through to the next source of water.

As it darkened, de Sousa called a halt, and the men stripped the saddles from their horses. The two black men conversed softly between themselves and disappeared into the bush. The captain remained silent, seemingly unconcerned about their disappearance. A half hour later, they returned with a few wild melons; these were green and round with speckled white patches. They called them *nanas*. These cracked open like a watermelon, revealing a green-white pulp which they extracted with their hands and ate. The contents were neither sweet nor sour, just bland and tasteless.

Exhausted, they huddled in their saddle blankets, which afforded at least some protection against the hordes of mosquitoes, using their saddles as pillows.

Werner struggled through the early dark hours of his stint at sentry duty. The morning chill seemed to penetrate to his very bones. Shivers racked his body. He groaned; he had an excruciating headache. Even after the sun rose and bathed him in warmth, bouts of shivering would still rack his body. God only knows what, but I hope I'm not coming down with something, he thought. He said nothing to the others, hoping to keep his condition to himself.

Once astride his horse, however, it was sheer agony, the horse's motion seeming to aggravate his condition, his headache ready to split his skull. And it did not go unnoticed; Philippe was the first to comment.

"*Mestre*, I think you have the mosquito sickness. I can see you are cold in this hot sun. Does your head hurt?"

He nodded his head carefully in affirmation.

"Something is wrong; it's getting worse. I'm about to fall off this horse."

"*Merda*! It's malaria," the captain said, bringing the party to a halt. "We can't let you ride. We'll have to build a travois so that you can lie down. Your horse can pull it. Let's do it now."

It was a difficult job. They had no axes and rope, but had to hack branches from trees with their knives. Paulo found a type of African vine, very flexible but strong and they used this to tie the various wooden poles together. In addition, Philippe and Paulo wove a net from the vines making a bed on the travois. Crude but practical, the captain thought. Hopefully, it would withstand the rigours of travel. They had a long way to go.

Werner's condition rapidly deteriorated, and he was soon showing the first signs of delirium, rolling his head from side to side and murmuring under his breath.

"What are we going to do with him?" the captain asked aloud, addressing nobody in particular.

"*Capitano*, we must take him south to the Finnish mission in German territory. They have doctors and medicine," Philippe said.

"How do you know this?"

"I lived there for a while—I know where it is."

"But that will take days!"

"It will, but I can make a medicine from some leaves which will help."

The captain estimated that if they turned south they would encounter the Kunene River again where it turned westwards towards the Atlantic Ocean. They would need three days for the journey. They were still in territory controlled by the Kunahamas. They would have to proceed with extreme caution. But they had no alternative, for without medical attention Werner might not survive. De Sousa considered Werner a friend; he would do whatever it took to save him.

By the next day Werner had lapsed into total delirium, rambling in German and Portuguese with the occasional English phrase thrown in. He barked out military instructions in German, de Sousa fortunately not understanding these. Then followed hours of unconsciousness, his body shivering and his teeth chattering. On the third day, he started to perspire profusely. The captain called a halt near a stream containing rock-pools filled by the recent rain. The captain and Philippe took turns bathing him with cool water, trying to lower his temperature; his body was so hot to the touch it seemed on fire. Philippe disappeared into the bush, returning an hour later with a collection of leaves. He mashed them, mixing the sap with water and dribbling this into Werner's mouth. That night, the captain took a chance and shot a gemsbok, barbecuing the meat over hot coals.

The next day they crossed the Kunene River again at a point where the water shallowed as it passed over a string of rapids. They now moved in a southerly direction into SudwestAfrika but remained on guard even when they finally crossed the border. This was no more than an imaginary longitudinal line, not something the Kunahamas or Hereros recognized, certainly not in this time of conflict.

"How long before we get to the mission?" the captain asked Philippe.

The black man stared into the distance. The land was now flat, without stone or hill. Obviously a flood plain, the captain thought, a seemingly endless flat expanse of dried silt, which stretched into the distance, heat mirages dancing on the horizon.

"Another day if we do not have to turn to miss lions and elephants. There are also many buffalo, all dangerous," Philippe eventually replied.

He was right. During the course of the next day, only once having to circumvent a pride of lions shading under a very large camel-thorn tree, they came upon a settlement, a congregation of small adobe huts and primitive buildings built of mud, brick, and stone with corrugated iron roofs. A small church with a squat steeple, its sides corrugated iron, stood proud of the rest of the buildings. A few wells dotted the settlement, while a windmill, its vanes slowly spinning in the light breeze pumped water into a round brick and cement built reservoir. Three children were drawing water from one of the wells, hauling the filled buckets to the surface by a rope running over a pulley. They were overseen by a black man, probably their father, who stared at the four horsemen as they rode into the settlement. Corrals on the outskirts of the settlement contained a few cattle, goats, and horses. A few scraggly chickens roamed between the buildings, scratching and pecking in the dust. This was no new settlement; this mission station had been in existence for some time, a haven of peace in this war-torn country.

As the horses came to a halt outside a large building, three women emerged, all dressed in identical light blue frocks with skirts reaching to the ground. They were obviously of Nordic origin, their complexions light, their skin like white porcelain, and their hair, the little that showed from beneath their bonnets, a sun-bleached blonde. The white starched bonnets were similar to those that Catholic nuns wore, but of a different design. They immediately undid the ropes that secured the unconscious Werner to the travois.

Assisted by Philippe and Paulo, they lifted Werner from the travois and carried him indoors. He was covered in dust. The woman who appeared to be in charge addressed de Sousa in German, and he shook his head and replied in Portuguese. Philippe, who understood both, translated, informing the captain that they asked that he follow them indoors.

"What are they going to do?" de Sousa asked, looking at Philippe with concern.

"They will look after my *Mestre*. They say we must stay in another building; this is the hospital. Don't worry, I know this place, and I know some of the people."

The captain looked suspiciously at Philippe.

"What do you mean; you know some of these people? You speak German, where did you learn to speak the language?"

Philippe did not know what to say.

"I am from Angola, but went to school here at this mission school. That's where I learnt to speak German. I don't speak it well."

"Huh! You are a strange one. Are you Angolan?"

"Yes."

Where did Senhor de Almeida find you?"

Philippe realized he would have to lie and proceeded to tell the captain what his master had told him to say.

"In Angola."

"He was in Angola before?"

"Yes, when he left, he took me with him to Mozambique."

The Captain shook his head.

"Strange – he never mentioned that he had been to Angola before. Are you sure?"

"Yes, that's when he employed me."

The captain mumbled under his breath, but did not pursue the subject further although it was evident he was puzzled. He decided he would have to talk to Werner; this Philippe, Werner's manservant, intrigued him – who was he? Where did he find him?

Captain de Sousa found the Finnish missionaries to be a strange lot. They did not treat the indigenous people as servants, but rather as equals, although the blacks carried out all instructions as if they were servants, treating the missionaries with the right degree of respect. In Angola, the whites treated blacks as the property of the government and who were forced to take employment when offered. It was no better than slavery; they just gave it a different name – contract labour. If you had the misfortune to be black and the government found you were unemployed, you were forced to work for a specific period for the government, building roads or similar projects, or you were assigned to a plantation or ranch which had approached the government for labourers. If you refused, you were jailed. Wages were barely above subsistence level, but no negotiation was permitted.

Captain de Sousa was given a small room in an adjoining building. Its interior walls were whitewashed with lime that reflected the light, creating a bright but sterile mood. It contained a narrow cot and a table against the wall on which stood an enamelled basin and a jug of water. The bed was complete with white linen, surrounded by a mosquito net which hung from the ceiling. A window opened to a courtyard from where he could hear voices, even though he was unable to understand the language.

The Finnish nurse was in her forties, her face Nordic pale notwithstanding the harsh sun. That she was a missionary was obvious, her disposition serene and aloof, a large crucifix hanging from a blue and white ribbon round her neck. The captain was acutely aware that she was a Protestant. She spoke to the captain and Philippe translated. He could bathe if he wished in a separate room, which she indicated down the passage. This contained a large zinc bath surrounded by slatted wooden floorboards. The captain nodded his head in approval and asked if water could be brought as he wished to bathe now. She smiled and said she would see to it.

Werner slipped in and out of consciousness, vaguely aware of people around him and of being laid on an oilskin-covered examination table. His clothing was removed and he felt someone bathing him, the water cool on his body.

"Mein Gott!"

The two nurses halted their washing and looked at each other questioningly, surprised by the doctor's outburst.

"Carry on, carry on," she said.

He opened his eyes. A beautiful face, surrounded by dark brown hair, peered down at him, the forehead furrowed in concern. For a moment, a fleeting glimmer of recognition manifested itself, but faded, the beautiful face lingering, as he again lapsed into unconsciousness.

The dark-haired woman, the source of the surprised exclamation, proceeded to examine him, taking his temperature with a rectal thermometer, looking into his nose and ears, listening to his chest with a stethoscope and thumping his body with her fingers. She inserted a catheter into his penis to obtain a urine sample. At her request, the nurses turned him on his side, and she efficiently administered two injections to his buttocks, a quinine solution, and a sedative, then scribbled her findings on his chart.

Although still racked with fever, the injection began to take effect and he slipped further into a drug-induced deep sleep. His shivering subsided, his body relaxed. Although it was midday and the heat oppressive, they kept him covered with a blanket.

She was shocked. She remembered him; he was the German marine officer on the SS Tanga. To see him here, in the company of what appeared to be a Portuguese officer was a surprise. From the man's servant, they had gathered that the men had fled southern Angola where they had been attacked by the indigenous people. But how had he got to Angola and why was he there? He was a German officer; he would not be permitted in Angola. And the other white man, who was he? Surely, the Portuguese would not have permitted German military personnel entry into Angola.

Pastor Vlotzka Haiddenon, the chief theologian of the mission, chose not to interfere, leaving the administering of the sick to Doctor Eggers. She had joined the mission about a month back and already she had proven to be an extremely competent physician. His degree was a doctorate in theology, so he was unable to be of assistance in medical matters, but he had great faith in her abilities and considered her a godsend in this remote region. Qualified woman doctors were unheard of, certainly in German SudwestAfrika. Why she had chosen to practice her profession in this area was beyond him and when asked, she invariably evaded the question. This did not concern the missionary; he considered it improper to delve in her personal affairs. It was none of his business. She was not particularly religious; he would have preferred that she was, but rationalized this was a gift horse—don't look it in the mouth, he told himself.

These men, however, were another matter entirely. He needed to report their arrival to the authorities; they had arrived on horseback, fully armed, accompanied by two servants, no clothes, and without camping or any other basic equipment. There were few white men in this region. Already, it was rumoured that they were the sole survivors of some ghastly insurrection in Angola. Astonishingly, the sick man was in possession of a considerable amount of money, most of it in Portuguese Escudos, although he did also have both German and English currency on him. This money was contained in a money-belt, which the nurses had removed. This was now in the Pastor's office under lock and key. Who was he?

At dinner, he felt compelled to discuss the unforeseen arrival of these men with his senior staff.

"I will have to report these men. The authorities are sensitive to movements across the border. It's the gunrunning that concerns them and the amount of money carried by your patient is worrying. Why on earth would he have so much money on him?" he asked, shaking his head, indicating his disapproval.

The young doctor looked at the *Pastor* seated at the head of the table.

" "He does not strike me as a dishonest man," she said quietly. "*Pastor Dokter*, if I may, I suggest that we wait until the patient recovers from his delirium, then we can speak to him. Now, he is still incoherent."

She hesitated. She was about to tell the table that she had met the patient onboard the ship from Germany, but for reasons she could not place, decided not to do so. Better he told his own story when he was able to.

"How long before we can speak to him?" the *Pastor Dokter* enquired.

"I imagine within a day or two. He is strong and should recover quickly now that he is receiving proper medical attention."

"Well . . . in that case, I will accede to your request. Where is the Portuguese gentleman?"

"He declined our invitation to supper and preferred to take his meal in his room; not being properly dressed was his excuse," a senior assistant missionary replied.

"I believe the man's uncomfortable, being a Catholic amongst all us Lutherans. Well then, Doctor Eggers, I'll wait to hear from you about our mysterious man's progress."

Werner opened his eyes to see the young doctor standing next to his bed.

"I know you," he said, his voice no more than a whisper.

"I know. We met on the ship and you rescued me on the train," she replied smiling.

"Of course, now I remember."

"What are you doing here? Pastor Haiddenon wants to report your arrival to the authorities at Ondongua."

Werner's eyes closed. He still was exhausted,

"Better that you sleep. We can talk later to-day," she said, realizing that it was still too early to press him for information.

The next day he awoke feeling famished. His fever had disappeared, his temperature was normal.

"You've improved, but you will continue to suffer bouts of fever for a while," she said, recording his temperature on the chart.

"I do feel better, in fact I'm hungry."

"I'll arrange breakfast. How about a boiled egg, a roll and coffee?"

"Fine, but make that two eggs and a roll."

She raised her eyebrows in pleased surprise.

He had just finished his breakfast when she entered the room again, sitting on a chair next to his bed.

She placed her elbows on her knees and leant forward, speaking in a low voice.

"You need to tell me what is going on. Pastor Haiddenon is curious; he thinks that your friend is an Angolan military officer and knows that you have a huge sum of money in your money-belt. He says he needs to report you to the military commander at Ondongua."

"Where's my money?" he asked, his concern evident.

"I told you before, but you probably don't remember. It's safe with Pastor Haiddenon. But let me finish; they don't know you are a German officer. What's all this secrecy?"

"It's complicated."

"Isn't it always? And who is the Portuguese officer? What's he doing here?"

"We were attacked in Angola and fled south. They brought me here because my servant knew of your hospital. That's all I can tell you." He paused for a moment and then added, "I would like to speak to Captain de Sousa. Could somebody please ask him to come here?"

"Very well, I will say nothing and leave you, but you owe me an explanation—just remember that. I'll call Captain de Sousa."

De Sousa arrived, freshly shaved, his clothing washed; he looked quite presentable. He smiled at Werner, clearly relieved at his friend's condition.

"Christus! It's good to see you've recovered!"

"Yes, I'm feeling a lot better. And you? What's happening?"

"Nothing really, I've been waiting for you to get better." The man's smile disappeared, replaced by a concerned frown. "I can't speak the language and your *cavalerico* has to translate every time I say anything. There's no doubt that these people are extremely curious about us . . . but then, my friend, so am I. I have been speaking to your *cavalerico* – there are a few peculiarities in your story that we need to discuss."

"Such as?"

"You speak all these languages, you have a way about you that indicates a military background, and when delirious you speak German and give orders in German. First, I thought you some sort of spy, but why? Portugal and Germany are friends. Who are you really?"

Werner stared at his friend.

"That's ridiculous," he finally said.

"Is it? I'm your friend first, and then a Portuguese officer, so will you tell me?"

For a moment, Werner was at loss. Without help, it was obviously a near impossible task to deal with dos Santos, the gunrunner. And that was his mission; he constantly needed to remind himself of that. Dos Santos could move through Kunehama territory with impunity, free to deliver the rifles from Huambo across the border—he had to be stopped. But Werner did not have the faintest idea as to where dos Santos would deliver these in SudwestAfrika.

He took a deep breath.

"Dos Santos is a gunrunner," he said, looking the Portuguese officer in the eyes.

"OK, I know that, but what has that got to do with what we are discussing?"

"Everything!"

The officer turned round and walked to the window, staring out into the courtyard. He lit a cigarette, blowing the smoke into the open air. Werner realized his statement had caught the man totally by surprise. He did not press him but patiently waited a reply. Finally de Sousa turned round and leant against the windowsill, staring intently at Werner.

"So?" The officer clearly expected Werner to add to his statement.

The bastard, Werner thought, now he wants to play a game – but he's telling me nothing! What am I going to do? I've already said too much!

"So, we agree, he's a gunrunner. Are you trying to sell him rifles?" de Sousa finally asked.

"No! Well, yes. Let's say I'm pretending to sell him rifles."

"So then you must be trying to stop him?"

"Yes! I'm trying to stop him."

Werner was exasperated.

"Interesting. Why didn't you say so in the first place? Because so am I and in fact, so are others in the Portuguese government."

They laughed, the relief at having broken through some invisible hurdle evident.

"You're a German officer, aren't you?"

Werner did not reply.

"OK, don't say anything. I knew I was right! What do we do now? This is your territory."

"I think we stick to our story. As soon as I can travel, we leave here and intercept dos Santos when his rifles cross the border. I can call up reinforcements."

"What rifles are you referring to?" de Sousa asked, looking somewhat bewildered.

Werner told his friend in detail what had transpired that night after the captain's column had left.

"Okay, we knew about those rifles. The weapons won't cross the border here," De Sousa said emphatically

"What do you mean, you knew?"

"Well, some people in our military intelligence know. They gleaned information that dos Santos will take these rifles to Namibe, on the coast in Angola, that's in the south, and then use a fishing vessel to take these still further south to a place on the coast of SudwestAfrika. There is a huge lagoon with an outlet to the sea on the coast just below Walvis Bay, that's a small British enclave on the coast."

"Yes, I know the place, Sandwich Bay is it? I saw it on the map."

"Well, at high tide a small ship can cross the sandbar and enter the lagoon. Although surrounded by a sea of dunes, it's unique in that it has fresh water. An underground river seeps below the sand dunes into the lagoon. There was more to Major Olazabal's column than just a show of strength for the benefit of the Kunehamas; Major Olazabal and I had proposed to intercept dos Santos' wagons when he moved south. Very few knew of the plan. That piece of shit has been selling guns to our enemies as well as our own people for the past two years. Initially, we were suspicious of you, especially when we heard you wished to go inland. You were nearly arrested! You remember the judge, de Mello? Well, he voiced misgivings about you, he didn't think you were what you pretended to be."

"How do you know about Sandwich Bay?" Werner asked.

"I've been there by ship. It's an oasis in the dunes. The lagoon is surrounded on one side, that is, where the dunes slope into the lagoon, by a vast impenetrable mass of reeds, reaching far above a man's head. The lagoon is tidal, the sea rushes in and out. The wind is ferocious;

the coast is extremely dangerous. However, in the early hours of the morning, with the correct tide, the wind is nearly calm and a ship with a shallow draft can enter."

They heard footsteps. Somebody was approaching the room.

"So do we agree, we stick to our story – you know, what we said before, we fled conflict in Angola and wish to return?"

"Yes."

Captain de Sousa bowed to Pastor Dokter Haiddenon as he stood at the door. The pastor was a portly man, dressed in a grey striped suit. He was in his mid-fifties, both his hair and full beard grey and streaked with white. A pince-nez was perched on the bridge of his nose, attached by a black ribbon to his waistcoat. Werner thought that men of God had a special way about them, evident in their mannerisms. They always looked humble although this did not necessarily mean they were; they merely looked it. This missionary displayed the same traits.

A chair was placed next to the bed, but the pastor ignored this, choosing to stand.

"Are they looking after you?" he asked.

"Thank you, I'm extremely grateful to you and your staff," Werner replied.

"That is a considerable amount of money you were carrying."

"Yes, I know. I'm a manufacturing representative. I was trading in Angola and got caught up in a rebellion."

"Yes, we have heard of an enormous loss of life in southern Angola. They say about four hundred souls were killed. We have prayed for their redemption."

"We were lucky to escape with our lives."

The pastor shook his head, both his anguish and disapproval evident.

"These wars are tragic, they know no boundaries. Now, I need to report your arrival here to the local military command. Where will you be going when you leave here?"

"We will return to Angola. You have probably realized that my companion is a Portuguese officer?"

"Yes, I have. I will report that you arrived needing medical attention having fled from the Kunehamas after the battle and are now returning. Your money-belt is safe in my office. You can collect this whenever you wish."

"I would like to make a donation to the mission."

"Thank you," the pastor unbent slightly, "that will be appreciated."

Persuaded by Doctor Eggers, the men decided to remain another week at the mission to enable Werner to regain his strength. By the next day, he was able to leave his bed and take stock of his surroundings. During the morning, the small hospital was a hive of activity. The missionaries had established a medical clinic which drew the sick from the surrounding Ovambo area. The Ovambos were the dominant tribe in northern SudwestAfrika. The sick and frail would arrive daily before sunrise, limping and shuffling with small children on their backs or in-tow. They would form a queue, standing or sitting on the ground for hours, patiently waiting to be attended to. The clinic opened its doors from about seven in the morning and by lunch time, the staff had usually dealt with the last patient.

Werner sat on the hospital porch on a crudely constructed bench. The captain, impatient to be on his way, joined him. The two men discussed their next course of action, both adamant that dos Santos needed to be stopped. The captain was convinced that dos Santos would use the current insurrection permeating southern and central Angola as an opportunity to transport his rifles to Namibe without interference. He would encounter no government patrols; in fact, the Kunehamas would provide protection.

"I believe he left Huambo shortly after us and by now must be only be a few days from Namibe. We will never be able to intercept him. Anyway, what can we do with only a few men? We have no reinforcements available. I'm sure absolute chaos still reigns in southern Angola," the captain said dejectedly, smoking one of the pastor's donated cigars. He blew smoke towards the corrugated roof of the veranda.

"God! This would be better with a beer, glass of wine or better still, some port."

"Better still with female company," Werner chuckled.

"Of course. All we have here are nuns and doctors. Quite awful, they're so career-orientated. They certainly don't appear to have any interest in men."

"Christus! Have a heart, they're missionaries!" Werner said, laughing.

The smile disappeared from his face, and his expression grew serious again as both men lapsed into silence, pondering their predicament.

"Maybe I'm wrong. Maybe he won't make for Namibe. If I were him, I would make for the border. Who is going to stop him? Certainly not the Portuguese!" de Sousa said. There was silence for a while, then de Sousa spoke again.

"I would like to suggest we send our two servants out as scouts – they can use our horses and pretend to be Kunehamas. They can ride back until near to Huambo and scout around—listen to bush talk; you'll be amazed what you get to hear. If dos Santos is in the southern area, everyone will know, orders will have been issued that he and his men not to be harmed. If I'm right, we can lead him into a trap."

De Sousa stubbed the cigar into the sole of his boot and flicked the butt over the veranda railing.

"That's quite an undertaking! Who's going to help us – we certainly can't take them on alone?" Werner queried.

"Surely you could spirit up some German reinforcements?"

Werner guffawed, a loud sound in the stillness. "I need to think about that," he replied, a plan beginning to take shape in his mind.

He mulled over the captain's suggestion for a moment. Of course, he could send a cable to Major Zietzmann; the military was bound to react. He had no idea of the strength of the military forces in the north of the German colony. This was Ovamboland, and the Ovambos were not at war; that was about all he knew.

"We need to send the two men off. I'll get my money-belt back, give them some money to use for supplies and if they need to buy their way out of danger."

The two black men saw no danger in returning to Angola in the guise of Kunahama warriors; they both spoke the language fluently. De Sousa suggested that they pass themselves off as members of the attack force involved in the conflict with the Portuguese. If asked, this was where they had acquired their horses and guns. They listened attentively to his instructions and all agreed on a place to meet on their return. Eight days was considered sufficient for them to establish dos Santos' whereabouts and the direction his wagon train was heading. Werner re-emphasized their mission; they were merely to observe and not to make direct contact with the gunrunner under any circumstances.

Samantha Eggers no longer hid behind her professional façade, and from time to time, even bestowed an occasional smile on Werner. She realized that the officer was on some covert military mission and that the less she knew the better. He on the other hand pressed her for information; where was the nearest telegraph office, did German patrols come through this area and if so, what was their strength and where were they garrisoned?

"I don't know what you are planning," she said, concerned. "But I hope this will not involve the mission in anyway?"

"Good Lord, I would never permit that."

"So, something is going on?"

"We are here only because I needed medical attention, otherwise we would be hundreds of miles away."

The day after Philippe and Paulo departed, a mounted column of Schutztruppe arrived at the mission, part of the force garrisoned at Ondongua under the command of Major Ferdinand Graf zu Dohner, about sixty miles from the mission. He told them that, although peace reigned in this part of the colony, discontent still simmered amongst the Ovambos, but, he proudly added, the Schutztruppe was ready to deal with any insurrection.

"Does the town have a telegraph office?" asked Werner.

"Yes," replied the sergeant. "It is for military use only, but the local civilian population are allowed to use it. Do you wish to send a telegram?"

Werner hesitated. Certainly, he needed to send a telegram but did not know quite how to do it, certain that the sergeant and others would read the contents.

Yes, but it is in Portuguese."

"That's OK, who cares? It's not the first time a Portuguese telegram has been sent from there. You'll be surprised at the number of Portuguese in Ondongua."

Werner drafted the telegram, addressing it to the Portuguese Consular Office in Windhuk, to a Senora Mato, the undercover name given to Werner by the German authorities. This would alert the Intelligence Division, who would intercept the telegram before any attempt could be made to deliver it. Major Zietzmann was the ultimate recipient.

After some thought, Werner drafted the following:

CONSIGNMENT IS ON ITS WAY SWA VIA PORT NAMIBE STOP SEA ROUTE FINAL DESTINATION SANDWICH BAY STOP WE ARE IN SWA NEAR ONDONGUA

STOP AWAIT YOUR INSTRUCTIONS STOP REPLY C/O ONDONGUA STOP DE ALMEIDA

He handed this to the sergeant in a sealed envelope and mentioned that he and his colleague would possibly visit Ondongua during the next few days for supplies before returning to Angola.

The two black men rode rapidly north, crossing the border where the longitudinal line met the Kunene River. It was obvious that the rebellion had spread rapidly south. The first villages they encountered were deserted, the men having joined the Kunehama rebellion and their womenfolk hiding in the bush, afraid of Portuguese reprisal raids. They soon made contact with Kunehama raiding parties. That they were on horseback was a Godsend. The rebels believed the two men to be scouts sent out by the tribal chiefs to reconnoitre, and treated them with deference and answered all questions without hesitation. The rebels controlled all territories in southern Angola. Philippe audaciously cross-questioned the rebel commanders as to the whereabouts of a small wagon train that would have recently departed Huambo making its way south under the protection of Najamo, a Kunehama kingpin. Although the Kunehamas knew of Najamo, none knew of such a wagon train.

Philippe and Paulo penetrated further into Angola, changing direction and riding north-west in the direction of the coast and Namibe. The bush gave way to rolling savannahs, the area sparsely populated. Huge herds of springbuck, buffalo and gemsbok roamed the plains, the area unaffected by the rebellion. It seemed their quarry had disappeared into thin air; they persisted, forced to ride further north on the outskirts of the desert.

On the third day, they halted atop a shallow hill, the only high ground for miles around. They hobbled their horses, leaving them free to roam and graze on the sparse grass. They lit no fire, but ate the biltong they had brought, salted venison marinated in vinegar with herbs and then dried in the wind until it was as hard as rock. They washed the meal down with water. The sun set rapidly, the evening sky filling with a multitude of stars as it darkened. There was no moon and the air was crystal clear.

Philippe rose from his haunches and stared into the distance towards the north.

"Look! A fire."

Yes, there was a light in the distance. It was not a star on the horizon.

"It's a campfire, but it is a long way from here," Philippe's companion volunteered.

"It could be dos Santos."

"Who else, my friend, it must be him."

"Don't be so sure. But we'll need to check."

"OK, let's sleep, but we must rise early and move before daybreak. Just before it gets light we can stop and hide, and watch them from a distance. If they are travelling south, they will move towards us. We'll need to be careful."

Philippe patted his companion on the back.

"Don't worry, even if we are seen they'll think us rebels. But still, better they don't see us."

Dorothea was at odds with herself. She was devoting far more of her professional attention to the young officer than was necessary. He was rapidly regaining his strength, the malaria bouts now under control, the quinine doing its work. She enjoyed talking to him. Every evening, after work was done and the sun slipped below the horizon, the white mission staff congregated on the veranda, nurses and mission teachers, Dorothea and Pastor Haiddenon. Both de Sousa and Werner would join them.

She thought him rugged and attractive and even though a military man, he seemed caring and compassionate. He was certainly different from the local Europeans, who usually treated the black inhabitants abominably. *Untermenschen* was the descriptive word—all who were not white and European fell into that category; they were considered no better than slaves and treated accordingly. Werner acknowledged that this was their country and that they had first right to it, a sentiment certainly not shared by many, some of whom considered such remarks subversive. Even de Sousa surprised her. Rumour had it that the Portuguese were particularly harsh and cruel, still practicing slavery, wrenching blacks from their families and tribal lands and sending them to Brazil, never to see their homeland or their families again. De Sousa had more than once voiced his abhorrence and the wish that the Portuguese authorities would deal harshly with those traders. Embarrassed, but feeling obliged to make some sort of excuse for this reprehensible practice, he reminded them that the colony was, until recently, used as a dumping ground for criminals and other exiles, and that perhaps no better could be expected from people who really represented the dregs of society. Some, he added darkly, had infiltrated the provincial governments and accounted for much of the corruption found in the lower levels of administration. Unfortunately, for a price, some officials closed their eyes.

The same could not be said of the Boers. They had trekked between 1880 and 1890 from the South African Boer Republics across the Kalahari Desert to escape British rule, enduring tremendous hardship before finally settling in the Angolan highlands and along the Kunene River. Most belonged to strict religious sects, Protestants in a predominantly Catholic country, aloof and jealous of their heritage, but fair and correct to the extreme, paying their workers for work done, if not with money, then in goods. They treated the indigenous people with kindness and respect, but mixing with them was taboo; they immediately ostracized anyone who crossed the colour line.

Werner fretted. Five days had passed. He knew dos Santos was underway with the rifles he had seen at Huambo, but where to? He found it difficult to appear nonchalant and unconcerned. If another smuggled shipment of rifles found its way to the Hereros, he would blame himself.

"Are you always this quiet?" Dorothea asked, sitting opposite him in a cane chair on the veranda.

"Yes, I suppose I am. I'm not one to make small talk."

"I can't help but get the impression you are troubled. Is anything wrong?"

"No, I'm fine. I must thank you for bringing me back to good health. I'm lucky to have found you here. Thank you again."

"I'm glad I met you. You probably thought me rude on the ship," she found herself saying before she could stop herself.

He did not reply.

His presence at the mission disturbed her; she often finding herself thinking of him, her mind wandering. In his company, she was both excited and confused at the same time. Quite ridiculous, she thought. What is this man to me, she asked herself, surely just another patient? But she knew it was something more.

Every evening all would sit down to dinner at the huge, long table with Reverend Haiddenon seated at the head.

It was only once Werner had accepted an invitation to this table that Louis eventually joined them. Although he had taken his meals in his room, the missionaries had persisted with their daily invitations to dinner. Werner ascribed this to the fact that being missionaries, persistence was a necessary trait, the conversion from heathen to Christian known to take time. Louis wasn't quite sure what Werner meant. These Protestants sometimes had the strangest senses of humour, he thought.

The theologian asked that they all join him in prayer, a protracted process in which Werner never felt entirely comfortable. He imagined de Sousa found it even more difficult though the man's expression revealed nothing as they stood behind their chairs with heads bowed. It was evident that the theologian and his assistants took their Christian convictions seriously, their demeanour sombre, seldom laughing and joking, the ladies always subdued.

"I've noticed that your servants are no longer with us," Pastor Heiddenon remarked.

The man misses nothing, Werner thought.

"That's right; we've sent them on a private mission. They should return in a day or two."

"Presumably, you'll be leaving then?"

"Yes, we are impatient to be on our way."

"And where will that be taking you?"

"Ondongua," Werner replied.

"Are you not returning to Angola?"

"Once we've concluded our business in Ondongua, we will head back. Hopefully, the Portuguese will have brought the rebellion under control by then."

"Not likely, our war here or rather the German's war has waged for some years now. How can you hope that peace will prevail so soon in Angola?"

"The rebels are not as organized there as they are here. I believe a strong military presence will see a rapid return to peace."

"Why don't you stay here and wait until it is safe?" Dorothea asked.

"Unfortunately, we have serious matters to attend to and the Captain wishes to return home; he has a wife waiting for him." Werner replied smiling.

After dinner, the three men made themselves comfortable on the veranda, the theologian generously offering each a cigar. Soon cigar smoke drifted away in the still evening air.

Suddenly the stillness of the evening was interrupted by the sound of approaching horses. Philippe and Paulo rode into the forecourt.

They had awakened in the early hours of the morning, the sky still dark, and made immediate preparations to stalk the camp in the distance. They tethered their hobbled horses to bushes in a dry arroyo, tying blankets over their eyes to ensure that they stood motionless and silent. The two men walked towards the encampment they had seen. The fire had died during the night but reappeared as the camp awoke and someone stoked the embers and added fresh wood. About two hundred yards from the camp, the two men dropped to the ground and slowly crept forward. Fortunately, the oxen and horses were corralled on the opposite side of the camp in a makeshift boma. They stopped about forty yards from the perimeter and lay motionless on the ground, waiting for the sun to appear above the horizon. With the sun directly behind them, it was unlikely that they could be seen.

Philippe estimated that the camp contained about twenty men. Most were black but he did see four white men. He saw no sign of dos Santos. The man's sheer size would give him away; if he were there, he would be immediately recognizable. There always was the possibility that the man was still asleep in a wagon, but Philippe believed this unlikely. Surely this was be the whole group?

"Philippe!" Paulo whispered fiercely, his face revealing his concern. "The fat one's not there. I can't see him anywhere!"

"I see that. That's strange."

"Where do you think these wagons are heading?"

"Not Namibe. Ondjiva, I think. That's on the way to SudwestAfrika, but more towards the sea, towards the Raucana waterfalls. This track goes that way. They probably chose that route to avoid German patrols. There are Hereros in the Kaokoaveld near the Kunene River. That's across the river, I'm sure that's where they're going."

"Look, they've all got rifles."

It was true; both black and white men had rifles. That was unusual; seldom did blacks carry rifles. The Hereros and Kunehamas were the exception; they were at war. Philippe had no doubt that this was dos Santos' wagon train.

Still on their stomachs, the two men slowly retraced their steps. They retrieved their horses and staying below the skyline, walked their horses away from the camp along the course of the dry riverbed. Only when they were a few miles away did they mount up. Their task done, they rode off at a good pace towards the border keeping a lookout for rebels. They rode for thirty-six hours, stopping only to rest and water their horses, making it back to the mission by the next evening.

Werner and de Sousa excused themselves and stepped down from the veranda to speak to their servants. The two black men were exhausted, their bodies streaked with dust where this had stuck to their skin. Similarly, dust caked the sweat-stained hides of the horses, their mouths foaming at the bit, their heads drooping with exhaustion. They had ridden their mounts near to collapse.

Werner acknowledged their greetings.

"I'm glad you made it back safely. Thank you," Werner said with relief etched on his features.

Philippe and Paulo collapsed on the ground next to the corral, leaning back against the posts, their chests still heaving from the hard ride.

Werner waited until Philippe had regained his breathe.

"Well, Philippe, what can you tell us?"

"They are heading towards Ondjiva, but dos Santos is not with them. There are about twenty men with rifles. Four of them are white. We didn't see any rifles in boxes."

"That's not possible, he must be with them!" de Sousa interjected.

"He's not with them!" Paulo repeated.

"Shit! Where is he then?" Werner said exasperatedly.

"I think he's looking after a second consignment," de Sousa said quietly.

"Sweet Jesus, what do you mean, a second consignment?"

"He's done this before, sent out two consignments. The man's devious – full of tricks," de Sousa replied.

"Captain, where would he be taking it?"

"To Namibe," the Portuguese officer said, an expression of uncertainty on his face. "Or so I think. I'm sure he is sending that shipment by boat from Namibe to Sandwich Bay, just as I told you."

"Well, Captain if that's the case, I have to get hold of our intelligence people. We've got to stop him. What about the wagons we saw?"

"Werner please, my name's Louis. I'd rather you called me that. As Paulo has said, I think his men are bringing these across the border. Probably in the vicinity of Raucana."

"OK, Louis," Werner inclined his head in acknowledgment. "We leave for Ondongua at first light. Let's hear what my CO has decided should be done."

The ride to Ondongua was boring, the terrain completely flat, no rocks or stones whatsoever. It was obvious they were still crossing the same vast flood plain interspersed with thorn trees, the countryside typical of the rest of Ovamboland.

Ondongua was a sprawling Ovambo settlement, huts surrounded by high wooden-poled picket fences scattered at random, the ground between the huts nothing but dust and sand as all grass and other ground vegetation long since been worn away or destroyed by the summer sun. Pathways, deeply worn tracks in the ground, connected the huts and kraals. These were six inches deep in powdered dust.

The German military was encamped a few hundred yards from the settlement where the surrounding bush commenced, their tents erected with exact precision, the canvas canopies forming a straight line. A large single-storey building—it really was no more than a large hut built from mud-brick with a corrugated iron roof, served as the command post, the German imperial flag fluttering from a flagpole. The telegraph wires were clearly visible as they exited the roof of the building and connected to a string of poles which disappeared into the distance. In fact, there were two sets of lines, one obviously connecting with Windhuk via Tsumeb, Otjiwarongo and Okahandja, while the other disappeared in a northwest direction towards Ondongua, the Ovambo tribal chief's place of residence.

Werner and Louis made their way directly to the command post. After the bright midday sunlight, the interior was dark and it took a few moments before Werner's eyes adjusted to the gloom. A rough counter blocked further entrance to the hut, and a Schutztruppe sergeant in full uniform rose at the approach of the men. It was evident that he was surprised to see two white civilians.

"Good day, gentlemen, have you lost your way?" he asked in German, his eyebrows arched in an obvious attempt at humour.

"Guten Tag," Werner replied. "In a way, yes. A rebellion in Angola and need for medical attention brought us south to SudwestAfrika."

"Oh yes, I heard about you. You were at the Finnish mission at Olukonda. One of our sergeants reported your presence to our CO. You speak German extremely well."

"I spent many years in Germany and am, in fact, a representative for a number of German manufacturers who sell goods to the Portuguese. I'm actually expecting a telegram; my name is Joachim de Almeida. Where can I enquire as to whether you have received a telegram for me?"

The sergeant smiled.

"You're at the right place," he said

He extracted a yellow envelope from a cubbyhole in a large bookcase which stood to one side and handed this to Werner.

Outside, they found a bench under a tree where Werner sat down and opened the telegram. It was from Major Zietzmann, not that this was the name the Major used. The sender was Senora Mato, the Major's undercover name. It was in Portuguese. It read:

CAN ONLY SPARE MOUNTED COLUMN OF THIRTY MEN. WILL ARRIVE ONDONGUA ON 14^(TH) COLUMN UNDER COMMAND OF RITTMEISTER V BRANDT STOP PLACE YOURSELVES AT HIS DISPOSAL WITH YOUR FULL COOPERATION STOP TRACK DOWN SHIPMENT APPROACHING BORDER STOP V BRANDT AWARE YOUR BACKGROUND STOP WILL SUPPLY FURTHER INSTRUCTIONS STOP MATO

Well, Werner thought, the telegram wasn't exactly written in code, but no doubt, the Major knew what he was doing. The chances of a security breach were probably remote; what clandestine agent would be on the lookout for secret messages between Windhuk and Ondongua? Werner handed the telegram to Louis.

"Who is this Rittmeister von Brandt? Are we going to have to do what he tells us to do?" Louis asked, his concern obvious.

"Hell no, Louis! I've met him, in the desert when the rebels ambushed the train from Swakopmund to Windhuk; he's a decent fellow. Yes, he'll be in command, but rest assured, the Major would have told him to take advice from us. After all, we know what's going on. Don't worry, we will intercept the wagon train Philippe and Paulo saw and destroy it. The good Rittmeister certainly can't do it without us. He wouldn't even know where to find them."

"Well, we better. If we don't, the Hereros will get those weapons. I see the Major has said nothing about the possible shipment which soon will arrive at Sandwich Bay?"

"I don't think it's being ignored. It'll take a few weeks before it gets to Sandwich Bay. There is still time to deal with it."

The sergeant appeared in the doorway and beckoned Werner and Louis nearer.

"The Major would like to see you. Please follow me."

They followed the soldier into the back room which served as the Major's office.

The Major, standing in the middle of the room, struck an imposing figure. He was in full uniform, his boots polished to a mirror shine, his uniform pressed as if ready for any parade ground inspection. His moustache was an exact copy of that of the Kaiser, the pointed ends pointing vertically upwards, and his brilliantined hair was combed straight back slick against his scalp, the first tinges of grey discernible around his ears and temples. The all-important monocle was clamped in his left eye. Lavish furnishings transformed the office into a piece of Germany: the walls were whitewashed and adorned with paintings, most portraits of men in uniform, some obviously of bygone eras. Werner realized that these probably were portraits of the Major's ancestors. Others depicted hunting scenes. A thick Persian carpet covered the floor and in a corner, a bust of the Kaiser stood on a pedestal. An imposing desk took up the larger part of the room and two deep-red buttoned leather chairs claimed a corner, a low coffee table between them.

"Major Ferdinand Graf Zu Dohner," the Major announced himself, holding out his hand in greeting. Good God, Werner thought, a duke in command of this forlorn place! This one had to have been really bad to be stuck out at this end of the world. The aristocratic families in Germany would often ship their black sheep to the colonies, hoping that they would get lost, preferably for good. Werner had a sneaky feeling that the Major probably fitted the bill admirably. He wondered what the man's transgressions had been.

"I have had word that you are to wait until Rittmeister von Brandt arrives tomorrow. Would you good gentlemen care to inform me of the purpose, both of your arrival here and that of the Rittmeister with his troop tomorrow?"

Werner thought it best to say as little as possible.

"We are to act as guides. We know no more than that."

The Major's face was cold.

Rittmeister von Brandt greeted Werner by name before he could draw him aside to hush him and whisper that he was now Portuguese, his name Joachim.

56

"Sweet Jesus, if it isn't the Scarlet Pimpernel; now he's Portuguese and even speaks the language fluently. Do you think I can trust you?" the officer said, laughing. "Zietzmann said that I was to listen to you and do what you suggest. Is that safe? You look like a spick farmer."

Werner frowned at him. Derogatory remarks about the Portuguese would not go down well! Fortunately Louis had no idea what was being discussed, as they conversed in German.

Jurgen was surprised to learn that Louis was a captain in the Portuguese colonial forces. Conversation was difficult, with Werner having to translate between the other two men. Jurgen listened to their story with amazement, but realized the seriousness of the situation when he heard how they had barely escaped with their lives when fighting the Kunehamas.

"The battle is currently a major topic of conversation in military circles and certainly general knowledge in SudwestAfrika," Jurgen commented.

A sergeant approached the men and saluted Jurgen.

"Herr Rittmeister, Major Graf zu Dohner has requested that you accompany me to his office." The sergeant did an about-turn and marched smartly back towards the command post building.

"Careful, Jurgen, the Major has not been told anything," Werner whispered quickly. "I have the impression his nose is out of joint because Zietzmann has left him in the dark."

Jurgen strode into the Major's office. The post's commanding officer bristled with controlled anger. The Major stood in front of his desk. Jurgen threw him the smartest parade ground salute, clicking his heels and announcing his rank and name and stating that he and his column were reporting to Ondongua as ordered by Major Zietzmann.

"What is the purpose of your mission? I've was merely told to expect you. This is highly irregular."

"Herr Major, with respect I must tell you that all I'm permitted to tell you is that I and my troop are to intercept a wagon train, and to that end I am to allow the two Portuguese gentlemen to accompany and assist me. This is a secret mission."

"This is most irregular," the Major repeated. " This area is under my command. I will take this up with the OKH in Windhuk."

"Herr Major, this mission is sanctioned by the OKH."

"Nonetheless, they could have used my troops. Will you require assistance?"

"No. No, Sir."

"Well, in that case, it is pointless saying anymore."

"Thank you, sir."

Jurgen threw the Major another smart salute and left the office.

Werner raised his eyebrows enquiringly.

"Well?" he asked.

"What can I say? The good Major is seriously pissed off. He considers it an affront that he was not included in these deliberations. As he puts it, this is his command after all. Christ, I didn't know what to say! Whatever else we do, let's do everything by the book and not give him any reason to get nasty. Believe me, he's fuckin' mad! Who knows, maybe he doesn't like Zietzmann."

Werner translated. Louis found the Major's attitude amusing. Then on a more serious note, he reminded Werner that they should be after the wagon train as soon as possible. The Rittmeister agreed. They allowed the men were allowed only an hour to refresh themselves and have a quick meal. By midday, the column, now with Jurgen, Louis and the two servants in tow, resumed its mission.

The belated summer rains were about to arrive in full fury. Massive concentrations of cumulus cloud built up during the afternoon, the sky darkening. Violent flashes of lightning and thunderous claps of thunder heralded the first raindrops, which in minutes turned into a torrential downpour, a cloudburst, the column leader scarcely able to see more than twenty yards ahead. The ground was soon awash, the horses stepping through inches of water. The troops had quickly donned oilskin rain-slickers but these were no match for the rain. Soon everyone was drenched.

Louis brought his horse up close to Werner and shouted across to him through the rain.

"I hope it's not raining where dos Santos' wagons are. The rain will wash away their tracks: we're supposed to intersect these on the heading we're on now. That'll make it very difficult for us to find them."

Werner looked ahead. It was no good. He could hardly see anything. He called Philippe nearer.

"Will we lose dos Santos' wagons in this rain?"

"I don't think so, it's not raining like this over the whole country and anyway, the wagons are further west towards the desert. It probably won't rain there at all. We'll still find the wagons," Philippe replied, nodding his head as if he wished to give his statement further support.

Werner was relieved. They were hoping to intercept the wagon train during the course of the next day.

After about an hour the rain let up and the sky rapidly cleared, leaving the earth refreshed and transformed. Flying ants appeared. Swallows seemed to materialize from nowhere in their hundreds, swooping and diving on the ants in a feeding frenzy. The unique fresh smell of rain on dust permeated the atmosphere.

It would soon be dark. The troop quickened its pace. They found a natural clearing amongst the thorn trees where they halted to make camp. They pitched no tents. Certain that the gunrunners were upwind of them, they prepared a quick meal over a well-shielded small fire, and the men turned in, sleeping in blankets on the ground, using their saddles as pillows.

At first light, they broke camp and before the sun had crept above the horizon, were underway again, Rittmeister von Brandt impatiently urging them on. Philippe and two other black Askaris were sent to scout a few miles ahead. The idea was to see the gunrunners' scouts before they saw them; Von Brandt's scouts proceeded with the utmost caution. The Rittmeister and the Askaris had removed their uniforms and were now dressed similarly to the local inhabitants, with only rudimentary pieces of civilian clothing. As the sun warmed them, the Askaris bared their upper torsos, as was the custom.

Late that afternoon the scouts intercepted fresh wagon tracks, headed towards Rauacana. The number of horses accompanying the wagons indicated that this must be the gunrunners' entourage. The military column swung south in pursuit, travelling parallel to the Kunene River. Soon the scouts reported the wagon train a few miles ahead. Immediately the Rittmeister called a halt. They could rest and eat, but no fires were to be lit. Two NCOs joined the Rittmeister, Werner, Louis and their two servants to discuss a plan of action. Philippe confirmed that all the wagon train's men were armed and had their own horses, making them mobile and dangerous. If they were to be overcome, stealth was essential. A frontal attack would just result in too many casualties. A sneak attack under cover of darkness would give them the best chance of success.

After much deliberation, it was decided that Werner, Louis, Philippe, Paulo, one NCO and an Askari would spearhead the initial assault, approaching the wagons from the opposite side to where the gunrunners had their horses corralled. During the early hours of the morning, a slight wind blew towards the sea, a peculiarity along this desert coastline, so this would hopefully be downwind. At the first sound of gunfire, the Rittmeister would lead the rest of his men in a mounted charge on the camp. Werner and his men would don white bandannas to distinguish them from the enemy; nobody wanted to be mistaken for the enemy when the Askaris finally charged!

At about one o clock, the small group of men, strung out in single file and on foot, set out at a brisk pace towards the gunrunners' camp, Philippe and Paulo in the lead. They slowed down as they saw the faint flicker of campfire. The fires had been allowed to burn low, but it was light enough to see the wagon train lookouts on the outer ring around the wagons. There appeared to be four, one at each corner of the compass. Two, however, were seated on the ground and appeared to be trying to ward off sleep.

Now crouched low, the men slowly approached the campfires. Most of them were armed with rifles, but Werner had opted for a shotgun, both barrels loaded with buckshot. He also had a nine shot Parabellum automatic in a holster attached to his belt, as did Louis, only he had decided on two automatics, deciding to dispense with any rifle. About a hundred yards from the camp, they lowered themselves to the ground and laboriously crawled forward towards the camp. Werner wished he had donned thicker clothing; his knees and elbows soon hurt from the small cuts and abrasions inflicted by pieces of gravel and thorns. The Boers called these little thorns *duiweltjies*, little devils. Appropriately named, Werner thought. They were smaller than a marble, but rock hard and surrounded on all side with short sharp thorns. He gritted his teeth and continued to creep slowly forward.

In the moonlight, he could see Philippe in front of him. The black man slowly turned round, pointed at himself and his companion, and then pointed forward again. He slowly drew a finger across his throat. There was no misinterpreting their intention; they were going to stalk the sentries and slit their throats.

Werner shook his head. He thought the idea insane! That was not part of the plan. Philippe was not about to listen, however: he vigorously nodded his head signalling a very emphatic yes, and the two men crawled forward. Not to be outdone, Werner crawled towards the nearest wagon. As he neared the wagon, he saw Paulo rise from the ground behind the half-asleep sentry. With lightning speed, Paulo placed his hand over the man's mouth, jerking his head back and simultaneously slashing the blade of his knife across the man's exposed throat. There was a rush of air followed by a bubbling sound as blood pumped from the severed corticoid artery. He then slowly lowered the inert body to the ground. Werner was momentarily stunned by both the suddenness of the ghastly attack and the gruesome result.

The man's sudden death had alerted no one; the camp was still quiet. Werner crawled forward. Suddenly he heard a thump followed by a whoosh-like sound; the sound a man makes when he has the breath driven from his body by a tremendous blow. That was all he heard. He saw nothing, everything still appeared normal. A wagon towered above him. Sounds of snoring emanated from the top: he presumed that this must be the sleeping place of one of the senior members of the wagon train, as most of the men were in blankets on the ground around the fire.

Werner rolled under the wagon. The planking had wide gaps in it; he could see the moonlight through these slits.

"Aaaaaah!" A loud death shriek pierced the silence. There was a loud snort and then the sounds of a body stumbling around the wagon. The moonlight shining through the slits disappeared. Werner took the shotgun and thrust the two barrels against the slit in the floorboards. He squeezed both triggers. The roar of the shotgun in the confined space below the wagon was deafening. Wood splinters and dust flew in all directions, followed by a loud thud as something fell to the broken wagon floor. He rolled from beneath the wagon. A body hung half over the tailboard of the wagon, arms and head dangling down, blood glistening in the moonlight. Already he had split the shotgun, the two smoking discharged shells ejected by the action. From his shirt pocket, he shoved two fresh cartridges into the breech and snapped the action closed again, quickly drawing the two hammers back.

Pandemonium reigned as men shouted and gunfire erupted. He remembered the white bandanna; he pulled it from his pocket and drew it over his forehead. Nearby, he saw Philippe bending over a fallen man, a short stabbing spear in one hand and an enormous machete in the other; he had a wild look in his eyes, the whites clearly showing in the dim light. The scene had been transformed into something ghoulish and macabre.

"For God's sake somebody help me!" he heard, shouted in Portuguese. He spun round looking for the source. He saw Louis grappling with a huge man who had him by both wrists. He was no match for the man, who was slowly bending his arm backwards trying to force him to release the revolver in his hand. Werner did not hesitate; at point-blank range shot the man in the head. The heavy bullet blew the back of the man's head off.

"Sweet Jesus! That was close. Thanks."

Standing back to back, the two men surveyed the scene around them. In the seconds that had passed, some men were still trying to extract themselves from their blankets while others had already found their weapons. The air was filled with a cacophony of shouts, screams and gunshots. Werner and Louis blazed away with their automatics but the gunrunners had started to return fire, and the first bullets were whistling past their heads.

"Christ! Let's get out of here!" Werner shouted, dragging Louis with him to a wagon, taking cover behind the wheels. They saw no sign of their companions but from the shooting, it was evident they were very much alive.

Suddenly he heard the drumming of approaching hooves. It had to be the Rittmeister approaching with his troops. The riders swept into the camp, sabres drawn. The enemy, still in total disarray and shock, was no match for the mounted horsemen, who cut them down with pistol, rifle and sword.

It was all over in a few minutes. A pall of dust now hung over the camp, the air tinged with the smell of cordite. Somebody threw fresh wood on the fires, which soon caught and illuminated the surroundings. The dead and wounded lay scattered around the wagons, the cries of the wounded mixing with the heartbreaking sounds of dying horses. The troop had only one Sanitär, who had his hands full attending to those moaning and screaming in pain.

A concerned Rittmeister dismounted from his horse rushing towards Louis.

"I'm all right! Please, it's not mine," Louis shouted, realizing that Jurgen, seeing his face and hair spattered with blood from the man Werner had summarily dispatched with a shot to the head, thought him seriously wounded.

Jurgen looked at Werner.

"What's he saying?" he asked urgently.

"It's somebody else's blood!"

Jurgen's relief was evident, and he began to laugh. Werner paused, then joined him. The smile on Louis face broadened until he also laughed, finally releasing all his pent-up apprehension and emotion.

The Askaris rounded up the survivors. They had no way of knowing how many had escaped. A search of the wagons revealed the rifles still in their cases.

"Where is dos Santos?" Jurgen asked.

The NCO stepped forward.

"We have already asked the prisoners, Herr Rittmeister. They say he is with another wagon train, more wagons than this one, on his way to Namibe."

Werner realized that Louis had been right after all. Dos Santos was both devious and cunning.

"Well, we better get going in the morning. We need to catch them."

"Herr Rittmeister, they say he is probably in Namibe already. Besides, a large number of Kunehama rebels accompany him. Certainly too many for us to take on," the NCO fearfully added.

"Sergeant, let me be the judge of that," Jurgen berated him, his annoyance showing.

Werner decided to intervene.

"Jurgen, the Sergeant's right. This is not even German territory. It's one thing to catch them in the bush as we've just done. It's an entirely different matter attacking a Portuguese fishing village. That could create an international incident."

Jurgen said nothing; he merely nodded, indicating that Werner was right.

"Werner, ask Louis if he thinks the Portuguese can do anything," Jurgen asked.

Louis shook his head.

"What can my people do? Our army in the south has been virtually wiped out. It will take weeks before reinforcements arrive. We don't have a choice, we've got to go south to Sandwich Bay and intercept him when he tries to land his cargo in your country."

"Look, we've won this round. Let's get back to Ondongua and contact Zietzmann. Let him make the decisions. We can tell him what we've just learnt."

"Well, we'll have to be smart about it. It'll take dos Santos no more than a few days to sail from Namibe to Sandwich Harbour. OK, he may not have loaded the weapons on a ship yet, but how long can that take?" Werner replied.

The Askaris carried the wounded to the wagons where they were made as comfortable as possible. At gunpoint, the prisoners were ordered to climb aboard the wagons. Once seated, the Askaris tied their hands behind their backs. They were a sullen lot. Werner wondered what fate awaited them. Which court would try them, the Germans or the Portuguese? Did it really matter? Actually not, whether it was at the hands of the Germans or Portuguese, he was sure they would come to a gruesome end. In both colonies, the penalty for gunrunning was death by hanging.

The troops returned to Ondongua. Two of the wounded troopers succumbed to their wounds while en route. Rittmeister von Brandt called no halt to bury them but ordered their bodies wrapped in blankets and kept in the wagon, to be buried with full military honours at Ondongua. The troopers showed little compassion for their prisoners, however, withholding water and food until Jurgen was forced to intervene, commanding the troopers to look after the prisoners. This was done with great reluctance; the troopers considered them an unnecessary burden and if given a choice would have ended their lives right there and then.

Their return to the command post with both prisoners and the illegal rifles did nothing to improve Major Graf zu Dohner's demeanour. Affronted that he had not been party to the preparation and assault on the gunrunners, he was now meaner than ever. Jurgen chose to ignore him, which only exacerbated the situation.

From Windhuk, Major Zietzmann cabled the Portuguese military authorities and informed them of Captain de Sousa's role. As a result, they seconded him to Zietzmann's operation. Werner was elated that the two of them would continue to pursue dos Santos together. The Portuguese were unaware that Senora Joachim de Almeida was a German lieutenant masquerading as a manufacturer's representative, and as dos Santos had no reason to believe otherwise, hopefully the deal he and Werner had struck was still underway.

The command post's medical facilities were austere and primitive, with only a medical orderly and little in the way of medication. The arrival of the wounded on the post created a problem. The Major immediately dispatched a rider with a request that the Finnish mission make their doctor available. A day later, Dr. Dorothea Eggars arrived by horse drawn wagon, bringing two Finnish nurses with her. They immediately set up a temporary operating theatre and care unit. Only after she had attended to the wounded men's needs, did she allow herself to notice Werner. She had been clearly surprised to see him again, but now greeted him warmly. Concern soon replaced her joy when she realized that the wounded she was attending to were the casualties of an assault that Werner and Louis had been a part of. When questioned, however, Werner would not discuss anything related to the past week with her.

Alone with Werner, Louis broached the subject.

"Werner, the lady's upset, it's evident she cares for you," Louis said, having noticed Dorothea's concern for the young lieutenant.

"It's a whim on her part. It probably will pass. Don't forget, I was her patient once," he replied nonchalantly.

"Methinks you became more than just a patient. At least you could be more receptive."

Werner merely nodded. Louis persisted in bringing up the subject, believing himself an expert in the love department. In typical Latin fashion, he kept telling Werner how he should launch his campaign of seduction.

The Rittmeister had barely entered the small lazarette to check on his wounded men when Dr. Eggars confronted him.

"Herr Rittmeister," she addressed him. "A number of these men require specialized treatment. Unfortunately, such care is available only in Windhuk. I must insist that they are sent there as soon as possible. Here, we have done what we can, but if they don't receive specialized treatment soon, we may lose them."

"Doctor, please, I note your concerns. My men and I have been ordered back to Windhuk; we will leave to-morrow. These men will accompany us. However, I insist that you also join the train and attend to the men until they get to Windhuk. Your two nurses are to assist you. I will ensure that the mission is compensated for your time."

"*Herr Rittmeister!* I cannot leave the mission and neither can these nurses. They are missionaries!"

"You forget, doctor, this country's at war; you have no alternative. Please make the necessary arrangements. I, in turn, will ensure that you are returned to the mission as soon as it is possible, once we get these wounded into the military hospital at Windhuk."

Not waiting for a reply, Jurgen spun on his heel and walked out of the lazarette.

Dorothea realized that she had no alternative but to obey the directive. She was furious, but silently conceded that the Rittmeister really had little choice if his men were to receive the best medical attention. The condition of two of the wounded was serious. The two nurses were unhappy; they were devoted missionaries and had no desire to go to Windhuk. However, there was little they could do except accept the situation.

Hurried preparations were made to transport the wounded to Tsumeb, the last town on the northern railroad which connected with Windhuk. This was eighty miles from Ondongua. Two horse-drawn, well-sprung carriages were employed to carry the wounded. Fortunately, the terrain was flat and devoid of stones. The route the wagons took was mostly through soft sand. This area was an extension of the Kalahari Desert, a massive expanse of sand and bush, which stretches in a north-north-west direction across the border, hundreds of miles into Angola. Were it not for the soft sand, Dorothea doubted whether the seriously wounded would have survived the journey. Jurgen and his men, accompanied by Werner, Louis and their servants, rode ahead of the wagons, keeping a constant lookout for marauding Hereros.

At Tsumeb, a small frontier town, they boarded the train. This consisted mostly of flat-deck goods wagons to which a few passenger coaches had been hastily added. The troops occupied the first wagon immediately behind the three boxcars, which were attached to the train for the exclusive use of the troop's horses. As this was a narrow-gauge line, its speed never exceeded twenty-five miles per hour. No dining car was provided, and the stationmaster reminded Jurgen that his people must ensure they had sufficient food and water before the train left as there was little to buy on the way.

The train finally departed Tsumeb late that afternoon. As it approached its maximum speed it began to sway alarmingly, the passengers that were standing forced to find something to grab hold of to steady themselves. Werner immediately thought of the wounded. God knows how they felt; this could not be comfortable. Fortunately, it had recently rained, so the ground was still damp, which kept any dust to a minimum.

Werner preferred to stand in the corridor, hanging onto to the handrail. This was a lot more comfortable than sitting on the green leather-bound coach seats and swaying from side to side. Others had taken their cue from him, and there were now a number of people in the passageway.

Initially, Dorothea had busied herself making the wounded as comfortable as she could. Now she joined Werner and Louis in the corridor.

Hanging on to the rail, she brushed the hair from her face with the back of a hand. "Really, this is awful! We can't travel like this all the way to Windhuk! It's like riding a fun fair! I'm afraid it will jump the rails."

Unable to keep a straight face, he started to laugh.

Louis understanding the gestures and tone of voice, laughed too.

"At least we don't travel in toy trains in Angola. Christus, this is really ridiculous!" Louis said to Werner. Werner just rolled his eyes.

These bloody Portuguese: first – better lovers, now better trains – what next?!

A particularly violent sway of the carriage broke Dorothea's hold from the rail and flung her against Werner, who caught her against himself to keep her from falling. Immediately he was aware of her breasts against his chest and the smell of her.

"Sorry," he said, "But if I hadn't caught you, you would have fallen."

She was slightly flustered, her body as aware of him as he was of her. She moved away, walking carefully down the passage.

Louis noticed the fleeting seconds of intimacy between the two and looked knowingly at Werner, pursing his lips.

Bloody idiot, Werner thought, he is enjoying this!

The officers and troopers had bought a fair numbers of sacks containing bottles of beer in wet straw. These now swayed in most compartments. With little else to do and spurred on by the summer heat, a great deal of beer was being consumed. The train was taking on a slight festive atmosphere. Two NCOs were trying to draw the two nurses into conversation while in another compartment loud guffaws followed ribald jokes.

Werner and Louis had consumed a few bottles between them and both had relaxed their normal professional façade. Louis dug his elbow into Werner's ribs, bringing his mouth close to his ear.

"Come on, make a move on her – she's waiting for you."

Of course, he meant the doctor. He was starting to get under Werner's skin.

"Christ! This is not some Portuguese bordello! The doctor is a lady and I'm an officer. Don't be bloody mad!"

Louis immediately took umbrage.

"Don't knock Portuguese bordellos. Many Portuguese men frequent these establishments. Let me tell you, our women are ladies. They know how to treat their men."

"Well, that may be so, but I'm not about to come on to the doctor, if that's what you mean!"

"If you don't, you'll lose her. There are too many men here and she is truly beautiful."

Werner remained silent. However, he had to agree Louis was right; something definitely sizzled between them and both of them knew it.

Dorothea had disappeared. He wondered where she was.

Louis' eyes were slightly bleary and his grin, now sloppy, made him look decidedly stupid. He waved his empty beer bottle at Werner, who shook his head, indicating that he had had enough. Louis lurched off to their compartment to get another. The moment Louis disappeared, he walked down the corridor towards the adjoining passenger car. He stepped over the coupling onto the landing, the loud clackety-clack of the wheels and the banging of the coupling assaulting his ears. She stood in the corner of the landing leaning against the railing, staring out into the night as it rushed by.

"What are you doing out here?" he asked.

She turned to face him and smiled.

"The swaying made me feel ill."

"Can I get you something?"

"No, no. I'm fine now. But you can stay and keep me company."

For a long while, they both just stood there looking out, the lights radiating out from the compartments illuminating the bush rushing by. A violent lurch threw her against him.

Once again he caught her. This time he did not immediately release her but held her close, her shoulder against his chest. She made no attempt to break from him; instead she placed a hand on the arm that held her around the waist as if to say it was only natural that he be holding her.

Slowly his emotions got the better of him, and he lowered his head and gently kissed her hair above the ear. She drew her head back, as if to get nearer to him. He kissed her ears and slowly slid his lips down her neck. She turned her body to face him, lifting her lips to his. As they kissed passionately, she slid her arms around his neck, pulling him close. He felt his own passion and arousal and was aware of her heightened emotions. She did not object when he lowered his hands to clasp her buttocks and draw her lower body hard against his.

Suddenly she regained control of herself, drawing away from him, looking down at her feet, unable to look him in the eyes.

"I'm sorry. This should not have happened," she said, obviously embarrassed. Before he could say anything, she turned away and walked quickly down the passageway. When she got to the compartment, she insisted that the two NCOs leave immediately. They did: the NCOs knew better than to argue with a doctor. She entered and immediately slid the door closed behind her.

Werner was dumbfounded. It had all happened in seconds. He had wanted to say something but she had disappeared before he could get a word in. Overwhelmed by the unexpected change in their relationship and the few seconds of intense intimacy, he waited a few minutes to regain his composure and then returned to his own compartment.

Louis was sprawled on the bunk snoring, oblivious of what was happening around him, his body moving from side to side with the sway of the carriage, an empty beer bottle rolling on the carpeted floor. Just as well, Werner thought, heaven help me, should he ever find out what had happened!

Dorothea did not speak to him for the rest of the journey. Werner was morose, at a loss as to how to handle the situation and irritated by Louis who repeatedly enquired what was happening. Nothing! Werner would reply. This left Louis mumbling words like inadequate, feeble, and stupid under his breath.

The train journey took a day and a half. They arrived in Windhuk during mid morning. A NCO with three Askaris was waiting on the platform to greet Werner and his companions and see them settled in a hotel. Werner was informed that Major Zietzmann wished to see Louis and himself at three that afternoon and that they were to join him for dinner later and should dress accordingly. The NCO assured Werner that he would see to it that Louis was issued appropriate clothing, compliments of the German government.

Werner and Louis made the most of the few hours, soaking in a bath, getting a shave and having their hair trimmed. Louis was somewhat disappointed with Windhuk when compared to Luanda in Angola. Werner had to remind him that Luanda was three hundred years old, while Windhuk was not quite twenty.

"Nor was it built on a tropical seacoast. Families in Angola have been in the country for hundreds of years, establishing small empires and palatial homes supported by dozens of servants. Whereas the Germans have just got here," he explained.

His second meeting with Major Zietzmann was far more amicable, with the major jovial and receptive, keen to congratulate the men on their success against the gunrunners. To his surprise, the Major was even able to make himself understood in Portuguese, which certainly created an atmosphere in which Louis was at ease.

"Of course, the current tense situation in Angola must play into dos Santos' hands, as the Portuguese are having difficulty making their presence felt in the southern part of the country. That does not mean that we should relax our efforts. On the contrary, I propose to make an example of this man."

The Major paused, lighting a cigar.

"You say he is in Namibe?"

With a start, Louis realized that the question had been addressed at him.

"That is the information we got from the prisoners," Louis replied.

"Well, we need to intercept him. It's pointless trying to mount an operation from within your country. I'm trying to get the Imperial Navy to assist, but strangely, they have no ship that can assist us. I know, that sounds ridiculous, us being at war, but then there is no war at sea at all. They say there is no call for the Navy to be present."

"I don't imagine that dos Santos will use an ordinary fishing boat to smuggle these weapons into Sandwich Bay. He will surely consider some resistance from us a possibility and will prepare himself for such an event. Knowing him, he will make sure that he is able to defend himself. However, an attack from the sea may surprise him," Louis added.

"OK, he needs a craft small enough to pass over the sandbank that bars the lagoon's entrance at high tide. The current at Sandwich Bay is quite treacherous, or so I'm told. Therefore, a steam-driven boat will be essential. Probably, something between forty and seventy feet; certainly nothing bigger than that. At most, he will have about ten to fifteen men aboard, all armed to the teeth of course"

The major blew smoke at the ceiling.

"Well, we'll certainly need something of similar size," Werner countered.

"Yes. I have found a forty-foot steam-driven cutter. It was used to tow barges from outlying ships anchored off Swakopmund to the small jetty behind the breakwater. It's not armed at all. I'm told she's an absolute bitch, has an inherent vicious roll, guaranteed to make the best seaman ill. Any voyage from Swakopmund to Sandwich Bay is bound to be an unforgettable experience." The Major was unable to hide the twinkle in his eyes he watched Louis' face

"I'm for it, but then I won't be aboard – you will be," he continued. "What do you say? Otherwise, it will have to be a land-based operation and that will probably not allow us the opportunity to catch him. Yes, we may get the rifles, but not him."

"Who will command this? We don't have a captain! What about navigation and all that?" Werner asked.

"I've found an old Navy sea-dog who has just gone on pension and decided to retire in Swakopmund because he liked the place so much. Surprisingly enough, he jumped at the opportunity. However, I should warn you—I'm told Kapitän zu See von Moelkte is difficult, a proper pain in the ass."

For a moment, all were silent, digesting the Major's latest information.

"Gentlemen, we don't have a lot of time. Oh, incidentally, Captain de Sousa—you've been placed under my direct command." With that, the Major slid a folded sheet of paper over his desk towards Louis. Louis read it. It was short and to the point – obey the Major's instructions to the letter. The commander-in-chief of Portuguese colonial forces had signed it. However, it did include his superiors' admiration for the interception and destruction of the gunrunner's wagon train in Angola.

"Sir," Louis said, addressing the Major, "It will be a pleasure to serve under your command."

"Thank you."

Werner smiled, relieved that he would have Louis at his side in the fight against dos Santos. The Portuguese captain knew dos Santos and was aware of what to expect. More importantly, he despised the man and wished to see him and his operation destroyed.

Werner looked at Louis who gave him a barely perceptible nod.

"Major, we need to get to Swakopmund and meet the good Captain von Moeltke."

"Excellent! I will assign Rittmeister von Brandt to you, with fifteen men. Oh and incidentally, Lieutenant, you've been promoted to captain."

The major removed a box covered with red velvet from the drawer of his desk and slid this over to Werner. Werner slowly lifted the lid of the box to peer inside and saw his new symbols of rank, two shoulder boards, each board with two parallel silver bars in which nestled two stars.

"Thank you, sir."

"You certainly earned them. Congratulations. And you, Captain de Sousa, are bound to be in for a surprise on your return to your country."

CHAPTER FOUR

The three captains stood on the foredeck, all in uniform; even Louis was in a German Schutztruppe uniform with all insignia removed other than the shoulder boards depicting his rank.

Although it was already nine in the morning, there was no sign of the sun, the sky an endless blanket of low-lying fog. The sea was dead calm, its surface oily smooth except for long undulating swells which slowly moved in from the southwest. The boat slid over these as it chugged southwards. Black smoke bellowed from the high stack mounted over the wheelhouse at the stern, where two black men, stripped to the waist, took turns keeping the boiler stoked with coal. Although she was sturdy, conveniences aboard the tugboat were spartan. The twenty-three persons aboard shared one head and a small stove, and except for a few privileged, any sleeping had to be on deck. The Major was right; she was a bitch, rolling like some drunken whore in a seaport bordello, her for'ard mast swinging in a wide arc, the motion guaranteed to persuade the weak-stomached to lose their last meal.

In Swakopmund, engineers had feverishly worked on the boat. A steel gun platform was riveted to the forward deck plates just behind the entrance to the fo'castle, on which a converted three-inch howitzer had been mounted, its barrel able to traverse just more than 180°. The only restrictions on forward fire were the forward mast stays. The cannon, however, was known to have a vicious recoil and both Werner and Jurgen were dubious as to how many shots they would be able to fire before the weapon tore itself from its mountings. The nineteen troopers, which included two NCOs, were all armed with rifles.

Major Zietzmann had not been entirely truthful about Kapitän zu See von Moeltke. On seeing him for the first time, any expectations Werner may have had that he was about to encounter a captain of the line were instantly dispelled. The man must have come up for retirement before the turn of the century—there was nothing recent about him. He was certainly too old to be commanding a ship about to enter battle, an obnoxious fellow whose vocabulary contained the foulest language. When agitated, which was more often than not, he would wave around his large clay pipe, giving vent to his feelings, berating the crew, the tugboat, the soldiers and the rest of the world in a seemingly uninterrupted tirade. That the man had a penchant for schnapps was an understatement; Louis was convinced this was his sole source of subsistence.

Werner's suggestion that they make better speed sent the man into a near apoplectic frenzy; von Moeltke considered the request an insult.

"Do you not realize she is already at full speed, flat-out in fact? Look at the boiler!"

He pointed to a brass plaque attached to the boiler; Werner had to crane his neck forward to read it, so much grime covered it.

"Do you see that? What's it say?" the seadog asked sarcastically, a cloud of foul-smelling tobacco smoke engulfing them in the close confines of the wheelhouse come boiler-room.

"It's in French, I think."

"You're fuckin' right. This is a piece of French shit, built in Le Havre. God only knows how she landed up in our hands. Do you realize that if I push her any harder, she will start to behave like a French tart? Trying very hard not to give what you want from her! You have to treat her gently if you are to get anywhere with her, if you know what I mean. She is already close to working herself to death!"

Werner quietly wondered when the old man had last had a piece of French tart, or whether he could even remember what that must have been like. However, he seemed to understand the complexity of the piece of machinery before them. That was something to be grateful for. He looked at the old mariner. He wore a uniform of sorts. God knows when it was last cleaned, and the front was spattered with the remnants of many past meals. Over this, he wore some sort of pea jacket.

"I understand. How fast are we going?"

"About six knots, but I could give you eight for a short period if you really fuckin' needed it," he said, exposing a few tobacco-stained teeth as he broke into a grin for the first time. For a moment, Werner thought he saw the man's eyes twinkle. Christ! Was he looking forward to a last encounter on the high seas before he died, a *Götterdammerung!?*

As the mist dispersed and the sun came out, an awning was hastily erected over the forward deck to provide shade. The wind had come up, and the boat was ploughing through a fair chop which occasionally threw a spray of seawater over the bow. Most of the men now frequented the gunwales, their stomachs desperately trying to rid themselves of their contents.

By nightfall the fog appeared again, making everything damp and unpleasant, and the soldiers huddled under their blankets as they slept on the deck.

The boat steamed abeam of Sandwich Bay at about two o clock in the morning. The steady thump of the steam-engine was suddenly silent, the only sound the lap of the waves against the hull and the faint hiss of steam. All navigational lights had been doused. Far in the distance, towards the east, they could hear the boom of surf, its sound a constant warning that to approach spelt disaster; this was a treacherous and unforgiving coastline and graveyard to many a ship.

The three officers approached the Kapitän in the stern.

"The bastard never sleeps! Just being near him is an ordeal," Louis whispered. He found the captain abhorrent, always swearing, burping and farting. Werner just smiled.

"Gentlemen, we are about five miles off the coast. Unless you have something particular in mind, this is the best place to be, way out here. This coast is too damn dangerous."

"Captain, if we remain here, dos Santos is bound to see us and will be suspicious. We need to take the boat into the lagoon."

The captain looked at the three men, sucking on his pipe, making a disgusting sound as the air bubbled through the accumulated spittle.

"Christus!" Louis quietly said, wrinkling his nose.

"What did the wop say?" the sea captain asked.

"Nothing, it was just a general remark, you know, something in Portuguese. Can you take us in?"

There was a long silence.

"Only during the day and then only at high tide. That'll be around ten. If the mist has cleared by then."

"Okay, let's do it. Dos Santos can't be far off. Like us, he'll have no alternative but to approach during the day and at high tide."

The captain allowed the boat to drift, the Benguella Current slowly taking it north, its movement assisted by the southwesterly swell. At nine that morning they got underway, the mist still present but already showing the first signs of breaking up. As they neared the coast, the sea's mood subtly changed as the bottom shoaled; the boat was now in the grip of a ground swell. To the east they could see the dunes, and to their surprise a swathe of reeds surrounding the lagoon on the landward side where the dunes swept down directly into the water. Here, the water from the Kuiseb River was forced underground, its passage barred by fifty miles of row upon row of some the highest sand dunes in the world. From underground, the water seeped into the lagoon, displacing the sea and creating an oasis.

Jurgen had told them that the place was not entirely deserted. Years ago, a few stragglers from some Strandloper tribe, beachcombers of Hottentot descent, had settled here, finding the place perfect as fish, small game and abundant waterfowl supplied them with ample food. The lagoon was naturally protected, access made near impossible by land other than by a narrow causeway between water and dune which became visible only at low tide. Few ventured into the lagoon from the sea, as this required a special boat with a shallow draught and a more than fair degree of seamanship.

As they neared the coast, they could clearly see the entrance to the lagoon. The tide had just changed, and the sea was starting to flow through the mouth. As it rushed over the sandbar, it created a barrier of small waves, continuously cresting and breaking.

"We need to be damn careful here!" Von Moeltke said. "We could easily be swamped."

With that, he opened one of the many valves that protruded from the boiler and the thumping of the steam engine took on a more urgent note, the deck vibrating beneath their feet. The boat suddenly showed a surprising burst of speed, a white bone firmly clenched between its teeth as it sped towards the turbulent water discoloured by the sand and agitated by the action of the waves over the shallow sandbank.

The calmness was an illusion. As they neared the sandbar, the waves seemed to grow in height. The captain's remarks now took on a different meaning. He was at the rudder, his pipe clenched firmly between his teeth, his concentration focused.

The boat did not quite match the speed of the incoming waves. As they entered the mouth, a following wave rapidly developed a towering crest and threatened menacingly, raising the stern of the boat. Clearly, the boat could broach, slewing it sideways, spilling all into the water. Not to mention that any water cascading over the unprotected rear of the boiler could also have explosive results.

"Lieber Gott! This is bloody dangerous," Jurgen said, hanging onto to a mast stay as the boat speeded up, similar to a surfboard before an advancing wave. The captain was proving to be an expert after all, masterfully handling the boat, keeping her stern up against the racing wave and sliding before it into the calmer inner waters of the lagoon, where the mass of moving water seemed to lose its momentum, breaking well behind the boat.

Louis extracted a large bandanna from a pocket and mopped his brow.

"Whew! You know, I think I'm actually beginning to like the old man, even if he does stink and fart. Just as long as he can keep me out of the water."

Jurgen wanted to know what he had just said. Werner translated, both men then doubling up with laughter, much of it out of sheer relief.

The captain forced the boat stern-first into the tall green stalks, until it was near invisible from a distance. The activity disturbed a host of insects, which now buzzed around the men and crew who swatted wildly trying to keep them away. Eventually, the insects settled down but not before most had acquired a few dozen bites.

The captain busied himself overseeing the operation of the boiler, which continuously belched black smoke. Not knowing when dos Santos would make his appearance, it was crucial that they maintain steam pressure so that they could immediately be underway if so required. However, smoke would be a definite giveaway. The stokers had to ensure the coal in the boiler never smouldered, only slowly adding coal to the fire, so removing any trace of smoke.

Another concern was the whereabouts of the contingent of Hereros who were supposed to receive the weapons once these were landed. It was doubtful whether dos Santos would accompany these on their journey inland. The whole operation had to have been well orchestrated; messages had to pass between the gunrunners and the rebels, rendezvous had to be arranged and payments made. How was this done? There had to be some undercover group within the colony, an organization whose people were not even remotely considered subversive. Major Zietzmann had touched on the subject but had not elaborated. He had merely said that he would ensure that a detachment of troopers were deployed in the desert on the southern borders of Walvis Bay, the small British enclave about forty miles south of Swakopmund. This was part of the British Cape Colony, the only natural harbour along the coast, which had served as a whaling station and had access to fresh water. The British had annexed this ten by fifty mile seemingly useless stretch of desert with little opposition from the Germans, and had little other presence in the area. The Germans were free to travel as they wished. A German military force camped on the borders of Walvis Bay would not give rise to concern.

Werner felt frustrated. Somebody had to receive the weapons. Where were these people? It was possible that the German military detachment might have intercepted them, but that would be contrary to the plan. The idea had been to deal with the recipients after they had received the weapons from the gunrunners.

During the night, the fog slowly moved in from the sea. When he awoke the next morning, the boat was fog-bound, the men not being able to see more three or four yards. There was not a breath of wind stirring: it was deathly quiet, except for the distant sound of the surf. This never stopped.

Dos Santos was expected to-day. If he were to enter the lagoon, it would be later in the morning, when the tide was at its highest. Jurgen ensured that his troops readied themselves, checking their weapons and laying out their ammunition. The three men assigned as gun crew readied the howitzer. They had only brought twenty rounds of ammunition as this was considered sufficient. Now all they could do was wait.

Within a few hours, the fog had cleared completely, and the sky was now crystal clear.

"A sail!"

The three military officers crowded into the bow. A sailing ship had appeared beyond the spit of land to the north, about three miles offshore. Wisps of smoke could be seen from a small funnel visible through the masts. Jurgen peered through his binoculars. He could see men on deck. Already the sails were coming down, the ship now making way under steam. Abeam of the lagoon entrance, she turned sharply to port heading straight for the entrance. The ship resembled a Dutch barge, about forty-five foot long and wide at the beam with a shallow draught. For stability under sail, she was fitted with two huge drop-keels, one on each side of the hull, that could be lowered into the water to function as a keel to minimize any sideways drift. No flag fluttered from her stern.

Werner actually smelled von Moelkte before he saw him, and he turned to find the captain next to him, his pipe clamped between his teeth.

"I'm surprised, that's a fuckin' Channel barge. Find them in Holland, there are not many of them around. A surprise to see one here. The only other place I've seen these is in the Congo, particularly around the river mouth. The Portuguese use these in Cabinda and on the Congo River. No doubt, that's where he acquired it."

"Can he outrun us?"

"You're damn right, he can. Those boats are fast, what with their swallow draft and huge sails. Steam-assisted she'll have a good turn of speed."

"Damn! We must stay hidden and hope he gets close to us. This is the deepest part of the lagoon, up against the dunes. Let's hope that this is where he proposes to anchor."

With the wind close on her stern and the steam-engine running, the sailing ship cut through the water, riding the waves as they had, and swiftly entered the still water of the natural harbour. As predicted, the boat headed for the deepest part of the lagoon.

"If we let them get too near to us, they'll see us," Jurgen whispered. "I'm going to let the men open fire once she is in close range."

Werner nodded.

The barge slowly crept forward, seemingly headed straight for the tugboat hidden in the reeds. The gun crew had swivelled the howitzer around on its pedestal until it was pointed at the barge, and the barge was no more than three to four hundred yards distant when Jurgen gave the order for the cutter to break out of the reeds. Von Moeltke opened the steam gate valves, the propeller churned the water at the stern and the boat surged forward, its bow bursting out of the reeds.

Everyone heard the shouts of surprise as the barge crew saw the tugboat.

"Fire!" Jurgen shouted.

Louis yanked the lanyard. With a roar, the cannon belched smoke, a shudder passing through the ship as it absorbed the shock of the recoil. Immediately the breech was slammed open and the spent shell ejected, clattering to the deck. A massive fountain of water erupted just ahead of the bow of the barge, which was still headed straight for them. Already, the crew had the next shell in the breech.

The barge frantically swung to port, exposing her starboard side. Suddenly, part of the gunwale dropped down, obviously hinged.

"For Christ's sake! Get down! Down! That's a machine-gun!"

The crew and troopers immediately dropped to the deck, but the machine gun was already chattering loudly, wood splinters and ricochets flying in all directions as part of the gunwale disintegrated. Two of the gun crew went down, one writhing on the deck, shot in the stomach. Jurgen rushed forward to assist the remaining gunner re-aim the heavy weapon, dropping to the deck every time the machine-gunner walked the spray of the Maxim's bullets towards the gun, tearing the rest of the tugboat's gunwales to shreds. Fortunately, the hull plates withstood the deadly onslaught. A few seconds later, the big gun roared again, and the shell exploded on the hull of the barge blasting a huge hole, shattering the thick plank, a hole big enough to drive a small wagon through. The explosion had also torn the wheelhouse apart, shredding the planking, and the shattered remnants had been blown high into the air, falling into the lagoon with multiple splashes. The Maxim gun crew had not avoided the blast; flying shrapnel decimated them.

A jagged cry of success broke out amongst the surviving tugboat crew.

"God knows where the man got a Maxim machine-gun! Watch out, he has a new gun–crew!" Jurgen shouted, warning the others as dos Santos' men took up position behind the machine-gun.

Again, the lagoon reverberated with its deadly chatter, the cutter's men flinging themselves flat on the deck in turn. The fusillade passed overhead like a swarm of angry bees. Clearly, the new gun-crew had still to master the use of the gun.

Von Moeltke lay flat on the aft deck, keeping an eye on the boiler. He had stuck a long pole into the rudder post that protruded vertically from the stern, and this pole now pointed for'ard allowing him to steer the cutter while still prone. Amazingly, he still had his pipe clenched in his mouth.

"You better fuckin' do something fuckin' soon about that fuckin' barge!" the old sea dog shouted.

"Can you ram her?" Werner shouted.

"I can bloody well try! Get your men away from the bow."

The engine's revolutions increased as von Moeltke strained the last vestiges of power from the steam engine. The deck shivered from the vibration of the overstressed engine. The barge stood broadside to the cutter, its engine stopped by the first hit from the cannon. The machine-gun continued to rake the deck, fortunately its aim erratic. Suddenly the water below the stern of the barge swirled violently as the propeller thrust the boat forward, the helmsman desperately trying to bring the barge to starboard.

Werner never understood how Jurgen had managed it, but somehow the cannon had been reloaded under intense fire from the barge. Now it roared again. Fired at point-blank range, the shell tore into the innards of the barge and exploded, opening the hull below the waterline so that Werner could see daylight. The barge began to list.

The cannon was not going to fire another shot, however: the enormous recoil had torn it from its mountings and the howitzer, still attached to its gun platform, was now lying on the deck, the deck plates ripped from the boat's structure. Miraculously, Jurgen had escaped injury and was sitting spread eagled on the deck where he had been tossed. The trooper who had helped man the gun had not been so lucky. The cannon had struck him full force as its pedestal toppled, pinning him to the deck.

No more than a splintered wreck, unbelievably the barge still floated. Von Moelkte continued to steer the cutter towards the barge, rapidly closing the remaining distance. Doing a good ten knots, the cutter's bow ploughed into the barge, cutting the weakened vessel in half. The stern sank, and those members of the crew still alive jumped overboard and began swimming towards the shore some two hundred yards away. Jurgen's troopers opened fire with their rifles, spouts of water erupting around the swimmers.

"Cease fire! Damn you, I said cease fire!" an agitated Jurgen shouted.

"Let them kill the bastards!" Von Moelkte yelled loudly from the stern.

Jurgen swung round to look at the old man lifting himself from the deck, his pipe still clenched in his teeth. The tugboat's engine had stopped, the boiler loudly hissing steam. The two stokers lay crumpled on the deck, not moving.

"Cease fire!" he shouted again and then shouted furiously at Von Moeltke. "We don't shoot unarmed men swimming the water."

"They're fuckin' gunrunners, you must shoot them."

"Sorry, I can't."

The old mariner shook his head in disbelief.

"What kind of soldiers are you?"

He stomped off to join Werner, for'ard inspecting the damage. It was going to take a while to extract the cutter's bow from the barge's hull which now held them trapped.

The swimmers had reached the shore, only six men. Or wasn't one of them a woman? Louis thought he recognized the huge bulk of dos Santos as the enemy thrashed their way through the reeds and climbed the dune. The troopers on the tugboat opened fire again but they were out-of-range and disappeared over the crest of the dune.

There was nothing they could do. More than half of Jurgen's troop was down, most struck by machine gun bullets.

It was a scene of carnage, the deck slippery with the blood pooling on the planks. Eleven men had lost their lives; five more were injured.

"Can we get underway again?" Werner asked the sea captain.

"I think so, damage seems to be superficial, but I must do an inspection."

"Please do it immediately. Where's Louis?"

"Over here!"

Werner heard a shout and turned towards its source.

Louis stood on the forward deck of the Dutch barge. He beckoned Werner to join him. The bow of the cutter was still stuck in hull of the barge and with little difficulty he hauled himself back onto the for'ard deck of the sailing ship. If the cutter was in a bad way, the barge was worse. The cannon had wreaked havoc, and dead and wounded blacks covered the decks above the water on the sinking barge. Werner was amazed to see three cases of rifles, the same cases he thought he had seen in dos Santos' storehouse, still lashed to the deck. There had to be more.

"Are you all right?"

"Christus, I don't know how we survived that? That Maxim was a surprise. Where on earth did they get that?"

"Probably was part of a consignment originally intended for the Boers. Some enterprising Portuguese official probably sold it with the rifles."

"Rest assured, I will see to it that I get to the bottom of this. Some Portuguese officials don't know what awaits them."

"That gun could have wiped us out, but fortunately it's damn heavy. And not easy to operate, it needs to be continuously thumped with the palm of your hand to get it to spread its fire." He paused, looking at the cases. "Where are the rest of the cases?"

Louis turned his thumb downwards.

"At the bottom of the lagoon."

"Well, that's good. They'll be useless in a few days even if wrapped in grease. The water will see to that."

"What are we going to do with these cases?" Louis asked.

"Let them sink with the bow when we back the cutter off. We can't transfer them, they're too heavy."

Louis nodded in agreement.

"Kapitän, can you get us loose from this boat?" Werner shouted.

"Get aboard, I'm doing it now."

"What about the wounded?" Louis exclaimed, pointing at the wounded on the barge.

Jurgen stood on the foredeck of the cutter looking at the two men; he understood Louis' concern even though he did not understand his words. He said nothing; he just shook his head. There was no misunderstanding his intentions.

The two men were shocked but they clambered aboard the cutter. Von Moeltke immediately manoeuvred the boat astern. With a cracking and grinding of timbers, the bow of the cutter broke free from the barge. No longer buoyed by the cutter, it slowly began to sink. The lagoon was quite shallow and although the two sections of the barge now lay on the mud, the top of its mast still protruded above the surface. Debris floated around the wreck, slowing drifting before the light wind towards the reed-lined shore.

Louis stared at Werner.

"What's wrong?" he asked defensively.

"So, you have to thump a Maxim machine gun with the palm of your hand to get it to traverse? And that from a civilian?"

Werner just shrugged his shoulders, deciding to say nothing.

Jurgen ordered the captain to take the boat ashore. The sooner he made contact with the small German force which had taken up position near Walvis Bay, the sooner his wounded would receive medical attention.

"Where the hell are the Hereros?" Werner asked.

"Pray God they don't arrive now. That'll just finish us off," Jurgen replied, just as concerned.

Somebody had to be in the vicinity to receive the arms shipment. Somewhere out there in the sand and dunes lurked a rebel detachment, awaiting the arrival of the barge.

"Any suggestions?" Jurgen asked.

Speaking to Werner in Portuguese, Louis volunteered to take a few men and establish a lookout post on the crest of the highest dune. Jurgen considered this an excellent idea. So, armed with sufficient water and some cans of food, they slowly climbed to the top of the nearest high dune. Louis was surprised, he could see for a good few miles. He thought he could actually see the encampment of the Schutztruppe detachment on the borders of the Walvis Bay enclave to the north. He also caught a glimpse of the runner they had sent out, who seemed to be making good time through the dunes.

He had to admire dos Santos' planning. Never had the Germans ever considered Sandwich Bay as an ideal location through which to smuggle contraband cargo. Its location made it virtually inaccessible other than by sea. The sand dunes barred the use of wagons, the soft sand and steep inclines created a formidable barrier. He could only imagine that the Hereros would arrive with pack animals, allowing them to break the crated rifles up into smaller loads, light enough to carry on packhorses. A sense of foreboding haunted him. He knew the Hereros were not far away. Why they had not yet appeared was inexplicable – something was about to happen.

He swung round to look out to sea and recoiled with shock. A few miles off the mouth of the lagoon, a warship lay stationary. The Imperial German ensign fluttered on the stern. His binoculars swept the vessel from stern to bow. He saw the guns on her fore and aft decks as well as the three tall funnels, all emitting smoke. From her size, he thought the warship to be a frigate. He trained the glasses on the bow of the ship and could just make out the name – "ss Leipzig". He was astounded. Where had the ship come from? Major Zietzmann had told them that the Imperial Navy had no ships in this area. As he watched, three large boats were lowered, still attached to their davits. From their size, he thought one of these had to be a cutter, smoke already pouring from the small funnel on its stern. He made a quick decision. Speaking in Ovambo, he told one of the men to stay while the other was to accompany him. Using long strides, they half slid and ran down the steep side of the dune.

Werner noticed them stumbling down the dune. Why was he coming back? Louis pointed out to sea and then made a waving motion with his hand moving it horizontally from right to left, indicating a ship sailing on the water. He again followed this with an arm pointed out to sea. Bewildered at first, Werner soon caught on. He started to climb the dune, glad that he was wearing knee-high riding boots, which prevented sand from spilling into them.

They met a few hundred feet up the seaward slope of the dune. Werner stopped and looked out to sea. The boats were now in the water and were already en route to the lagoon entrance; two boats towed by the cutter, the funnel belching smoke, the boats fully laden with naval troops, their rifles clearly visible.

"Donne wetter! Where on earth did they come from?"

Louis stared at him. Werner quickly repeated himself in Portuguese.

"I thought you said your Navy had no warships in this part of the world?"

"Well, that's what Zietzmann said. It appears he was wrong."

"Thank God, he was wrong! These chaps are just in time. I was getting extremely worried; the Hereros have to be around here somewhere."

Both men watched the cutter navigate the turbulent and dangerous entrance to the lagoon. The two trailing boats had put out oars and used these to assist the cutter through the breaking waves and stop the boats from broaching. The sailors knew what they were doing; they passed through the surf without incident other than a good soaking. Nothing unusual for navy boys, Werner thought.

The bows of three boats ground into the shallows of the lagoon, the troops immediately leaping into the water and coming ashore, led by a uniformed officer complete with cocked hat and sword. He clicked his heels and saluted Jurgen.

"Leutenant Dorfling of the "ss Leipzig," he announced stiffly. "Fregattenkapitän Schneider sends his compliments and asks whether you require any assistance."

"Assistance! My God sir, you come at a most fortunate moment. I have wounded who are in need of urgent medical attention," an astonished Jurgen replied.

Quickly, the men loaded the wounded onto the naval cutter, which was ordered to return once they were aboard the frigate. Jurgen took the opportunity of filling in the naval lieutenant.

"Leutenant, I'm concerned the Hereros could be upon us at any moment. The rifles lie at the bottom of the lagoon, but they do not know this and no doubt think Dos Santos awaits them. They must be on their way here to collect these," Jurgen concluded.

By agreement, the naval lieutenant dispatched the bulk of his men to the top of the dunes where Louis' lone Askari still maintained a lookout. Two groups of four men were sent along both sides of the lagoon shore to take up station about a half mile from where the boats were beached, to protect the causeway.

By evening, no enemy force had made an appearance. The cutter had returned with blankets and provisions. An encroaching fog bank had left the Fregattenkapitän no option but to take his ship out to sea and it was no longer visible. It was unlikely that the Hereros would arrive or attack at night. Nonetheless, Jurgen considered it prudent to post sentries around the camp and a lookout was continued from the top of the dunes. The men slept in their blankets on the beach.

Jurgen awoke, his eyelids heavy with small droplets of dew. A thick grey blanket of mist hung over the mirror smooth surface of the lagoon, restricting vision to no more than a hundred yards. Unable to see the crest of the dunes, he threw back his blankets and shook his boots to rid them of any scorpions. Being an officer, he endeavoured always to present a picture of neatness and decorum, so he hitched up his jodhpurs and pulled down his tunic. But on closer inspection, he decided it was pointless. His uniform was no longer blue grey, but blackened from the cannon's cordite flashes and the cutter's coal dust. His tailor-made tunic had been torn in a number of places and his left knee poked through a hole in his jodhpurs. His hands and face were dark with grime and blood. At the water's edge, he scooped up handfuls of water to wash. The water was brackish, but it certainly could be drunk. He was surprised, expecting seawater. Amazing that fresh water could push its way through this colossal barrier of dunes and then seep into the lagoon.

"Morning, you look bloody awful."

Werner stood, his hands on his hips looking down at him. Jurgen laughed. Werner had obviously washed his face, but it was in stark contrast to the rest of him.

"If only Dorothea could see you now!"

"Don't start that crap; I've already had enough from Louis. He just won't leave me in peace!

"Hmmm, touchy this morning," Jurgen muttered.

Werner ignored him.

"Come on, let's see what our Navy guys have got for us to eat."

A sailor on board the cutter was handing out sandwiches of rye bread with smoked sausage and they joined the queue of men waiting to be served. The sailors had put together a few makeshift benches. The naval lieutenant and Von Moeltke occupied one of these, drinking their coffee. Werner and Jurgen joined them.

"Fine morning, what?" the old sea dog said, ever-present pipe in his mouth. He too was a picture of soot and grime. "The lieutenant tells me that they will help me to get the cutter out to sea. That old tub rolls like a bitch, she's not really made for the open sea, but after her performance in the lagoon, well, she deserves some tender-loving-care."

"I concur. She certainly did give a good account of herself."

"Well, it seems we have to wait, the frigate will not make an appearance before noon when the mist lifts. Any news from our runner?" Jurgen asked.

Before anyone could reply, a sailor sprinted up to the officers.

"Sir, mounted horsemen approach from the north along the beach, they are Schutztruppe."

"Thank you. Come, gentlemen, let's meet our other reinforcements."

About sixty horsemen approached, mostly Schutztruppe with a few Askaris. It was evident that the horses had not been properly watered for a while. If the captain had proposed to make a dramatic entrance, the horses stole the show as they strained against their reins to get to the fresh water. The captain relented, giving his horse its head, and soon the animals were lined up along the shore drinking.

"I have seen no sign of the Hereros," the captain said, saluting smartly, "although an intelligence report mentioned a large force of mounted Hereros who broke through the Khomas Hochland and had descended the plateau in the region of the Naukluft."

Werner looked at Jurgen quizzically.

"It is a canyon cut through the mountains as the river makes its way to the sea. The river then disappears into the desert, about ninety miles from Sandwich Bay."

"We think it is this band which was to intercept the rifle shipment," the captain explained.

Werner wondered how long dos Santos and his surviving crew would last. The group had little or no water, no food and certainly were not equipped to undertake any trip into the desert. However, they had been unable to mount any pursuit and dos Santos had now disappeared.

Suddenly there was shouting from the lookouts at the top of the dune. Jurgen, the newly arrived captain and the naval lieutenant quickly climbed to see what had attracted their attention. From where the sea had broken through the sandbar, the lagoon lay parallel to the coast, berms of sand twenty or so feet high separating it from the sea. The lagoon was less than a mile wide at its widest. On the opposite side it was hemmed in by the sand dunes, their steep slopes virtually disappearing straight into the water leaving only a narrow causeway. The lagoon was a long body of water, mostly no more than a fathom or two deep but at least ten to fifteen miles long, separated from the sea simply by this narrow strip of beach.

Facing south, they trained their binoculars on the strip of land. The large column of horsemen approaching were immediately identified as Hereros.

"Where the hell did they come from? There is no way through these dunes from that direction," Jurgen exclaimed.

"Well, it doesn't matter now, they're here," the Schutztruppe captain retorted.

"It will be difficult for them to mount any sort of attack. The dunes are too steep. This is like Thermopylae; a small band of men could hold them against all comers."

"They have seen us!" the naval lieutenant shouted excitedly.

The column had reined their horses in, and some were dismounting, their rifles in hand, giving their riderless horses over to be lead to the rear. A few ineffectual shots rang out, but the troops were still hopelessly out of range of the Hereros' rifles.

Werner still had his binoculars glued to his eyes.

"Christ!" he said, not lowering his binoculars, "I think I can see that bastard dos Santos."

Louis moved in next to Werner.

Taking the glasses, he peered through them.

"The bastard! It's him all right. And would you believe it, he has his bloody woman with him. The man's insane! Who brings a woman with on a trip like this? The bastard should be dead! " Louis spat in Portuguese.

The Hereros had begun to dig mounds into the sand for shelter from the troops advancing along the causeway.

"This is going to be a standoff. We're going to sit here all day, exchanging fire and getting nowhere. Is there no way around them?" Werner asked

"No, the dunes are too steep for the horses and if we try it on foot, they'll pick us off like in a shooting gallery," Jurgen replied.

"I've an idea."

The naval lieutenant had a sly grin on his face.

"I suggest we engage them with return rifle fire. I'll also put a few men with rifles in the cutter to approach them from the west. Meanwhile, we signal the "Leipzig" to open fire with her turret guns." He pointed to the top of the dune. "We can act as an observation post from up there, directing fire. Those are three and five and half inch shells; that'll scare the shit out of them."

"And how do you propose to signal the "Leipzig"?" Jurgen asked.

"Look."

The naval lieutenant pointed to the top of the dune. The officers could just see a sailor standing, legs apart, with a small flag in each hand.

"That's navy semaphore!" Werner blurted out. Semaphore flags had never crossed his mind.

"Sounds good to me," Jurgen smiled. "When's the Leipzig due back in?"

The lieutenant shrugged his shoulders, spreading his hands.

"So what do we do in the meantime, just shoot at each other?"

"I suppose so."

The Hereros and the troops were now returning desultory fire, the naval and Schutztruppe troops having dug in behind their own heaps of sand. The distance between the two was about four hundred yards; close enough to ensure that all kept their heads down.

The officers returned to the boats near the shore. Another sailor with a flag in each hand was jerking his arms about at second intervals, communicating with the top of the dune.

"They have detected the "Leipzig" steaming towards us," the naval lieutenant volunteered, watching the man at the top of the dune. "She's seen the Hereros and is now turning broadside to the shore."

"Get her to fire a shot at them."

A flurry of signals followed and few minutes later there was a low whistle as a shell arched over the lagoon and imbedded itself deep in the sand along the ridge of dunes; it exploded, throwing a mass of sand and dust high into the sky. They heard the explosion only as the horizon turned flamingo pink. The shallow lagoon and its mud was a source of food and home to thousands of seafowl, flamingos, pelicans and myriads of others. Another flurry of signals followed, but this shell was at least three hundred yards off target. It erupted in the lagoon about fifty yards short of a concentration of Hereros on the shoreline, an enormous fountain of water and mud bursting into the sky. The last of the flamingos took to the sky. Although short, it was clear that the second shell fall was too near for comfort, and there much consternation amongst the Hereros. Again, they heard the whistle. This time the shell drove itself into the mud at the water's edge, just yards from the enemy prone behind their berms. Its explosion flung sand, men and equipment in all directions. These were armour-piercing shells, which penetrated deep into the mud before exploding, with spectacular result.

Jurgen and the Schutztruppe captain galloped the mounted troopers down the causeway, past those still prone on the ground and charged into the scattered enemy, shooting and slashing at those desperately trying to flee along the causeway. Those Hereros whose horses had not bolted, remounted and fled from the charging troopers. The German troopers did not follow, certain they would ride into a deadly barrage of rifle fire. Those Hereros still on foot scrambled for their lives, some frantically climbing the steep incline of the dunes and disappearing over the top, others running into the shallow waters of the lagoon. Again, the Leipzig's for'ard turret belched flame and smoke along the lagoon shore to explode amongst the fleeing Hereros, giving them further impetus to rapidly depart the skirmish. When the enemy had all disappeared, the troopers broke off the attack and returned.

Louis was grinning as he met Werner and Philippe, still flushed with the excitement of the battle and their victory.

"Merda! It was good to be on the winning side again," he said in Portuguese as Philippe grabbed the horse's rein and he dismounted, a bloodied sabre in his hand. "We must have dispatched at least fifty of them and the ship's cannons killed still more."

"Did you see dos Santos?" Werner asked.

Louis shook his head.

"Damn, the bastard's got away again! Are we never going to catch him?"

Louis grabbed him by the arm. "We will, I just know we will. He's on the run now, a worried man. He knows he's a target and it's obvious we are not about to give up. I wouldn't want to be in his shoes."

"Christ! And he has that woman of his with him, or so it seems. That definitely complicates matters."

"Don't you worry about that, leave her to me; you obviously don't know how to handle women anyway," Louis declared a mischievous smile on his face.

Werner glared at him for a moment, and then smiled. Nobody would have ever guessed that his friend was a senior officer in the Portuguese colonial forces. There was nothing smart about him. In fact, he looked like a vagrant. His chin and cheeks sported a few days of stubble; he was filthy dirty, his face and arms scratched and covered with dried scabs, his shirt and trousers torn and his boots scuffed down to raw leather in places.

Werner chuckled.

"Fuck you," he said and walked off, smiling as Louis' loud laugh rang out behind him.

CHAPTER FIVE

For three days they had urged their horses on, and they were now on the outskirts of the desert, where it met the escarpment. Here the mounted column swung north, so the precipices, steep slopes and gullies of the steep gradient that rose to the top of the plateau three thousand feet above them dominated their view. On the horizon they could vaguely distinguish the start of the dune-sea from which they had emerged only a few hours ago.

Their troop consisted of only forty men. At Sandwich Bay, Werner, Louis and Jurgen had decided to pursue dos Santos and the Hereros, remaining on their trail while not trying to engage them. Consensus had it that the gunrunner would now try to make for Angola and must therefore travel north to avoid making contact with colonials or troops. The route they had chosen was desolate and virtually uninhabited. If they were seen, those who saw them would present no threat. By the time they could alert the authorities, a garrison seventy miles away, dos Santos would be long gone.

Crossing the sea of sand had been a gruelling ordeal for Werner's group. The wind was relentless, never abating, and they rode in a continuous dust storm with bandannas tied over their mouths and noses. Knowing the desert, the men had made sure that they carried sufficient water but Werner was alarmed to see just how much water both horse and man required in these conditions. They barely made it to the first natural well at the foot of the escarpment.

The scouts inspected the ashes of the recent campfires around the water hole. It appeared dos Santos and his men were no more than a day ahead, a group of nearly a hundred strong. The troops were exhausted, and Jurgen decided to call a halt and rest up for a day, confident that dos Santos would soon have to do the same and would therefore not get too far ahead.

Some enterprising karakul farmer who had long since deserted this region had erected a windmill in a slight depression. Driven by the wind, its spinning metal vanes glinting in the sunlight, the windmill pumped a steady trickle of water into an excavation dug into the ground to act as a reservoir. This was the only water for miles and attracted game and fowl of every description. Desert quail, their warble ringing across the desert floor, swooped down to the water in their thousands, as did black-necked ringed doves. Hundreds of guinea fowl dashed out of the scrub to quell their thirst, ever alert to danger. Herds of gemsbok lingered nearby, their long straight horns and black and white faces unmistakable. These desert oryx did not need to drink water as they could obtain moisture from the roots and bulbs they grazed on, but would not ignore the luxury of a waterhole. The springbok herds numbered in their thousands: Werner estimated one herd to be more than ten thousand strong. He marvelled at nature's ability to provide for such numbers in this wild, sun-scorched region. The evenings were cool, becoming near freezing in the early hours of the morning, the clear cloudless sky at night allowing the heat to radiate off. Once the sun rose in the morning, the temperature rapidly increased. By ten, it was already blistering hot. Any exposed skin soon burnt an angry red, and some form of headcover was essential if heatstroke was to be avoided.

The long shallow depression brought the underground water table nearer to the ground surface. This sustained a band of vegetation almost a kilometre long, comprised mostly of thorn bush and trees with dry desert grass in between. The men dismounted and hobbled their horses, all seeking shade under the umbrella of the larger trees. The scene was dwarfed by the sheer immensity of the plateau to the east, its rock face towering a thousand or more feet above the campsite.

Werner collapsed on the bare ground, lying back on the sand, his arms pillowing his head, his campaign hat over his face.

It was tacitly accepted that Jurgen, who had spent a few years in the colony, knew best how to out think the enemy and anticipate their moves. He joined Werner on the ground.

"Of course dos Santos is running north. He has to avoid the Schutztruppe. Between us here, and where I imagine he probably is now, there is a strong troop presence. Most of the conflict is still in this mid to northern region."

He paused for a moment.

"I think dos Santos will split his men, sending them north and northwest to draw attention away from himself. He must realize we are after him. Of course, we don't know how many men he will keep with him, but I think he'll keep his group small, no more than twenty to thirty. That'll enable him to move faster. If I were him, I'd probably choose a route passing west of Usakos, going on to Omaruru, then west of Outjo and finally into Ovamboland. I'd cross the border where we last encountered his wagons. But it's the rainy season now – he'll only be able to cross the river where it is fordable."

Werner's reply was muffled by his hat.

"Makes sense. Should we reduce the size of our detachment to pursue him, and take additional horses so we can increase our pace?"

"Sounds good. Once we're near to Usakos, I'll send most of the men to the garrison in town, and keep their horses. They'll just have to march the last few miles."

Werner dozed off, to be awakened by a laughing Jurgen.

"Just look at that! Your Portuguese friend's got the right idea."

Louis had stripped off his clothing, and his body was pale in the harsh sun except for his face, neck and hands, which were burnt red. Impervious to the stares and chuckles of the black

Askaris, he waded out waist-deep into the muddy reservoir, ignoring the green algae floating on its surface.

Somebody shouted from the shade.

"Watch out a catfish doesn't take that worm of yours for bait!" Loud guffaws followed from the assembled black men, who found humour in the simplest of things. Louis turned his back on the whistles and catcalls.

"Fuckin' Portuguese wop; serves the bastard right. The idiot thinks he's God's gift to women and says I don't know what to do with them," Werner murmured.

"What's that comment all about?"

"You don't want to know."

"Well, I don't know, from what I see out there," Jurgen chuckled, "he seems to be quite formidable—he just might have a point!"

"Christ, another fuckin' idiot," Werner said, heaving himself up from the ground, leaving Jurgen sniggering behind him.

As they had anticipated, the guerrillas scattered, and they were unable to establish which splinter group contained dos Santos. The groups had not split off simultaneously, but had broken away one by one at fifty-mile intervals. The *Schutztruppe's* numbers were too small to permit them to follow each splinter group.

Jurgen and his men rode north until abeam of Omaruru, about forty miles west of the town. Omaruru was situated on the narrow gauge railroad that ran north to Tsumeb, the same rail line on which they had previously travelled south accompanying the wounded to Windhuk.

Now, convinced that dos Santos would attempt to cross the northern border into Angola, they decided to break off pursuit and head for Omaruru. From there they could contact Major Zietzmann. Not all had been in vain; the Hereros had not been able to take delivery of the consignment of rifles smuggled in through Sandwich Bay, and this was now lying at the bottom of the lagoon. At least, the major had to be pleased about that.

In Omaruru, they found billet with the local military garrison which numbered a few hundred men. Cables were immediately despatched to Windhuk advising Zietzmann of the latest developments. While they awaited further orders, Werner persuaded the local quartermaster to part with an officer's uniform, not a perfect fit but still making him look quite presentable. Louis spent a few hours in the small village and returned in new clothes from head to foot, quite the gentleman. A shave and trimmed hair transformed them both.

Notwithstanding their backgrounds and colour, over the weeks the bond between Werner and Philippe had developed into an extraordinary friendship, a somewhat unique situation in this fiercely segregated country. Werner had acquired a deep respect for the black man: his dedication to his duties no matter how menial the task, his unwavering loyalty and unflinching bravery was exceptional. He was awed by Philippe's bush skills – he found his way through country that was not properly mapped yet, and had a seemingly miraculous ability to track man and beast and to find water in the desert when he'd had never been there before.

If Philippe had ever harboured any disdain for Werner, this had long evaporated. He saw in Werner of man of enormous resolve and strength, a fair man, a man of compassion. Philippe had long ago read the young white man's body language and reactions. When they rode into a kraal, Werner showed proper deference to the local headman: he did not summarily assume authority over them, he did nothing without permission and was always grateful for any assistance the locals rendered. If he believed payment was called for, he voluntarily paid. Within the confines of taste and culture differences, they shared much. More importantly, they trusted each other.

Werner and Louis sat down to lunch in the officer's mess, Louis resplendent in his new clothes and Werner in a new Schutztruppe uniform, his epaulettes displaying his new captain's rank.

"Werner, in town this morning, I found a small trading store, belonging to a Portuguese family which has lived here for some years. You can't imagine how surprised I was, to find Portuguese settlers in this town, somebody I could speak to! And I've just recalled something that bothered me. The storekeeper said that I was the second Portuguese who had come into his shop within the last week. He said he never sees any Portuguese. I wonder if it could be dos Santos?"

Werner's fork hovered over his plate.

"Did you ask him any questions? Like, was he alone or did he give a name or where the man was from?"

"Quite frankly, I didn't even think of it."

Werner shoved his chair back.

"Come on, let's go."

"Christus, I haven't even eaten! Where to?"

"To your Portuguese shop, come on!" he replied, his mounting excitement evident.

They trotted their horses through the dusty streets and dismounted in front of the trading store. Being past midday, it was now closed. Everything closed for lunch in the colony. A pathway connected the store to the back of the house next door. Both men walked down a cobbled path, flanked on both sides with flowers of all description in full bloom. Somebody was obviously an ardent gardener, Werner thought, probably the wife. On their knock, the door immediately opened.

Werner stood back, hoping his uniform and rank were not intimidating.

"An ill-timed intrusion, I know," Louis apologized, "but my friend has a few important questions. We are assisting the German authorities on behalf of the Portuguese government on a matter of the utmost importance."

The trader did not ask them in, but merely stood in the door, his expression neutral.

"When I visited your shop earlier, you mentioned I was your second visit from a Portuguese person recently?"

"Yes, senhor."

"Can you describe this man?"

"Certainly, I won't easily forget him. He was exceptionally big, burnt by the sun. He had recently hurt himself—I remember, his arm was bandaged and he had scratches on his face." With his arms outstretched, the trader indicated a huge gut. "He had an enormous stomach."

Louis looked at Werner.

"Was he alone?"

"No, he had a woman with him. A mulatto. Very beautiful," the trader's hands indicated a curvaceous body.

"Did he say anything else?"

"Well, being Portuguese, obviously we talked. He said he was hoping to start a trading business here. He asked me many questions. He said he had injured himself falling off his horse. Christus! He was so big; it must have been a hard fall."

The trader smiled at his own joke.

"He said he was going north."

"Did he say how?"

"No, I assumed by train."

"Did she say anything?"

"No, she seemed afraid of him. My wife tried to speak to her while she bought a few things, but she said very little."

Louis realized the man had little more to add. "Thank you very much, senhor, you've been a great help. We apologize for disturbing your lunch."

"Is everything all right?"

"Not to worry, it's fine, you've been a great help," Louis repeated.

Lifting their hats, they said goodbye and left, leaving a somewhat bewildered trader on the porch.

"It's him . . . I just know it," Werner blurted out, once they were out of earshot.

"I agree. Do you think he is going north by train?"

"I don't know. Let's go to the station."

The stationmaster and his staff had taken off for lunch, as no train was expected before five that afternoon. On the platform, they found a hawker who sold beer. He said they would only be back at three. With little else to do, they bought a few beers and then sat on a bench in the shade of the platform canopy drinking these.

Promptly at three, the stationmaster arrived. He recalled the Portuguese gentleman, who had had difficulty making himself understood. He had wanted to return to Angola, and had bought two tickets on the northbound train. In fact, to Tsumeb, he added.

They rode back to the barracks and sought out Jurgen.

"We've got to get on this evening's train. There is no time for cables. The commander has to allow us use of the phone; we have to get in touch with Major Zietzmann."

Initially the garrison commander was reluctant, as the phone was a new installation, available for use by district commanders alone, but he eventually relented. After an endless delay, they got Zietzmann on the line. The connection was faint.

"We need your permission to board a train to Tsumeb with the troops," Werner shouted, having updated the major on the latest developments.

"Of course," agreed Zietzmann. "I will telegraph orders to the garrison commander at Tsumeb and Ondongua. He will ensure that you are provided with everything required to mount a pursuit operation."

Within an hour the cable had arrived from Windhuk, authorizing their departure by train to Tsumeb. The men scrambled, mobilizing rapidly, and men and horses were already on the platform when the northbound train arrived that evening. The local garrison commander had supplied fresh horses and new riding tack, weapons, food and first aid supplies for the eight of them; the three white men, Philippe, and four of the Askaris who had accompanied them from Sandwich Bay.

No-one knew how many men had accompanied dos Santos. The bookings clerk recalled that others had also bought tickets for the train and space for horses on boxcars on that day, but could not recall how many or whether they were all part of a group. However, he did mention that he was surprised that blacks had bought space for animals on the train, as black men did not often own horses and certainly never used the train to transport them.

"Well, we don't quite know how many, but it seems we are up against at least eight to ten of them," Jurgen commented as they boarded the train.

"Don't worry, this time we are going to take this bastard out," Werner declared. His desire for revenge was becoming overpowering.

"What do you think dos Santos is planning to do from Tsumeb? What route will he take to Angola?" Werner asked Louis in Portuguese.

"The eastern and central part of the border is too dangerous for him. He'll go west: probably first to Ondongua and then to the mission. Or he might even pass it before going north. Everybody around here knows about the mission station. Anyway, that's the way I would go," Louis replied.

"Philippe?"

"The *Capitano* is right. He must make for the mission if he intends to go west," the black man murmured quietly.

"Can we catch him?"

""No, I don't think so, he's got a head start. He'll get to the mission before us," Louis said resignedly.

Werner found himself thinking of Dorothea and the brief but intensely passionate moment on the train, when he had been so aware of her. He knew he wanted to see her again, and it seemed Fate seemed to want to thrust them together.

The train arrived in Tsumeb in the early hours of the morning. Dos Santos had indeed been and gone. His group of black riders and their buying of supplies and additional horses had drawn attention although no suspicions. The Kunehama uprising in Angola was a source of concern to the inhabitants of northern SudwestAfrika, as many believed this could spark a similar revolt amongst the Ovambo tribe. Under the circumstances, none considered dos Santos' departure with an escort unusual: the man required protection, as did his wares, and the situation in his country was still troubled and tense.

Major Graf zu Dohner's reception was cool, his attitude abrupt and condescending. Once again Major Zietzmann had chosen to mount a pursuit operation in his district without requesting his assistance. He felt slighted and annoyed, but he had no alternative but to accept the situation – Zietzmann's authority came direct from the OKH. His previous complaints had been ignored; he was not about to make fool of himself again.

They saddled up and left before daybreak the next morning.

Dos Santos had chosen to cut out Ondongua. He purposely avoided the main trail that headed towards the west and the Finnish mission, cutting a new route through the bush. Jurgen hoped this would have slowed the gunrunner down; he had often been forced to hack a virgin path through the veld.

They pushed their horses hard, hoping to make the mission before sunset. When they halted, thirsty and exhausted, about a mile from the mission, the sun was already below the horizon and darkness was rapidly approaching.

Jurgen called the men together.

"I think we should send Philippe forward to see what's going on. Agreed?"

"Yes. Good idea. He will easily blend in and shouldn't raise any suspicions, that is, if dos Santos is even there," Werner replied doubtfully.

Louis seemed to pick up the gist of the conversation. "He's there, of that I'm sure. This is the last water. I remember this from when we brought you through on the travois."

Philippe quickly removed his clothing and produced a *chenga-lappi,* worn by all male Ovambos, a leather loincloth of two squares of soft leather. Both squares hung from a leather thong around his waist, one covering his front the other his rear. When he added a leather braided necklace, he was transformed; he now appeared no different from other local Ovambo males they had seen.

Philippe handed Werner his rifle.

"Please, look after this for me, Ovambos don't have rifles," he said, producing a spear with a flourish as his face broke out into a huge grin. His white teeth flashed. "In the dark, this is better."

The African danced from foot to foot, throwing the spear from hand to hand.

"The bastard's enjoying this!" Jurgen gasped incredulously. "He's going out there on his own and he thinks it's fun. Christ, he doesn't seem to understand he could get killed!"

Following the wagon tracks and not attempting to conceal himself, Philippe jogged towards the mission in the receding twilight. He hoped that no-one would enquire who he was. The mission residents knew him; he would need to proceed with caution and not blatantly show himself. He needed to avoid being recognized and jubilantly greeted by an acquaintance and drawing attention to himself. He also needed to avoid one or two women whom he had promised he would return to! As he neared the settlement, he slowed to a walk then strode boldly into the compound. There were numerous people still about, the women busy around their cooking pots hung on tripods over fires just outside their huts, their men seated on small benches smoking and talking, the children playing in the dust within the light of the fires. He carefully skirted the fires, staying in the shadows, closely examining the individuals, trying to recognize any of dos Santos' group. Those dressed similarly to him, he rejected; dos Santos' men would be properly clothed. He saw none who appeared suspicious in the village.

A large fire was burning near the corral, surrounded by a number of people with cooking pots also hanging from tripods. As he neared, he saw they were dressed in civilian clothes. Certainly not locals; this could only be dos Santos and his men. He melted into the background, into the deepest shadows where the firelight would not illuminate him.

Philippe carefully scrutinized each individual. Although he was hoping to see dos Santos, when he did actually spot him, he involuntarily drew in his breath with an audible hiss. There was no mistaking the man; he sat on a large log, using his fingers to pick food from a plate on his lap. To his left sat the same woman he had seen at dos Santos' trading store in Huambo. Assuming that all his men were here, the gunrunner's small group totalled ten men, plus dos Santos and the woman. Their horses were corralled nearby; some twenty animals. With that many spare horses, it was clear that the man planned to travel fast—very fast. It would be very difficult for Werner and his men to keep up; they did not have that many spare mounts.

The group were speaking amongst themselves and Philippe could clearly understand the Herero dialect they spoke. Dos Santos's voice was loud and demanding, and as Philippe listened intently, it became strident. He carefully peered out at the fire and saw the silhouette of the huge man standing over the woman, waving his arms and shouting. They spoke now in Portuguese. Suddenly the gunrunner lifted his hand and slapped the woman across the mouth. She fell to the ground. Dos Santos towered over her, silent, glaring at her as if he dared her to either speak or rise.

Philippe did not know what to make of the altercation. Was this an exception or a common occurrence? With Portuguese colonists, you never knew: their interaction with one another was often volatile and at times, quite explosive.

Slowly he backtracked, slinking from the group towards the mission building, where he silently entered the dark courtyard, careful to remain in the shadows, hugging the building walls. Light filtered through the curtains of a few of the rooms. He peered through a window, the curtains of which had not been properly drawn, and saw the missionaries standing behind the chairs which surrounded a large rectangular dining table, over which hung two large coal oil lanterns. The bright light illuminated the room where the occupants were about to commence dinner.

"Was machst Du denn hier?"

He froze at the sound of the female voice behind him. He had his back to the junction of the veranda where it stood proud of the building wall. He slowly turned round. She stood in the shadow of the porch, the last light of twilight not sufficient for him to identify her. Slowly she moved forward until she stood against the porch railing. It was the lady doctor who had attended to the lieutenant when they were last here.

"I recognize you. You are Lieutenant von Dewitz's servant, aren't you?" she asked.

He nodded, raising a finger to his lips and shaking his head silently.

Her voice was barely more than a whisper.

"What are you doing here? Is he also here?"

Again, he nodded his head. She looked round the forecourt as if she expected to see the lieutenant. Before she could say anything further, he pointed towards the east, his fingers still to his lips. He then slowly backed off until he disappeared into the dark.

Dorothea was bewildered, unable to grasp the necessity for the secrecy and stealth or why the black man had so hastily withdrawn. She could still picture the lieutenant, his slightly aquiline nose, his strong hands, the blond hair on his arms which had shimmered in the light when she first laid eyes on him on the examination table, his chest bare. He had looked dreadful, still racked by fever, obviously dehydrated, his face a sickly pallor. Since her return from Windhuk with the two nurses, he continuously intruded on her thoughts, leaving her irritated and confused. At night in bed she became aware of an inner ache when her thoughts dwelt too long on him. The black man had indicated that the lieutenant was nearby; why had they not approached the mission? And why was his servant wearing only a loincloth?

"Doktor!" The Pastor impatiently called her to dinner; as she entered the dining room, all the others were standing behind their chairs, patiently waiting so that they could commence grace. The Pastor gave her a reproachful look. She apologized.

The three men listened attentively to Philippe's report on the camp.

"We can't attack the camp, innocent people could get killed," Werner argued, concerned for the missionaries' safety but primarily that of Dorothea. "We are going to have ambush them when they leave for the border."

Louis and slapped his thigh and turned away in disgust.

"What's wrong?" Werner demanded.

"The man will get away. I know him! But we've no alternative . . . if we cannot attack tonight, or at the latest tomorrow morning, we'll have to scout around the mission and set ourselves up on the other side, at least a few miles away from the mission," the *Capitano* replied. He was clearly concerned at the delay.

Werner translated.

"He's right, Werner, we've got to get ahead of them tonight," Jurgen said.

"It'll take us until tomorrow morning to get into position. We'll get no sleep."

Jurgen shrugged his shoulders.

"Can't be helped. Okay, I've decided, let's go," he said, getting up from where he was sitting, indicating his agreement with Louis.

Werner laughed, looking at the Portuguese captain and then turning to Jurgen. "The bastard wants to get this over with because he just wants to get home."

Jurgen nodded. Not that he blamed the Capitano – he wanted to go home as well.

With Philippe and a scout leading the way, they led their horses through the bush, keeping well away from the mission, not wanting any sound, in particular a neigh from the horses, to alert dos Santos and his men. They knew the enemy must be nervous, as they were still deep in German territory. They were bound to have placed sentries around their camp.

Only at four in the morning did they stumble upon the trail leading west which dos Santos and his men would need to travel to cross the border into Angola. This area was an extension of the semi-desert that dissected much of southern Africa; a flood plain that was completely flat. There were no rocks, only sand. During the summer season, the run-off from the rains would accumulate in the vast shallow Etosha Pan, a huge dry lake for most of the year, a white dustbowl at times, but home to hundreds and thousands of African animals of every description. The bush, while not impregnable, was quite dense, with large camel thorn trees every fifty to sixty yards and smaller mopani trees and brush in-between. Jurgen ordered the men to take up ambush positions on both sides of the trail using whatever bush, trees and ant heaps they could as cover.

Jurgen was convinced dos Santos would have scouts reconnoitring ahead of his group, primarily to avoid accidentally running into a military patrol. He proposed that they intercept these lookouts and eliminate them, hopefully without raising any alarm. Philippe was to remain dressed as a local in his loincloth. All he had to do was draw the attention of the scout momentarily, enabling the Askaris to approach stealthily from the rear, getting close enough to silence them. Usually, scouts moved a good half-mile ahead of a mounted troop and it would take dos Santos a short while before he caught up, by which time Jurgen's men would have taken up their ambush positions again. A simple plan, Werner thought, but nonetheless risky. Philippe ran on ahead so that he could approach from the west as if he was walking towards the mission. He concentrated on coordinating his approach so that that he would meet the scouts at the point where his comrades were ready, hidden in the bush. Timing was crucial.

Although the sun was still to appear, the dawn's light already suffused the landscape, the sky a swath of purple to the east. Philippe saw the first scout appear on the trail in the distance, his horse approaching at a slow trot. He emerged from the bush where he had been hiding and walked leisurely down the wagon tracks. No other scout could be seen. The black man had a rifle in one hand, its butt resting on his boot in the stirrup, the barrel pointing skywards. As is custom, Philippe raised his hand in greeting and followed this with a few words of greeting in Ovambo. The scout reined in. Philippe kept walking as if he had every right to be there, planning to pass the scout on his left.

"Stop!" the scout shouted, lowering his rifle and pointing it casually at Philippe, who immediately stopped, appearing unconcerned, waiting for the man on horseback to speak. "What were you doing in the bush? Why were you hiding?" he demanded in Ovambo.

"Having a shit. What's it to you?" he replied indignantly, hoping to imply he had every right to be there and not be questioned.

"Hmm, are there any others?"

"No, I don't have a shit where there are others."

At that moment, another black rider burst from the bush.

"What's going on? I heard voices," he asked. The first rider explained, pointing at Philippe, and the new arrival visibly relaxed, seeing no danger in a single individual.

"Where have you just come from?"

Philippe pointed vaguely towards the northwest.

"Have you seen any German soldiers?"

Philippe did not immediately reply, pretending to give the matter serious thought. He saw two of his black comrades emerge from the bush behind the two riders. They had stripped to the waist. Both clutched short stabbing spears. They slowly crept up behind the two mounted scouts. Philippe realized he had to distract the riders.

"What are you doing here with rifles?" he asked belligerently, not answering the question.

The second rider laughed loudly.

"Who are you to ask?" he demanded, pointing the barrel of his rifle at Philippe's chest.

The Askaris had crept up close to the horses. Simultaneously now they spurted forward, covering the last five yards in an instant, lashing both horses on the flanks with the butt-end of their spears. Both horses leapt forward in fright, catching the riders off-guard. As the first horse bore down on him, Philippe lunged upwards with his stabbing spear, the forward motion of the horse driving the spear into the man's chest just below his ribcage, the metal tip tearing deep into his lungs and heart. There was a shrill death shriek and he toppled from his saddle, his horse bolting westwards along the trail.

A shot rang out. The Askari had grabbed the other horseman by his clothing and were dragging him from the saddle, but he had fired his rifle. He fell to the ground with a loud thump and the Askaris plunged their spears into the man's chest. Damn! Surely dos Santos must have heard the shot and the cry, Philippe thought. There's no mistaking a death scream. What would he do?

Philippe and his two accomplices melted back into the bush. Werner and his men remained hidden, hoping that it would seem the two black horsemen had been killed by locals. They didn't wait long.

The guerillas approached rapidly, their horses trailing a cloud of red dust. They reigned in at the sight of their fallen comrades, alarmed, and quickly formed a circle in order to cover all sides, staring into the dense bush.

"Fire!" Jurgen shouted.

At near point-blank range, the fusillade of shots found their targets easily, men dropping from the saddles and horses rearing up. It was over in seconds. Those who struggled to their feet were summarily despatched with the short spears. No quarter was given: the eyes of the Askaris were wide with a killing madness Werner had yet to get used to.

"Christus!"

The dead men represented only about half of dos Santos' force. And dos Santos and his woman were not amongst them. They must have remained behind awaiting the return of the recon group. What would he do now?

"He won't attack. He doesn't know our strength," Werner said, reading Jurgen's mind.

"I know. I think we should attack immediately while we still have him off balance and out in the open," Jurgen frowned.

There was a moment's silence.

"Okay, my decision."

Jurgen spun round and shouted at the men.

"Everybody mount up, we going after them, right now."

They ran to their horses and swung into the saddles, checked their weapons and galloped back east along the trail towards dos Santos. Stealth was no longer important.

They had ridden no further than half a mile down the trail when a shot rang out and a bullet hit an Askari high in the shoulder. The men reined in, dropping from their horses, desperately looking for cover. Fortunately, the Askari appeared to have only a flesh wound and was still mobile, holding his shoulder while blood flowed from between his fingers. Dos Santos' men had taken up a defensive position along the track, but an untimely errant shot from a nervous adversary had destroyed their element of surprise.

"I can see men on horses returning to the mission," Louis said to Werner in a subdued voice. "What's going on?"

"Did you see dos Santos?"

"No, but I definitely saw a woman, it has to be that Maria woman of his; maybe he was in front and I couldn't see him."

"How many?"

"Three or four, I think. That means they've left some men between the mission and us. If we go back, we'll have to fight our way though. Christus, what a cock up!" Louis groaned.

"We've got to go after him."

Werner spun to face Jurgen, his voice rising.

"And how do you propose we deal with this rear guard unit he's left?" Jurgen asked sarcastically.

"Without dos Santos to lead them and us back in German uniform on German territory – what would you do if you were them?"

"Run and avoid a fight."

"Exactly, they know we don't give a rat's ass about them and that we're after their boss. They're no longer interested in his fight: especially if think they're not going to see him again."

Jurgen remained silent, contemplating their predicament.

"Well, Jurgen, what are we going to do?" Werner asked impatiently.

"We are going to give them the opportunity to leave peacefully."

"You're crazy!" Werner retorted.

Jurgen ignored him. He took a white shirt from Philippe and ordered an Askari who was conversant in Herero to accompany him. They rode forward about a hundred yards, Jurgen waving the shirt. He then stopped and waited. About a minute later, a rider emerged from the bush also waving a white clothing item in his hand. The two riders slowly advanced on one another until ten metres apart. They spoke for a few minutes, then both Jurgen and the guerilla wheeled their horses round and returned to their groups.

"Well?" Werner demanded.

"We gave them free passage, provided they left immediately for Angola and never returned. They accepted."

"And dos Santos?"

"They refused to answer any questions."

Werner had no idea what dos Santos would do once he got back to the mission. He knew there would be no negotiating with the man. He was deeply concerned about Dorothea; he knew the gunrunner was ruthless.

Jurgen turned to Philippe again.

"You're going to have to pretend to be an Ovambo again. Go and find out what's going on at the mission. Just be careful, don't get too near."

Philippe returned in the early evening, by which time, the three white men were sure something dire had befallen their friend.

"Where the hell were you all this time?" Werner berated him.

Philippe looked at his master somewhat disdainfully. There was no need to use crude language.

"Being very careful, I don't want to die. That man, dos Santos, is there. He has a few of the nurses and the white doctor on the veranda. He has guns pointed at the women. The rest of his men, I saw three in total, are guarding the mission perimeter. I'm sure that if we try anything, he'll kill the women. He thinks you'll never let anything happen to the women."

All were silent while they contemplated their next course of action.

"Philippe, make sure the rest of the men have their uniforms on again. We're going back to the mission," Jurgen finally said. He then addressed his companions, "We're going back, and we'll decide what to do when we get there. And Werner, just please don't try any heroics. Okay?"

Werner nodded. He remained silent. The gunrunner had to be outsmarted, but now he was holding Dorothea hostage. He could hardly contain his rage. The man knew that by holding the women hostage they would not dare mount an attack. Werner knew that dos Santos would not leave the guarding of the women to his men: the hostages represented his ace card—his ticket to Angola.

"Werner, you know we're going to have to let him go; we don't have a choice. He's got us by the *bolas*," Louis said quietly, aware of what thoughts raced through his friend's mind. "Let him go to Angola . . . once there, he'll let the women go. Why should he hold them? He does not believe the German army will follow. He thinks we are the German army."

"For God's sake Louis! I've got to free her!" Werner retorted, his voice full of anguish.

"I know and I understand your feelings, *compadre*, but let's do this intelligently. Let's talk about it. I hate the bastard as much as you, and you know I would never allow him to harm those women. But we need to be realistic."

CHAPTER SIX

Werner lay prone in the dust, resting on his elbows behind a large fallen tree trunk. With his binoculars glued to his eyes, he slowly swept the mission from left to right, placing dos Santos' perimeter guards. Through a gap in the buildings he could see into the forecourt. There was no mistaking dos Santos. He was seated with another of his men on the veranda, their guns trained on the missionaries lined up on benches opposite them. Dorothea sat next to the Pastor.

Jurgen's group had arrived at the mission some time ago; it was the crawl to get nearer without detection which had taken so long. This was a stalemate situation—they dare not open fire, and the enemy knew it.

Suddenly dos Santos stepped down from the porch, pushing Dorothea and the Pastor in front of him, a pistol at their backs.

"Ahhoooooy! Can you hear me?" he shouted in Portuguese while he walked towards the gap in the buildings. He stopped in the open ground just outside the small complex, making sure his two hostages stood in front of him, shielding him from an overzealous soldier.

Jurgen lifted a hand.

"For God's sake, don't shoot."

The gunrunner shouted again.

"He wants to talk," Werner spat

"One of us should go forward. I doubt whether he knows you are in the group. He probably believes he was intercepted by a normal German patrol at Sandwich Bay, which then called for reinforcements. It hasn't even crossed his mind that you and Louis are involved here. Rather let me go forward and speak to him," Jurgen said.

You don't understand Portuguese," Werner replied.

"One of my men knows the language, enough to make himself understood; I'll take him."

Unarmed, Jurgen slowly approached the man standing in the dust, the woman in front of him. He noticed that dos Santos' arm was still heavily bandaged. At least the bastard hasn't got away unscathed, he thought. The huge man looked haggard: the long journey through the desert on horseback had taken its toll.

Dorothea looked at Jurgen, obviously terrified, but showing a brave face.

"Are you all right?" he asked her in German.

Dos Santos shouted something in Portuguese.

Jurgen raised his hands palms out indicating that he understood, the gunrunner did not want him to speak to her.

Jurgen's eyes never left dos Santos. He watched intently as he spoke to the Askari who then translated.

"He says that if you let him ride on he will take only the women with him who he will release once inside Angola. He will allow one of your Askaris to ride with him, the man must be unarmed, and he will leave the women in his care to lead them back to the border."

Jurgen realized that he had no option but to agree. If he did not, it could lead to a gunfight with the women caught in the middle and he was terrified that dos Santos would shoot them as he had threatened to do. He had no alternative – dos Santos controlled all the options. He nodded; the gunrunner would be allowed to leave just before daybreak. The troops would keep their distance.

Throughout the night the truce was maintained. As the first sign of dawn appeared on the horizon, dos Santos and his men rode out as Werner and the others watched from a distance, powerless. During the night, Werner had convinced Jurgen to let the troops cross the unmarked border into Angola, if only for a few miles. Once dos Santos was a few miles ahead, they mounted up and followed. It was only late the next day that the gunrunner crossed into Angola.

Surprisingly, dos Santos had kept his word and left the women encamped under huge baobab tree, a few miles within Angolan territory. He had added a surprise – he had abandoned Maria and left her along with the Finnish nurses and Dorothea. The men rode into the camp and found the four women seated around a campfire, with the Askari who had accompanied dos Santos seated on the ground nearby.

Dorothea could not believe her eyes. She had not expected to see him here. She stood shakily as he dismounted and approached her.

"Are you all right?" he asked, taking her hand, not able to resist having some physical contact with her. He ached to take her in his arms.

"I'm OK," she replied, hanging onto his hand, desperately wanting to collapse in his arms.

Relief slowly replaced Maria's initial shock. She had not fared well. It was obvious that she had been beaten: her face was swollen, her lower lip cut, her clothes were torn and dirty, and her hair stiff and thick with dirt. Louis was speaking to her in Portuguese, trying to comfort her, and tears of relief were streaming down her cheeks. Werner watched, and vowed that he would deal with the gunrunner, no matter what it took.

They decided to stay the night at the camp, giving the women a chance to rest before returning to the mission. To pursue dos Santos was out of the question; this was Kunehama territory, the country was embroiled in civil war, their force was too small to deal with any attack. Fortunately, the Kunehamas seldom ventured so far south.

At first light, they returned to the border, riding slowly, resting frequently, as Maria was in pain from the beatings she had taken and the other women saddle-sore, unaccustomed to riding long distances on horseback.

The three officers discussed their next moves. Jurgen was adamant that once they got to the mission and the women were in safe hands again, the trio should head back to Windhuk. Any incursion into Angola was out of the question. This was Portuguese sovereign territory, which had to be respected. A German military incursion in force was not possible.

"What I don't understand," said Werner, "is your attitude, Louis, or rather your government's attitude towards dos Santos. I've known you for a while now and I've realized that you have long harboured suspicions, serious suspicions I gather, that dos Santos is master-minding a gun-running operation. You already believed so before we met. Why the hell didn't you people do something about it?"

Louis did not reply, but merely stared straight ahead.

"What's going on?" Jurgen asked, curious about the terse interchange. Werner translated.

"I agree. Come on, Louis, tell us what's going on. Christ man! We've been through a lot together. At least tell us. Your government should have nabbed him long ago," Jurgen demanded.

"Okay."

The Portuguese captain sighed. "Yes, I and a few others have known for some time. Unfortunately, my government is corrupt. Or rather, the local provincial government is. And dos Santos enjoys protection from people high up, powerful people. Do you recall meeting Senhor de Mello?" he asked Werner.

"Yes, wasn't he the local judge president for the Benguela province, the *jurisdicao?* I met him at that dinner we had the first day I arrived in Benguela."

"That's right. Well, unfortunately he'll ensure that no action is taken against dos Santos. The judge is politically powerful—he's related to the country's Governor-General in Luanda – for Chrissake, he's the governor's brother-in-law!"

"Now isn't that fuckin' convenient."

"Every time we've brought some evidence before him and have wanted to arrest the man, our efforts have been brushed aside with the comment we have no proof and that we are responding to unfound rumours."

"What's he saying?" Jurgen queried urgently.

"He's saying some political bastard is protecting dos Santos."

"Christ! These dagos are all corrupt."

"Shhhh! Christ! Don't let him hear that," Werner retorted, not wanting to offend Louis.

"Hell, he can't understand me. Anyway, he's different. He's a damn good soldier. I would trust him with my life."

"I'm sure he would be glad to hear you say that," Werner replied, unable to disguise his sarcasm.

"Well, you don't have to tell him," Jurgen said, swinging his horse around and riding back to the women a short distance behind them.

"I'm pretty sure dos Santos doesn't know that we, that's you and I, were involved in the attack on his boat and the pursuit through your country. You've been in uniform most of the time and really not distinguishable from the rest of the German military. I believe you could return to Benguela in your original role, the manufacturing representative."

Louis knew that if he was to destroy dos Santos' operation, he would need the help of his German friend.

"I couldn't get away with that. Anyway, what happened to me when we were attacked? How did I get out of there alive? Weren't we all supposed to have been killed by the Kunehamas? He'll wonder how we managed to survive."

"Easy, you and I escaped with our servants. We returned to Angola together. The more I think about it, the better it sounds. Yes! That's what we should do – return together to Benguela saying we survived the Kunehama attack on the Kunene and fled to SudwestAfrika, returning to Angola by sea. It may be our only chance to get at dos Santos. As far as I'm concerned, he doesn't really give a damn. I believe he knows I suspect him, but realizes I can do little without the authority and backing of de Mello."

Werner remained silent, chewing over Louis' proposal. It just might work, he thought.

"It sounds fair to me. If we are wrong, we'll soon find out. Only he will be a lot more wary of you. He may have recognized you, although, as you say, we have always been at a fair distance from him and then, when near, you were such a mess, your mother wouldn't have recognized you!" Werner laughed.

Louis chuckled: "You could be right. Then it's back to Angola by sea as soon as possible after we've deposited the ladies. Am I right?"

Werner nodded.

Werner stayed close to Dorothea on the ride back, ready to console her after her harrowing experience at the hands of dos Santos. She had withstood the ordeal rather well, certainly a woman of inner strength and resolve. They avoided any serious discussion on dos Santos or Werner's future movements or plans, but spent many hours discussing her life in Germany and the path to SudWestAfrika. He realized where she had found the courage to study medicine, a profession that was still male dominated, which was still unkind to women attempting to enter its specialty. He gathered that her father had supported her choice of profession and, in fact, had encouraged it.

It was evident to them both that this was no longer a casual acquaintance, but in the brief period they were together, the opportunity never arose to take it any further. He desperately wanted to be alone with her – to hold her in his arms and tell her of his feelings towards her. The mission never allowed this to happen: they were never really alone, others were always circumspectly in close proximity.

The next available ship which would dock at Lobito and Luanda would only arrive in Swakopmund in four days time. Major Zietzmann arranged for Werner and Louis to leave by train for the coast a day before.

The authorities had no use for Maria. However, at this stage, they considered it too dangerous to return her to Benguella. At Louis's request, they decided that she should continue by ship with them onto Luanda, the capital of the Portuguese colony, where there was little likelihood of her encountering any of dos Santos' acquaintances. Initially, she would spend a few weeks with a close aunt who, she said, would be only too pleased to have her visit for a while. Hopefully by then dos Santos would be dead or behind bars: retribution was swift for those involved in gun-trafficking. The Portuguese dealt as ruthlessly with gunrunners – it was either a firing squad or the gallows.

The general idea was to keep their return to Angola low-key. Louis believed that Maria should keep out of the limelight for a while to ensure that dos Santos never got to hear that she had returned. He was bound to have contacts in Luanda. At first, Maria flatly refused any offer of financial assistance, saying indignantly that she was quite capable of looking after herself, but then realized that she would need clothing and other essentials.

Maria's spirits were high, a caged bird suddenly freed. Unable to speak any language other than Portuguese and some local black dialect, she remained close to Werner and Louis. Although still bearing a few faint bruises from the beatings dos Santos had inflicted, the fear that previously haunted her eyes was gone, and her face split into a smile at the slightest provocation. From the ample funds Werner had at his disposal and at Major Zietzmann's insistence, Maria bought a wardrobe of clothes sufficient for her trip to Luanda. Major Zietzmann could not disguise his initial dismay when she glided into his office dressed in the latest fashion from Europe. She was transformed, a smouldering beauty not to be ignored.

"My God, captain, she is magnificent," the major said, raising his eyebrows, knowing she could not understand German. "Tell her I would be honoured if the three of you would join me for dinner at the Kaiserkrone Hotel this evening. It's Friday, they serve a fantastic meal with lots of beer and wine. There's even dancing."

For a fleeting moment Werner wondered what Frau Zietzmann would say, should she ever get to hear of this. The major, in the company of a woman as beautiful as Maria, would not go unnoticed.

"Fear not, captain. I'm not married," Zietzmann said, reading Werner's mind.

Caught off-guard, Werner merely smiled. He then translated, omitting the bit regarding the Major's social status. Maria graciously accepted, obviously excited at the prospect of being entertained by these three personable men.

Punctually at eight, they arrived in the foyer of the hotel. The furnishings were over the top, as was the choice of colours – an abundance of red drapes and silken walls into which were woven elaborate designs. The sofas and lounge chairs were upholstered in buttoned red leather, enhancing the atmosphere of opulence. Numerous large chandeliers lit the foyer, and through the large double doors, now folded and retracted into the wall, they could see the guests seated at the tables that surrounded the dance-floor. A string quartet on a raised dais played soft music. Nobody danced, it still considered too early. Werner looked around. The elite of the colony was gathered here.

Major Zietzmann, resplendent in full dress officer's uniform, had unobtrusively assumed the role of escort to Maria. He presented his arm to her, and they entered the dining room, the two junior officers following. Recognizing the Major, the maitre d' rushed from behind his desk to meet them, his hands submissively clasped in front of him. A hush descended on the diners as he led them to their table. Werner wasn't quite sure whether it was because she was an astounding beauty or the fact that she was coloured or a combination of both. Her light brown skin was in definite contrast to that of the rest of the ladies present.

As they threaded their way through the tables, the Major nodding his head to a few other diners in greeting, Maria received many an appraising, and appreciative, glance. She glowed, and the top of her breasts, revealed by the low and wide neckline of her deep-red evening gown, jiggled provocatively with each step. There was no mistaking the mischievous spark in the Major's eyes; if it had been his intention to draw attention to himself, he had certainly achieved that. The men could not ignore Maria, and their own escorts were clearly disconcerted with the attention this strange woman was receiving.

"Major, if I may say, you've created quite a stir here. We are receiving more than the usual furtive glances. Would you ascribe this to Maria?" Werner ventured.

"Most certainly, this bunch of stuffed shirts occasionally need to be reminded that there is more to life than the aristocracy, money and overplaying the role of gentlemen. They carry this charade to the extreme – what they need is a wilder and more wanton approach that jerks them back to reality – something that awakens that primordial spirit that lurks in all of us. Just look at them, this good lady certainly has a number of them thinking with their peckers. Good female company is not easy to come by in the colonies. Let the bastards eat their hearts out."

Werner laughed, enjoying the Major's unexpected candour.

"What did he say?" Maria asked.

"Well, he said you are absolutely beautiful and that the rest of the men seem to think so as well. Wait until they start dancing, you won't be short of partners."

She giggled, thoroughly enjoying the attention.

The cuisine was typically German, the choices restricted to pork and beef – eisbein, gammon steaks, sauerbraten and schnitzels, all served with potatoes or spätzle, sauerkraut and an assortment of vegetables. The major took his time carefully studying the wine list, finally choosing an imported Beaujolais from France, no doubt for the sake of appearances. Christ, Werner thought, most of the colonists would not know a Beaujolais from a Burgundy! The heavy German food was not quite Louis and Maria's fare, nevertheless they seemed to enjoy the meal.

During dinner, the Major purposely ignored the war, steering the conversation to Germany and in particular, Berlin, the city that was his home. He talked about what a beautiful and joyous place it was, the heart of Europe, waxing lyrical about the hustle and bustle, the sidewalk cafés and coffee shops, the incredible industrial transformation the country was experiencing and the euphoria that accompanied this economic metamorphosis, pausing after every few sentences to allow Werner to translate. Maria appeared captivated. Werner was not quite sure whether this was merely put on for the Major's benefit or whether she truly was enthralled. Nonetheless, the magic worked and the Major was clearly smitten with this beautiful mulatto woman. The numerous furtive glances she received from other male diners verified that he was not alone.

The first couples took to the floor. The major did not hesitate, springing up to face Maria and bowing from the hip, his intentions obvious. She rose, presenting her hand to him, and he led her onto the floor. She stepped into his arms, her left hand resting lightly on his shoulder, her face tucked in between his chin and shoulder, not quite touching. The Major was an adept dancer: as a cadet officer he had seriously dedicated himself to the compulsory dancing lessons which were part of the *Offiziersschule* curriculum. This now paid dividends. To the tune of a popular Viennese waltz, they glided across the floor. The Major was acutely aware of the nearness and scent of the beautiful woman he held in his arms.

Louis said little. He did not have to understand German to know what was going on.

"God, I hope he doesn't try and ravish her on the dance floor. Does he have to stare at those bobbing tits all the time!" Louis whispered to Werner, afraid that others would overhear him.

"Don't be stupid – the Major's a gentleman, and don't worry – nobody here speaks Portuguese," Werner hissed.

"Don't bullshit me! Major or no major, this guy's got the serious hots for the woman and, boy, is she playing him."

"That's what's wrong with you Mediterranean types, you're always thinking with your dicks!"

"You ramrod German types, what do you know about women and love? From what I've seen, you probably would do yourself a favour if you did the same; the German Fraulein Dokter will not wait forever for you. Of course, you do realize that this woman here has eyes only for you, yet you don't respond. My friend, the doctor is far away, opportunity beckons right here."

"Don't start with me!"

Werner scowled, looking away, clearly exacerbated.

"Really, I have to say this – you're such an idiot. Maria only sees you – she's really not interested in the Major. But you're too late my friend, if you make a move now the Major will strip you of all rank!" Louis laughed, a smug expression on his face.

Well, let the Major have his fun, Werner reflected. Why should he try and intercede? He had Dorothea—or rather he wished he had. Hell, he had nothing!

The Major and Maria returned to the table. She was clearly enjoying herself, flushed with excitement, a dazzling smile on her face. Already a junior officer was approaching their table, no doubt intending to ask her for the next dance.

She did not hesitate and addressed Werner in Portuguese.

"Joachim, please dance with me."

The Major realized what she had said and added his support.

"Yes, Captain, dance with the lady before she is overwhelmed by the rest of the officers here," he insisted.

He had no choice, lest he look like a complete idiot. He rose, bowing to her, and she took his proffered hand. As the music commenced, a popular tango now doing the circuit in Europe, Maria beamed. She obviously loved the tango, Werner thought.

She danced superbly, and he was conscious of his thigh brushing hers as they emulated the exaggerated long steps required.

"Are you sad you don't have the lady doctor with you tonight?" she teased.

"No, she is nothing to me," he lied.

"I don't believe you – something is happening between you two."

"Unfortunately there is a war on. Some things are best left forgotten."

"Well, I'd like to help you forget. I owe you so much. If you had not come along, I would still be with that brute. You saved me."

"I never saved you."

"Of course you did, you forced him to abandon me. If you had not pursued him that would not have happened. Let's not argue," she pleaded.

For a while they were silent, gliding in circles around the floor.

"Will you escort me back to our lodgings tonight?"

Werner hesitated.

"I think the good Major already has those intentions."

"I know, but he is not my type. I think I'll develop this terrible headache and insist that you take me home."

This damn woman was creating a predicament. He dare not cause affront to the Major. Go with the flow, he thought, don't be confrontational.

She had no lack of admirers, and danced with several officers bold enough to approach the Major's table. Louis also danced with her, the couple never silent – prattling in Portuguese, giggling and laughing. Werner was uneasy – he hoped he was not the subject of discussion. Recalling Louis' preoccupation with his love life or lack thereof, he was unable to reject the notion out of hand.

Her performance was superb. They had returned to the table. Within the space of a few minutes, her demeanour changed. As another officer approached the table, she let the man understand that she was not well and was about to leave. The Major was unable to disguise his disappointment but insisted that he personally escort her home.

"Tell the Major that I'm not well at all," she instructed Werner. "He does not speak Portuguese – better you escort me back so that if I'm in need of assistance I can at least converse with you. Tell him I thoroughly enjoyed his company and look forward to seeing him again."

Somewhat reluctantly, the Major conceded to her wish, ordering Werner to escort her to her lodgings. "Should her condition worsen, do not hesitate to seek medical attention," he insisted to Werner.

Werner and Maria took their leave and walked out of the hotel. They stepped onto the pavement to be greeted by a cool evening breeze, a relief after the warm dining room. The terminus for the horse-drawn tramway was directly opposite the hotel, the last tram patiently waiting to depart.

"Let's take the tram, it'll be fun. It stops outside our hotel anyway," Maria said, giving his arm a squeeze.

The skirts of her gown rustled loudly in the quiet confines of the carriage. Besides them a few hotel workers returning home after their shift seemed surprised to see this couple in full eveningwear boarding the tram.

As the bells of the Lutheran Church of Christ struck ten, the tram got underway. The carriage was not lit; the only light to be seen was that of the street lamps and a few shop windows that slowly flitted by. Maria sidled closer to him and placed her hand on his lap. He drew back slightly, acutely aware of her touch and fragrance.

"My God, captain, don't be so pompous, you need to relax," she whispered.

"I'm fine."

"You're not! You're like an adolescent on his first date," she said teasingly, her fingers resting warmly on his inner thigh. She removed it when the conductor approached, but promptly replaced it once the man returned to his post on the boarding platform.

He felt a buzz of anticipation, an apprehension of things to come. His senses were heightened – as Zietzmann had said, he was reacting to some primeval instinct hidden deep within the recesses of his mind. Christ, he thought, this woman has no inhibitions. Yes, she clearly was a lady; the product no doubt of a good Catholic upbringing, schooled by nuns, well-mannered and endowed with the airs one expects of an ex-debutante. But it seemed she had discarded all attempts at pretense – she knew she was in charge and subtly manipulated the situation.

They alighted from the tram opposite the Thuringer Hof Hotel where Major Zietzmann had billeted them. The hotel was one of the watering holes of the town and although it was now late, quite a number of patrons, primarily Marine officers and their women, were still in the lounges. The doors were wide open to allow the small orchestra to be heard. To cater for the conscripts and subalterns, a separate large bar had its entrance directly out onto the pavement. Here the atmosphere was less refined and the atmosphere more raucous: the floor strewn with sawdust, the men lined up along a huge bar with a wide counter, most now well inebriated. No self-respecting officer ventured into such a bar.

Werner and Maria walked through the foyer to reception, her arm entwined in his. Even when approaching the concierge, she did not remove her arm. If he read anything into their intimacy, he was too circumspect to reveal anything.

"A drink?" she asked.

"In view of your feigned illness, better not go into in the lounge," he replied.

"In my room then," she said firmly, ordering from a passing waiter.

Her room had a small entrance foyer that led into a larger lounge come bedroom furnished with a couch, two armchairs and a small coffee table. The sleeping area consisted of a large carved wardrobe with mirrored doors and two large beds with ornate wooden headboards tucked up against the opposite wall. The thick red velvet curtains were drawn across the open windows, and the noises from the street below were just audible through the drapes.

A discreet knock on the door heralded the waiter. He placed a bottle of wine and two glasses on the table and surreptitiously pocketed the tip Werner held out for him.

Werner raised his glass to her.

"Prosit," he said.

She whispered in response and took a sip of her wine, her large blue eyes studying him over the rim of her glass. Faintly, he could hear the music below. It was a popular Viennese waltz. She placed her glass on the coffee table and stepped closer to him.

"Why is it that you reject me always, when you know how I feel about you?"

"I'm not rejecting you. It's only that I'm not ready for any relationship at the moment."

"I never intended that we have a relationship, as you put it, but only a . . . dalliance, if you like. I know I excite you. Is it the doctor that you want?"

"I really don't want anybody at the moment."

"But surely you must have needs?"

He laughed. This woman was direct.

"Yes. I do have needs."

"Well, kiss me then," she smiled, moulding her body to his.

He could feel her breasts pressed against his chest. A quiver of excitement coursed through him. He was unable to deny the physical attraction she had awakened. He pulled her close, his hands sliding down her body, cupping her buttocks, drawing her up against him so that his hardness pressed against her.

"Oh yes," she whispered.

He nuzzled her neck and then slid his lips down, his tongue probing her cleavage, his chin pressing aside the neckline of her dress to reveal her white breast and erect nipple. He took the nipple into his mouth and rolled it with his tongue. She moaned softly.

She turned in his arms, her back facing him.

"Undo me."

He slipped the buttons at the back of her evening gown, then slid it off her shoulders. She turned to face him again, revealing magnificent breasts buoyed only by her corset. She unbuttoned his tunic, tugging it off his shoulders. His collarless linen shirt followed. She stepped out of her gown as he pulled the last stays out of her corset.

Naked, they collapsed on the bed, their bodies entwined. Slowly his face lips over her, repeatedly tasting her skin, licking her body.

"Please, please – now!" she pleaded.

He thrust into her.

CHAPTER SEVEN

When the ss Usambara, still shrouded in mist, dropped anchor in Lobito Bay during the early hours of the morning, most of the passengers were still asleep. Werner and Louis, Philippe and Paulo were the only people who disembarked. Maria had confined herself to her cabin lest she be recognized.

At first glance, the town did not seem to have changed. However, they soon realized that it now contained a significant military presence, and the atmosphere amongst the inhabitants was no longer laid back. The men sensed a new underlying tension. The death of so many at the hands of the Kunehamas had shrouded the town in a pall of mourning and sorrow. Bands of bandits still roamed the banks of the Kunene River and many had fled the countryside for the safety of those towns with garrisons stationed, as these guaranteed a degree of safety. It was clear that the new military command, swelled with new troops from Luanda, was preparing to wreak vengeance on the Kunehamas.

Louis immediately took carriage for home. The officers had agreed to meet as soon as possible once Louis had reported to whoever was in command. Both men and their servants would resolutely stick to their story that they had fled the battle on the Kunene River and crossed into SudwestAfrika, with Werner desperately requiring medical attention. Louis would make no mention of any involvement with the gunrunners or voice any suspicions regarding dos Santos.

Louis' arrival stunned his family. His wife had adamantly believed that he had survived the battle despite no confirmation, but the survivors who had escaped the carnage had already made their way back to safety, without him. She rushed into his arms, tears of joy streaming down her face. His six-year-old daughter could only hug his leg, shouting: "*Padre! Padre!*"

The hotel owner was overjoyed to see Werner and Philippe again.

"Madre Dias!" she exclaimed. "You're back – you survived! Thank God."

She beamed from ear to ear. "I kept your room and your things. Somehow I knew you would be back. How is Captain de Sousa?"

"He's fine. We both got off the ship this morning. He immediately went home to his wife. He was worried that she thought him dead," Werner replied.

"Senhor de Almeida, we were so worried for both you and the Captain and, of course, for everybody else. It has been terrible. So many died, so many husbands and sons lost." She covered her mouth with her hand, close to tears. "Oh, before I forget, a cable arrived for you a few days ago."

She rummaged in the desk, and handed it to him.

He stepped back from the reception desk and ripped open the sealed envelope. He extracted a yellow sheet of paper:

ORDER FOR 270 RIFLES COMBINED WITH SHIPMENT FROM STEYR WAFFENFABRIK STOP CONSIGNMENT LOADED SS TANGANYIKA ESTIMATED TO DOCK LOBITO 5 APRIL STOP DOCUMENTS ACCOMPANY SHIPMENT
KRAUSE
MAUSER WAFFENFABRIK
OBENDORF AN NECKAR

So, the next shipment was on its way. All that was needed now was a plan to rope in de Mello, dos Santos and their merry men. Dos Santos must have paid handsomely for the shipment lying at the bottom of the lagoon at Sandwich Bay. Hopefully, an irrecoverable loss – anything to hurt the man's pocket. Werner assumed that dos Santos must already be back in Huambo. He must have realized that the German military had executed the prisoners taken when they overran his wagons. They were hanged at Tsumeb after a short trial that was no more than a sham. The Germans did not even wait for the wounded to recover. What would his next move be?

As the sun sank below the horizon, Werner strolled into the lounge for the usual *aperitivo* that accompanied every sunset. Louis, his young wife on his arm, gave him a warm smile. Bowing from the waist, Werner took her hand in his and kissed it. Louis was dressed in a brand-new uniform, certainly more impressive that its predecessor, his rank of major now prominently displayed. At least, Major Zietzmann had been true to his word.

"Senhor de Almeida, I hope you don't mind if I address you as Joachim?" Louis said for the benefit of those within earshot who had heard the rumours that the two men had escaped with their lives.

"Of course not and I shall call you Louis. After all, we owe each other our lives," Werner replied, both men laughing.

Louis' wife interceded. "You may call me Rosetta," she said, stepping forward and kissing him on the cheek. "Joachim, I personally thank you for saving my husband. His coming back was like a miracle from God. Thank you."

A bare-foot African in a white smock and knee-length black pants with a red sash across his chest from shoulder to waist served their drinks.

"I see you're a major now."

"Oh yes. What a surprise! This morning I reported to the local commanding officer, Colonel de Oliviera. He gave me the good news about my new rank. I even received a letter of commendation from General Cadiz in Luanda. All I now need is a medal," Louis said good-humouredly

"Damn right, you should get one, you saved my life! What about this man?"

"I know him well. He is from Luanda and has had a lot of experience dealing with the blacks. He arrived here a week ago with five hundred troops. Apparently, or so he tells me, the revolt is a direct result of the dissatisfaction amongst the blacks with the conscripted forced labour system that the government introduced a few years ago. Confidentially, if I were black, I would do the same; it's an inhumane system – nothing short of damn slavery. De Oliviera is a good fellow, certainly no friend of you-know-who."

Rosetta interceded.

"A successful man like you, yet Louis tells me you're not married? That's a surprise," she chuckled. Then added, "Please, I don't mean to be rude, just curious."

"Well, I've never really met the right woman," Werner replied, improvising a smile to indicate that he did not mind the question at all.

He realized that Louis had not told his wife who he really was or what the two of them eventually hoped to accomplish.

"He says you are a good businessman and have already obtained an enormous order from dos Santos in Huambo. I know a few women who would like to meet you. I could arrange some introductions – Benguela is a lonely place."

Louis had stepped back from his wife. Now looking intently at Werner, he shook his head, mouthing a distinct "No!"

"It wouldn't be fair; I'm only staying a few weeks and will be away for most of the time. But thank you anyway," Werner apologised. Louis nodded his head in approval.

"Well, if you ever feel lonely, let me or Louis know."

The two officers met for lunch the next day at a popular restaurant. The sat on the bougainvillea enclosed porch, hidden from prying eyes. Once their meal was finished, they ordered coffee while Louis lit up a cigar. He threw the spent match into the ashtray, drew hard on the cigar then blew a thick cloud of fragrant smoke towards the beams of the ceiling.

"Well, my friend, what now?" he asked, contemplating the smoke that wafted beneath the ceiling.

Werner told him about the cable he received.

"Watch – dos Santos will clear the consignment here in Lobito and ensure that you get paid before he even attempts to move it. He'll want no questions asked – the goods must belong to him. Then he'll send everything to Huambo except the rifles – these he'll leave here."

"Why leave the guns here?" Werner asked.

"Because he will consign these by sea to Namibe or take them there himself. And once there, the rifles will disappear."

"So you're saying we are going to have to deal with him in Namibe?"

"Yes. Only this time we'll have the whole Portuguese government behind us. De Mello must realize he's playing with fire if he tries to protect him. Anyway, that's my theory."

"Christus! Why can't your people just arrest him? You have sufficient proof. I would even be prepared to be a witness. Indirectly, he and de Mello and whoever else is involved are responsible for the deaths of hundreds of others."

"There's actually more to it than you know. I wasn't permitted to tell you anything else until now. But now that your country and ours are talking to one another, albeit very confidentially, General Cadiz has permitted that I bring you into the picture. It's not only the gun-running – it's diamonds. This is what de Mello and dos Santos are really after. And they are backed by a couple of other high-ups in this corrupt colonial government we've got here. Never forget, blood's thicker than water and this certainly applies here. We believe that de Mello and possibly the Governor-General are caught up in this. But we have a problem – de Mello has somehow managed to get Colonel de Oliviera replaced by one of his cronies, a Colonel Batista. Believe me, a real arsehole and as crooked as they come. He'll arrive in the next day or two. De Oliviera has been ordered back to Luanda under some stupid pretext, all the Governor-General's doing."

"That's not good. But what's this about diamonds? This is the first I've heard of this."

"Government geologists made this discovery near Caconda in the Huambo region, not far from the Kunene River – slap-bang in Kunehama territory. Some of the local indigenous crowd just wanted to barter some stones for goods and these were traced back to the Caconda region. Well, you can imagine the reaction. Intelligence is that it is unique, a narrow kimberlite pipe, near vertical which breaks the surface. The pipe contains diamonds in profusion. Quite easy to mine as well. One of the old aristocrat families has an enormous ranch in the area, I don't think anybody really knows how large this is, the area has not even been properly surveyed yet. That's not unusual, most of Angola has yet to be surveyed. The area is unclaimed territory, and guess what; de Mello wants it and so does his brother-in-law, the governor. I'm sure that a claim has been or is in the process of being registered. However, the governor and de Mello would have to proceed with caution – you know, abuse of position and all that. If either of them step in, well, even the aristocrats are going to jump around. Everybody will want a slice of the action. By keeping the area inaccessible by using the Kunehamas, they believe they can have the lot, with the Kunehamas doing the spadework. But of course, they'll want some sort of compensation : that's where the rifles come in. They have to put up a front – dos Santos is the frontman together with some Kunehama sub-chief. This is why it's being kept quiet."

"How do you know all this?"

"We have somebody on the inside. I can't tell you more."

Werner shook his head and then ran his fingers through his hair, clearly frustrated. This was getting a lot more complicated. He beckoned the waiter for a fresh coffee.

"So now what? My only concern is the guns. I've got to stop that."

"This all goes hand in hand."

Louis lent forward in his chair, anxious to emphasise the salient point.

"We're going to finish this off in one go – first dos Santos and his guns and then de Mello. Many of those loyal to de Mello were killed in the massacre. This has been a serious blow to his organization. To exploit the diamonds, they have to keep the Kunehamas happy. That's why your consignment is crucial – they have to keep supplying weapons to the Kunehamas and Hereros. In reality both tribes are one, merely divided by a white's man border. If we catch them red-handed passing these weapons over and we get somebody to talk or come up with some other proof of de Mello's involvement, then we've got this beaten. Just remember, he needs the Kunehamas to get the rifles to your country. There's no love lost between de Mello and the blacks; this is pure business. If this goes wrong, then de Mello and his merry-men will revert to being the enemy again – no access to the mine."

"Trust the Portuguese to complicate things," Werner sighed resignedly, unable to hide his frustrations.

"Hey, hey, don't worry, this will work out. Just go about being the businessman you're supposed to be. Go out there and sell. I'll tell you what I next propose soon enough. Pity Maria isn't here; at least meanwhile you could have some fun," Louis said mischievously, his mouth drawn in a smirk.

"Fuck off!"

For two weeks, Werner went about his business, pretending to be a successful agent for various manufacturers, calling on shops and trading stores in the town and immediate surrounding area. Surprisingly, his goods found great appeal: his prices were fair and the sales he garnered lucrative, and he placed numerous orders with his principals in Europe. Rifles were purchased, but it was obvious that these were intended for over-the-counter sales and the quantities ordered were small. The only large order was from the Boer Protection Society and this group was nothing more than the local militia. They ordered thirty Mauser K88's.

Werner and Louis had considered it prudent not to see each other too often. Colonel Batista, the new commanding officer had arrived by ship a few days after they met for lunch, accompanied by his own staff officers. Colonel Oliviera departed for Luanda on the same ship with his own staff officers in tow.

One evening as Werner descended the stairs, the hotelkeeper, as ever in a low-cut blouse which exposed her voluptuous bosom, came round from behind the reception desk and caught his arm, steering him towards the lounge.

"Senhor, I must introduce you to one of the most important new arrivals in the district," she excitedly exclaimed.

Werner immediately recognized dos Santos. The huge man, dressed in a black suit, his shoes highly polished, stood with his back to him speaking to de Mello and a colonel of the Portuguese colonial forces dressed in full uniform. Louis, also in uniform, was amongst them. Drinks in their hands, the four men were conversing. Demurely, the hotelkeeper waited next to the colonel for him to acknowledge her presence.

"Colonel, I would like to introduce you to Senhor de Almeida."

As the men shook hands, de Mello recognized Werner. "We have met before," he said.

"And we too have previously met. How are you, Senhor de Almeida?" dos Santos stated loudly, taking Werner's hand.

"In fact, very well. It's good to meet my most important client again – truly a pleasant surprise. What brings you to Benguela? And Maria, is she here?"

The colonel said nothing but merely watched the interaction. It appeared that dos Santos was pleased to see Werner. Clearly, he did not associate him with what had transpired during the past few weeks.

Werner was aware of the colonel quietly appraising him. This was not a man to be trifled with – there was nothing soft or compassionate about him. Smart in his blue colonial officer's uniform hung with gold braid, the colonel struck an imposing figure. A tall man with dark hair faintly streaked with grey. His eyes seemed dark and pitiless. His features were hard, accentuated by a thin moustache and black eyebrows. This was a hard man who expected to be obeyed without question. Louis' demeanour spoke for itself: he realized he was subordinate and was not about to forget it.

"Senhor de Almeida, I've already heard about you."

The colonel indicated dos Santos with a wave of his hand. "I hope you are doing fair business in this town."

"Colonel, I cannot complain. However, if I were permitted to venture further into the hinterland, I certainly would be able to do a lot better."

The piercing black eyes scrutinized Werner carefully before the colonel replied.

"Out of the question. It's still far too dangerous. But I'll keep your request in mind."

"You enquired about Maria," dos Santos interrupted. "I had to leave her in Huambo. She's still recovering from a bout of malaria and with the war situation I felt it safer to leave her there, protected by my people and the locals who are well disposed towards us."

De Mello congratulated Werner and Louis on their escape from the battle with the Kunehamas and briefly enquired as to Werner's health after his bout with malaria and his recuperation at the Finnish mission. Clearly, this man is well informed, Werner thought.

Werner turned to dos Santos. "As you hear, I too was ill. Right after fleeing the battle, I came down with malaria. With the passage north cut off by the Kunehamas, Major de Sousa took me south to the Finnish missionaries. Fortunately my cavelherico knows the place. I think if he had not done so, I would not have survived."

"The major is a resourceful man. Well, I need to speak to you, soon. Business. Can we meet tomorrow after breakfast?" dos Santos asked.

"But, of course."

"Until tomorrow then. Please excuse us, we're about to start a business dinner."

Werner rose early and sat down to breakfast as soon as the dining room opened. He was the only diner. He asked that his final cup of coffee be served in the lounge, where he awaited dos Santos' arrival.

He gazed out to sea. A drab grey hung over the sky, as it usually does in the early hours of the morning along the African west coast where the cold Benguela Current still influences the climate. It would only clear around mid morning.

Heavy footsteps announced the approach of another guest. Werner turned and saw dos Santos enter the lounge. He was dressed in beige jodhpurs, his legs encased in highly polished, dark-brown riding boots that reached to his knees. Encased in a white linen shirt, his huge belly hung over a wide brown belt, which at his side at a holster attached, the butt of the firearm visible.

They exchanged morning pleasantries as dos Santos joined him.

"I take it that our business arrangements proceed smoothly?" dos Santos enquired.

"Oh yes, I've received a cable from Germany – the consignment is on the water aboard the ss Tanganyika which is due to dock in Lobito on about the 10th May."

"Good, good. Has our barter arrangement proceeded well?"

"Yes, the bank has finalized everything. When the consignment arrives, it is yours. My principals were extremely happy with deal."

"I should think so, they will profit handsomely on the sale of all those goods in Europe," dos Santos commented.

"There's merely the small formality of signing and handing over a few papers confirming your ownership. As requested, the business of customs clearance is yours to deal with. "

"Wonderful, of course, I've arranged everything," dos Santos smugly replied, clearly pleased that no hitches had been encountered.

I'm damned sure you have, the young officer thought. No doubt with de Mello's intervention and assistance, certain formalities would be overlooked. He was appalled at the thought that if he and Louis did not come up with a plan, they, and he in particular would be instrumental, no – directly responsible – for providing Germany's enemies with five hundred plus brand-new rifles!

"I'm actually looking to buy another consignment of rifles and other items."

Werner unconsciously raised his eyebrows. The gall of this fellow! The man must be insane – a second consignment of that size must surely be suspicious. Somebody was bound to take note.

"Well, I don't know," Werner hesitated. "I wonder whether my principals will entertain another barter deal. It is far too cumbersome, with them being in Germany. It would have to be cash or bank draft, I would think."

"I've not got cash but I have something as near or better if you would care to see. However, I must insist on your confidentiality. Can you do that?"

Now he was intrigued. What the hell was this renegade up to? Werner found it difficult to believe that this commanchero – an appropriate description, he thought – had absolutely no inkling that he was talking to the man who was hell-bent on engineering his demise.

"A business deal is always a deal. If you require my confidence, you can rest assured I'll say nothing. Of course, I would have to involve my principals but . . ."

"Naturally," dos Santos interrupted. He removed a rather small string-tied black leather container from his pocket, resembling an old-fashioned money pouch. He undid the knot and then slowly poured part of the contents into the palm of his other hand. There was no mistaking the flash and faint sparkle of the clean translucent pebbles as they poured from the pouch.

"My God, those are diamonds," Werner gasped.

"Shhhh – quiet! Here, look at them," dos Santos hissed, pouring a few of the stones into Werner's palm.

"Where did you get these?" Werner enquired softly.

"No matter. The question is, would you accept these in payment? You must realize that when your principals dispose of these in Europe they will make huge profits on the sale thereof."

Werner pretended to show the degree of excitement to be expected from somebody suddenly confronted with a bag of diamonds.

"I do. I'm sure we can come to a business arrangement. What exactly are you looking for?"

Dos Santos removed a sheet of folded paper from his shirt pocket and handed it to Werner. He held his hand for the diamonds, then poured them back into the pouch and pocketed it.

"That is my list. Read it some other time. I must be on my way. Remember, not a word."

Dos Santos left the lounge, leaving Werner stunned at this sudden turn of events. The gun-traffickers already had the diamonds – this confirmed that the riches of this mine was no myth and that it was already in production. No wonder de Mello and his associates were prepared to take these risks – it was all for money. The mine could set them up for life. With this type of fortune at stake, the gunrunners would go to extremes to protect their operation. He and Louis would have to proceed with extreme caution; was it possible that they were already being watched?

Werner made his way to the rear of the hotel, walking around the outside of the building and entering the premises through the rear gate. There he sent a worker to find his cavalerico. Soon Philippe approached from the outside rooms, built along the perimeter of the property. For the benefit of any onlookers, Philippe greeted him deferentially.

"Philippe," Werner said, handing the man a folded sheet of paper. "I need you to find Paulo, and get him to deliver this note urgently to his master. Under no circumstances must any other see it. Paulo must wait for a reply, and you must bring this back to me today. Louis will understand the urgency – you must wait!"

"This could be difficult, Paulo is at the garrison and we are not allowed to enter."

"I know, you'll have to change your clothes, something older so that you look like the other locals. Just be careful."

Philippe nodded and trudged back to his quarters.

It was late afternoon before Philippe returned. Werner hardly recognized his cavalerico; barefoot, dressed in ragged trousers and faded shirt, he looked just like any local. He had found an old sweat-stained discarded campaign hat, and he wore this jauntily on his head, the shadow cast by its wide brim hiding his features.

Werner took the note Philippe proffered. "Any problems?" he asked.

"They were inside the fort; I was not allowed to enter. I asked for Paulo saying I was family and that I had important news to give him. One of the black troopers at the gate knew him and fetched him. I gave him the letter, but I had to wait a long time before he came back with your answer. I only got this letter a short while ago."

"Thank you," Werner said.

Werner waited until he was alone before he opened the note.

"TEN THIS EVENING AT MADAME MANCHATAS"

He had never heard of the place. He returned to the hotel and sought out the hotelier.

"This Madame Manchatas, do you know where it is?" he asked.

Her eyes were round as her hand covered her open mouth.

" Really, Senhor de Almeida! This is embarrassing. Men of your standing should not frequent such an establishment. It is best that one ignores its existence. It is a house of ill-repute!"

Bloody idiot, Werner thought, trust Louis to come up with a meeting place like this!

"Quite so, but where is it?" he insisted.

Reluctantly, the hotelier gave him directions. From the tilt of her nose, it was obvious that her esteem of him had diminished.

What on earth was Louis up to? Surely there were better places to meet.

Werner found a carriage and gave the driver the address. The place was on the fringes of the town, an imposing one-storey building with a long first floor porch which stretched the width of the building. A number of carriages stood in the street, the drivers smoking and talking to each other. Light music drifted into the street, interspersed with laughter and other sounds of joviality.

Werner strode up the entrance steps; a door attendant greeted him politely and opened the door for him. He entered a huge foyer stuffed with strategically placed settees and armchairs. It was immediately evident that this was a whorehouse.

"I see you are surprised," he heard behind him. He spun round to find Louis, dressed in civilian clothes, laughing at him.

"You're mad – why meet here? I had to ask for directions. That woman at the hotel reception nearly fainted when I asked where this place was. Christus, she now thinks I'm some sort of sex maniac. To crown it all, I had to be insistent when she did not immediately tell me where."

Louis doubled up with laughter. Werner did not share the joke.

"Please, my friend, this was not intended to embarrass you. This is truly the safest place to meet. Never will you find de Mello and his crowd here. If they needed any of the services this place renders, they would have them delivered. People of their standing are too private. I am sure that our enemies will never know we met here. And anyway, this is the best whorehouse in southern Angola."

"That does not impress me at all."

"Come, let's find ourselves a corner in the lounge," Louis said, moving forward confidently.

"You've been here before?" Werner asked incredulously.

"Yes, actually the grande dame here is a far distant relative of mine – an aunt, I think."

The found themselves a quiet corner and ordered drinks from a roving waitress, whose attire could not have been more revealing. She displayed a good portion of her ample bosom, dressed in some sort of corset with a short skirt revealing net stockings secured by black suspenders and tucked into laced-up ankle high boots. Her face, although pretty, was over painted, the bright red lips a harsh smear on her mouth, the eyes hidden behind black kohl. A small tiara perched atop her upswept black hair winked as she asked whether they required anything else. Werner frowned at the insinuation contained in "the else".

"No," said Louis grinning, "Not at this time."

Once she had brought their drinks, Werner told Louis precisely what had transpired between him and dos Santos that morning.

"God, another five hundred odd rifles. These would only be used against us. We cannot let that happen."

"I know, but we have to play along. We thought they still had to mine the diamonds," Louis replied. "You're telling me they already have access to the diamonds from Caconda. Now they can finance anything they like – buy anybody. But with Colonel Batista in command, things are difficult. I cannot just do whatever I wish. I will have to rely on you."

Louis finished the last of his drink, signalling the waitress for another.

"Listen, assuming I go along with this, I've absolutely no idea of the value of an uncut diamond. I wouldn't know a rough diamond from a piece of glass. I can't shop these around. How do I know that whatever diamonds he gives me will represent fair value for my consignment? Anyway, at it is, this is a no go situation. This will have to have Zietzmann's ok. God, they'll shoot me! I've got . . ."

"Christus, stop worrying, we'll work this out. Perhaps . . . yes, Batista is planning a campaign and he wants me to command it," said Louis thinking furiously.

"How's that going to help me?" Werner demanded.

"This campaign takes the railroad up as far as the British have built it so far; I think that's about forty or fifty miles from here. Then we ride south, actually quite close to Caconda – a small diversion would take us right there. I could see what's going on."

"Is dos Santos going along?"

No, this is a purely a military operation, he's staying, probably waiting for the shipment you have arranged from Germany."

"Well, that doesn't help that much: what the hell are we going to do?" Werner said with barely concealed irritation.

For a while, both remained silent, each deep in his own thoughts.

Louis suddenly clicked his tongue then raised his hand, his index finger pointing upwards, his face lit with inspiration.

"I've got an idea, but I've got to borrow Philippe. We use him and Paulo disguised as locals; they speak the language fluently. They reconnoitre Cacondo for us and find out what's going on. They should be able to do that within two weeks. Meanwhile I'll plan my campaign and you await your shipment. Dos Santos will take the guns to Namibe but won't try the Sandwich Bay stunt again. He'll probably go south and smuggle these across the border. You better think of a way to stop him."

"Me and who else?" Werner asked incredulously.

"I'll speak to a chap I know in the Boer militia. We'll try to get twenty men together. I don't think dos Santos would have more than that in his own group. You can track them south until they cross the border. If dos Santos uses a Kunehama escort, those blacks won't cross into German territory."

He pondered Louis' proposal. It seemed the best plan so far. It was the only plan so far! Probably the best plan under the circumstances, he thought gloomily.

"I'll get a Boer by the name of Van Reynecke to contact you. He'll put the men together –you may have to help with some financing, but you've got money so that shouldn't pose a problem. I should be leaving in about four day's time – we meet here two days from now at the same time."

With no alternative, Werner agreed.

The men finished their drinks; Louis rose from his armchair and turned to Werner.

"I've got to be going; Rosetta's waiting for me at home. But you can stay and have some fun," he said, a lecherous grin on his face.

"Louis, I'm warning you, leave my private life out of this," Werner said with unconcealed contempt, his eyes flashing.

His friend laughed loudly at his own attempt at humour. Werner did not find it amusing at all.

CHAPTER EIGHT

It took Philippe and Louis four days to prepare for their scouting trip to the mine near Caconda. It was not a matter of simply riding out on horseback. Firstly they had to procure the appropriate horses. Kunehama tribesmen did not own steeds that had known the luxury of stables and the care of grooms; their horses, although actually quite sturdy and spirited, still appeared to be ragged hags, their coats dull and patchy. Well-groomed animals would be an immediate giveaway.

There was only one way to acquire these – buy them. Eventually, they found two suitable horses, and purchased these complete with saddles and tack. The tack was old, having been patched and repaired so many times that the leather had long lost its shine. In fact, everything should have been discarded long ago.

Louis had come up with a brilliant idea; the two men would masquerade as close family of a well-known Kunehama called Kavela, a sub-chief who, unknown to his people, was sympathetically disposed towards the Portuguese military. To ensure he remained so, a vital source of intelligence, the military made certain that he was continuously remunerated – not necessarily with money, but rather with concessions and above average prices for the goods and produce he bartered or sold. The two men were not going to meet this man but would merely use his name.

When they left Benguela on horseback, Philippe and Paulo looked the part – young warriors in loincloths, their feet bare, complete with spear and shield and sisal sacks of provisions slung over the backs of their horses. They had no rifles but each man carried a revolver hidden in their sisal sacks.

They rode east, following the railroad the British were constructing, until they reached a siding at the small village of Norton de Mato, where they turned south, now taking a direct line to Caconda. The deeper they penetrated the hinterland, the more dangerous the situation became; Caconda was close to the Kunene River and close to the centre of Kunehama territory. They soon encountered mounted patrols, all armed with Mauser rifles. However, their story that they were on their way home to Kavela at Matala was accepted without incident.

The men rode hard, covering the hundred and forty miles in four days by starting each day before sunrise and only stopping when the last light faded. It was now the rainy season. Every afternoon was greeted by an enormous cumulus cloud buildup followed by the violent thunderstorms heralding torrential rain, a frightening cacophony of thunder, wind, lightning and water.

Still miles from Caconda, they hobbled their horses in a concealed depression in the hills and proceeded on foot. They did not know if the mine was guarded, And if so, whether there were merely a few sentries posted or whether they would encounter roving armed horsemen.

No longer following a trail, they scouted the mine all day, moving from cover to cover with the utmost caution; they encountered nothing except animals. Just before the first signs of sunset, a loud boom was followed by a tremor beneath their bare feet as a shockwave passed beneath them. They looked at each other in fear, not sure what this signified. They had never been near mine workings. However, the incident was not lost on them; they realized they were close, and proceeded with even more caution, melting completely into the dense bush, carefully picking their way forward.

They smelt the first sentry before they saw him. Through heavily intertwined branches, they spotted a black man smoking a pipe, his rifle on the ground next to him. Slowly they backed off until they had put a good hundred yards between themselves and the lookout.

"Should we kill him or just skirt around him?" Paulo asked matter-of-factly. He regarded the taking of a life as nothing unusual.

"Killing him may raise an alarm. We'll go around; the bush is so thick we could pass within spitting distance and he would not know. Anyway, he's bored – he's not even keeping proper watch. Did you see where his rifle was?" Philippe shook his head.

It had started to rain again, the thunder a low rumble in the distance.

The men crept forward and passed within a few yards of the lookout sitting on a rock under a tree, now covered by a slicker which hung over his head like a pyramid with only his face visible.

After another hundred yards, they came to the fringe of a large clearing where all the bushes had been removed and the ground cleared to about halfway up a hillock. In one spot against the hill, the ground had been excavated to a considerable depth, revealing a deep depression. Surrounding this, various pieces of machinery were visible, the purpose of which was lost on the two black men.

It was now raining hard, the torrent sending all the workers scurrying for shelter. A number of hastily erected huts were visible surrounding the cleared area. These were all just thatched roofs of grass and banana leaves supported on long poles, with a large overhang. The two men could clearly see the labourers huddled there for shelter. There was another hut, which stood apart from the others; this was much larger and better constructed. All it seemed to contain was a long flat table. Around the table stood three white men, closely examining whatever was on the table, moving and spreading the contents of the table with their flat hands. Nearby a corral had been erected in which a few horses stood with their backs facing the driving rain.

Water poured down the cleared slopes of the hillock, forming rivulets of dirty brown water which made its way to the valley below.

"If it keeps raining like this we won't be able to cross the rivers," Philippe said to his companion.

"I know."

"What do you think we should do?"

"I think we just stay here for the night and watch again tomorrow when it not raining."

The men retracted their steps until they were well back from the sentry. They erected a makeshift shelter from branches and large leaves and sat under it, eating jerky and rusks. Afterwards they rolled themselves in their blankets and slept heavily.

The next day they again approached the clearing, but ensured they were closer to the hut in which the white men worked. The mine was a hive of activity, large rocks being removed from the depression, clearly the remnants from the dynamite blasting they had heard. These were fed through a steam-driven roller mill from where the crushed stone passed through a series of tubular sieves which rotated, sorting the broken rock into various sizes. Labourers carried buckets of this sorted gravel to the large hut.

"What are they doing with that gravel, look – there come two of them with another bucket?"

Two labourers approached the large hut, stumbling as they struggled to carry the heavy bucket. They entered the hut and poured the wet contents on the end of the table, where the white men then flattened the heap over the table's surface, using pieces of flat wooden board.

It slowly dawned on the hidden men that they were looking for the diamonds in the gravel.

Sometime during the morning, the men in the hut stopped working, all congregating around the only other item in the room, a strongbox that stood on a short sturdy square table. Opening, they extracted a few pouches. These they placed in a saddlebag and handed it to one of the men.

"The man's taking the diamonds. I wonder where he's going?" Philippe's voice was a whisper.

"That well-used trail going towards Huambo—I'm sure that's where he'll be heading, back to dos Santos' place," Paulo replied.

"OK, let's follow."

Hastily retracing their steps, they crept past the sentry and when at a safe distance, jogged rapidly to where their horses grazed.

Mounting, they rode off in a northeast direction to intersect the trail. At the track, they reined in and dismounted, crouching down to carefully study the many hoof indentations in the mud.

"Three of them. They're ahead of us but not by much," Philippe said.

Paulo agreed.

"We've got to take the diamonds from them," Philippe said, his voice resolute, smacking the palm of his hand with a fist as if to emphasis his statement.

"That's not what we were told to do!"

"I know, but nobody knew that we would get this close to the diamonds."

"Well, how do you think we should do this?" Paulo asked, his face reflecting his concern, unable to ignore his sudden sense of foreboding. He wondered whether his master would approve.

"We'll wait until they camp for the night. They know they're in Kunehama territory and feel safe. Huh, we'll get them! We sneak up, kill all three, and take the diamonds – it'll be easy, they'll be asleep. Others will think the Kunehamas killed them, having mistaken them for other degregados."

"You're sure they will think that?"

Philippe shrugged his shoulders nonchalantly. "It will work, anyway what does it matter what they think. We'll be long gone."

They followed the trail, ensuring that they did not accidentally get too close to the three men and reveal themselves. As soon as the short twilight shed the last of its glow, Philippe called a halt and they led their horses off the track. It was raining again; visibility was no more than a few yards. Under the canopy of a large tree which afforded some shelter against the drenching rain, they dismounted and hobbled their mounts. Then they pulled their blankets around their bare shoulders in an attempt to ward off the chill brought on by the rain.

As is usual, by midnight the storm clouds had disappeared, and the half moon and stars were again visible. They resumed the pursuit, slowly leading their horses in the darkness along the trail, the mud deadening all sounds. After a short while, they could see the first flicker of a campfire far in the distance.

"That must be them," Philippe whispered, bringing his horse to a halt. "We need to get our horses around them to the opposite side, ready to flee if we need to. We don't want to have to back track if things go wrong."

Paulo agreed. They detoured into the bush to skirt around the camp and keep a fair distance away from it. Once off the trail, the virgin bush and trees hampered their progress and thorns scratched and hooked everything, often drawing blood. It was too dark now to clearly see these obstructions and they only became aware of them when they stumbled into them, softly cursing. About a mile north of the camp, they again moved towards the trail, soon striking it. They tethered their horses a short distance from the track, under a large tree with a recognizable enough shape in the poor moonlight should they have to find it quickly.

They discarded their shields and armed with spears and revolvers, they stealthily slunk back towards the camp. On the very edge of the area illuminated by the fire, they lay prone, carefully studying their surroundings. As was expected, they could see a sentry. He was sitting on a fallen log, his blanket wrapped around his shoulders, his rifle resting on its butt between his legs, the muzzle pointing skywards. He stared into the fire, seemingly oblivious of his surroundings.

The trio's horses were tethered a short distance from the camp. Philippe pointed to the horses and then himself and Paulo, indicating that they make their way there. Paulo understood. They cautiously made their way to the horses and once near, Philippe took cover in a large bush that was in a direct line with the camp and the horses. He slowly pushed himself backwards into its leaves. He extracted a length of piano wire from a pouch tied to a leather belt around his waist. The wire had two small hand-carved wooden handles at each end.

Philippe nodded at Paulo who moved slowly towards the horses, not to spook them but just to get them to move. There was some unease and agitation, the horses' heads came up, a hoof stomped on the ground. The guard's head swivelled round to look at the slight disturbance as he realized the horses were jittery. He threw the blanket from his shoulder. Philippe heard the slide of the rifle's bolt action as he worked a cartridge into the breech. The man now stood crouched looking in the direction of the horses, his rifle at the ready. He slowly walked forward. Paulo had moved away from the horses and had taken up station in the surrounding bush. The man approached slowly, looking from side to side. Philippe held a handle in each hand, the steel wire forming a loop: he could faintly see the glint of the wire in the moonlight. He let the man pass until he was a yard ahead of his concealed position, then he stepped out. There was a blur of movement as he swung the loop over the man's head, immediately jerking the handles in opposite directions pulling the steel noose taut. The thin steel wire closed the man's windpipe. He desperately tried to get his fingers under the garrotte, silently gagging, his eyes bulging from their sockets, trying to scream, his mouth open but emitting no sound as his feet drummed on the ground in his final death throes. Paulo sprang from the bushes, his spear in hand. He ran forward, driving the weapon upwards under the man's ribcage, piercing his heart. His death was silent. Blood from the jugular artery severed by the piano wire spurted onto Paulo's chest, the wetness glistening in the weak moonlight. They left the guard where he had fallen.

Philippe and Paulo crept stealthily towards the fire and the two men still sleeping on the ground. The horses had settled down again, no longer agitated. At a pre-arranged signal, they leapt forward plunging their spears into their victims. The air was suddenly rent by blood-curdling screams, abruptly cut off. All was still again. Philippe rummaged quickly through their saddlebags, but found no pouches. He then proceeded to go through their pockets. The concerned expression on his face changed to a triumphant smile of glee as he held up three blood-drenched pouches in his hand.

They doused the campfire using mud and sand. Paulo unhitched the dead men's horses, shooing them so the animals galloped into the bush. Leaving the bodies where they lay and taking nothing else, the two assailants retraced their steps to their own horses and rode off down the trail, with the intention of putting as much distance between themselves and the camp as possible before sunrise.

As the first hint of dawn filtered over the horizon, they guided their horses off the trail into the virgin bush towards Chongoroi, a small village situated on the road from Sa Da Bandeira south of Benguela. The further west they rode, the less the likelihood of them riding into a

Kunehama patrol. Unless their deaths were discovered soon and word sent out to be on the lookout, there seemed little reason for any Kunehamas to treat them differently.

As Philippe had anticipated, their track west brought them to the Catumbela River, now a raging torrent of muddied brown water sweeping the accumulated debris of a few years before it. This river moved northwest, finally reaching the sea at Lobito Bay. Crossing the river was out of the question and there was no way round; they would have to wait for it to subside.

Paulo washed the blood from his torso before scrubbing the pouches containing the diamonds, their drawstrings still tied, to remove all traces of blood. Philippe then placed them in a leather bag he wore attached to a homemade wide rawhide belt, its ends knotted around his midriff.

Waiting for the river to subside, they travelled along the shore, moving well away from the water to blend into dense bush that thronged the riverbanks.

"Often, the water in the river never quite makes the journey to the sea, it just disappears into the sand. But this is a flood and will still be a flood when the water gets to the sea at Lobito Bay. Of course, I have to tell you there's a mighty big waterfall between here and the sea," Paulo said, chewing on a piece of jerky.

"In that case, let's stick with the horses. We'll cross the river where we can and keep close to it for a while. But we need to get further west towards the sea to avoid running into any Kunehama patrols."

Two days later, they skirted the outskirts of Chongoroi, the last real stronghold the Kunehamas had established on the western side of their influence. Colonists had not settled that area, and the civil war had hardly touched it.

Nonetheless, the two still proceeded with caution, avoiding any human habitat. The last fifty miles to Benguela took them across the coastal plain, where the going was easier and they made good time.

The officers met in Major Zietzmann's office in the Alte Feste administration building.

"Coffee, gentlemen?"

They both nodded. The major lit up his cigar and leaned back in his chair.

"Well, my friends, we still have a lot of work to do. We need to deal with de Mello and Colonel Batista. I believe this will prove to be something entirely different, requiring all your cunning and guile."

"Major, my first question is, do I dare go back to Angola? Do they not know who I really am?" Werner asked.

"I really doubt it," Jurgen said. "Dos Santos only knew after his capture that you were a German officer. Before that, he had no reason to believe you were involved. He never had an opportunity to convey this information to anybody. Now Louis, well . . . he's a different matter entirely. He officially deserted his command. Believe me, Colonel Batista will be dying to get his hands on him for that infringement alone, never mind the rest!"

"I've no excuse to offer Colonel Batista for my absence. He will also know that my batman was missing. What do you think he will make of that?" Louis asked.

"Look, don't concern yourselves yet. I'll make contact with General Diaz and explain this new predicament. Let's hear what he suggests. Meanwhile, Major de Sousa, you should continue to recuperate."

Major Zietzmann looked at Werner. "And you, Mr de Almeida, must prepare to return to Benguela on the next ship," he said with a cynical smile.

"Where do I tell them I've been?"

"I doubt whether de Mello or Batista will even enquire. They have little interest with you, and they certainly will not be approaching you for weapons. However, they are involved with the Kunehamas and Hereros, and that is a matter of concern. I'm sure you can think of something acceptable to account for your absence."

"Well . . . I suppose so," Werner hesitantly replied.

A week later, Major Zietzmann informed them that he had made contact with General Diaz, and that Louis was to return directly to Luanda. Werner, as Senhor de Almeida, was to board the same ship but to disembark at Lobito, to continue his role as a representative and await Louis' return. Briefly put, the Major said, General Diaz would advise Colonel Batista that Louis had been working for the General on a clandestine operation and that he had been urgently recalled to Luanda, with strict instructions not to divulge his movements to any other. It was hoped that his return by ship from Luanda would lend credence to his story.

The three men met for dinner at the Thuringerhof Hotel to discuss what to do with their ill-gotten gains.

"I think the diamonds should be left with a bank in safekeeping," said Louis.

Werner shook his head.

"No point in that," he said. "The stones need to be disposed of as soon as possible. Once they're converted to cash, it's highly unlikely we could be incriminated in any way."

Finally, it was decided that Jurgen would take these to Germany when he returned in a month's time. He could visit the diamond merchants in Antwerp with a few samples to gauge their worth, and if the disposal of the parcels was a relatively simple exercise, then he would do so, depositing the funds in a joint account with Werner and Louis affidavits. Everyone understood that this would take a while.

The two officers, with their servants, boarded the Portuguese steamer "Beira" at Swakopmund; Werner disembarked at Lobito and proceeded directly to Benguela, and Louis and Paulo continued on to Luanda.

Werner was glad to be back in Benguela. It was now autumn, the weather was pleasant, and the recent rains had saturated the ground, preventing the wind from raising dust. He rode down the main thoroughfare in his open carriage, Philippe trotting alongside as was proper, the duo a picture of affluence.

He swept up the stairs to his hotel, amused at the startled reception from the hotelier at his sudden appearance.

"Madre Diaz, Senhor de Almeida!" she said loudly, her hands fluttering over her ample cleavage. "Where have you been? We have been so concerned. Your luggage is still in your room."

But then realizing what she had just said, she quickly added, "Of course, you paid for the room well in advance and all is safe, but we've all been worried about your well-being."

"Senhora, business, I'm afraid, urgent business required my presence in Luanda. Regrettably I was unable to inform you of my urgent departure, but now I'm back."

He smiled beguilingly at her.

"I'm glad; you are our most important guest!"

"Did anybody enquire as to my absence?" he enquired.

"No, no. It was just I that was so concerned," she said, her voice now subdued.

Was he to read something into her remark or was this mere concern? Did the good woman have designs on him? Or perhaps his sojourns to Madame Manchatas had given her the wrong impression? She insisted on accompanying him to his room, Philippe in tow, lugging the additional luggage up the stairs.

"As you see, everything is as neat and tidy as you left it," she beamed.

"Thank you."

"Will you be coming back late tonight? I need to know so that I can make arrangements with the porter."

Inquisitive woman, he thought.

"No."

He waited until the hotelier had left, then spoke quietly to Philippe.

"Nothing is going to happen for a while. Would you not like to go home for a week or so?"

Philippe shook his head.

"I've no home, the army is my home and I must stay here and serve you."

Werner's emotional response to the man's loyalty was unexpected. He hesitated before replying.

"Thank you, Philippe, I will not forget that. All right, I've told you what's happening to the diamonds. Once the money arrives, you'll be a rich man. You will get your share when we finally get to Windhuk to stay."

The black man flashed his teeth.

"Then I'll buy cattle and find myself a good woman and go and live in SudwestAfrika. Maybe you and I can buy a ranch, a big, big ranch. I'll work for you. Maybe father a dozen sons!"

He spoke shyly, displaying that hint of embarrassment all Africans seem to show when discussing anything that remotely implied sexual activity. Werner clenched his teeth, fighting his emotion. He felt like a father to this man.

Philippe, my friend, that's a good idea."

CHAPTER NINE

Every morning after breakfast, Werner would unobtrusively stroll to the rear of the hotel. This morning the grooms were busy brushing down a dust covered animal, which he recognized as his servant's horse.

"Good morning, Mestre. Are you looking for Philippe?" the groom asked.

"Yes, is he back?"

The groom nodded, and pointed to the room which Philippe shared with a few others.

"He came late last night, I think he's still asleep – he brought another man with him."

Werner opened the door to the room. After the stark sunlight outside, he was unable to see at first and waited for his eyes to adjust to the gloom of the interior. An assortment of clothing hung from pegs driven into the wall. The room was empty except for the two occupants sleeping. He walked over to Philippe and shook his shoulder.

"I need to talk to you," Werner said.

He waited while the black man emerged from sleep. Philippe was still not fully rested and his features were drawn. Werner's nostrils stung with the pungent smell of rancid sweat: he must have collapsed into bed the previous night, too tired to wash.

"Give me a little while, I have Paulo with me," Philippe replied, indicating the man lying next to him.

"God, you both need a wash. Take your time, then saddle up. I'll meet you in front of the hotel. We'll ride out together and find somewhere private so that we can talk." He smiled, looking down at them. "I'm glad to see you both safely back here," he added, the conviction evident in his voice.

Werner rode out of town with the two cavalerico making up the rear, as was considered proper. Once far enough out, they left the main road and trotted along a side trail until Werner reined in under a huge acacia tree.

"This should be good enough."

Wordlessly, Philippe extracted the three pouches of uncut diamonds from his trouser pockets and handed them over. Werner looked quizzically at the two Africans. They were again dressed in civilian clothes.

'What's this?" he asked.

They both grinned.

"Open them," said Paulo.

Werner felt the pouch with his fingers and then, opening the drawstring, poured part of the contents into the palm of his hand.

"Christus! These are diamonds!" he cried.

"There's more, the other two also have diamonds in them," Philippe said.

"My God, it's a fortune! What did you do to get these?"

Patiently the two recounted what they had seen and how, when they realized that the men proposed to courier the diamonds to wherever, they had decided that it would be possible to intercept the group. They emphasized that there had been only three men, which made it easy, especially when it became evident the miners had not taken proper precautions to protect the parcel.

Werner was aghast. "You killed them? How could you do that, you didn't even know who these men were."

"They were the enemy; they were rebels working together with the Kunehamas and dos Santos. We heard the mine labourers talking – they talked a lot about dos Santos; he's their Mestre and he pays them. If they had known we were there, they would have killed us. We did the right thing. Without the diamonds, how are they going to buy rifles?" Philippe replied, clearly believing that their actions were justified.

There was nothing complicated about their logic, Werner thought.

"Of course, you know that you've caused them a lot of trouble. The loss of the diamonds is going to have many people trying to find out who killed these men. But you say nobody saw you?"

"No. Nobody saw us at the mine, and there was nobody around when we took the diamonds," Philippe assured him.

"I'll take the diamonds and speak to Major de Sousa. I'm sure that he will work out some sort of compensation for you – these diamonds are worth a great deal. Of course, these actually belong to the Portuguese government. Please do not talk to anybody about this. Do you understand?"

They both nodded.

"Paulo, go back to Major de Sousa. Tell him I must meet him, tonight at ten o'clock at the place we always meet. He'll know where. Tell him it's very important."

Werner was horrified by what these men had done. It had of course been tacitly understood that if they ran into any resistance or felt threatened they would kill. Ultimately, it came down to a matter of kill or be killed. Had they really had any option? He conceded they had a point: rather kill for the diamonds than allow these to be used to acquire weapons – every colonist and soldier in the country would agree that these two men had showed unquestionable loyalty and courage.

"Are you all right? Is there anything you need?" Werner enquired.

"No, we have everything."

He mounted up and rode off, leaving them to make their own way back to town.

As arranged, Werner met with Louis at Madame Manchatas. When he produced the first pouch of diamonds, Louis was dumbstruck. However, when a minute later he produced the additional two pouches, the man was astounded.

Louis hefted the three pouches in his hand as Werner briefly filled him in on all the details.

"Do you know what I'm thinking?"

"No," replied Werner, looking up. Then it slowly dawned on him.

"You're not serious?"

"Who's to know? We keep two pouches, share part of it with our two men after we have converted this to cash, and we're set for life! Or at least nearly. May be we should include Jurgen?"

"That's stealing!"

"Is it? From whom? The rebels? I think not. The Portuguese government doesn't even know about these. Once we hand the remaining pouch over, we'll never get another chance, the government will have confirmation of the mine and the riches it contains; they will be all over that place. You'd need to be invisible to get in."

"Hang on, OK. I need to think about this. I realize what you're getting at, but it's still stealing. But not bad stealing; is that what you mean?"

"Well, something like that. While the diamonds do play a part, it's really the guns that play the bigger role. The government can have the mine, sell it or do what they wish with it—but we keep two of the pouches."

Werner reserved his opinion, he needed to think about it first.

"What are we going to do with the diamonds right now?"

"No, no. Don't give them to me," said Louis. "I'm a Portuguese government employee, duty bound to hand them over, but if I don't have them . . ."

"What am I supposed to do with them?" Werner retorted, reluctantly taking the pouches back from Louis.

"Hide them."

"Ok, I'll think of something."

The two men ordered additional drinks, continuing to discuss the diamonds as well as what their next step should be. It was mutually agreed that at this stage that the best tactic was to wait: dos Santos must make the next move. Meanwhile, Louis would try to contact Major de Oliviera without raising suspicion.

Around midnight an exhausted Werner prepared to leave.

"What, not taking part in any fun here?" Louis nonchalantly enquired. "I told you, this is the best bordello around."

Werner gave him the usual two words as a farewell greeting. Louis thought it was hilarious.

"You know," he said, believing he had the last word, "it can't be all work and no play!"

Werner ignored him.

The next day Werner called on the local branch of the Banco Ultramarino to request a safe deposit facility. He slipped the two pouches of diamonds into the large document folders the bank supplied, together with a wad of documentation he had accumulated. This raised no suspicions; Werner's business dealing accounted for a huge amount of documentation and it was considered normal that he wished to place these in safekeeping.

Two days later, de Mello, dos Santos and Colonel Batista sat at a table in the corner of the hotel's dining room. They saw Werner enter but other than acknowledging his greeting, they ignored him. He had purposely chosen a table that enabled him to keep an eye on them, sitting just within his peripheral vision but not close enough to make it obvious. They appeared to be in a serious debate; at one stage, de Mello tried to subdue a heated exchange between dos Santos and the Colonel. Werner was convinced the fate of the diamonds had finally reached them. With the fortune involved, there were bound to be recriminations – somebody was about to take the blame!

Madame Rodrigues, the hotelier, entered the dining room. On seeing Werner, she drifted over with a rustle of skirts.

"Good evening Senhor de Almeida, may I sit?" she asked.

"Please," he smiled, gesturing to the only other chair at the table.

She sat, making herself comfortable.

"I wish to apologize. The other day when you asked, it was none of my . . ." she stammered.

"Please, think nothing of it," he interrupted her, knowing where the conversation was leading.

"But, I should . . ."

"Senorita, please. I would truly appreciate it if we did not discuss the matter. I implore you, let us keep it between it ourselves," Werner requested emphatically.

His attitude was not lost on her.

"I'm sorry, Senhor, rest assured nothing further will be said."

"Thank you."

The woman left. A short while later, the assistant manager approached Werner's table and handed him a wine list.

"Madame Rodriques insists that you accept a wine of your choice. It's on the house."

Obviously a peace offering, Werner thought. The good lady was concerned that she had offended him. May be she's just curious, he thought. He had been to Madame Manchatas three times in a relatively short space of time, and this woman knew everybody's movements. He wondered what she thought of him—no doubt, she imagined him to be a man with an unusual sexual appetite. He was amused, but also embarrassed; he would have to make damn sure Louis did not hear about this, he would use and manipulate it in an attempt at fun at Werner's expense. Damn that de Sousa again! Surely, they could have met somewhere else.

Whatever the subject of the heated discussion at the table in the corner, it was evident that nothing had been resolved. Suddenly, dos Santos rose and threw his serviette down on his untouched food. He stormed out, ignoring Werner as he passed, his face a caricature of fury. The first cracks in the ceiling, Werner thought – discord amongst the thieves, how wonderful.

Werner and Louis met again at the same hour at Madame Manchatas. The frequency of their visits was now raising a few eyebrows, especially from the women. Who were these men who visited regularly but never touched or even showed any interest? Every time they approached the pair, they were politely shooed away. Some even suggested they were men of a different sort, but then, why come here?

"Listen Louis, coming here is not good. I've already got the hotelier worrying about me and now these women are beginning to look at us askance."

His friend chuckled softly, finding Werner's remark amusing.

"Just think how much you could surprise them when you really let your hair down! Actually, for the sake of appearances that might not be a bad idea. Some of them probably think you've been coming here trying to build up courage to take one of them. That's it; they think you are a virgin," he replied, unable to hide a smirk at his latest piece of logic.

"Just leave it alone, will you!" Werner snapped, close to the end of his tether. "God, I think you suffer from some sort of sexual perversion."

This brought Louis close to collapse. He laughed so loud that others turned to look. Realizing however he'd overstepped the mark, he sat sipping his drink as he waited for his friend to calm down.

"I'm leaving for Luanda," he said finally. "I've told Colonel Batista a blatant lie, blaming family problems and requested a fourteen-day furlough. Rosetta and my daughter will be going with me; I've booked passage on a coastal schooner. Of course, I'm actually going to see Colonel de Oliviera and his superiors. I'll hand them the diamonds and report on what has transpired so far. I'm sure Batista knows – the mood today at headquarters was extremely tense, the man actually threw a tantrum for no known reason. But I'm sure it was the diamonds."

"Meanwhile what do you think I should do?"

"Just relax, make a few sales. Wait for the rifle shipment from Germany. I should be back from Luanda by then, hopefully with a plan of action. I take it our treasure is safe?"

"Yes, it is." Werner told him where he had deposited the diamonds.

"I must go, but will contact you as soon as I'm back. On a more serious note—and don't get upset. Take one of these ladies – you don't have to do a damn thing but you've got to go through the motions for appearance's sake. Just pay – do nothing if that's how you feel. These women don't talk outside the bedroom. At least then everybody will think it normal, you being here. After all, you're single, nobody will think your visit to a bordello is suspicious. Remember, this is Portugal, not Germany. This is the best meeting place; let's not change. I spoke to my aunt the grande dame; she knows who you are. She'll arrange anything you want. And if you wondering, Rosetta knows I'm here and knows my aunt would never let me stray."

Louis left. Werner realized his friend was right – pretence was all important. At least he would have an excellent excuse for being here, and de Mello and his merry men would not consider it strange if they were to hear of it. He might as well act the part. God, he thought, what one had to do for Volk und Vaterland! He wondered how Zietzmann would react to that in his report, especially if it was at the Kaiser's cost!

He returned to the hotel well after three in the morning, only to find the hotel doors locked. He had to ring the night bell several times before the night porter shuffled into view grasping a large key with which he grouchily opened up. No doubt, in the morning Madame Rodrigues would be told of his latest late night escapades, adding to his already dubious reputation.

In fact, after Louis' departure, the remainder of his evening at Madame Manchatas had been pleasant. Louis' aunt introduced him to what she thought was her best girl, or so she said. A recent acquisition from Portugal, she had added. Oh, she certainly was beautiful, but too young and still somewhat childish. What was pleasant was that she had not yet cultivated that inevitable hard façade, the hallmark of the trade. The three of them drank two bottles of champagne, which the aunt ordered at some horrendous price. They chatted, the young woman not offering her services and Werner not asking. This did not perturb the grande dame, probably because Louis had told her what to expect. Not so the hotelier, who seemed overly concerned about his regular evenings of debauchery.

The "ss Tanganyika" docked at Lobito on the 5th April. Werner stood on the small quayside with dos Santos as the barge approached; it was filled with crates and cargo.

"Those forty-four crates, that's all yours," Werner said.

Dos Santos nodded. The custom officers stood to one side, also waiting for the barge. Werner had no idea what the modus operandi was relating to the import of firearms. He was not particularly concerned: he had already been paid and the proceeds of the barter shipped to Germany. If the import of the firearms encountered a problem with customs then that was the buyer's quandary, not his.

Louis had returned two days earlier from Luanda where he had consulted with General Cadiz and Colonel de Oliviera. Both had initially considered it imperative that the arms shipment be confiscated on its arrival in Lobito, but on reflection decided it a pointless exercise if done when the crates came ashore. They believed de Mello would intervene, with the customs officers going through the motions, the shipment confiscated, only to have the weapons find their way back to dos Santos. Corruption was rife with in government circles, and de Mello's tentacles were everywhere in southern Angola.

After consultation with German Intelligence it was decided to step back, let the gunrunners clear the firearms and not intercept these before they crossed the borders of SudwestAfrika. Only then would the authorities strike. The apprehension, or death for that matter, of Portuguese nationals would not create an international incident, as they would have been caught on German soil with the incriminating evidence. It would be impossible for any Portuguese authority to intervene with such overwhelming evidence. Of course, this would not take care of de Mello or his protector, but General Cadiz believed that this would resolve itself. Precisely how, he never indicated.

The customs officers had taken possession of all the documentation, and as the derricks swung the crates ashore, these were carefully inspected. The crate numbers were compared with those on the manifest and a few cases opened supposedly at random for inspection.

Werner had difficulty concealing his surprise and annoyance. The customs officers blatantly overlooked the crates containing the rifles. None of these were opened. With twenty-five rifles to a crate, this accounted for twenty-two of the crates, yet not one was opened.

Werner had no doubt that de Mello had a hand in this blatant disregard of proper custom procedures. The officers were not only in his employ, but also in his pocket it seemed! Fuming, there was little he could do other than pretend to be unobservant and happy that all formalities had been completed without a hitch.

Dos Santos had arranged for four wagons on the quayside to load the cargo. All the rifle crates were loaded into two of these wagons. Finally, the wagon train was ready to depart.

Dos Santos turned to Werner and held out his hand.

"Senhor de Almeida, it has been a pleasure doing business with you. I hope we shall do a great deal more. It seems we have the makings of a mutually beneficial business relationship. You will recall my discussion with regard to further shipments, and I hope that you have given my proposal serious thought. Please consider my order as confirmed. In fact, if you produce a cable from your principals confirming shipment, when and where loaded, what ship and date of departure, I will consider this sufficient to effect payment."

Werner shook the man's hand, ensuring an expression of pleasure on his face at receiving this further order. He had obviously established his bona fides, and dos Santos was not wary of him at all.

"Excellent! I'll place the order and as soon as I have the confirmation, I'll be in touch."

Dos Santos took the reins of his horse and swung into the saddle, a signal to his men, who rapidly mounted behind him. He raised an arm up high and then let it fall in an easterly direction. The wagons lurched forward, his men taking up position on both sides of the wagon train. The gunrunner turned, waving farewell. Reluctantly Werner returned the greeting.

Philippe held Werner's horse in check as he prepared to mount. There was no ignoring the dejected expression on his cavelerico's face.

"Are we going to stop him, Mestre?"

"Yes, but not here. In SudwestAfrika."

This seemed to placate the African. He nodded his head, satisfied for the moment that something would be done.

CHAPTER TEN

Dos Santos sat on a folding camp chair staring into the recently lit campfire, smoking a cheroot, a small tumbler of Portuguese brandy in his hand as he waited for his servant to prepare supper. The last of the day's light was rapidly disappearing, the evening star Venus already perceptible on the western horizon. They would soon cross the border into German territory, but there still remained a formidable obstacle, the Kunene River.

The Kunehamas' insurrection had come as a shock to all. The loss of three hundred plus, including one hundred and fourteen white men, had galvanized the Portuguese into action. The Portuguese government had reinforced the colonial forces, resurrected all militia forces, and launched a retaliatory action against the Kunehamas. For the first time, the military employed artillery. They moved into the Huambo province, using the partially completed British railway line that had rapidly penetrated the interior from Lobito to Katanga, to provide logistical support.

The military advanced in force and dealt ruthlessly with any resistance. The revolt collapsed, with the military setting up garrisons as they advanced. The rebels, many of whom who had been the contract labourers subjected to forced labour on ranches and plantations, simply returned to their places of employment, pretending to have been no more than fugitives from terror who had fled to save their lives and hidden in the bush trying to avoid the conflict.

Those who continued to oppose the government forces were systematically driven south, no match for the superior forces that now confronted them. Portuguese retribution was merciless: they assailed tribal strongholds with shell and cavalry charges, massacring the inhabitants, giving no quarter.

In order to avoid the Portuguese patrols, dos Santos was forced westwards into the desert wastelands that hug the coastal region of southern Angola, a seemingly endless plain with little vegetation and water.

"Mestre?"

He looked up. One of his scouts was standing a respectful distance away requesting permission to approach. Dos Santos beckoned him near.

The man, a tall and powerful Kunehama, was traditionally dressed, except for the rifle in his hand and the bandolier of ammunition over his shoulder. He also wore a sweat-stained campaign hat, which any other would have long discarded, it was so holed and torn.

"What is it, Dom Alphonso?"

Dos Santos addressed the man by his "Santu", the Christian name the missionaries ensured all who were baptized and passed through their system were given. The "Dom" prefix was a sign of respect, but dos Santos seldom used it. Alphonso, however, was special; virtually irreplaceable in fact.

"We are being followed."

"Who can follow us in this desert, it's so flat surely we would see them?"

"It is only two men, Mestre."

"How do you know this?"

"I was sent to shoot a gemsbok for the pot. I wounded the animal and had to chase after it on foot. It had run north back to the trail we came along. I crossed the spoor of their horses. I followed them and eventually saw them in the distance. They were following our wagon tracks. If I had been on horseback, they would have seen me."

"Could you see them well?"

"Not too good, but I saw one white and one black."

Dos Santos was dismayed. That the party that shadowed them included a white was ominous. His initial thought was that it was impossible; they had taken extraordinary precautions to cover their tracks.

"Are you sure about this?" he queried.

"Yes, Mestre. Why would two men without wagons be this close to us in the desert, but avoid our camp?"

A valid observation. He could not argue.

"You're right. Thank you Dom Alphonso, I'll think about this."

He called for his lieutenant, a deputy he had appointed years ago, a degregado, a tough, sullen brute of a man, a man without conscience who had barely escaped the gallows in Portugal for heinous crimes. Anything that required force and brutality seemed to be this man's specialty. Alvarez was large, but not given to any fat, his torso strong and powerful, well honed muscle. He was more squat than tall, with a full black beard and piercing black eyes.

"Alphonso tells me we are being followed by two men. One is white."

"What can two men do to us? We are twenty-one," he responded shrugging his shoulders with indifference.

That answer was too simplistic—something was going on.

"I don't think they want to attack us, I believe they just want to know where we are going. It's got to have something to do with the rifles. How far still to the river?"

"About twenty miles."

"Well, we should be there by day after tomorrow, if not tomorrow night."

"Yes," the deputy replied. "But I don't think we will be able to cross. The river is still in flood."

"I don't like this – why follow us unless they know what we are carrying and what we are trying to do? I don't want anything to jeopardize this. Sandwich Bay, those men from the mine – I'm not about to take anything for granted," dos Santos growled, his mind already analyzing his options and deciding on an appropriate course of action. "No, we must do something. Within the next day or two. Let's talk tomorrow."

The terrain was impossible. To try to get any nearer to the camp would expose them. Louis and Paulo lay on the bare gravel of the desert looking down towards the camp which dos Santos had pitched in a light indentation. There were only two wagons, the oxen already outspanned. Bales of hay lay strewn on the ground, the oxen and hobbled horses feeding on these.

Louis turned to Paulo. "If we don't get our horses to water soon, we'll have a problem," he whispered.

"Capitano is right. The river is a day's ride. Dos Santos will get there tomorrow night or the day after."

"Do you think they know they are being followed?"

"Never, we've kept too far back. I think he is going to cross the river just before the Raucana Falls, that's the only place near here that is shallow. But he'll have to wait, the river's in flood, we've had too much rain."

Louis was concerned. Their plan hinged on a number of ifs, and if any number of these occurred, the plan was shot – dos Santos would dispose of the weapons and with that would go their proof. The man had to be dealt with once and for all.

Werner had returned to SudwestAfrika. According to plan, from Swakopmund he was to contact Major Zietzmann and relay the latest developments. All were convinced that dos Santos would cross the border with the weapons, but precisely where was anybody's guess. Werner's task was to persuade the Major to send an armed detachment from Ondongua westwards, across the flood plain and through the northern sector of the Etosha Pan to intercept Dos Santos as he crossed the Kunene where it formed the border between the two countries. No-one had any idea what arrangements dos Santos may have made with the Hereros. It was also possible that he might trek southwards, passing through the eastern fringes of the Kaokoveld and meet up with the recipients of the rifles further south on the fringes of the Namib Desert.

Originally, Louis' group had consisted of three, but Philippe had left them two days ago, heading for the Finnish Mission. Werner had said that once they were reasonably certain what dos Santos' intentions were, they should cable Major Zietzmann. Louis had drafted a cable in Portuguese using Werner's pseudonym for Philippe to hand to Doctor Eggars. She could arrange to have this sent from the telegraph office at Ondongua.

"May be we should skirt around and make for the river and let them catch up with us. At least we will have grazing and water for the horses," Louis said.

Paulo shook his head.

"Major, we can't do that. They send men out to hunt for food. They can take any direction – they could discover our tracks. Best we stay behind them."

"Mmm, maybe you're right, Louis reluctantly conceded.

The horses were a good mile back. Unsaddling, they prepared to spend the night. After a mundane meal of jerky and biscuits washed down with water from their water bottles, they slid into their bedrolls, leaving the horses tethered to their saddles on the ground. They used these as pillows, hoping that the horses' movements would deter any snakes coming near. The area was invested with puff adders and horned desert vipers. At night, these are drawn to body heat: without proper precaution, you could have a reptilian companion sharing your bedroll!

Alvarez lay on the ground with the tracker alongside him. Behind them lay a further three African men. It was three in the morning, and a quarter moon provided just sufficient light to make out the outline of the horizon. A hundred yards from them, they could see the horses of those who followed their wagon train. The horses were hobbled and unsaddled, their riders asleep. No fire burned.

Dos Santos' instructions had been explicit – kill them, remove and bury their clothing and saddles. Take the horses. Leave the bodies to the lions and hyenas. It was unlikely that any trace would ever be found in this remote region.

Paulo awoke suddenly. He had no idea what had woken him, but then he was a light sleeper. The horses were restless. Was there a predator in the vicinity – had the horses picked up the scent? He was uneasy. If it was a lion, the horses would be panicky; it had to be something else. He leant over and shook Louis.

"Major, quiet! Something is wrong," he hissed.

Louis was immediately alert.

"What is it?" Louis whispered.

"I don't know, but it's not a lion, something else," Paulo replied, rising from his makeshift bed, his rifle already in his hand.

Louis followed suit. Both men crouched, their rifles cradled in their arms, slowly looking beyond their campsite for anything out of the ordinary.

"Something is out there, I think it is men, not animals, otherwise the horses would be a lot more restless," Paulo said. Still whispering, he added urgently, "Get down on the ground, quickly, now. Crawl away from the camp."

Louis threw himself to the ground and quickly crawled after Paulo into the scrub.

The tracker tugged at Alvarez' shirtsleeve as he lay prone next to him on the ground.

"They think there's something wrong, probably the horses gave us away. What do you want to do?" the black man asked, his voice barely audible.

"We have to go after them."

He signalled those behind him, lifting a finger to indicate one man, and then swept his arm in an arc to his left. Repeating this, he swept his arm to the right. Two men crawled out from the group of three, one moving left, the other right in a flanking movement around the campsite.

Paulo had taken up position behind a desert saltbush, a dense collection of thick vertical stalks growing to about shoulder height, his short stabbing spear in one hand, his rifle in the other. Louis crouched behind another similar bush. They did not have long to wait before a man approached, running low to the ground, a huge machete in his hand. Paulo let him pass, then quietly emerged from behind the bush, grabbed the man by the chin and drove the spear into his body, thrusting it upwards below the ribcage. Louis had his hand pressed hard over the victim's mouth, but the dying man's scream pierced the night before he convulsed, arching his back as his life slipped away.

The need for stealth evaporated. Confident they outnumbered their prey, Alvarez and his men charged forward into the camp, not entirely sure whose scream they had heard. Louis raised his rifle and fired. One of the men fell to the ground. The remaining two swung round towards the rifle flash, no more than ten yards away. Before Louis could reload, his assailant was upon him. He swung the butt of the rifle at the black man, catching the man's neck and flinging him sideways to the ground, but not before his spear caught him just below the shoulder. The downwards thrust raked across his ribcage, burning a path to his navel.

Alvarez stormed forward, his revolver in his hand and only saw Paulo when a few yards from him. Paulo's arm was raised, ready to fling his spear. Alvarez fired at point-blank range and the bullet hit Paulo in the shoulder. His spear fell from his hand. Alvarez fired again, but Paulo had already dropped to the ground. Alvarez grinned as he skidded to a halt in front of the prone black man, raising his revolver to administer the coup de grace. A shot rang out and his head exploded. Paulo turned to see Louis, his arm still outstretched, revolver in his hand, his blood spreading a large blotch onto his shirt.

They waited silently, listening to the sounds of someone crashing through the scrub as he fled from the skirmish.

"I suppose he must be the last," Louis said, jerking his head in the direction of the fleeing man. He held his arm across his body, trying to stem the blood seeping through his shirt. His companion was battling to stand up, bleeding freely.

"Major, we must ride. Dos Santos will come with the others," Paulo said, trying to roll his bedroll with one arm.

"Here, let me help you."

Louis rolled up the bedrolls and with difficulty, they saddled both hobbled horses. He handed his companion his horse's reins and boosted him into the saddle, both gasping with pain.

They rode off, travelling east, trying to put as much distance between themselves and dos Santos before sunrise. Without light, it would be impossible to follow their tracks; dos Santos would have to wait until daybreak. From the blood trails, dos Santos would realize that they were wounded. Would he follow?

Although sore and uncomfortable, Louis was not too concerned about his injury. Yes, he had lost some blood but nothing like Paulo; his wound was bad, and the blood was pumping slowly but continuously from the bullet–hole. He didn't know whether it had hit bone. They needed to stop but first had to lose dos Santos. Paulo realized this, and he grimly hung on, swaying from side to side as he clung to the saddle pommel with his good arm.

Only once the first morning light bathed the landscape, did Louis stop. They halted on a shallow knoll, which enabled him to see a good few miles. He saw no-one behind them. Paulo's shirt and trousers were saturated with blood, his face was grey and drawn.

"Don't worry, I'm going to do something about this," Louis said, as he helped Paulo dismount. He tore up a shirt and made two plugs, inserting one in the entrance hole of the wound and the other in the jagged exit hole. Strapping Paulo's chest and shoulder tightly with the rest of the shirt, he hoped this would help to stem the flow. It would work so long as they did not have to ride, Louis thought. Fortunately, the bullet had exited. Infection was the next problem.

He then attended to his own wound. This was only a flesh wound, but ugly, the cut about a quarter of an inch deep, the skin peeled open, his ribs and stomach muscles exposed. Similar to Paulo, he wrapped his torso tightly with torn clothing. They both urgently required medical attention; the only place he knew of was the Finnish mission. That had to be at least a hundred miles away, at best a two-day ride.

Paulo lay on the ground, his eyes closed. Louis lifted his head and trickled water into his mouth.

"Nobody seems to be following us. I'm going to let you rest as long as I can. But as soon as it starts to get too hot, we have to ride again. We need to find water. And we both need medical attention; the only place is the Finnish hospital."

"As soon as you get to the river, you must make a travois," Paulo whispered.

"Christus! I wouldn't know how to do that, but I'll try."

Paulo managed a weak smile.

Dos Santos was furious. The wide-eyed black, almost gibbering with fear, had ridden into camp with a garbled story that his comrades had been killed and Alvarez shot in the head. The gunrunner lost control. He cuffed the black about the head, knocking the man to his knees.

"You useless piece of shit! Why did you run? You should've stayed and fought back!" he shouted, kicking the man in the rear as he raised his arms to protect himself from the vicious blows. The other blacks looked on morosely, too afraid to intervene.

Dos Santos was in a quandary. He realized he should initiate a pursuit, but if the men were wounded, they probably could not come after him. He was loath to leave the wagons; he would have to send more of his men after them. Finally, he decided to press on: it was better not go after the two, but rather try and finalize the weapons deal as soon as possible.

By mid-morning, Louis had no alternative but to hoist Paulo into the saddle and force him to ride. It was now too hot; they simply had to get to water. The plugs were working to stem the loss of blood, but Paulo hovered on the brink of unconsciousness, occasionally slipping into delirium, but hanging onto the saddle with sheer determination.

Late that afternoon they made it to the river. Louis helped his cavalerico slip from the saddle, making him comfortable under a large tree. He shot a duiker, a small buck often found near water, and skinned this, roasting the meat over a fire. He tried to feed some of it to Paulo but he ate very little. Using Paulo's machete, Louis sought out suitable saplings, cutting and trimming these to build a travois. It was an arduous and difficult task but he finally surveyed his finished creation dubiously; the question was whether it would last.

The next morning before dawn, he strapped his wounded companion to the travois and set out for the mission. He followed the course of the river, hoping to find a place to cross the still raging torrent.

Dos Santos' wagon train had resumed its journey south, with the man now extremely alert, surrounding the moving wagons with scouts to warn of any approaching horsemen. They finally reached the river at a point a few miles upstream of the Raucana Falls, and its spray and mist were discernible in the distance. At the point where the wagons now stood, the river was usually at its shallowest, the horses and wagons able to ford the river. However, it was still in full flood and impossible to cross. The blacks reckoned it would be two days before they could cross, and that only if it did not rain.

Dos Santos seethed with impatience, knowing that he needed to conclude the deal with the Hereros before any further pursuit found him. He was further incensed that he did not know exactly who was pursuing him; surely not the Germans, he was still in Angola! De Mello and Colonel Batista should have seen to it that this did not happen. He dared not be apprehended while still in possession of the rifles. And whoever it was, they were well organized. The loss of his first consignment, then the Sandwich Bay ambush and now he was again being chased! Add to this the sorry mess of the death of the diamond couriers and the loss of a fortune in gemstones—this was now serious!

"Dom Jorge!" he shouted for his new assistant. "I want an armed perimeter guard right round this camp – four hours on and four hours off. Don't let anybody near. Is that clearly understood?"

"Yes, Mestre," the man replied fearfully.

It took two full days for the water to subside. The crossing was still dangerous, but Louis could wait no longer: Paulo's condition was critical, and he had to get him to a doctor. He had found a dugout canoe drawn up on the riverbank. It had not been used for a long time and was dried and cracked but it was still able to float. He laid Paulo in the canoe, tying the bow with a length of rope to the saddle-pommel of Paulo's horse. He was sure that the river was now shallow enough to allow him to walk across; it was the strength of the current that concerned him. Knowing his horse would follow, he led Paulo's horse into deeper water, the dugout trailing behind, the current pulling it to the side at an angle. He goaded the horse on, swimming alongside it as the water deepened, hanging onto the pommel, kicking his legs trying to assist.

They were halfway across when the river knocked the horse off its legs and the current swept them downstream. Desperately the horse swam, slowly pulling himself and the canoe across while Louis hung onto the pommel, helpless to assist. He felt the horse's hooves touch the bottom as it found purchase, and they stumbled from the river.

Louis was relieved but exhausted. Paulo was oblivious of what had just occurred. Using his own horse, Louis returned to the opposite bank to retrieve the travois and the rest of their gear. It was another hour before they were ready to ride. The water had soaked his wound, and the strain had re-opened it, soaking his shirt with fresh blood.

Utterly exhausted, Louis rode into the forecourt of the mission just before midday of the following day, having ridden most of the night. He had skirted around a pride of lions, having to fire shots to scare them off.

The nurses immediately carried Paulo into the small hospital section. Dr Eggars came out, taken back to see Louis again and in an Angolan officer's uniform. She looked around for Werner, then took him by the hand and led him indoors into a room containing an examination couch a chair. The racks on the wall were lined with medicine bottles. She sat him down and removed his shirt, and then cut away his makeshift bandages. At the sight of the now festering wound, she screwed up her nose and led him to the table.

"Where's Werner?" she asked.

He did not understand, but heard the word "Werner" and realized she was enquiring as to his friend's whereabouts. He made like a train with his one arm and said:

"Windhuk."

Then with his finger, he pointed to the ground, indicating that his friend was coming here.

She smiled, clearly happy at what Louis had indicated. She gave him a sedative and left him to sleep.

CHAPTER TWELVE

Werner sat in the compartment, fully clothed at four o'clock in the morning, swaying from side to side with the motion of the train as it chugged through the bush, still fifty miles from Tsumeb. Jurgen was asleep, sprawled on the opposite bunk. The story had spread that Louis had thrown caution to the wind, and without authority he and Paulo had left Benguela at night to find dos Santos. Colonel Batista had no idea where he was. All he knew was that it was some family crisis, but Rosetta de Sousa and daughter could also not be found; it was assumed that she was in the company of her husband. Werner thought Louis' unilateral action foolhardy: what chance had two men against who knew how many? Dangerous, he thought, not wanting to dwell on the possible outcome. Meanwhile, the two pouches containing the diamonds which he had retrieved from the bank burnt a hole in his pocket.

From Benguela, he had sent a deliberately vague cable to Major Zietzmann, informing him that he would report to Windhuk shortly. The Major issued instructions for him to be given immediate access to a phone, and from the garrison commander's office in Swakopmund, he had waited patiently for an hour or so while they placed the call. Finally, he was able to speak to an unhappy Major who was insisting that he be briefed on the latest developments. As this was not possible over the phone, Zietzmann insisted that Werner and his Askari leave for Windhuk on that evening's train. Informed of the urgency of the matter, the garrison commander personally assisted Werner and Philippe to the station!

In Windhuk, Werner briefed Zietzmann and Jurgen. In detail, he recounted how they had acquired the diamonds, although he mentioned only one pouch.

"Where are the diamonds?" asked the Major. With a self-satisfied smile, Werner handed over the pouch.

"Of course, these are actually the property of the Portuguese government," he said, "but in view of the affiliations between Colonel Batista, de Mello and the Hereros, both Major de Sousa and I decided that they be given to you, sir."

The Major undid the drawstring and poured the contents of the pouch onto the blotter on his desk.

"Lieber Gott!" Jurgen said with a sharp intake of breath. Though uncut, the stones were large and would fetch a handsome price: a small fortune in fact.

"This is what my Askari took off the men they killed. As I said, dos Santos had offered to pay me in diamonds for the next shipment he ordered. I had to make a decision at the time; I said I would accept: really, I had no alternative but to agree. That was when the mine was still a rumour and before we sent the Askaris to investigate."

"Herr Hauptmann, you were correct to do so. He would never have understood your reluctance to accept diamonds in payment. No sane man would do that – think of the profit to be made on the resale of those diamonds in Europe. You would've jeopardized the whole mission," the Major replied.

Zietzmann carefully retrieved the stones and returned them to the pouch.

"I'll issue you with a receipt which you can give Major de Sousa when you see him. At least he will be able to tell his superiors the stones are in safe hands. I don't need an incident with the Portuguese!"

The Major then turned to Jurgen.

" Herr Rittmeister, you need to intercept dos Santos as he crosses the border. I've ordered your troop to be increased to eighty mounted men, all veterans – no new recruits. Under no circumstances are those rifles and ammunition to find their way to the Hereros. By the time you get there, it may be that dos Santos has already crossed the border. If that is that case, you will mount a pursuit, and this time, stop at nothing to apprehend him. Do whatever is necessary."

He paused, then looked off into the distance.

"In fact, off the record, it would be far better if no arrests are made, if you know what I mean."

"Major, the Kunene is in full flood due to the heavy rains in southern Angola. It is impossible to cross with loaded wagons. He will be stranded. And if dos Santos is heading for the Kaokoveld, then he must cross just above the falls. With the river swollen, that's the only place where his wagons can ford. We need to get there as soon as possible," Werner said.

"You will both leave on the next train north. I've managed to pry a Maxim and crew out of a fellow officer and friend of mine. Those damn things are like hen's teeth. These machine guns only recently have been issued to the Schutztruppe."

"What about Major Graf zu Dohner at Ondongua? He's bound to interfere. When we last saw him, he had his nose seriously out of joint – all this action in his area and he and his men sidelined."

The Major withdrew a cigar from an ornate box on his desk and proceeded to cut and light it.

"God, the man's an idiot, but unfortunately, he's an aristocrat and a duke to boot, even if he's some Junker family's black sheep—probably got the gamekeeper's daughter or the kitchen help pregnant; these scandals usually involve a woman. Just ignore him. If he resorts to his customary difficult attitude, by all means tell him you are following my orders. I'll sort something out with the General. He incidentally doesn't think too highly of our dear Graf either."

Close on eight the next morning the train pulled into Tsumeb. In Windhuk, two additional boxcars and a passenger coach had been added to the train to accommodate the additional men and their horses. The Maxim machine gun was mounted on a small wagon drawn by two horses.

It took an hour before the column departed. Jurgen was hoping to reach Ondongua no later than noon the next day.

It was now nearly autumn, the late afternoons still greeted by a rapid build-up of darkening cumulus clouds, then lightning and thunder, followed by the short but heavy deluge so typical of an African thunderstorm. Fortunately, the ground was damp, with no dust or standing pools of water, and the column made excellent progress. The troopers were all veterans, and they knew what to do and what was expected of them.

An unusually amicable Graf zu Dohner welcomed them in Ondongua. The two officers realized that there must have been an exchange of messages between the good duke and Windhuk, no doubt initiated by Zietzmann. The duke had seen to it that tents were erected for their anticipated arrival, his Askaris tended to their horses and for the officers, while he laid on the best dinner: cold beers and wine from the Rhine, venison steaks, and apple strudel with cream to finish. The excellent meal was wasted on Werner. He was impatient, unable to wait for the morning, desperate to be on his way again, as he found his thoughts alternating between dos Santos and Dorothea.

They arrived at the Finnish mission at Olukonda in the late afternoon. As they rode into the forecourt, he saw Dorothea smiling and waving to him. They dismounted and formally shook hands with Pastor Haiddenon.

"You certainly are busy men," the missionary said to the two officers. "I never expected to see you so soon again. You will be surprised to learn that I have your Portuguese officer friend and his servant in my hospital."

"In your hospital! How is Louis?" Werner asked, unable to conceal his concern.

Dorothea had taken his hand, standing up close and looking up at him, her first public display of affection.

"He will be fine," she smiled. "He has a long gash from his shoulder to his stomach, a flesh wound, ugly, but I've sutured and cleaned it. His servant, I think his name is Paulo—well, he's not so good. He has a gunshot wound in the shoulder – no bones broken, but an infection has set in. He's running a high fever but we are watching him round the clock. These blacks are resilient and he is particularly strong – I'm hopeful."

She still held his hand.

"Can I speak to them?"

"No, they're both sleeping, but you should be able to speak to Louis tomorrow morning."

The oil lamps in the dining hall made the room uncomfortably warm, and as soon as all had eaten, the group retired to the verandah, where a cool breeze from the west offered some relief. The evening star hung low on the horizon of a crystal clear sky, the last shadows of the day no more than a grey smudge on the horizon. Werner stood at the verandah rail, Dorothea leaning against him, thrilled at his nearness.

"So, you're leaving again tomorrow?"

"Yes, as soon as I've been able to speak to Louis. I need to catch him early in the morning. We want to be on our way by sunup."

"You're still after dos Santos, aren't you?" she asked, taking hold of his arm, a vivid picture of the man coming to mind.

He did not reply. She nuzzled her head up against his arm and whispered.

"Come back."

He was up and dressed by five the next morning, Philippe had woken him with a steaming cup of black coffee to fight off the early morning chill which had descended on their camp alongside the mission. Before it was light, he and Jurgen strode to the hospital section where Dorothea greeted them. She gave Werner a quick peck on the cheek, causing Jurgen to lift his eyebrows in surprise.

"He's awake," she said.

Louis lay on the hospital bed, his chest bare. Dorothea was an ardent supporter of the new belief that air was necessary if wounds were to heal rapidly. His scar, the sutures clearly visible, was yellow from the iodine that had been painted on. .

"God, I'm glad you're safe. What happened?" Werner asked.

Louis told them the story, as Werner translated for Jurgen.

"Where is he now?" Jurgen asked.

Louis gave them a position on the river where he thought dos Santos would ford the river with his wagons.

"You may be a bit late. He probably would have crossed yesterday or will do so, today."

"Scheisse!" Jurgen exclaimed when Werner translated. "We have to get going. If he meets up with the Hereros before we get there, we're going to have a serious fight on our hands."

"Have you told Jurgen about . . . ?" Louis asked as Jurgen left.

Werner shook his head.

"I will," he said.

They went next door to check on Paulo, but he was still asleep, heavily sedated, his shoulder bandaged.

As they left the room, Dorothea pulled him back and placed her lips to his, pressing her body to him. He took her into his arms and passionately returned her kiss. They drew apart, and she snuggled her face into his neck.

"Be careful, come back – I need you," she whispered, then broke away and fled down the passage.

CHAPTER THIRTEEN

From many miles away, the Raucana Falls revealed its position, the mist rising into the sky, the inevitable rainbow visible and the roar of the falls just audible. Louis had said that dos Santos would cross just above the Falls. Although no longer in the flood plain that drained into the Etosha Pan, the ground was flat and featureless, except for the scrub bush.

A scout appeared, reining in next to Jurgen and speaking rapidly.

"He says dos Santos is gone," Jurgen translated to Werner.

Werner swore.

The column broke into a canter as they neared the riverbank and burst into a clearing. It had obviously been a campsite, with water-doused campfires and wagon tracks clearly visible.

"The scout says he left yesterday."

"How many were they?" Werner asked.

"No more than Louis told us. It seems they have not yet met up with the Hereros, which just may be a Godsend. Let's water the horses and be on our way; with these tracks, he's going to be easy to follow. It seems he's moving in a southwest direction. My God, that's rough terrain – you don't want to get lost there," Jurgen replied.

"That's a very bad place, little water and lots of wild animals. The wind blows so strong that it even blows small stones before it. This happens nearly every afternoon. Many people have been lost there and never found again." Philippe shook his head. "A bad place," he repeated.

"Well, we've no choice – we have to follow," Jurgen said, making it clear that he did not want to discuss the option again.

It was stifling hot, and most of the soldiers had stripped off their blue grey tunics, and were clad now only in their singlets and braces. The scouts were far ahead, at least five miles further on, so that should they encounter any Hereros, the enemy might believe them to be individuals or a small group. These men were not in uniform: all were dressed as locals, hopefully to mislead the enemy.

The further southwest they rode, the more rugged the terrain became. The flood plain gave way to rocky outcrops scattered with large flat stones. These pieces of the strata layers were easily seen in the rock faces. Arroyos separated the hills, dry riverbeds lined with sparse vegetation. It was evident that dos Santos' wagons were finding the going difficult. Philippe had told Werner that the Raucana Falls demarcated the beginning of the coastal plain, where the ground dropped sharply, the river's strong flow cutting through the plateau to the coastal plain. This was now thirty miles behind them to the northeast. It was clear that dos Santos was making for the coastal plain, believing that it was extremely unlikely that he would run into a German patrol in this desolate region.

Philippe was right – they saw animals of every description; lion, desert elephant and rhino, leopard and cheetah, the scavenging jackal and hyena. It was obvious that the white man had not yet hunted this region, it still an animal paradise. The animals were not shy, just curious.

As the sun sunk, the western sky was a golden streak across the horizon. As the last light waned, the scouts returned. The column had halted in a deep arroyo to camp for the night. Already, the wind had risen; it had a tinge of dampness, moisture from the sea where it had originated. The deep riverbed afforded some protection, but still it howled driving sand before it, unpleasant and making everyone irritable.

Werner and Jurgen sat in two folding camp chairs around a small fire, shielded by an expanse of bush along the arroyo bank. Philippe approached and squatted down on his haunches within a yard or two of the men. Jurgen passed him a water bottle. Philippe drank long, screwed the cap on, and only spoke once Jurgen had taken the bottle.

"We have found him; he is only a few miles ahead. He's still alone—there are no Hereros. The wagons move very slowly, with difficulty. I'm waiting for Joseph – he scouted far ahead and towards the southeast. We thought we may find the Hereros and decided to send him; he knows this area well. We think they must be near."

Both men agreed; the Hereros had to be near, dos Santos could not travel much further with the wagons.

It was well after nine when Joseph silently entered the camp, leading his horse. Philippe rose from where he was seated to greet him, and both men stood in deep conversation. They finally approached the officers.

"He's found the Hereros, they are camped at least ten miles from here. There are more than fifty men on horses – all armed. They also have fresh horses with them," Philippe said, lowering his head. Then completely out of character, he added his concern and a warning. "It is a large force. They are careful, they have made only one small fire."

The two men looked at each. Werner shrugged his shoulders, leaving it to Jurgen to make a decision.

"Well, they will meet up with dos Santos tomorrow," Jurgen said. "There's not much we can do now. It's too dark and there is no moon. The terrain is too dangerous to make any attempt to attack at night."

"Be sure, the Hereros will be in the saddle at first light and will be with him before we can attack. We don't want to be badly positioned when the Hereros attack, we need to choose the spot," Werner countered.

Jurgen frowned. He did not agree. He wanted to initiate the attack at first light and hopefully deal dos Santos a crushing blow before the Hereros arrived.

"Mestre, he is camped in the mouth of a small gorge he must pass through. This will be easy to defend. He is sure to put sentries on the hills," Philippe interjected, humbly bowing and looking away, clearly contrite for being so bold as to interrupt.

Jurgen spoke adamantly.

"We attack at dawn. The Maxim must be placed on an elevated position so that it can cover us should the Hereros attack. I want everybody mounted up and ready to ride by first light."

The word spread. The troops checked their kit before turning in, as there would be no time in the morning.

The soldiers broke camp, their horses saddled up and ready to depart at the first sign of daybreak; they actually began to move out while it was still dark. At the first touch of dawn, the troop broke into a canter, Jurgen wanting them to be upon dos Santos before he and his men realized what was happening. This was not to be. Dos Santos' sentries alerted their camp to the approaching column when still a mile or two away, immediately firing shots into the air, their prearranged signal of approaching danger.

Dos Santos had foreseen the possibility of such an attack and prepared to deal with such an eventuality. He had the wagons drawn across the mouth of the gorge as an additional precaution, and his men took cover behind these, with their horses and other animals deeper in the gorge, protected from gunfire.

Jurgen was not about to attempt to overwhelm dos Santos with a charge on horseback, his men riding into a curtain of rifle fire. He called a halt and the troops dismounted, spreading out over the ridges that overlooked the river. They took up position on the skyline giving themselves a view of the campsite below. However, as soon as the enemy perceived movement on the skyline, backlit by the dawn, they opened fire. If the Hereros were approaching, they would hear that dos Santos was under attack.

"We've got to know what those bastards are going to do. Get Philippe and one other to skirt the camp and find a lookout position, so that we can be warned where and when the Hereros will approach. "

Jurgen called a sergeant over and sent him off to find Philippe.

Sporadic gunfire continued. The range was excessive, at least five hundred yards, but still the occasional shot rang out.

"God, an outright charge against their camp will be too costly. Dos Santos knows that, he'll just sit and wait for the Hereros to arrive. We have to think of something else. We can't cross the ridge into the open; they'll massacre us. Order the men to stop shooting; except for our snipers, they're only to shoot if something moves. Let's pin him down. I want to see what the Hereros are going to do," Jurgen ordered.

Philippe soon returned.

"The Hereros have already entered the gorge—they should be with dos Santos any moment now. They've left a rearguard. There must be about a hundred of them. Also, I saw there are a few pools of water at the end of the river."

Jurgen swung round to face Werner.

"Christ! With water they can stay in there as long as they like."

"I'm wondering what's going to happen now. He's actually delivered the rifles – I'm mean, he's not going to carry on into SudwestAfrika, he'll want to head back," Werner spat angrily. "The deal is done, or what do you think?"

"You could be right. All he has to do is abandon the wagons and ride. We'll have to go after the Hereros to get the rifles; that's not his problem anymore."

"Well, my orders are explicit – apprehend dos Santos, and that's what I'm going to do if he makes a break for it," Werner said his voice fierce, his facial expression hard and determined. "I'm going to hunt the bastard down."

"Listen Werner, we can't split up the troop, there're just too many Hereros. We have to stop the rifles first and then hunt him down – we can't do both simultaneously if they split up."

"I've got to . . ."

"Enough!" Jurgen shouted, interrupting him. "The rifles first, that's an order!"

Seething, hardly able to control his anger, Werner stalked away towards the ridge which would give him a view of the camp. He had no choice; Zietzmann had placed Jurgen in command.

"Hauptmann von Dewitz!" Jurgen shouted. "Get back here immediately!"

Werner stopped in mid-stride, in two minds as to whether to obey.

"You heard me, Werner," Jurgen said menacingly.

He did an about-face and returned to stand before Jurgen, snapping to attention in front of the officer.

"Get off your high horse, that's not necessary. Calm down; I promise, you'll get your shot at dos Santos one way or another, but we cannot break up the troop yet. Right now, the rifles are the most important item. The Hereros cannot get to use these. You and I have to cooperate and remain unified."

"Jawohl, Herr Rittmeister!" Werner said loudly, unable to suppress his sarcasm. He clicked his heels in a parade ground salute.

Jurgen looked at him with a slight smile on his face, and then spoke quietly, intent on having the last word.

"Herr Hauptman, just fuck off."

. Werner did not consider it prudent to respond!

Werner's anger slowly evaporated. His friend was right—stopping the guns was imperative.

"Ok, now that you are thinking clearly, this is what we're going to do. I want you to take about thirty men, all mounted, and prepare a cavalry charge. You'll have to move to the other side of the gorge. I'll take command of the rest and with Feldwebel Wirtz and his Maxim machinegun crew, we'll start to harass those behind the wagons."

"What do you think they will do then?'

"I don't know—I don't think the machine gun will flush them out, but I'm hoping that the Hereros will at least split, some of them coming up the gorge to support dos Santos, making any charge on the rear a lot easier if it is not so heavily defended."

In order to avoid a downward trajectory which made aiming the machine difficult to aim and operate, Feldwebel Wirtz insisted that the crew manhandle the Maxim down to the riverbed, where they positioned the gun behind a small buttress of rocks. This turned out to be a dangerous task. Dos Santos, seeing the gun and realizing what the Schutztruppe intended, ordered his men to concentrate rifle fire on the gun crew. The bullets ricocheted off the rocks, forcing the crew to take cover behind the buttress. The Schutztruppe on the ridges retaliated, laying down a barrage of covering fire. Finally the crew maneuvered the gun into position and returned fire, walking the shots towards the wagons. The heavy and unwieldy weapon chattered in short bursts, the bullets leaving a trail of spurting sand and flying rock fragments.

Philippe had left his companion on a high point overlooking the southern entrance of the gorge with instructions that should the Hereros start to enter the gorge he was to signal by waving his arms, as he was still clearly visible against the skyline.

Werner had proceeded to a point about a half mile from the entrance of the gorge, but ran into some resistance as the Hereros had left a few men keeping watch over the fresh horses they had brought, a lookout for any sneak attacks. Leaving three or four men to provide initial covering fire, Werner's men forced their reluctant horses down the slope further upstream; they then approached the men by walking their horses along the riverbed. The nervous rearguard opened fire when they were still well out of effective range, but immediately those troops left above the slope opened fire. This was Werner's signal to attack. The troop drew sabres and charged, the air rent by bloodcurdling screams and shouts that were magnified in the confines of the ravine. Werner led the charge, pistol drawn.

The combination of volleys from above with the sight of a group of screaming horsemen as wide as the river, charging up the riverbed with sabres flashing was a test for any opposing force's resolve. Confusion broke out in the Hereros' ranks and they panicked, abandoning their horses. Usually brave fighters, never shirking combat but returning bullet for bullet, they found cold steel an entirely different matter! They had an abject fear of hand-to-hand combat. They fled towards their main troop, hopefully still stationed at the entrance to the gorge.

The German forces now had the enemy pinned down.

Werner left only four men overlooking the gorge, and with the rest walked the horses forward towards the lip of the gorge, expecting to encounter rifle fire at any moment. Sporadic shots greeted them, and they dismounted and took cover. He took stock of his situation; he had lost four men, two killed and two wounded. Two men had accompanied the wounded to the rear, further depleting his strength. The Hereros had established a half-moon defence around the entrance to the gorge, and they were well-concealed behind rocks and boulders, almost impossible to flush out with any direct action. His troops also took up a defensive position, similarly protected from any assault. It seemed to be stalemate.

Leaving his troop under the command of a Feldwebel, he returned to Jurgen and reported his current situation.

"Well, at least we have them bunched up and appear to have the upper hand, but if they initiate a combined charge towards the rear, I doubt whether your men will hold; we need to give you additional support. Let's look at our options."

"Correct me if I'm wrong," Werner said. "but we are here primarily to stop the rifles and get dos Santos, not take on the Herero force while he escapes with the consignment – right?"

Jurgen nodded.

"If we attack your end, that is the wagon end, with a near full force, they would have to retreat into the gorge, abandoning the wagons and the rifles, or so I would imagine. At least we would have accomplished part of our objective. Do you agree?"

"You're right, but dos Santos could also retreat with the Hereros. But wait, I've just thought of something. He's not going stay with them for long –he'll want to get back across the border. He won't want to stay here – too dangerous, there's safety for him in Angola."

"Right. So?"

The two officers stood in the shade of a large rock overhang. Jurgen withdrew a tin from his tunic pocket and offered Werner a cheroot. They lit up.

Jurgen stared into the distance at the entrance to the gorge. Without turning around, he spoke.

"You know what he's going to do? They'll break open the crates and distribute the weapons and ammunition amongst the men. At least that way they'll get most of them out. We have to attack soon! A full frontal attack with our whole force on the wagons, leave the rear open so that the Hereros can make their escape; if that assists dos Santos, well, too bad. At least, we'll have the rifles and ammunition."

That did not suit Werner – he had to get dos Santos. His friend read his mind.

"If he gets away, I'll give you a good portion of my men so that you can pursue him while I'll take care of the rifles etc. What do you say to that?"

"Ok." That was all he was going to get – it was his best option. "All right, let's do it!"

Jurgen called his sergeants together and outlined his plan. They recalled all the men from the other end of the gorge, leaving an escape route for the Hereros, hoping they would take it once a full attack on the wagons started.

Although now reinforced by a number of Hereros who had come through the gorge, the defence perimeter created by dos Santos could only take a limited number of men. An onslaught from above and both sides of the river, compounded by concentrated machine gun fire would be more than he could resist for long. The only alternative was retreat and regroup. They tried breaking open the crates and handing the rifles through to the rear, but Jurgen's snipers, with particular orders to be on the lookout for precisely that, picked off those attempting to hand rifles down a line. The plan was abandoned and the wagons retreated into the gorge where they were safe from rifle and machinegun fire.

Word arrived from the scouts that the enemy was emerging from the gorge's upper end. Jurgen ordered that no attack was to be initiated against them. To engage in a fight in the open would be too dangerous as the enemy was numerically stronger: fighting them in the gorge would be no better than a standoff.

"Rather allow them to escape to fight another day, provided we have possession of the rifles and ammunition," he explained.

The Schutztruppe soon overran the wagons. Most rifles were accounted for, as the enemy had managed to salvage only about a dozen. The Maxim had wreaked havoc: the wagons were badly shot-up, the timbers shattered and riddled with holes. It was questionable as to whether they would make it back to Ondongua.

The Hereros did not flee, but took up position on the other side of the gorge, placing men on the ridges from where they could engage any approaching force from a distance. They knew that in the open they were numerically stronger. Neither force dared move troops through the gorge, both adversaries ensured that the passage was blocked.

The spare horses taken from the Hereros were hitched to the wagons and despatched, retracing their steps to the border where they would go on to Ondongua via the mission. The main troop of Schutztruppe was to shadow the wagons and ensure that the Hereros did not carry out any sneak attacks. Only when they were out of danger did Jurgen split the force, retaining twenty men to escort the wagons while the rest together with the Maxim and its crew were assigned to Werner to continue the conflict with dos Santos and his motley band of Kunehamas and Hereros.

Akai, the leader of the main Herero troop sat under the stunted thorn tree on the banks of the dried river, cautiously watching a seething dos Santos sitting opposite him. Things had not gone well at all. The Germans had the rifles. The question was who would pay. Akai looked at the fat man sucking on the broken-off pipe-stem, now only a stub in his mouth, through which he blew an occasional large cloud of evil-smelling tobacco smoke. He despised the white man, especially this fat pig opposite him; he only sold rifles to the Hereros for the money – nothing else. Akai knew him for what he was, a cruel, insensitive man who pillaged and murdered and sent other black men into slavery. Unfortunately, the Hereros needed him – for rifles, ammunition, and explosives. This was the only reason he showed the man any respect.

"We should not have abandoned the wagons!" dos Santos said with savage irritation.

"I know, but was else was there to do?" Akai calmly replied, hoping that the white man would behave; he would not allow him to speak down to him.

Dos Santos realized he best be circumspect and hold his tongue, the Hereros could kill him and his men them right there and then and no-one would ever know what had happened.

"Those rifles are lost; we'll never get them back. You must go back to Angola and arrange another shipment," Akai said.

"I know, but there is something wrong somewhere. The Germans seem to know every time we cross the border. Even when we go by sea, they are waiting for us. I'm even having problems in Angola – there, our assets are being stolen. There's a leak somewhere."

"It's that woman of yours. When I was in Huambo I saw she was not happy to be with you," Akai said, wondering why any woman would want to spend time with this man anyway – he was grotesque.

"She's gone!" Dos Santos did want to go into detail. He looked at the black man opposite him, the man's thin face, the black frost of his tightly curled hair touched with grey, his clothes loose on his frame, the hardship of perpetual conflict and the lack of proper food etched in his face. Still the eyes burned with a stern resolve and fire; dos Santos knew this was not a man to be crossed.

"Just as well," Akai sighed, rising and replacing the battered khaki officer's cap he wore, his only sign of rank. "I will now leave with my men and you take your men and head back to the river. You let me know in the usual way – I'll be ready for the next shipment—with your payment."

Akai knew that they could never win the war, but Hannu Zeraua, their chief was right: to give in to the Germans was to give in to slavery. He thought back to the status his family had enjoyed before the Germans came, when peace reigned and all were happy, their wealth reflected in their vast herds of cattle. No, rather die fighting. This was his people's land. The Germans had come with their ships, their trains, built towns, tore up the land and built farms. They never asked for land, they just took it. He could still see the disbelief and fear in the eyes of the farmers they had beaten and hacked to death in the beginning; they had never believed that those they had treated so abominably would rise up against them. 'Did they really think we would just let them go on treating us as they did?' he thought. Even the Portuguese: they were just as bad, sometimes even worse.

Dos Santos watched the tall African walk to his horse; a young black boy, who could not have been more than fourteen or fifteen, held the reins.

"My youngest son, Jaakko," Akai proudly announced, proprietarily placing his hand on the boy's shoulder.

Dos Santos merely nodded, forcing a smile. The boy meant nothing to him, and he was more concerned with his own thoughts, trying not to reveal that stomach cramps plagued him, brought on by the flood of recent disasters. The loss of money was the most serious: he had other shareholders. The mere thought of de Mello and Batista made him cringe and clench his teeth in frustration. Then there were the ramifications of this latest escapade gone wrong, and the consequences he was yet to face. He knew the Germans would now pursue him relentlessly; he would need to be extremely careful.

His scouts had confirmed that the Germans had left, retracing the wagon trail back to the river. He knew they would turn eastwards once the terrain improved, leaving the way clear for him to make an escape. He would delay his departure until he knew they were a good distance from the trail he would take north. Only then would be safe for him to leave.

Werner thought the machine gun would be of little support, as it not easily moved from position to position. Dos Santos' men were all on horseback, they would be in and out of range within seconds. He did not believe dos Santos fool enough to follow the shortest route to the border. The river would soon or had already subsided, and he would then able to cross at any of various points. Which would the man choose? Werner thought the best route would be across the flood plain that fed the Etosha Pan, as the terrain was a lot easier. Still, he strung scouts out across the approach to the river over a wide area, stationed at least twenty miles from the river at intervals of a few miles. He instructed them to merely observe and report, but ensure that they were not observed.

For four days they waited, before a scout stationed on the eastern side reported dos Santos on the move. Werner recalled all the scouts and they moved off towards the river. Philippe indicated that it seemed highly likely that dos Santos was riding in the direction of a ford on the border where the Kunene suddenly turns northwards into Angola; this would be one of the first fords to become passable as the river subsided. Not having much of a start on the gunrunners, Werner hastily placed his men in a defensive half-moon circle around the access to the ford. Meanwhile, he established that river had subsided, but was still dangerous, although men on horseback could cross. He chose a clearing at the ford to place the machine gun, which would allow it to traverse a wide arc of fire.

As dos Santos approached the river, he sent two men ahead to reconnoitre the ford. He halted his column, but allowed no-one to dismount; he was not discarding the possibility of the Germans trying to ambush him; they knew he had to cross somewhere.

The two scouts discovered Werner's fresh tracks. Stealthily approaching, blending in with the bush, it did not take them long to spot a soldier in blue grey; they cautiously backed off to report to dos Santos. They had no idea of numbers but knew a reception awaited any who was fool enough to approach the river here.

The Germans never saw the scouts.

Werner fumed with impatience. His scouts had spotted dos Santos and his troop approaching, but what had happened? Where were they? He called his cavalry sergeants and scouts together.

"Something gone wrong, I'm sure they've spotted us."

"Mestre, it must have been the horses, they will have found the spoor, they are very careful. Maybe they'll cross somewhere else on the river, maybe more west," Philippe said.

"Feldwebel Arends, take ten men and ride west. If you find them, avoid engaging them. I'm sure they'll probably find you first. They know we are here," he said grimly, and then turned to the others. "I want the rest of you men to maintain a state of readiness. At the first sounds of gunfire, we're going to their assistance. All troops are to standby their horses, ready to mount at an instants notice. Feldwebel Schwiegers can take ten men and protect the machine gun here."

Arends rode off with his men, maintaining a well drawn-out single file, ensuring they would not be bunched up in the event of an ambush. The only sounds were those of the horses.

The men were visibly tense; they could no longer surprise the enemy, they knew they had been spotted.

As dos Santos approached the river, he swung west, following its course but keeping parallel about a mile away. They soon came upon a tributary; flowing towards the river, it was now a mere trickle. It had gouged a donga in the flat terrain, about twenty feet deep, with near vertical sides. He ordered his men across the donga to take up position along the bank of the stream, well hidden behind whatever was available. He was convinced the Germans were following and would approach from the east. They would have to cross the donga to get to him.

Feldwebel Arends was not a newcomer to the colony. Years back, he had already shed that ruddy, burnt complexion associated with all military men arriving in the colonies for the first time and making their acquaintance with the African sun. His skin had taken on a light mahogany hue, no longer soft-looking. He sported an imperial waxed moustache, not too ostentatious, and prominent crow's feet in the corner of his eyes from squinting into the sun, the folds radiating white streaks if he lifted his eyebrows. The hair visible below his campaign hat revealed speckles of grey; there was no doubt that he was a veteran of many campaigns. He knew the bush, and he knew his adversary. Once they hid, it was near impossible to see them before they saw you, and because of this knowledge, alongside him rode his most trusted Askari, Moses, a Damara man with incredible eyesight and knowledge of concealment in the bush.

"*Oubaas, das ist gefährlich!*" the scout said quietly, reigning in his horse.

The sergeant stopped. If his scout said it was dangerous, he knew he had to listen.

"What do you see?"

"I don't see anything. But I can feel something."

The man's uncanny intuition had proved itself before. This was a good time to heed it. The sergeant signalled for his troop to dismount, leaving the horses in the care of the youngest.

The noon sun was blistering hot, the contrast between shadow and sunlight severe, making it difficult to distinguish any shape in the deep shadows of the stunted trees and bushes. The men took shelter deep in the shadows, rifles at the ready. Through the foliage, they could vaguely make out the depression before them, which the scout said was a small river. The scout indicated with a raised hand that the sergeant should hold his position, and slowly crawled forward. He removed his Askari hat and held this in his hand; he had left his tunic with the sergeant and his upper body was bare. About a hundred yards from the stream he raised his hat on a stick just above the bush line, moving it slowly from side to side. A shot rang out. The bullet showered him with leaves and twigs and he immediately hugged the ground.

Werner heard the distinct echo of the shot as it rolled over the plain, and immediately ordered his men to mount. They soon covered the distance to the soldier tending the sergeant's horses. Here, they all dismounted and cautiously made their way forward until they found the sergeant and his men concealed in the bush. The sergeant and scout quickly briefed Werner on the current situation.

"Is there anywhere near here where dos Santos can cross the river?" Werner asked.

"Yes, we are directly opposite it. If you go directly north from here you'll find it."

"I'm sure that's where he intends to cross. Sergeant, send some men around them and block off their route to the south so he won't be able to fall back. I want to persuade him to go north towards the river. I'm going to advance on him, leaving the north open and allow him to get close to the ford."

"*Mestre*, he'll escape!" Philippe said with surprise.

"No, he won't. Send a scout to lead Feldwebel Schwiegers and his Maxim to this ford."

The black man smiled in understanding.

Werner knew it would take the machine gun crew a few hours to get their weapon in position. Meanwhile, he made the men wait, silently cursing the inactivity, not understanding why their captain did not launch an attack. They knew the enemy was just across the river.

It was well after five in the afternoon that he ordered the attack, moving the men forward to the river. The moment the gunrunners discerned movement in the bush, they opened fire, with volley upon volley pinning the troopers down. The troopers returned fire, but neither side did any damage, as everyone was well hidden. Certain that both the gun and his detachment in the west were in position by now, Werner ordered the men to advance until they had taken up position along the banks of the stream and could clearly see the opposite side of the donga.

He listened to the exchange of fire, pondering the situation. Suddenly his face lit up, and he smiled at the sergeant.

"Sergeant, have you noticed we've got the wind at our backs? Have them men tie some kindling together to make a few torches and set the bush alight on the opposite side, even if they have to go slightly south to avoid the gunfire. Let's see what the bastard does when he see a bushfire racing towards him. May be we can roast his bloody hide!"

Smoke soon begun to spiral from the opposite bank as the fire quickly took hold, fanned by the wind. Suddenly, with a roar it blossomed into a wide swathe of flame, clouds of black-grey smoke billowing into the air, the wind driving the fire line before it. It was now an out-of-control bushfire. They could not see the gunrunners because of the smoke, but the fire moved steadily in a westerly direction; the only escape route open to dos Santos was north, towards the river.

Dos Santos wavered. For some inexplicable reason, the Germans had not blocked the route north. He couldn't go west; he would have to continuously retreat before the bushfire to avoid being engulfed. Any escape route south would only lead them further into German territory. It had to be north, it was the only option. He ordered the men to mount up and they galloped north. He knew the Germans would soon be in pursuit. What bothered him was what awaited them at the river. Surely, they had sent a troop to cover that escape route, but how many men did they have? They had broken their force up into three contingents and he knew approximately where these had taken up position. There could not be that many men at the river. Still, he sent a few scouts ahead, while his main troop slowed down.

As the scouts broke through into the clearing, the Maxim opened up, the bullets raking the horses and scouts with little spurts of dust. Horses collapsed, their riders tumbling like limp sacks from their saddles.

"*Dummkopf!*" Feldwebel Schwiegers shouted, leaning over and cuffing the errant gunner behind the Maxim across the head, knocking his campaign hat off. "Idiot, I told you to wait! Now they know we have a machine gun here."

Dos Santos had heard the bark of the machine gun and reined in the rest of his men.

"Split up!" he shouted. "Towards the river, skirt the gun, keep out of range. When you get to the bank, go back along the water's edge to the ford. The machine gun won't be able to cover both flanks. As soon as you can, cross!"

Feldwebel Schwiegers realized his predicament. He could cover only one side under fire; he chose the east to at least keep his own escape route open. The other troops concentrated their fire on the west, where the fordable portion of the river was quite wide, a stretch of rapids where the water flowed rapidly over numerous ledges of stone that formed the bedrock.

Suddenly, from the south, Werner and his men galloped into the clearing. Within seconds, he had absorbed what was happening. Dos Santos and his men were in the river, waist deep in the water and slowly picking their way across the stones and boulders over which the river raged, using their horses to shield themselves. Accurate rifle fire had taken its toll; already he had lost a few men and horses.

As Werner watched, dos Santos' horse collapsed, struck by a bullet. The river immediately began to pull it down stream. Dos Santos lost his grip and the water immediately swept him off his feet. Werner grabbed hold of the nearest horse's reins and swung into the saddle. Philippe and a few other troopers followed suit. They raced along the riverbank watching dos Santos struggling in the river, trying desperately to swim to the opposite bank. Already he was being carried away by the strong current into deep water. Dos Santos had realized that he would not be able to cross; his only option was to stay in the centre and hope that he could outpace the horsemen on the bank, whose passage was often obstructed by the dense riverine bush. Ahead, the river made a sharp turn to the right, and the current was drawing him to the left close to the bank, which rose sheer about fifteen feet from the water's edge.

Werner raced ahead. As he got to the edge, he flung himself from the saddle and as dos Santos swept past no more than twenty-five feet away, treading water in the current, he dived in, swimming strongly towards the gunrunner. He was determined to get his man. As he approached the gunrunner, dos Santos turned to face him, a knife appearing in his hand. Werner dived deep into the murky water, swimming underwater beneath dos Santos' kicking feet, to grab his legs and pull him under. Both men broke the surface, dos Santos coughing and spluttering as Werner lunged forward and grabbed the hand holding the knife. Dos Santos' huge fist caught the side of Werner's face, nearly knocking him out, but somehow he managed to keep a grip on the man's wrist. He opened his eyes to see dos Santos' startled look of recognition.

"De Almeida—you! You're a German spy, I should have known. *Merda!* I'm going to kill you!"

The man was incredibly strong. Werner realized he would not be able to overpower him. With his free hand, he struggled to draw his Parabellum from its holster but before the automatic could clear leather, dos Santos pushed him under, sitting on him to drown him. He had the man's wrist in a vice-like grip but knew he could not hold on for much longer – he had to get air. He let the automatic slip from his grip, his lungs screaming for relief. He fought to break to the surface. His world was changing, he was in a dark tunnel and he could see a circle of light receding at the end. He still had dos Santos' wrist in a death-grip, but he was no longer even aware of it. As if in a dream he became aware that the gunrunner's hold on him had slackened, and the knife was falling from his grasp. In blind panic, Werner kicked, driving his body upwards, his mouth open, sucking in huge gasps of air as his head broke the surface. As he retched, he looked dazedly at his opponent, amazed to see him unconscious, his head lolling in the water, his dark curls plastered to his forehead. Werner couldn't understand it. Then he saw Philippe a few feet away in the water, beaming at him with that usual huge white-toothed grin.

"My God, you were just in time, he was going to kill me. I could no longer hold him off. Thank you!" Werner smilingly spluttered. "I didn't know you could swim."

"*Mestre*, there's a lot you don't know about me."

Between the two of them, they propped dos Santos up, keeping his mouth and nose above the water, letting the current take them along the riverbank.

"Mestre, we better get out of the water soon, there are a few small waterfalls close by."

"I hear you, there's another turn in the river ahead. The men must throw us a rope," Werner replied, waving his hand at the men ashore who were keeping pace with them.

Philippe caught the rope and tied it to dos Santos' midriff, and the men ashore hauled them in.

Dos Santos was slowly coming around, gagging and spluttering.

"What did you hit him with? God, he was nearly dead!" Werner asked his *cavalherico*.

"I had a *knopkierie*, but I lost it in the river."

"A *knopkierie*, what's that?"

"A wooden club, made from a small tree trunk with a root attached at one end. The root is whittled until it looks like a ball. You did want him alive, didn't you?"

"I suppose, but if he had died it wouldn't have mattered," Werner replied.

"What about the rest of his men?" a sergeant asked.

"There can't be many of them, your men picked off quite a few in the water. Let them go, without him they're nothing. You're probably wasting your time chasing them; they've long disappeared or crossed the river."

Dos Santos started to remonstrate with him loudly in Portuguese.

"You won't see the month out, you crook! Either my men or the Hereros will kill for taking the diamonds!"

Werner swung on him, his expression reflecting total surprise and curiosity.

"What diamonds? I know you wanted to pay me in diamonds, but I never took any diamonds. But I'm now curious, where are you getting these from? I'm sure the Portuguese government would like to know too," Werner insisted, not missing the look of concern that crept into dos Santos' face.

Dos Santos realized he had made a mistake and clammed up, realizing that it was possible Werner did not know about the mine or where the diamonds had come from. He shrugged his shoulders, remaining silent, looking away, implying that he had no more to say.

"It doesn't matter. You won't be selling any more guns. They'll hang you and I want to watch you swing, you bastard! And I'll catch the rest of your cronies as well."

"It's all falling into place, it's you, and Major de Sousa, isn't it?" dos Santos' eyes suddenly widened. "Merda! It's that fuckin' bitch, she showed you the guns! Maria, that bitch!"

Werner ignored him, calling for four men to tie dos Santos hand and foot.

"And if he tries to escape, shoot him," he said.

CHAPTER FOURTEEN

Werner's column arrived at the mission Olukonda in the late afternoon, just as the sun was about to dip behind the horizon, casting long shadows across a quadrangle already in shade. The mission was a mass of soldiers, all the different detachments having arrived almost simultaneously. They had pitched camp just a short way from the buildings, near to the corrals, and their campfires were already burning.

He dismounted to see a grinning Jurgen walking towards him. His friend put his arm round his shoulder.

"Well done, my friend, you have him at last. I knew you could do it!"

"No, not me, Herr Rittmeister, we! And don't forget Philippe, he should get a medal!" Werner replied with emphasis. "Anyway, without your help, we would never have got him. Watch out, he's like an eel; we'll have to watch him carefully until we hand him over. We've got to find somewhere to keep him for the night."

"Don't worry, I've found just the place. When I heard he was captured, I started to look. The good pastor, rather reluctantly, I may add, has volunteered his creamery – it has only one door and thick walls to keep the room cool. He won't get out of there."

"Well, put four men around it at all times – good men."

"Don't worry, I've it in hand. Incidentally, the pastor has again invited the officers to dine with him and his staff. I took the liberty of saying you would be delighted, as I know Dorothea will be there."

"What a good friend you are," Werner replied facetiously.

Jurgen laughed. "Paulo is out of danger, but it will be a while before he can leave the hospital. Louis is making excellent progress. Already he can walk, but only doubled over, as the stitches have not yet been removed. Your Portuguese friend is waiting to congratulate you!"

Dorothea was not in the hospital. Apparently, a complicated childbirth demanded her attention at the nearby maternity clinic, or so they told him. Louis grinned at them both from his bed, naked to the waist, his stitches proudly displayed. As they shook hands, Werner told Louis about dos Santos.

"Listen, *compadre*, he knows of your involvement with me, and has sworn to get us. Not that I'm worried, he'll swing—and soon. But if word gets to de Mello and Batista, Benguela could become quite dangerous. He accused me of stealing his diamonds. I feigned ignorance and questioned him. He quickly shut up. I didn't let on that we knew where the mine was."

"What's this all about?" Jurgen asked.

"Listen, friend, you better tell our friend here the whole story, I wouldn't want him to think we are hiding something from him," Louis laughed. "He's one of us!"

Both men watched Jurgen carefully as Werner explained that there were actually three pouches of diamonds, that he had only handed in one and that they had decided to split the other two pouches between the three of them and the two black servants.

"Werner, tell him that nobody knows about the two pouches of diamonds – nobody!"
Werner did so.

Jurgen kept them in suspense, his expression unreadable as they anxiously waited to see how he would react. If he complained, they would have to fabricate some excuse and belatedly hand the diamonds over to Major Zietzmann.

Finally, Jurgen looked up, staring first at Werner then Louis.

"I think that's a bloody good idea!" he said, his cackle reverberating through the small room.

"You bastard," Werner said, relieved.

The tension broken, they all shook hands, sealing their agreement.

"Where are the pouches?" Jurgen asked.

"I've got them hidden. We'll have to do something with them in Windhuk. Ok, back to Louis' problem, what are we going to do with him? If we send him back to Angola, we could be sending him to his death. Colonel Batista will be waiting for him. God knows what he has already found out."

"Let's wait until he recovers fully. We'll let Zietzmann decide. No doubt, he'll contact General Diaz in Luanda – let's wait, let both them wait."

"Christ! Not here in the middle of nowhere, I hope," Werner complained.

"No, no. As soon as they are able to travel, both Louis and Paulo are to leave for Windhuk. I'll get Zietzmann to arrange it."

Werner translated all for Louis, who nodded in agreement.

As they walked back to their tents, they passed a windmill continuously pumping water, keeping the reservoir filled to capacity. Neither Werner nor Jurgen had bathed for days and grabbing the opportunity, they stripped off their uniforms and plunged into the brick-built round reservoir. Jurgen produced a piece of soap, and they lathered themselves richly.

"Christ, I hope this doesn't supply the drinking water," Werner suddenly said.

"Who cares, a bit of soap has never killed anyone," Jurgen replied, chuckling before he immersed himself completely to wash of the soap suds.

"Are you men mad? How dare you swim in here? And all this soap. People have to drink this water! Get out immediately!" Pastor Haiddenon's red face stared at them over the rim, almost apoplectic, beside himself with fury.

Both men hesitated – they had no clothes on.

"Get out! Get out!"

Well, if that is what he wants, then that's what we'll to do, Werner thought and climbed out of the reservoir.

"Mein Gott! You haven't even got any clothes on!" the shocked pastor shouted.

The commotion had drawn Dorothea and the nurses to the porch, and when Werner climbed the bricked steps and emerged from the water in all his naked glory, there was a distinct ooh and several loud giggles. Only then did he look up, to see the women staring at him. Jurgen was right behind, cackling loudly; he covered his privates with his spread hands, finding the whole incident hilarious, especially when he saw the pastor avert his eyes and look away. The man looked like he was about to cry. The women, their hands covering their mouths, quickly turned away and retreated into the building, but not before all had seen the amusement on their faces.

"If anybody says anything about swinging . . ." Werner muttered.

That was just too much for Jurgen; he collapsed with his back against the reservoir, sliding down the side into a sitting position, bent over with laughter. Those of the troops who had seen the performance joined in until it seemed everybody was laughing, except the good pastor – he was still in a state of shock, his mouth hanging open.

Philippe handed each of them a large linen towel. He looked at Werner's nakedness and rolled his eyes exaggeratedly, screeching with laughter. The pastor walked away, mumbling under his breath, words like 'unbelievable, disgusting, no common decency, disgrace to the German officer corp' clearly audible.

"God, what a mess. I've haven't even said hello yet and here she sees me with my dick swinging, and never mind, her nurses as well. Christ! This is embarrassing."

"Actually, you're lucky, the water was warm. Can you imagine what she would've seen if the water had been cold?" Jurgen collapsed with laughter again.

"Why don't you just fuck off?" Werner retorted, realizing that there was nothing he could do. What was done, was done.

Cleaned up and neat, the two officers arrived at the mission's dining room. The mission staff were already standing behind their chairs waiting for them. He looked at Dorothea; she looked up fleetingly at him, and he caught his breath. Was she crying? She definitely had tears in her eyes. No, she was laughing quietly, as were all the other women! Not a few of them were giving them both furtive looks from under lowered brows.

The pastor rapped the table to get their attention.

"Enough! I insist that you all behave yourselves. That was an unfortunate incident and it is to be forgotten," he said pompously. "Do I need to remind you that this is a religious mission and you are all to behave like dignified people before I commence grace?"

A hush descended on the table as they were all suitably chastised.

It was wonderful to sit at a proper table and have a decent meal again. The conversation centered round the capture of the gunrunner, as all wanted to know how this had been achieved. The pastor gave strict instructions that none of the staff was to approach the creamery; the prisoner was an army matter. The pastor slowly regained his composure and eventually even managed to smile occasionally.

"What do you propose to do with the man," he asked wording the question badly, really meaning to ask where they would take him.

"He will hang," Jurgen said, before Werner could reply, adding that gunrunning carried the death penalty. The pastor blanched. The women were appalled. Werner kicked his friend under the table.

A long silence ensued.

"So, *Herr Hauptmann*, for how long will we have the pleasure of your company?" the pastor finally asked Werner.

"We'll leave in the morning for Ondongua," he replied. Nobody asked any further questions about the prisoner, all were aware that the troopers would take dos Santos with them.

After dinner, they congregated on the veranda, the men lighting cigars which the pastor had generously offered. Werner stood at the railing looking out at the night, blowing smoke into the light breeze, Dorothea standing next to him, furtively taking his hand.

"I suppose you have to go." Dorothea hid her disappointment; she had hoped he would stay a few days.

"I'm afraid so, we've got to get this man into proper custody before something goes wrong. There're still Hereros out there somewhere. Although I don't think they would come running to rescue him."

"When will I see you again?"

"I don't know." He squeezed her hand. "But I'm happy to be here with you again," he whispered.

She stepped closer until she could feel him against her side.

Werner looked around. Jurgen was talking to the nurses in German. Louis had joined them on the veranda, dressed in a gown, still bent double. He had finally settled down on a bench, and the pastor was conversing with him in broken Portuguese or Spanish: Werner wasn't sure which, but they seemed to understand each other.

"Let's get away from here," he said.

She nodded. They walked to the end of the landing, expecting someone to ask where they were going. No-one did.

Once around the corner, she led the way to her clinic, which was in a separate cluster of buildings. She produced a key and opened the examination room, pulling him in and closing the door. He stood there, expecting her to light a lamp; she did not. Instead she turned, stepped towards him and put her arms around his neck, drawing his face down and placing her open lips on his. They kissed passionately, their tongues probing, his hands grabbing her buttocks, drawing her to him. She moulded her body to his, and he felt the stirrings of arousal, as he became aware of her quickening breath and her pelvis and breasts pressing against him.

He opened the top buttons of her blouse and then let his lips slide down her cleavage.

"Mein lieber Gott!" she whispered in his ear.

He undid the rest, stripping her blouse off. Her eyes were closed, her head thrown back. He undid the cords of her corset, which voluntarily loosened, exposing the fullness of her breasts. He kissed them, taking a nipple into his mouth; it was hard and erect. She moaned.

She fumbled to undo his tunic, tugging at it to remove it, then kissed the scars and welts on his upper body. He could no longer contain himself. He swept her into his arms, carrying her to the large examination couch. He slid his hand under her skirt, her wetness amplifying his arousal. Urgently, he pulled off her skirt and underwear, then shed his own clothing. They lay on the couch, their bodies entwined, exploring each other, lost in ecstasy. Finally, he entered her.

Afterwards she lay next to him, her head on his chest, her fingers running through the curls of hair on his chest.

"We can't sleep here. We have to go, they'll wonder what happened," she said.

"I know."

Reluctantly they got up and dressed, touching each other repeatedly, as if they each needed reassurances.

The illicit half hour had felt like minutes. Sheepishly, they left the clinic, strolling to the corrals as if they were still taking a walk. The others were still on the porch. They walked round the complex and then leisurely approached the porch to join in the discussions. Nobody said anything about their absence.

They arrived at Ondongua without incident, glad to hand dos Santos over to the local garrison and Major Graf zu Dohner. It was now his task to ensure that the prisoner was delivered safely to Windhuk.

CHAPTER FIFTEEN

Louis rode in through the Benguela fort gates with Paulo trotting alongside, flanked by two Portuguese cavalrymen. The guards who manned the gates snapped a smart salute, which he nonchalantly returned. This was General Diaz's idea—arrive with aplomb; he believed that this would put Colonel Batista on the back foot.

Batista had been briefed, but given no details of the activities the General had supposedly required Louis to attend to or why the cloak-and-dagger mantle had been cast over these. The General had even apologized for the surreptitious manner in which he had availed himself of Louis' services. Apparently, this had appeased him somewhat.

Louis was quickly ushered through to Batista's office. This was no military office: the room was far too elegant, dominated by an exquisite, leather-topped, ornate desk with matching chairs. A bookcase on one side contained row upon row of books, while a sideboard took up the expanse of the other wall. A large silver tray contained various crystal decanters filled with an assortment of spirit. Alongside this was another, heavy with crystal glasses and tumblers. A huge portrait of Carlos I, King of Portugal, looked down from the whitewashed wall.

The Colonel did not bother to return Louis' formal salute.

"At ease, Major. Take a chair."

Louis sat, his feathered cap balanced on his lap.

"Your latest behaviour was certainly not conducive to a good inter-officer relationship. You must realize you are under my command, irrespective of what General Diaz now tells me. As I sit here, I cannot but question your loyalty," the General snapped, making sure his tone indicated who the superior officer was.

"Colonel, I must apologize, but this operation was already underway before your arrival. No disrespect was intended, but the General was adamant that I disclose nothing and when recalled to Luanda, the only option was to take leave of absence without permission. I assume the General has cleared this with you?"

"I understand, but I want an assurance from you that there will be no reoccurrence of such insubordination. Absence without permission I will not tolerate. It would seem the General has more than a passing interest in you, would you not say?"

The bastard's fishing, Louis thought. He chose to ignore the remark.

"Colonel, rest assured this will not be repeated."

"In that case, the matter is closed."

The Colonel opened the single file on his desk.

"I have a rather distressing matter here which I would like you to investigate. Three men were murdered on the trail from Huambo to Cacondo. At first, it was thought to be the Kunehamas, but we have since established that this was not the case. The men were merely killed, but nothing seems to have been taken. Of course, this is out of character if this was a racial attack or robbery."

Louis was uncomfortable; he hoped the Colonel could not read anything in his behaviour.

The Colonel slid the file over his desk.

"Here, study the file. If you have any questions take them up with Lieutenant Marques; he has been in charge of the investigations. He has been ordered to hand this over to you. I need you to find not only the perpetrators, but also the reason for the murders."

Louis stood, snapping a salute as he about-turned. Once outside, he breathed a quiet sigh of relief. Inside his own office, he asked Paulo for coffee and then sat down to study the contents of the file. The lieutenant appeared to have investigated the crime thoroughly. The names of the three men were recorded, with a note that two were degregados who had arrived in the colony three years ago on the same ship. It stated that the men had last been seen together two days before, in the town of Cacondo. Investigations had not been able to establish precisely what their business was in the town. The lieutenant incorrectly assumed that they were returning to Benguela after supporting the army with its retaliatory action against the Kunehamas. Louis knew this to be false. No mention was made of a mine in the Caconda vicinity or that they were possibly employed in the area. The closing remark mentioned that on their arrival in Benguela from Portugal, they had been employed for a year or two by Antonio dos Santos, a prominent trader in the Huambo district.

Louis sought out Lieutenant Marques, a young man in his mid twenties who had arrived in the colony six months before.

"Lieutenant, why were you given this to investigate?" Louis asked.

The question surprised the lieutenant.

"Well, I think it was because, at first it was thought to be an attack related directly to the rebellion and therefore an army matter, but I soon realised that this had other motives, as nothing had been stolen. The bastards would have ransacked the men's belongings, but nothing was touched. I put this to the Colonel, telling him that I thought this a matter for the Guardia. Strangely, he thought not: he ordered me to continue my investigations. "

"Interesting. What are your personal feelings about this, in strictest confidence, of course?" Louis enquired, raising a questioning eyebrow.

"Well, if this was a vendetta, these take a while to develop and word gets round. There was nothing like that. I thoroughly investigated the site. They were overwhelmed while they slept.

Something must have been taken from them or else why kill them? One of my Askaris heard a rumour about a mine, but we drew a blank there."

"Thank you, lieutenant; you've been very helpful."

Louis needed to know the mine's exact locality; this had also been requested by General Diaz.

"Paulo, can you take me back to where you found the mine?" he asked.

"I think so. But we must not go in uniform."

Louis obtained the largest detailed map of Angola he could find. Many areas had not yet been properly surveyed, but were just blank blotches on the map with no detail. Placing the map on the desk and turning it until he had aligned it to the compass, he showed Paulo where they stood in relation to Benguela and asked him to point out in which direction Caconda lay. A futile exercise; Paulo could not equate the map with real surroundings.

They would just have to go. Louis made arrangements for the trip saying that he personally wished to inspect the murder site, a normal request in the light of the investigations.

Having little else to do, Werner asked to accompany Louis in the search for Caconda. They decided they would meet on the trail where no suspicions would be aroused. They would travel as transport men, each owning a wagon loaded with general merchandise that they intended to sell in Caconda. Paulo and Philippe would accompany them, assisted by two additional oxen men.

Three weeks later, they entered Caconda. By now both men sported unkempt beards, their clothes were dirty and everything was coated with dust. The black men wore only their loincloths and satchels, their feet shod in rawhide sandals. No-one had washed since leaving town, and they all generated that smell of stale sweat that's guaranteed to keep anyone with a degree of refinement at more than arm's length!

Caconda was typical of a frontier town, consisting of one wide dusty main street sandwiched between a few hastily erected mud-brick buildings, sheds and huts. Large acacia trees grew between the buildings and along the road. The place was crowded with Africans, most of them refugees from the civil war looking to the local garrison to protect them. Only a few whites were visible. Several wagons and carriages plied the streets as did a number of horsemen, but for the most, the inhabitants were on foot, congregating around the large trading stores. There were no hotels, although the two cantinas did a good trade. One of these, "The Red Hornet" belonged to a close relative of the grande madam, as Louis put it, of Manchatas, the brothel in Benguela, and Louis persuaded her to give him a letter of introduction. If that was what it could be called, really it was no more than a note, merely stating that she would be happy if the owner, her brother, would assist his nephew in any way possible.

The two men walked into the cantina, dust flying as they stomped their feet and beat their hats against their high boots. The barman turned round as they took up position at the bar; he was huge, with hands like hams and forearms like an ordinary man's thighs. A white grubby apron was tied round his waist.

"Bueno, gentlemen. What'll it be?" he asked.

"A large jug of beer, the largest you've got!" Werner said.

The barman guffawed.

"You two men could never finish my largest jug," he said jovially, laughing at his own joke.

"All right, enough beer for two really thirsty men and also for our servants outside; they've worked hard."

"A kind gesture, sir. They'll appreciate it."

With astounding alacrity, a large jug appeared with two glass beer mugs. Werner poured, immediately downing half the glass. The beer was surprisingly cold and refreshing.

"Do you know where I can find Senhor Sardinha?" Louis asked the barman as he did the same.

"That's me," the man said, pointing a finger as thick as a sausage at his chest. "And why are you looking for me?"

Louis pulled the note from his pocket and slid it across the counter. The barman's face broke into a smile as he read it.

"Heh, heh, so you are my nephew!"

The man stretched his hand over the bar, and both men vigorously shook hands. Werner winced at the strength of his grip.

"Well, do you see my sister often?"

Louis didn't know what to say.

"Yes, we meet there often," he eventually replied.

"You only meet there?" the barman exclaimed, his eyes round with surprise. "I would think you more than just meet there – she has the most beautiful women working for her. I wish . . ." He stopped and looked around to make sure he could not be overheard. "I wish we had some of them here!"

Louis just smiled.

"Okay, what can I do for you?"

"We need somewhere to park our wagons and feed our oxen. We need to buy fodder for the animals and food for ourselves."

"You can do all that at the back where I live with my wife. The grounds are big, there are corrals and water and I have two huts you can use. The fee is reasonable, your meals you can have here. I'll arrange for fodder to be brought by the local hostler."

The barman mumbled some figure in escudos that he thought to be a fair fee. Louis paid, then bent closer.

"I have a lot of questions," he said, "but I don't need others to know I'm asking, if you know what I mean. My aunt said that I could rely on you to be discrete."

"For my nephew and my sister, but of course. She lent me the money to start this cantina."

"Maybe we could sit down after supper. We'd like to buy you a drink or two."

So it was arranged.

The four servants ate huge meals, massive pieces of meat and cooked maize smothered in rich gravy. This they washed down with two large jugs of beer, the envy of the other not-so-fortunate servants in the yard.

Philippe and Paulo then left and mingled with the crowds, trying to get a feel for the place, for what the latest gossip was, where people worked and what the chances were of making money. They returned that evening at six and reported back to Werner and Louis.

They had hit pay dirt. There was the odd murmuring of a mine and of diamonds.

"Can you take us there tomorrow?" Louis asked.

"Yes, but we must leave in the afternoon and move up to the mine in the dark so that we can look at it from the edge of the bush when the sun rises – then we will not move again until it's dark, otherwise we may be seen," Philippe cautioned.

That evening they finished a bottle of the best scotch whiskey with Senhor Sardinha, compliments of Werner.

"So, do you know Antonio dos Santos?"

"Yes – he's been here a few times. He's the biggest trader in Huambo."

"Do you know what he does here?"

"I don't know, but he does visit Don Pereira, he's got the biggest plantation and ranch in this area, a very wealthy man."

The barman lit a cigar taken from Louis.

"Do you know this hacienda?"

"I do."

From a tube, Louis unrolled a map, the same map that he had shown Paulo at the fort.

"Can you show me where this hacienda is?" Louis asked.

It was obvious the Senhor Sardinha was also not acquainted with maps, but once Louis had taken him through it, pointing out certain features, rivers, towns and mountains, he pointed in a northwesterly direction.

"The plantation is about twenty-five kilometres from the town," he said.

"Have you heard talk of any mines around here?" Werner enquired.

The man shook his head.

"No – not around Caconda," he said.

They thanked him and bade him goodnight.

"Nobody is going to start a mine without first registering their claim. But first, we have to establish the exact location of the mine. Hopefully, we'll be able to do that tomorrow. Without that, the deeds office in Luanda will reveal nothing. And I have this feeling that Don Pereira has something to do with this. Maybe the mine is on his land?" Louis commented while they strode to their hut.

"Well, Louis, if the rumour is already going around that a diamond mine exists, Batista and de Mello are not going to keep their secret for long," Werner said.

"After we get back from the mine, we should take the one wagon and travel to the ranch, masquerading as general dealers selling our wares. We can have a look round then and find out what we can," Werner suggested.

"That's OK by me."

The mine was easy enough to locate. Fortunately, the area around Caconda had recently been surveyed, and this was expressed topographically on the map, so they had been able to pinpoint the location of the mine with a fair degree of accuracy. Although the mine had lost three men recently, it had not influenced the mine's activity, and the black miners were still blasting and the whites still sorting through the gravel. However, it was evident that security had been beefed up, and there were now a number of armed men evident.

The four men left Caconda in the early hours of the morning, their ox-wagon trekking slowly along the road to Pereira's plantation. Senhor Sardinha had given them specific directions. Late that afternoon they arrived at the entrance to the plantation, an elaborate archway with "Hunter's Rest" carved in Portuguese into the large Angolan teaks beams supported by two huge pillars. The surrounding bush was densely carpeted with luxuriant grass; excellent cattle country. But it was clearly sisal which accounted for the farm's main source of income. The fields stretched as far as the eye could see. Wild rubber trees had been tapped, and small containers hung against the tree trunks, the bark slashed to resemble a fish's vertebra, guiding the white latex sap into the buckets.

They spent the night just within the farm's entrance, at least one of them standing watch on rotation; there were still lion, leopard and hyena in the area. Early the next morning they made the eight-mile journey to the hacienda, stopping along the way to show their wares to the workers they passed in the fields and plantations. There were hardly any purchases, as most of the workers had no money. Well before they arrived at the hacienda, three riders approached from that direction. Dressed in white blouses and shiny leather breeches belted with ornate silver buckles, their long boots polished to a bright shimmer, their black flat-topped hats casting shadows over their faces, they reined their magnificent horses in alongside the wagon. Werner signalled the oxen-team leader to halt the animals.

"Buenos Diaz Senhors, what brings you here?" one of the three asked, clearly the leader. By his attire and attitude, Louis recognized him as one of a dying breed, the last of the followers of the Portuguese monarchy, an aristocrat, one of those who believed that the world was theirs by God-given right.

"We are general dealers, trying to sell our wares," Louis replied.

"You speak educated Portuguese, how is that?" the leader asked, trying to control his horse, which was skittering from side to side.

"Before the Kunehama uprising, we had a general dealership. Unfortunately, this failed, the revolt driving our clients away. We are now trying to salvage the business."

This seemed to appease the horseman.

"The revolt has affected us all. I'm Eduardo Pereira, the son of Don Hernando Pereira who owns this hacienda. Maybe we will buy some of your goods. You're welcome; it's only a mile or two to the house."

The three men rode ahead, conversing loudly and laughing as they rode three abreast. The trail circled a kopje and suddenly the hacienda came into view. It was a sprawling cluster of adobe white buildings built on the slopes of a hillock; all the roofs were tiled, their ochre colour shimmering in the sunlight. The buildings were surrounded by low white-washed walls and huge trees, clearly old, that provided abundant shade. As they entered the outer walls of the hacienda, the young Pereira directed them to the corrals that adjoined the hacienda.

"Senhors, you can outspan there, I'm sure my father will be round shortly," the young man shouted, waving his hat in greeting as he galloped off.

"They don't strike me as the type to get involved with gunrunners," Werner said.

"Not gunrunners, but maybe diamonds. What do you think? Remember, friend, we are now also involved in diamonds," Louis retorted, giving Werner a slap on the back, then dodging the small cloud of dust, which erupted. "God, you need a wash," he added humorously.

"You can be happy you can't see yourself," Werner retorted.

The two men left the outspanning of the animals to their servants, pulled off their shirts and headed for a long trough containing clean fresh water pumped from a windmill.

"Werner, what you don't know is that the loss of Brazil as a colony cost the Portuguese aristocrats dearly," Louis spoke slowly as they sat in the shade of the trees, waiting for Don Pereira to arrive. "The aristocrats had invested fortunes in the colony. Those who decided to stay with Portugal and pulled out of Brazil lost handsomely. I believe the Pereiras were victims. To maintain this lifestyle takes a lot of money. I'm not sure they've got it."

Werner swept his arm from left to right.

"You've got to be kidding, just look around you. Here's money all right."

"I think it's an illusion. Therefore the temptation of the diamonds. Wait and see."

He looked up.

"Here comes the Don himself."

Two men approached, one following discretely behind the other. Don Perreira flicked a riding crop against his shiny black boots as he walked towards them. It was evident that this man was a cut above the rest: his bearing alone indicated that he had been born to this station and all others were mere peons. He sported a silver-grey pointed goatee beard which matched his hair, tied back with a thin black ribbon into a ponytail with not a strand out of place. He wore black trousers with an exaggerated high waist, similar to those Spanish flamenco dancers wear, tucked into calf-high boots. His shirt was collarless, of snow-white cotton, the plain neckline half-closed with a drawstring.

The figure behind him was also a white man, obviously a manager or overseer, with nothing ostentatious about his dress. Both were unarmed.

Werner reeled mentally, almost unable to contain his shock. He recognized the second man; he had been at dos Santos' trading store. The livid scar from ear to mouth on his left cheek was a trademark not easily overlooked. The man was subjecting them to close scrutiny, making no comment but not greeting them. He gave no indication that he recognized them, but Werner felt uncomfortable; the man concerned him.

"Buenos Diaz, Senhors! What brings you to my abode?"

The Don stood in front of them, not offering his hand in greeting, just flicking the crop against his boot.

Werner repeated the same story they had given his son.

"Well, you are welcome to persuade my workers to consider your wares, although I doubt you'll be very successful. Caconda is not far away and they visit the town regularly."

"Thank you, Don Pereira. Your hacienda is impressive," Louis said, turning to admire the buildings on the hillock.

The aristocrat ignored the comment. His attitude said that as simple peons lucky enough to be traders, their judgement was of no interest to him.

"Senhor, I must insist that you stay in sight of the hacienda and not move around my property. I have pickets out protecting the property because of the rebellion. They would not hesitate to shoot if they spotted strangers."

He glanced at Philippe and Paulo as if to emphasize the warning.

"Of course, we'll adhere to your request. Thank you again, you are kind to allow us to trade here. Perhaps you would like to take a look . . ." Louis replied.

"Personally, I've no interest in your goods."

Don Pereira turned around and retraced his steps, his overseer in tow, the two men conversing in low tones.

Louis waited until they were out of earshot.

"That damn mine is on his property. It can't be more than a few miles away. He doesn't want us stumbling on it."

"Of course, the mining rights may not be registered in his name. You know how these things work – anybody can lodge a mining claim. That's how it works in Germany anyway," Werner said.

"It's the same in Portugal and the rest of the world. You realize now why we need to go to Luanda?"

The following day the men made a show of presenting their wares and were kept busy by a steady stream of customers who surprisingly, purchased a fair number of items.

The day thereafter, they returned to Caconda.

That evening they shared another expensive bottle of whiskey with Sardinha while he served his customers, a boisterous lot of traders and wagon-men.

As the last of the customers left, Sardinha joined the two men at the table. He sat down and poured himself a generous shot of whiskey.

"You're my nephew and I don't know what you're up to or what you've done, but there have been a few people in here enquiring about you and your friend. I never said you were family.

172

I just said that you were passing through and we were just making conversation." He paused, "So, what's going on?"

"I thought something like this would happen. Who are these people that enquired?" Louis asked.

"I suppose friends and employees of Don Perreira."

He shrugged noncommittally.

"Did one of them have a distinct scar on the left side of his face?"

"One fellow, a pretty morose character, had exactly what you've described. Do you know him?"

"Do you?"

"No."

"What do you know about this man Pereira?" Louis asked his uncle.

"Look, there's no doubt he's a gentleman, well-mannered and caring. He looks after his people – both black and white, though when need be, he can be tough. Firm but fair, you know."

How could a man of Don Pereira's calibre be mixed up with someone like dos Santos?

"Well, never mind. We've seen what we've wanted. We'll be returning to Benguela tomorrow," Louis said, not wanting to divulge too much and wishing to end the conversation.

Sardinha looked at them.

"Just be careful – these are dangerous times. Just a short while ago three men were brutally murdered on the trail between here and Benguela."

Neither Louis nor Werner commented.

They left Caconda early the next morning. Louis was concerned for their safety, convinced that their arrival at Don Pereira's plantation had given rise for concern. Somehow he knew that Don Pereira realized that they were there to sell more than just general goods.

"Be vigilant," Louis said. "I have a bad feeling."

He was not wrong. Just before sunset, Philippe rode forward from the rear.

"Mestre, a group of men are coming, from Caconda."

The two officers turned, looking back along the trail. About a half mile behind, six men approached at a canter. Werner could make out two whites and four blacks. Paulo and Louis held their rifles upright at the ready, butts resting on their stirrups. The horsemen pulled up alongside in a cloud of dust as Louis called a halt to the wagons. All the group carried weapons, the blacks with rifles out of their rifle boots lying across the front of their saddles, the white men with their holster flaps undone, the butts of their revolvers visible. This was ominous. The leader's livid scar was unmistakable.

"Buenos Diaz," Scarface snarled, looking at Louis intently. "I recognized you. I could not remember where at first, but then it came to me. You're an army officer and your friend, he was with you, I think some representative for an overseas company, no? You both arrived at

Huambo and visited my employer, dos Santos. What's an army officer doing pretending to be a general trader?"

All weapons were trained on the four men.

"If I'm a Portuguese officer, which is correct, then I don't need to give you an explanation. Knowing who I am should have been explanation enough for you."

Werner couldn't believe his ears. Why was Louis telling them this?

Scarface casually lifted his rifle and fired a shot in front of Werner's horse. It reared up, and he had his hands full, fighting to stop it from bolting. Louis laid his hand on his revolver, and the other men in Scarface's group raised their rifles. The atmosphere was electric with tension.

"Senhor, my men could kill all four of you right now and nobody would ever know who did it. In fact, they probably wouldn't even try and find out who did it. All would think that it was the Kunehamas."

"Just like the three men who were murdered a while back?" Louis retorted.

"What do you know about that? Those men worked for us – they were my friends!" Scarface shouted. Then realizing he had said too much, his attitude changed.

"I'm Major de Sousa of the Portuguese Colonial Forces under the direct command of Colonel Batista based in Benguela Province who, incidentally," Louis sarcastically added, "ordered me to investigate the death of your friends. I thought it a good idea to arrive here incognito. Actually, an excellent idea. It appears I was right! What is your name?" Louis was now on the offensive, and Scarface quite taken back by the change in events.

"Senhor, your name," Louis insisted loudly, his voice sharp.

"Eduardo Morreira," Scarface replied reluctantly.

"And you say these three men were in your or your boss' employ? Who might that be? Quickly now, Senhor Morreira, I don't take to threats kindly."

"They worked for Senhor dos Santos."

"And where is Senhor dos Santos now? Is he in Caconda? Or is he here? If so, I would like you to take me to him immediately."

Scarface lifted his shoulders in a gesture of resignation.

"I'm sorry, Major, he is not here and neither is he in Huambo. We are concerned, he is overdue."

"Overdue! How come? Where did he go?"

"South, Major, with a group of men. They went hunting."

Louis pretended to be surprised, an incredulous expression crossing his face.

"Hunting, with a war on? Really, that's strange indeed. Brave men, I would say."

Scarface remained stony-faced. He'd already said too much.

"While we're at it, what were the three murdered men doing in Caconda for dos Santos? What business does dos Santos have here?"

"I don't know, Senhor dos Santos does not tell me his business.

"Pity, it was a truly unpleasant business as I'm sure you have heard. I may have to issue a warrant for your arrest and have you interrogated in Benguela. "

Scarface paled.

"Please, Major, I truly know no more than I've already told you."

"Well, we'll see about that. I will now resume my journey and I hope that you will not harass us further. Good day, Senhor."

Werner took the cue, shouting to the oxen men to get the wagons in motion. He was thunderstruck by the turn of events. The unadulterated gall Louis had displayed in the face of the threat these men portrayed was masterful. Scarface was now completely on the defensive, probably wishing he had never ridden out here. Accompanied by cries and the crack of whips, the oxen bellowed as the wagons began to roll, leaving the group of horsemen standing in the dust. Werner looked and Louis and winked.

"A truly excellent performance, maestro."

Louis merely smiled.

"I believe there's much consternation in the enemy's camp. De Mello and Batista must find themselves in a difficult position without dos Santos to run their show. We're probably forcing them to come out into the open – reveal themselves, very dangerous, indeed," Werner said.

"Well, we just have to keep on piling on the pressure," Louis added. "I believe you should go to Luanda. I know a reputable firm of lawyers who can assist you. Well, actually I don't know them – they come recommended by Colonel de Oliveira. They can look after the deeds office search and establish who holds the mining rights. Also, it will give you an opportunity to meet with General Diaz. He did indicate that he would like to meet you."

"Why don't you go?"

"No, what pretext could I use? Batista would not let me go unless the General intervened. I don't think that would be wise."

CHAPTER SIXTEEN

At the hotel in Benguela, the concierge handed him a note from Judge de Mello. The local Juiz requested that on his return, he join him for an aperitivo. Werner looked at the note; it was dated today. It was impressive, written in longhand on excellent paper bearing the province's judicial seal. Judge de Mello must think I'm still in town, he thought. A good thing, but no doubt in due time the judge will find out that I've been seen in the company of de Sousa, both disguised as general merchants. What questions would that give rise to? And how would it affect his friend, Louis?

Werner attended to the few items of business he still had, and promptly at six that evening entered the lounge.

It was autumn, the evening cool enough to require warm clothing. The moment the sun disappeared behind the sea, the temperature plummeted, and the hotel staff had lowered the canvas awnings that surrounded the huge balcony bordering the lounge and dining room.

With the utmost difficulty he maintained a straight face as he took in the scene. De Mello had already arrived: aperitivo in hand he stood in the centre of the lounge, immaculately dressed, bracketed by Colonel Batista and Louis, both in full uniform. He approached the trio with the slightest of smiles on his face, the portrayal of relaxed composure.

"Senhor de Almeida, good evening. So good of you to come. I see you got my note. Of course, you know the Major; I believe he was a captain when you last saw him. And this is Colonel Batista, commander-in-chief of the province's military forces."

They greeted one another.

"The Colonel and I have been introduced previously," Werner remarked.

The waiter brought Werner his aperitivo, and the four men made small talk.

"We are about to have dinner. Will you join us?" de Mello asked.

Werner acceded, although he wondered what the reason was for this sudden desire by de Mello to socialize. He was sure that neither de Mello nor Batista had yet received a report from their accomplices, whom he believed included Don Pereira, about the events in Caconda. Louis' demeanour gave no hint.

The dinner proceeded without incident as they discussed the rebellion and other generalities. The Portuguese were waging attack upon successful attack of retribution against the Kunehamas, and there were now only small pockets of resistance left to deal with, most of these far in the hinterland towards the east.

Finally all the crockery had been removed. The waiters served coffee with the customary liqueurs, and the men went through the ritual of lighting up cigars.

De Mello sucked in smoke and exhaled slowly towards the ceiling, leaning backwards in his chair, appearing to be totally absorbed.

"Senhor de Almeida," he suddenly addressed Werner, still staring at the ceiling. "Have you seen Senhor dos Santos or have you heard from him of late? I seem to remember the two of you doing business together."

Somebody kicked his shin under the table; it was a damn hard kick, it had to be Louis. He glanced at him but could read nothing in his expression. He too was absorbed with his cigar.

"Funny that you should mention that; I've heard nothing from him for a while. I presume he must be away or in Huambo," Werner responded, hoping that his attitude of indifference would have the desired effect and that it was Louis would want him to say.

"Did you conclude any deals with dos Santos?" the Colonel enquired nonchalantly.

"Gentlemen please, it would be improper for me to divulge my dealings with the man unless, of course, you could give me good reason to do so," Werner replied smilingly.

De Mello lent forward in his chair, his elbow propped up on the table, holding his cigar. "Senhor, this is important and as the local Juiz, I believe you would not compromise your ethics by doing so. We are concerned for dos Santos' safety."

Christ! Werner thought; the bastard's dead and they still don't know it! He shuddered imperceptibly as he remembered those last few hours.

Dos Santos had revealed nothing under military cross-examination, remaining sullen and unco-operative to the end. The military court was a long drawn out affair, but finally the two officers sat in full uniform against the rail that separated the court audience from the court proper. This was a closed session; not even the press were aware of any proceedings. No civilians were permitted: all present were there with special permission or had been ordered to be present.

Everyone had known that the death sentence was inevitable, but it still was a sobering moment when the Colonel made the pronouncement: that within ten days he would be taken to the gallows at the Winduk Prison and hanged by the neck until dead. Dos Santos stared straight ahead, expressionless.

The prison resembled a fort, an imposing building built of blocks of granite, its centre dominated by a manned watchtower allowing for all-round surveillance.

As arresting officers, Werner and Jurgen arrived in full uniform a half hour before six in the morning as commanded, and reported to the prison commander. The atmosphere was subdued.

They declined the offered coffee. Ten minutes before six, they followed the commander into the hall where they met with the members of the court panel who had passed sentence and who were also obliged to witness the execution. Major Zietzmann was with them. The prison commander led them up a flight of stairs to the execution chamber, a large bare room with an extraordinary high ceiling. A stout wooden floor supported on beams jutted out from the walls about twenty feet off the ground. The men entered the room from a door which led directly onto this wooden floor and the commander indicated where they were to stand.

Punctually at six, another door opened and a priest entered, followed by dos Santos, his hands bound behind his back. If the man was afraid, he did not reveal it, but his eyes blazed with blistering hatred as he recognized Werner.

The priest prayed continuously in Portuguese. A soldier led dos Santos by the arm to the gallows trapdoor, two painted footprints on the boards indicating where the condemned man's feet were to be positioned. Quickly, the soldier produced a wooden board with three straps with buckles, one at each end and a third in the middle. This was strapped to the back of his legs, a strap around the ankles, another around his knees and the third around his waist.

A black hood was placed over dos Santos' head, ignoring his sudden instinctive protestations. Immediately, the noose followed, quickly dropped around his neck; the slack in the rope was taken up by a large loop tied with thin cotton. The loop hung directly over the prisoner's head. The first rays of dawn pierced the chamber through narrow slits in the wall, casting long beams of light that stabbed into the gloom.

The commander, speaking in German, read the charge and sentence. There was no sound now from dos Santos. The officer stood back and nodded. The soldier standing next to the trapdoor jerked a lever back, and the spring-loaded trapdoors split in the middle with a bang. Dos Santos dropped like a stone, the rope jerking tight with a loud twang, motes of dust released from the rope swirling in the light that now began to flood the chamber. Trussed as it was, the body could not convulse, the legs twitching slightly for only a few seconds, then swaying inertly at the end of the rope.

Although he had mentally prepared himself, the execution still shocked Werner to the core. Yes, he hated the man and felt no compassion for him, but still he wanted to be ill. He stood, rigid with shock, his face as white as a sheet, not saying a word as he stared at the rope swaying like a pendulum shaft in front of him. It was a barbaric way to die.

Werner shook off the memories.

"Well, now that you put it that way, we did conclude a satisfactory deal, and in fact we are currently negotiating a second deal. I've placed the order for the goods but await payment – not that I doubt for a moment that there is a problem. It's been a pleasure doing business with Senhor dos Santos," he bluffed convincingly. "And I only expect payment when I produce proof of shipment, not before. I expect to receive these documents soon. May I ask what your concern is?"

There was a moment's silence as the Judge and Colonel looked at each other, before the Colonel gave de Mello an almost unperceivable nod.

"You must appreciate, this is rather sensitive . . . please, you must excuse me but I must insist that you maintain our confidence in this respect. Do we have your gentleman's word on this?"

"Of course, your lordship."

"The Colonel and I had entrusted him with items of considerable value, which unfortunately, appear to have disappeared. When I say considerable, I should actually say, immense. You can imagine our concern. Now it would seem he too has disappeared. The three men who were murdered on the Huambo-Caconda trail . . . that may also somehow be related to dos Santos' disappearance."

"I'm sorry to hear that. I am aware of the murder, as the Colonel has no doubt informed you."

"This last shipment," de Mello continued, "did he give you any indication as to how he proposed to pay for this?"

Werner went through a pretence of being uncomfortable, squirming in his chair, looking around, seemingly embarrassed at having to do something against his better judgement.

"Come, come, Senhor, this is important," de Mello insisted.

"Ok, yes, he did."

"And . . . ?" Batista asked, clearly unable to contain his impatience. "How was he going to pay you?"

"If you must know, Colonel," Werner responded with an appropriate amount of unease, " . . . in diamonds. Uncut diamonds, in fact."

There was a moment's silence.

"Did you not wonder where he would have acquired these?" the Colonel asked.

"Why should I? There are numerous diamond mines in Southern Africa, these could have come from anywhere."

The two men looked at each other again. Werner was ready to give his eyeteeth to know what was going on between them – what their thoughts were!

"Merda, the bastard," the Colonel exclaimed.

"Shhh, calm down!" the Juiz said.

"Gentlemen, please tell me what this is all about. Maybe I can assist," Werner said sympathetically.

De Mello sighed loudly, knocking back a generous tot of liqueur.

"I'm afraid our Senhor dos Santos has absconded with what is not his. I believe you won't be doing business with him again. In fact, I doubt we'll ever see him again."

"What about the shipment of rifles on the water; these are due here soon. Who's going to pay for these?" Werner exclaimed, allowing an expression of concern to descend over his face.

Louis now thought it time for him to join the charade.

"What shipment of rifles? How many?" he demanded, staring intently at Werner.

"About two hundred and fifty."

Louis swung on the Judge.

"What did I tell you? The man should have been arrested, but your people always said there never was enough evidence. Now he's gone, and with your money. Or the diamonds."

"Major, don't concern yourself. It's our problem; we merely wished to know if you knew of his whereabouts," de Mello wearily replied, clearly an unhappy man.

"When is this shipment due?" Batista asked.

"In about two week's time."

"Leave it with me, we'll think of something."

The Judge rose.

"Will you excuse us? The Colonel and I have a lot to discuss."

He looked at Louis.

"Major, please be the host and keep Senhor de Almeida company. Thank you." He then seemed to remember something and turned to Werner. "Did you ever meet that woman of his – that mulatto, Maria?"

"Why, yes, I have."

"I understand that she has also left."

"I wouldn't know that."

"Well, it may be that if we investigate her whereabouts, we may find him," De Mello said, thoughtfully.

Werner stared at Louis, dumbfounded. He turned to ensure they could not be overheard as he watched the two men leave.

"Christus! What next? If I didn't know I had the backing of both the Portuguese and German governments, I'd be running for my life!"

Louis chuckled.

"It's a fuckin' pantomime."

"God, what about Maria? They're going to go after her."

"You'll have to warn her once you get to Luanda, she'll have to disappear again," Louis muttered, not entirely pleased.

Werner had no idea what forces de Mello could call on to assist in tracing Maria, but he was sure these were considerable. He was a Judge and related to the most powerful figure in Luanda!

CHAPTER SEVENTEEN

In the seventeenth century, the Portuguese had chosen this bay as the ideal spot for their first European settlement on the southwestern coast of Africa. Surely, thought Werner, it must rank amongst the most beautiful natural harbours in the world.

He stood on the deck of the Portuguese steamer as it slowly entered the protection of the bay and surveyed the city sprawled along its shoreline. A spit of land, never more than a mile wide, branched out from the coast, creating a U with one arm parallel to the coastline penetrating far into the sea. The sweeping bay this created was protected from the southern Atlantic Ocean and open sea by the long narrow peninsula, really no more than a sandbar a few feet above the high water mark which jutted out.

Not too far from the equator, but well into the tropics, Luanda had all the makings of a paradise. Except for the harbour and its quayside and the few fishing jetties, a long pristine, near-white beach marked the edges of the half-moon bay, thronged by hundreds of palms. A coastal road ran parallel to the beach, with no structures whatsoever between beach and road. On the opposite side, typical Portuguese architecture had been used to construct single, two and three storey structures, no doubt the residences of the elite and near elite.

From the beach, the ground rose gradually, with the buildings behind the first row high enough to afford those living on the top floors a panoramic view. The harbour bustled with activity: a number of ships, steam and sail, sat alongside the quay, large cranes and ships' derricks were busily loading and unloading cargo. This was not a new colony; it was evident that the Europeans had been here for hundreds of years. With the abolishment of the slave trade, the Portuguese had opened their harbours, and entrepreneurs flooded into the colonies. Brazil still needed slaves, but this had now become a covert operation. Although Portugal maintained that the rumours were untrue and the trade had been eradicated, since the Portuguese had arrived in Angola in the seventeenth century, over a million slaves had been transported from this paradise to Brazil. The trickle of human cargoes still being sent out were now shipped from lesser ports.

Werner had boarded the ship at Lobito. It was flying the Portuguese flag, en route from the Far East to Europe having rounded the Cape of Good Hope from Mozambique to Portugal.

He was but one of a number of passengers who waited to disembark, some only sightseers on their way to Portugal from other colonies, others like him visiting for a while. During the voyage, he had kept to his stateroom, trying to be inconspicuous, appearing only to take his meals in the saloon, seated at a table on his own.

He walked down the gangplank, Philippe behind him with his luggage. It was not uncommon for the intelligentsia to have their servants accompany them, and he seemed to fit that category well. He showed their papers to the customs officer on the quayside who merely gave these a perfunctory glance and waved them through.

Neither of them knew their way around the city. They hired a carriage with driver on a continuous basis, signing a contract for a fortnight. The rate quoted was reasonable, and he was assured that the driver knew the city well. What they did not tell him was that the man hardly spoke any Portuguese and that a knowledge of the local dialect was necessary if you proposed to converse with him!

Once they had loaded their luggage, they set off for the promenade to book into one of the better establishments. The driver, with much arm-waving and loud conversation, managed to suggest that Werner try the Royal Beach Hotel, apparently frequented by the Luandan elite.

Werner took a suite for a week and arranged for Philippe to be accommodated in the black staff quarters at the rear of the building. The city was obviously booming, and with many families and businessmen in town from Portugal the hotel was almost full. Similar to Rio de Janeiro, the night came alive. The sea along this coastline teemed with fish and crustaceans, which together with the finest wine Portugal could produce kept couples in the many restaurants until the early hours of each morning.

Finding a map of the city was not easy. Finally, the hotel concierge parted with his, at a ridiculous price. However, it was an exceptionally good map showing both the old city near the port and the new part, the cidade alta. The old city, the baixa, was quaint, with narrow streets, old colonial buildings, white-washed churches and palms growing everywhere. The old style architecture lent a graciousness to the city.

Louis had given Werner various addresses and notes, which he studied, trying to pinpoint these spots as well as commit the overall layout of the city to mind.

The next morning he set out to track down Maria. The carriage driver's name was Josiah, and communication was difficult, as the language he spoke was different from that spoken in the south. He was a member of the Ndongo tribe, who had held out against the Portuguese for centuries, until their king Ngola Kiluange was eventually beheaded by the colonists. The Ndongo were a proud and defiant people, who had never really accepted Portuguese rule, and who were not prepared to trade their language, culture and customs for another. It was with difficulty that Philippe could make himself understood.

"Tell the man that if he does his job well, he will be rewarded with a handsome tip," said Werner. As understanding broke, Josiah beamed from ear to ear.

After breakfast, they found the carriage and driver ready to depart. In fact, he was so enthusiastic he had been there before sunrise just in case Werner chose to depart very early

They set off, Philippe sitting atop with the driver. The carriage was similar to a surrey but larger, with a black canvas canopy to shield the passengers from the rain and sun and two horses up front. The driver assured Werner he knew the place he wanted, as he knew the city well.

The city was pristine, with hordes of workers employed to keep it clean. The wheels rumbled over the cobblestones as the horses trotted past the hawkers thronging the streets, selling every conceivable item: clothing and hats, fruit and vegetables, brooms, exquisite wooden carvings, cooked corn on the cob and various other local delicacies.

Suddenly, the carriage stopped. Having studied his map carefully before their departure, Werner realized that they were still a good distance from their destination.

"What's happening? Why have we stopped?" he asked Philippe.

The two Africans chattered back and forth, trying to overcome their inability to understand each other.

Finally, Philippe turned round looking bewildered.

"I think he is trying to tell me that there is another carriage that has been behind us from the hotel. He's adamant that we are being followed. He says that when we stopped, it turned away into a side street," he said.

God, Werner thought, that can't be possible. Who could have expected him here? They had been extremely circumspect in their preparations; nobody had had any idea he was about to depart for Luanda from Benguela.

"Ok, Philippe. Let's carry on but keep a good lookout without it being too obvious. I need to think about this."

The carriage resumed its journey, but it wasn't long before they stopped again.

"Mestre, he's right, we are being followed."

"All right, carry on slowly."

This was serious. Somehow, they needed to outsmart their tail.

Up ahead was what appeared to be a local market in a small square, and the crush of people crossing from one part to another was forcing the carriages to slow or stop.

He leant forward and tapped Philippe on the shoulder.

"I'm going to jump off here. You continue and let Josiah lead them around the town for a while. With the canopy up, they can't really see if I'm in the carriage or not. I'll make sure they don't notice me jumping off. I'll see you at the hotel later."

"Yes, Mestre."

The carriage passed through the middle of the market, slowing down because of the number of pedestrians. The following carriage was similarly held up, and by the time the second carriage had broken through the throng of people, they had widened the gap.

Right in front of them was an intersection. Werner made a decision.

"Make a right turn here," Werner quickly instructed Philippe.

Immediately the carriage turned right into the lesser street and disappeared around the corner of the building. For a few moments it was out of sight, and Werner, valise in hand, jumped out, ducking and running towards the crowd, disappearing into its midst. From behind a stall, he watched the other carriage approach and when it drew abreast, he had an opportunity to see the occupants.

Two men sat in the carriage. There was no mistaking the ugly scar on the one's left cheek. Werner was shocked. How on earth had they got to Luanda so quickly and how had they found out that he would be here? And why were they following him? What was obvious was that de Mello had sent them to find Maria. And since last seeing de Mello and Batista, they had somehow associated him with Maria and dos Santos' whereabouts. Why else would they be tailing him? He was mystified.

Flagging down a passing carriage that plied the streets looking for fares, he gave the driver the street name, omitting the street number. Fortunately, the African driver spoke Portuguese. The carriage dropped him off at the entrance to Rau da Gama, and he waited until it had disappeared before he proceeded to walk the length of the street, following the street numbers unobtrusively.

He found No.54, but walked on past it. It was a two-storey building typical of the others alongside it, with a large entrance between two pillars supporting a portico. This was a middle class area, far from the hustle and bustle of the city centre, situated on the outer edge of the baixa, the old city. A brass plate affixed to the side of the entrance gave one name only, in large black letters, Pedro Williams. This surprised Werner; an English name in a Portuguese colonial city? Of course, he knew Maria was of mixed blood, but he knew nothing about her background at all. Somewhere in her ancestry, there must have been a union between African and European; it could have been European or Indian, maybe from Goa, he thought, that the small Portuguese colony in India, but it would seem that whoever the European, his name must have been Williams.

It was still early, so he decided to observe the building for a while, see who came and went. A short distance up the street, he saw a shop with a few tables and chairs on the pavement and an awning to protect the customers from the hot afternoon sun. Besides selling basic daily necessities to the local public, notices displayed on the sidewalk proclaimed it also served wine, coffee, and a few basic snacks. He entered and sat down, choosing a table that gave him a view of No. 54 Rau da Gama. He ordered coffee from the elderly storekeeper whose wife brought it to the table. It was excellent, probably from Brazil, he thought.

It was still morning, and the little shop was not particularly busy, just the odd customer from the surrounding area buying essential daily necessities. No. 54 remained silent.

It was an hour later that he saw two women emerge from the building, and turn to walk away from him. He was certain that Maria was one of them; he was again struck by that special beauty only mulatto women have. He still could vividly recollect the evening they had spent together, and he experienced a fleeting moment of intense anticipation. He immediately thrust this from his mind.

He quickly rose, dropping a few coins on the table to cover the cost and proceeded to follow the pair at a fair distance. The two women were in no hurry, strolling slowly towards to the local shopping area and market, each with a basket in hand, no doubt on their way to make their daily purchases.

As they meandered through the shops and markets stalls, he repeatedly checked behind. Neither they nor he were being followed. He had successfully lost his tail. No doubt, they'd be waiting for him at the hotel again.

About an hour later, after the women had spent an hour in a small sidewalk café, they parted, and Maria slowly retraced her steps to the house, carrying the heavy basket with her purchases. Werner quickened his pace until he was abreast of her. Without turning his head and looking at her, he spoke.

"Excuse me, Senhora; may I assist you with your basket?"

She purposely ignored him, staring straight ahead. No doubt, he thought, she thinks she's being accosted.

"Maria, let me help you."

She stopped walking and turned, an incredulous expression on her face, her eyes wide with surprise.

"Madre Diaz," she whispered, "It's you!"

He took the basket from her.

"Just keep walking. How have you been?" he asked.

"Very well, but lonely. My, my, am I glad to see you! I've been so worried about you, because I know dos Santos; he'll want to kill you."

She invited him to the house. He protested, thinking it not proper.

"Of course, you can come in. I've nothing to hide, neither have you! I've told my aunt everything; I had to so that she could fully understand my situation. She'll be pleased to meet you. Unfortunately, she'll only be back later this afternoon. She has some other appointment; she's separated from her husband and they are trying to work out an arrangement. Anyway, it's all really no concern of mine."

He reluctantly agreed.

They entered the tastefully furnished house. Bookcases and paintings adorned the walls; heavy curtains bordered the windows, the sunlight streaming through the drawn net curtains. The huge living room contained a few tropical indoor potted plants. Clearly, this was a well-to-do middle class dwelling.

"What does your uncle do?" Werner asked.

Maria removed her jacket.

"Oh, he's some government official, something in municipal services, I think. That's surely very boring, I think?"

"I suppose it is."

She had taken the basket from him, and he followed her into the kitchen where she packed the purchases away, some into the pantry and some out on the back porch into a large cool-room. He watched her, acutely aware of her exceptional beauty. Aware of him looking at her, she walked over to him, and pressed her body to his, her lips nearly touching his. She looked up into his eyes.

"I missed you so much. I've never forgotten that you saved me," she whispered, and then she pressed her lips to his.

His urgent need overwhelmed him, and he was immediately aroused. He could smell her, and the pressure of her pelvis against his was intoxicating. He kissed the hint of her soft silky breasts where they protruded slightly from her bodice.

Then he stopped.

"We must not, Maria. There are serious matters afoot."

"That can wait," she said trying to pull his head to hers.

"No, they can't; dos Santos' people are looking for you."

She jerked her head back, her soft expression replaced by shock and fear.

"Why are they after me? Does he want me back?"

"No, it's a long story. Sit down, I need to tell you what has happened."

He left nothing out. The news of dos Santos' execution shocked her, even though she hated and despised him. When Werner mentioned the diamonds, she said she had heard that they were involved in a mining operation, but knew no more than that. She had met de Mello on a few occasions – she had the impression he was the kingpin; all seemed a little in awe of him, and he issued all directives. She knew nothing of the financial arrangements, but knew of Colonel Batista, as his name had been mentioned a few times. Yes, she knew Don Pereira well, as well as his wife, a wonderful, refined woman.

"I spent some time at their hacienda as a guest. Every day the men staying there would ride off, only returning in the evening, dusty and dirty. Dos Santos, that ugly fellow Morreira, Don Pereira and de Mello. But I do not know what they had been doing. That degregado Morriera frightens me; he is dos Santos' hatchet man, a robber and a murderer," she said shuddering. She had no idea how he had avoided the gallows, but he had been transported from Portugal to Angola a few years back. An evil man, she said.

"I do not understand why they think I know where dos Santos would be! Why were they not told that the German military had executed him?" she asked.

"Hey Maria, I'm just a junior officer, I do as I'm told!" he laughed. "I'm not sure, but I suppose it is because the investigation is still ongoing, with both the Germans and the Portuguese wanting to apprehend de Mello and Batista. Now Pereira is involved and to that, you have to add in the diamonds."

"Will they find out he was hanged?"

"Yes, I'm sure they will; that's bound to leak out."

"What am I to do?" she asked nervously.

"You have to move again; I think your aunt should close up house and also leave. We'll help you find accommodation, but no family this time. Rent from total strangers using aliases. I'll being seeing General Diaz, and we'll help with money. You need to hide for a while."

"God, I want to be free," she wailed in anguish.

For how long would her past relationship with dos Santos plague her? Once again her life was being turned upside down.

Werner promised to call the following day at about five. Meanwhile Maria would discuss his visit with her aunt. Reluctantly, she let him go.

Finding another cab, he eventually got back to the hotel in time for dinner. He found Philippe waiting for him outside the entrance.

"Where's the carriage?" he asked.

"I sent the driver home. Those two men followed us around for quite awhile until they found out that you were no longer with us. When they rode past, I saw the same man who stopped us on the road from Cacondo. He tried to look away," Philippe said.

"I know; I also saw him."

"I'm sure they are watching the hotel."

"They must be. Philippe, listen; I don't want Josiah to come here. You must stop him before he gets here tomorrow morning. I'll meet you at the big Catholic church we passed in the old city. I'll walk, I'll leave the hotel using the back, well before it is light. I'll see you there. Okay?"

"I understand, Mestre."

The concierge handed him his keys and a message. It was from General Diaz advising him that a meeting was confirmed for eleven the next morning.

Werner bought a newspaper. Bold headlines announced that Portugal tottered on the brink of bankruptcy, and that the Portuguese monarch King Carlos I was under threat. There were rumours of him abdicating. Portugal had never recovered from the loss of Brazil as a colony and the continual near civil war situations in the colonies had taken a heavy toll on the treasury. Emerging nationalism, fuelled by discontent, threatened the existing government. There was speculation that the Governor-General of the colony would be recalled to Portugal. This could impact negatively on de Mello's plan, he being a protégé of the Governor-General: the meeting with General Diaz should be interesting, he thought.

The General's offices were in a fort situated in the old part of the city that overlooked the bay. At the entrance, the general's aide signed Werner in and escorted him to the General. The fort's outer and inner walls were enormously thick, built to withstand any naval barrage from ships in the bay. They were whitewashed, and the interior of the fort was cool. They met in a large hall, its centre taken up by a long table surrounded by a number chairs: the décor was opulent, the walls covered in light-green material with gilded edges. Large portraits stood guard around the room, past and present kings, governors and military officers who had served in the colony over the years.

The General looked splendid in his uniform, much adorned with medals and insignia. Werner estimated him to be in his fifties, with a distinguished grey trimmed beard and moustache, his rotund shape clearly a victim of good living. He wore a stern face as is expected from all senior officers but this did not belie the twinkle in his eye. He indicated that Werner should take a seat and asked his aide that coffee be brought.

"I'm somewhat confused; I don't know whether I should address you as Hauptmann von Dewitz or Senhor de Almeida," he laughed. "But whatever, espionage is a stupid but essential trial of our times. Anyway, I'm certainly glad to make your acquaintance."

"General, my Portuguese name, de Almeida, is probably preferable at the moment," Werner smiled.

"Quite so. I must tell you that I've been speaking and exchanging cables with your military commanders, who speak highly of you. I'm impressed."

"Thank you, General."

"Of course, from the newspapers you must realize that our country is in a state of political flux, not that this should influence the military, we serve whoever is in power. However, it may assist us in disposing of . . ." he hesitated for a second, merely mouthing the word 'Governor-General', " . . . those in charge and, in particular, our good judge de Mello. I believe his protector has no more than a few days left in this colony and probably will return to Portugal in disgrace. We need not concern ourselves with him. Already now, he is virtually without power and not able to assist his friend. You will excuse the riddles, won't you?" the General chuckled.

"Of course, General. I need to tell you that I've already encountered two of their henchman here in Luanda. In fact, I was followed yesterday."

"I'm not surprised, that consortium has its tentacles everywhere. Their actions are no more than treason, but proving it is another thing. Do you require my assistance in dealing with them?"

"No, I've given them the slip – I should manage."

"Good, I would not want them to think that we are aware of what is going on; not yet anyway. However, I thought it prudent that you have some protection. I've a letter here for you that you need only to produce. It is signed and sealed by myself and will immediately avail you of whatever assistance you may require from the military. Rest assured, no one would dare ignore it. Also, in the event of the police being involved, they will realize you are working for me," the General added, sliding the letter across the table.

"Thank you, General."

"Ah, yes. So you have a map for me, don't you?" the General asked.

Werner produced the tube and passed it across.

The general bent over the table and studied the map he had rolled out. He then pointed to the section of the map that revealed the Caconda area.

"I see you have marked the mine on the map and I see that it has been notarized, that's very good, that certainly lends it a degree of authenticity. I can tell you it has been established and confirmed that the mine is on Don Pereira's ranch, as was surmised. His property, his ranch; it is enormous, certainly the largest in the south. The records reveal, however, that the mining rights are not held by him, but rather by our friend de Mello himself. Don Pereira, we know, is not a willing partner. De Mello has some financial hold over him. Here comes the tricky part. For us to attain those rights, de Mello must either voluntarily relinquish his rights thereto, or he must be charged criminally. Alternatively, lose his life in the course of some proven criminal action. In that way, his deceased estate or heirs would forfeit their rights to the mining claim. We are dealing here with the worst of the worst; I need not tell you what would best suit us."

"General, what exactly is it that you wish me to do?" Werner queried.

"Hauptmann von Dewitz, I prefer your military title, now that we are discussing military matters. In conjunction with your General von Leutwein, commander-in-chief of the Imperial German forces in your colony, and Major Zietzmann as well as our Colonel Diaz and Major de Sousa, it was agreed that this should be a civilian operation headed by you, but secretly supported by us. The military is not to be involved. If this goes wrong, we will turn a blind eye. This is an undercover operation, with no-one being able to point a finger at either country's military establishment. Politically, it would be too sensitive. Remember, whatever happens to de Mello must be the result of a criminal action on his part, supported by absolute proof. Remember too, for all intents and purposes, you are currently a Portuguese civilian; you have papers to prove that, although I shan't ask where you obtained these," the General laughed. "No doubt, my friend Zietzmann's work! Don Pereira realizes that the degree of his present involvement could lead to his imprisonment and to the disgrace of his family. This concerns him. We need you to approach him, get him on your side and wrench control of the mine from de Mello and Colonel Batista. At the right moment, we will strip the Colonel of his command. However, let me repeat what I said, we don't want to see de Mello in front of a court. We believe his connections would get him acquitted. He would manipulate the trial and walk free, still as powerful as he is now."

"Who will assist me?" Werner asked, not quite believing what he was hearing. This sounded like a suicide mission!

"We will transfer Colonel de Oliviera back to Benguela, but still make him subordinate to Colonel Batista, until we are ready to dispense with Batista and for de Oliviera to immediately step into the breach. Both he and Major de Sousa will assist you. You must appreciate, it is essential that the military retain a low profile. At the moment, things remain politically volatile. Please, I don't expect you to respond now: you are here for a few days, think about it, and we will meet again in three days when Colonel de Oliviera will also join us. Should you assist us, it must be voluntary."

Werner left the fort, his mind in turmoil. They actually wanted him to get rid off, kill, murder, whatever, de Mello. Although it had never been said aloud, it certainly was insinuated. Did this have the blessing of the German high command? This was insane! This whole thing could blow up in his face. Nobody knew what was going to happen in Portugal; the country was still a powder keg. He couldn't even discuss it with Louis; he was out here on his own. The General had left him in no doubt that Morreira and his cronies were his problem. The letter ensured that no matter happened, he was indemnified, if that's what you wanted to call it. God! To crown it all, he thought, he and Louis had stolen the diamonds. What a cock-up! He had to stop them. If he didn't, he believed they would come after him. He wondered how Jurgen was making out.

At the designated time, he arrived at the Williams' residence. Maria greeted him at the door. She seemed to have recovered from the gloom and doom mood he had left her with. She introduced him to her aunt, a European woman approaching fifty. There was no doubt that she still was a beautiful woman, elegantly dressed, slim and petite, her hair perfect, leaving none in doubt as to her status. She was pleased to meet him, thanking him for saving her niece from that vile man dos Santos.

"He deserved his end, I have no compassion for him," she said fiercely. "I understand your concerns, certainly with the likes of those thugs, and we have already made arrangements to move. You need not bother. Not even my husband will know our whereabouts. But we will need some financial assistance."

Werner readily agreed, compliments of the Imperial German government. He made sure she knew that she was not taking it from him. Tomorrow they would lock-up the house, leaving all with the impression that she had gone to visit her sister in Ambriz, about sixty miles north of Luanda, and taken her niece with her. In fact, they would not be leaving Luanda at all. They had found a secluded house, which they'd rented on a weekly basis.

Werner wanted to leave and return to the hotel, but Maria was insistent that he take her to dinner, and her aunt leant her support.

"You need to go out, you've been cooped up for too long. Go, go!"

"You should have a string of suitors," Werner said as they swayed along in the carriage.

"I don't need any." Her beautiful blue eyes left him with no appropriate response.

He knew he was physically attracted to her. He never knew whether he imagined it or whether it was really so, but she seemed to gently flaunt herself, not in some degraded manner, but so subtly most would not even notice it. But he did, so aware was he of her sexuality. It was as if she knew he desired her and she was saying, I'm here, what's taking you so long?

They chose a secluded restaurant along the bay road, removed from the normal crowds, a restaurant in the baixa that catered for the local residents. It was open to the night air but roofed with tiles, and with all the food grilled on open fires, the ambience was unique; it seemed everybody knew everybody else by their first name. Maria was completely at home, not wearing her finery and jewellery, but clad only in a long skirt and white cotton blouse with a low neckline, which revealed the curve of her magnificent breasts. Her every movement and gesture caused them to quiver, and his eyes were invariably drawn to them.

They ate crayfish tails had been grilled over an open fire, perfectly spiced and accompanied by a garlic sauce only the Portuguese know how to prepare, filled with pieces of squid, mussel, shrimp and tuna. It was one of those meals not easily forgotten. The dessert was something indigenous; he knew it contained coconut and some liqueur – a truly magnificent end to a fabulous meal.

They both drank more than they should have, finishing three bottles of Langouste wine brought to the table in a primitive ice bucket beaded with condensation pearls. She was clearly besotted and she showed it, not caring whether others saw it or not. During the meal, she constantly rubbed her foot against his leg. He wanted to tell her to stop, but his reserve had crumbled, his emotions and arousal driving him to pay the bill early and leave an extravagant tip. Werner handed Maria into a four-wheel surrey with the canopy up, and they disappeared into the darkness of its interior.

He started to give the unknown driver instructions to her house. She interrupted.

"The Royal Beach Hotel," she said firmly. He didn't argue.

She snuggled up to him, laying her hand on his leg.

"You over-tipped the restaurant. For a moment, I thought he would kiss you," she chuckled.

"Maybe I did, but it was one of the finest meals I have ever had." He bent down and kissed the nape of her neck. She lifted her head, and his lips met hers for a long and passionate kiss as he slid his hand into her bodice, cupping her breast. Her erect nipple was hard against the palm of his hand.

The carriage came to an abrupt stop and a horse neighed. He looked up, but could not distinguish much as the street was too dark.

"What's wrong?" he shouted to the driver.

"Mestre, there's another carriage drawn across the road."

Werner was instantly alert.

Get down, quickly!" he whispered urgently to Maria, pushing her off the seat onto the floor so she crouched behind the forward panel of the surrey.

Werner stood up and leaned forward to see past the seated driver. The driver had not exaggerated; another carriage blocked the route, apparently having emerged from a small side street. It was now drawn across the road, the driver missing. He felt the hair in the nape of his neck rise. This was no accident. As he watched, two men emerged from behind the wagon, and he saw the glint of a silver revolver in the feeble light of the carriage's storm lamps.

"Senhor de Almeida, you and Maria please get off and get into this carriage—quickly now!"

It was Scarface; he waggled the revolver at them and then repeated what he said, his voice taking on a more menacing tone.

There was nothing to do, but obey. Werner helped Maria to her feet, and they climbed out of the surrey into the street.

Werner held onto Maria's hand. "What's the meaning of this?" he demanded, putting on a show of indignation.

Both men laughed.

"Merda! Don't play fuckin' games; I can't wait to shoot you. Get into the fuckin' carriage," Scarface demanded.

Werner and Maria sat on the rear seat next to each other, with Scarface on the opposite seat facing them. The revolver was still in his hand, resting on his lap. The second man climbed onto the driver's seat, and the carriage lurched into motion, turning right down the road, towards the harbour. Morreira's accomplice had knocked the other driver unconscious with a vicious blow to the head, and they abandoned the man lying crumpled in the street.

Werner's mind was blank, overcome by the shock of the sudden attack. Slowly, he started to rationalise their situation, aware of the danger they were in. He knew this was an execution squad; they would take them somewhere isolated, try and ring the whereabouts of dos Santos out of Maria, and then unceremoniously despatch the two of them. He didn't even have a weapon! What was he going to do? Maria sat quietly next to him, taking the sudden turn of events better than he had imagined, somewhat stupefied but not panicked.

"Raise your arms," Scarface commanded Werner, and then leant over and patted him down for any hidden weapons, his revolver never wavering far from Werner's chest. He ignored Maria.

Was it going to end like this? He watched Scarface; the degregado was vigilant, hardly taking his eyes off him, the revolver always pointed in his direction. Occasionally, when the carriage passed through a badly lit area, the interior of the carriage would be cast into near darkness, but their upper torsos remained silhouetted against the night sky and the faint running lights of the carriage. He knew that any untoward movement would draw an immediate reaction from Scarface.

He felt Maria pinch his thigh. He moved his hand from his lap to take her hand, thinking she wanted comforting. As his hand closed over hers, he felt something metal. At first, he did not realise what it was. Slowly, he took it from her; it was a pair of scissors! Not an ordinary pair, but those used for cutting and trimming hair, long and pointed. Where had she found that and what was he going to do with it?

As the carriage neared the harbour, it turned north. He recalled from the map he had that this led to the remains of an old fort, now a monument, built by the Portuguese to protect the bay. A half moon shone in the night sky, the sea breeze bringing some broken cloud with it that intermittently blocked out the moonlight. It was then particularly dark. They passed some traffic on the road but there was no way he could draw attention to their plight. They left the built-up area, and the road now meandered parallel to the beach above the high water mark. He could hear the small waves, the occasional palm rustling in the wind, accompanied by the sound of the horses' hooves and the creak of the carriage. The carriage came to a halt a few yards from the road. There were no lights, merely the moon disappearing in and out of the clouds.

Scarface opened the door and climbed down, standing on the sand facing them.

"Get out!"

Werner looked fleetingly up at the driver as the moon broke through a passing cloud. He was holding the horses in check, reins in both his hands. Werner got up quickly, not wanting Maria to alight before him. He clasped the scissors in his hand. As he stepped down from the carriage's single step, he accidentally stumbled in Scarface's direction. Scarface stepped back slightly, momentarily lifting the barrel of the revolver. Werner lunged forward, pushing him backwards. Scarface swung the gun barrel down and fired. Werner felt a tug at his shoulder; he ignored it, his mind resolute. As his body collided with Scarface, he brought up his arm and drove the scissors into the side of the man's face with all his strength. The point penetrated the temple just in front of the ear, the thin bone collapsing as the scissors were forced into the man's brain. He went down as if pole-axed, brain-dead before he hit the ground though his heart still beat, gushing blood from the wound over Werner's hand, wrist and arm.

The driver dropped the reins, scrambling to extract his revolver from his belt, and the horses moved forward. Maria did not hesitate; she leant forward, put her arm around his neck and jerked him off balance. As he fell backwards against her, she viciously bit his face. Werner scrabbled on all fours in the sand desperately looking for the weapon Morreira had dropped. The driver had now managed to draw his revolver, and was twisting around to target Maria behind him. Werner's fingers closed over the revolver, and he did what was quickest; he simply jabbed the barrel against the man's hip and pulled the trigger. The revolver bucked in his hand, the shot rang out, and the man screamed, dropping his revolver to grab his hip. Werner dragged him from the moving carriage. Maria had got hold of the reins and hauled the horses to a stop, applying the brake.

Werner looked at his arm; it was covered in blood. He did not know whether it was his or Scarface's. He felt no pain.

The driver lay on the beach, rolling from side to side moaning, blood oozing from the bullet hole in his leg.

"I think the bone's shattered," Werner said. "What are we going to do with him?"

"Kill him," Maria spat.

"For God's sake, I can't kill him in cold blood!" he exclaimed.

"Listen, my love, you have to, for our sake. You've already killed one. If you don't, they'll keep on coming after us, or rather me; I'll never be safe."

He pulled her close to him. "I can't do that," he whispered looking at her. There was blood around her mouth where she had bitten the man. He pulled a handkerchief from his pocket and gave to her, indicating she should wipe her face. He then bent down to look at the wounded man, who was now quiet. He had lost copious amounts of blood, and Werner could see a dark stain in the moonlight as it seeped into the sand.

"I think he's losing blood from his femoral artery, he's already lost consciousness," Werner said.

Maria looked at the man. Even in the weak moonlight, she could see how pale he was.

"There's nothing we can do for him. Just leave him. He'll never survive. Let's not stay and watch him die."

"Let's take the wagon. We can abandon it in town. There's blood on the driver's seat, be careful where you sit." He looked at her in amazement. "Where did you get the scissors from?"

"I had them in my bag from this morning – I always take my own scissors when I go to have my hair trimmed."

"Well, thank God, for that, is all I can say."

They drove the carriage back into town and abandoned it in a side street, quickly walking away towards the main thoroughfares and the city still teeming. Climbing into a roaming carriage, he instructed the driver to head for his hotel.

"Under no circumstances am I going to allow you to return home. Your aunt can look after the move. Don't worry, I'll send Philippe in the early morning to let her know where you are. Tomorrow afternoon you can go directly to your new residence."

"It's fine – she won't worry if I don't return tonight."

Werner had the taxi drop them off a block away from the hotel and they walked slowly, carefully scrutinizing the people still about. He decided that they should walk around to the back of the building into a delivery yard. Various other entrances led to the kitchens, and there was even a small entrance to the back of the reception area. They remained in the shadows, not wanting others to see the blood on his clothing.

Once in his room, he removed his jacket and shirt, relieved to see there was no mark on him. The bullet had passed through his jacket's shoulder padding, fortunately missing him. The blood covering him was not his own.

"You know, we are not safe even here. They followed me. Thank God, you're not hurt," he said.

"No, I'm not, and neither are you. We were lucky. First I'm going to have a drink and then a bath," she said treating his comments with some finality, as if she no longer wished to pursue the subject of their narrow escape.

He poured them each a cognac, which they drank quickly. They both had another.

"Now that I'm relaxed, I'll take that bath," she said, "you have the most beautiful bathroom. Hot water out of a tap and a nice white large bath. I haven't used one of those for a long time." She started to remove her clothing, making out as if she was oblivious of him, leisurely taking off each garment. His breath caught in his throat as her corset was discarded and he saw the jut of her breasts. This was followed by her knickers, and she bent to lay these on the bed, awarding him a clear view of her sex before sauntering off to the bathroom, swinging her hips provocatively.

He waited for her, drinking yet another cognac. He breathed deeply, wondering why she was spending so long in the bath; it seemed like she had been in there for ages. When she emerged from the bathroom, she was wrapped in a towel which she whipped off before sliding into his bed.

Werner disappeared into the bathroom, where in record time he stripped off his clothes, bathed and returned to the bedroom with a towel wrapped around his waist. As he got near the bed, she grabbed hold of the towel and jerked it off him.

"Well?" she arched her eyebrows questioningly. "What are you waiting for? Get in." She whipped the sheet back, making room for him.

Acutely aware that she could see how obviously aroused he was, he slid into the bed next to her. She turned towards him and her lips slithered down his chest and stomach. She took him in her hand, squeezing him and smiling provocatively as he gasped, then in one smooth movement, straddled him and guided him into her.

She looked at him lying next to her, still slightly out of breath, his chest rising and falling, the perspiration on his forehead glistening in the moonlight that streamed in through the open french doors that led to the balcony.

"Once you return to Benguela in a few days time, will I ever see or hear from you again?" she asked, kicking the sheet off the bed, wanting the breeze that drifted into the room to cool them.

He stared up at the ceiling. "I must be the most confused man in Angola. I never planned any of this; it just happened."

"Is it all just sex?" she asked.

"Oh, it's that all right, but it's a lot more; I've deep feelings for you," he replied. It was true, he did have feelings for her, but he also knew he was not in love with her. Nor did he have that all consuming infatuation that is supposed to qualify love. Actually, he didn't really believe he was in love with Dorothea either. Both were beautiful women, and he harboured strong feelings for both, even though they were worlds apart.

He sighed. First, he had to see this job through to its conclusion. Events over the last few months had profoundly affected his life; it wasn't a job anymore, it had become more of a quest. It seemed he no longer had control of his own destiny: he felt as if he was merely a passenger with little say as to how it would all end. Once it was over, maybe then he could regain some perspective and be able to make the right decisions.

"I'm a *mestiço*, does that bother you? I know that in your country any association with a *mestiço* is taboo," she said quietly, running her fingers through the hair on his chest.

"That's true." There was no ignoring that fact. Associating with a *mestiço* or having an affair was one thing, marrying one would be another: he would be quietly but definitely ostracised. "Look, let's not even think about that, let me first deal with dos Santos' friends."

The meeting with General Diaz and Colonel de Oliviera was very much a repetition of the previous one, where he was assured that he would have the full support of the Portuguese military for the clandestine mission. He was introduced to a Senhor da Silva, a prominent lawyer appointed by the Portuguese military, and told that it had been found that the registration of the mining claim was flawed and that this should have been registered in Don Pereira's name. Of course, this was merely an invented ploy, and the lawyer gave Werner a very officious looking letter with numerous stamps and seals, which Werner was to use it to persuade Pereira to stand up to de Mello, with Werner's support. Out of gratitude for his support, the government would then apply for re-registration of the claim, with the proviso that Don Pereira retained at least a forty percent equity in his personal capacity. They believed that this would be sufficient to persuade him to side with them. Naturally, he would also be exonerated from any wrongdoing.

If he had any sense whatsoever, Werner thought, Don Pereira would jump at the offer; a continued association with de Mello, be it willing or unwilling, could only eventually lead to his and his family's downfall. There was no other choice.

Both he, Colonel de Oliviera and two of his military aides departed Launda two days later. On his last day in the city, he met Maria for lunch, promising that although he was on his way to Benguela, he would be in touch with her. She smiled sadly at him, knowing full well that at this stage there were so many ifs and buts in both their lives, any such promises were meaningless.

CHAPTER EIGHTEEN

Werner's second entrance to Caconda was very different to his first. Philippe and he rode into town on horseback, now the successful businessman and member of the bourgeoisie, an agent for various European manufacturers, dressed in clothes that reflected his standing. Philippe, his *cavelherico*, was attired in a white shirt, grey trousers and riding boots and flaunted a new hat, now his prized possession. Both were armed with new rifles. They were accompanied by another black, actually an army scout in disguise, named Pedro. He did not enjoy quite the same status as Philippe, but his presence lent further support to the overall image that 'here rode a rich man'. Louis had insisted that the man accompany them; he spoke Portuguese fluently as well as being an excellent soldier. Werner had decided against using a wagon, but chose rather to use packhorses; this would enable them to travel faster.

They made straight for The Red Hornet cantina. Werner strode loudly over the planked floor towards the bar, seeing Senhor Sardinha behind it, polishing glasses.

The huge barman looked up, at first not recognizing Werner. Then his face lit up in surprise.

"My goodness, just look at the man. What a transformation!" Sardinha said, stretching his hand over the counter in greeting, obviously glad to see Werner. "You look like a successful businessman! Where's that nephew of mine?"

Werner shook the proffered hand. "He had to stay behind."

Louis' uncle immediately made arrangements for their accommodation at the rear of his business, although Werner was now invited to stay in the main house. His two *cavelhericos* led the horses to the back and preceded with unpacking while Werner remained in the bar.

"Are you going to be all right on your own? You're dealing with difficult people around here," the barman asked with concern.

"Certainly, there's nothing to worry about."

Without being asked, Sardinha pushed a large glass of beer towards Werner.

They chatted quietly, and Werner was hoping to pick up on rumours that would add to his information, but the bartender assured him that all was quiet.

"I've a favour to ask," Werner finally said, looking around the cantina to check if anybody was in earshot. He lowered his voice as Sardinha passed him another glass of beer.

"Could you get a message to Don Pereira asking that he meet me here? It's probably safer than at his hacienda. He's going to think this presumptuous of me, but just say I've a proposition he may find very beneficial. Tell him also, it may assist him in re-establishing his true independent status and not be tied to de Mello. Remember the name, de Mello, it's important. When he hears that name in this context, he will realize what I'm getting at. Can you do it?"

Sardinha looked at him sardonically. "I know who de Mello is. Do you think that it will work?"

"Of course it will. You don't know the whole story."

"None of my business, but I'll tell you what; as a favour, I'll personally deliver the message first thing in the morning."

"Incidentally, I have an important letter to hand to him from a lawyer, Senhor da Silva in Luanda: he specializes in property deeds and mining claims," Werner added. He slid the letter across to the barman.

Sardinha returned late the following afternoon from Don Pereira's ranch. They sat down in the house, each with a beer, Werner impatient to hear what had been said.

"You don't mind if I call you Joachim, do you?" Sardinha asked.

"It's fine with me, I've so many names," he laughed.

"Well, Joachim, initially he was extremely uncommunicative and very wary, actually belligerent, not prepared to meet you, saying his business was of no concern of yours. Of course, he had no idea who you were and when I told him that you had been in town a few weeks ago, incognito so to say, that just made matters worse. I got the impression that he was somewhat fearful, although I wouldn't know why."

"I do," Werner interjected.

"Anyway, I then handed him the letter. He didn't read it in front of me, but walked out onto the porch and stood there a long while before he returned. When he came back in, he was a little more relaxed and said that provided he could bring his eldest son and also provided this was all done in the strictest confidence, he would meet you Friday morning at ten, here at my house."

"Thank you, that's all I want," Werner responded. "Did he say anything else?"

"No, he's too wary. I left immediately thereafter."

Werner thought that Don Pereira would prefer to be as inconspicuous as possible, but this was not the case. He and his son rode into Caconda on two magnificent horses, strutting down the main street dressed as would be expected from members of the aristocracy. Well, so much for that, he thought, everybody knows they're in town; there goes the subterfuge.

Werner met them in the cantina. Both father and son were unable to hide their surprise when after a few minutes, they recognised him as the same man who had been on their land selling general merchandise some weeks ago.

"I demand to know what's going on here. I remember you. Where's your friend?" the rancher demanded, clearly unhappy at the thought that a general dealer could possibly know about his dealings with de Mello.

"Please, Don Pereira, all in good time. Let's sit down in private and I'll tell you all."

The rancher followed Sardinha and Werner to the house.

"It's de Almeida, isn't it? Well, Senhor de Almeida, I think you have a lot of explaining to do," the rancher said.

"Quite true. Before I say anymore, please understand that I'm here at the request of General Diaz, commander-in-chief of all Angolan colonial forces, who in turn acts on behalf of the absolute commander of all Portuguese forces in Portugal. I'm about to give you some secret information which, should you disclose to any other, could result in your arrest and prosecution."

"Let me be the judge of that. I don't understand why I'm being approached by you in an official capacity. Is this cloak-and-dagger meeting really necessary?"

"Please, they insisted that I warn you and that I have done. Actually, I'm an officer of the Imperial German Colonial Forces and seconded to the Intelligence Division under command of Major Zietzmann. A close rapport exists between General Diaz and Major Zietzmann. I'm further authorised to tell you that dos Santos was executed in Windhuk for gunrunning. I was a witness to the execution – death by hanging."

There was no mistaking the effect this had on the rancher: he blanched, the colour draining from his face.

"That cannot be true!"

"Believe me, it is. He was hanged on the 7th of June at six in the morning, after being tried by a military court. The arrest and proceedings are still a secret; in fact, you're privileged to know this. Do you realise that the diamonds from the mine you share with them are being used to finance the purchase of weapons which are sold to the Hereros and probably the Kunehamas? General Diaz says I should tell you that this amounts to high treason."

Don Pereira collected himself, remaining silent as he took his cup and drank some coffee. "Let's say I understand the severity of the problem. What do you want from me?"

"I want you to contact de Mello . . ."

Werner was interrupted by the rancher.

"What do you know about de Mello?"

"Enough to know that he is implicated in this, and the gunrunning, and that he is your partner, be this willingly or unwillingly on your part."

This information appeared to astound Don Pereira.

"But the man is related to the Governor-General?"

"We are aware of that. Again confidentially, the Governor-General is about to be recalled to Portugal. You are as aware as I am that Portugal is currently in political upheaval. Some fear that an attempt may be made on the king's life. In fact, I think we both know that the

Portuguese monarchy's days are numbered. I believe that within the next few years Portugal will be a republic."

"That's treason!" the rancher spat.

"It may be but I'm not a Portuguese national, so it's merely an opinion," Werner said smiling. "Anyway, as I was saying, please contact de Mello and ask him to visit you concerning the mine. Tell him that you've established that there is a serious problem, or anything similar that will bring him running. It's imperative that he come here."

"Why not go to Benguela?"

"No, it's got to be here; there's good reason for it."

He was not about to disclose that Louis was camped about ten miles out of town with a small troop of twenty men awaiting word from Werner.

"If you're trying to take the mine from him, he'll resist, with force if necessary. The man's dangerous – I know!"

"Don Pereira, he may have been dangerous, but he no longer has any support. The claim will be re-registered, with you as a partner to a bona fide mining group. If you wish, you can sell your share to the group, for a large amount of money. Also, you would be released from the clutches of de Mello and his consorts, and absolved from any prosecution, with your reputation intact. Is that not attractive?"

Don Pereira rose from the table.

"Let my son and I take a ride. We'll be back in an hour."

"I would suggest you let your son read the letter from the lawyer in Luanda and then tell him the whole story. I'm sure he'll find both very interesting."

Don Pereira looked at him, not saying a word.

They returned about an hour later and informed him that they would ask de Mello to come directly to the ranch. He also extended an invitation to Werner to reside at his hacienda, as he wanted him nearby when he confronted de Mello.

"De Mello will not arrive alone," he warned, "but will bring at least two of his men, probably from the mine, to the house. You should prepare yourself for such an eventuality."

"Do you have a flagpole?" Werner asked.

"Yes, but why?"

"Please fly the Portuguese national flag for the next few days."

"Why should I do that?" the perplexed rancher asked.

"I have a reason, but let's just say, as a show of loyalty to the government and king."

Werner had no idea when de Mello would arrive, if at all or how many men would accompany him. Neither had Don Pereira opened up: his intentions were still a mystery, probably inclining towards keeping his options open. Pedro, the additional *cavelherico* supplied by Louis came in handy, and acted as a messenger between Louis and himself.

Their arrival at the hacienda was a subdued affair. Don Pereira introduced Werner to his wife, Donna Rosa, a refined aristocratic lady whose dark hair streaked with grey belied the fact that she ran the household with an iron-hand.

There was little to remind him that he was literally in the middle of a yet to be properly explored wilderness. The hacienda was sumptuously furnished, all windows encased with shutters and heavy drapes, and a multitude of paintings adorned the whitewashed walls. Heavy oak and teak tables and chairs occupied the huge dining room and reception room, upholstered with the finest suede leather. Similarly covered cushions were scattered on the benches and the slate floors were polished to a high gloss and covered with beautiful rugs.

Over the next few days, Werner learnt to respect Don and Donna Pereira and their children. It was evident that they treated their employees fairly, always polite and never taking anything for granted, speaking civilly to them, a marked contrast to most colonists who treated the indigenous people as near slaves. The servants reacted accordingly, devoted to their employers and fiercely loyal.

Although a degree of reserve was evident, Don Pereira treated Werner well. The aristocrat would disappear every morning until well after noon, never giving any indication as to where he had been when he returned. As promised, every morning at dawn the Portuguese national flag was raised. Don Pereira never again mentioned de Mello, and all Werner could hope was that de Mello would arrive. Precisely when remained a mystery.

Ten days passed, and still Werner received no indication that de Mello would arrive. As they gathered on the large veranda to greet the short tropical twilight with a drink, Don Pereira drew him aside.

"I believe I should tell you that I've just heard that our governor-general has been recalled to Portugal. I can assure I have this news from an impeccable source. Apparently, his successor has already been appointed. Meanwhile an acting Governor-General will be appointed. Colonel Batista has also been relieved of his command, to be replaced by a Colonel de Oliveira, but I would be surprised if you did not already know this. Normally, these changes are accompanied by much fanfare and ceremony to express thanks for services rendered. This was certainly not the case here. I must say, in the light of what I've just told you, I have hopes that we may solve this amicably with de Mello."

"Well, Don Pereira, it is evident that change is afoot in the highest echelons of colonial government here in Angola. Have you any news about de Mello?"

"Yes, I have, not all necessarily good. He should be here in two days. He detoured to Huambo and is accompanied by ten men, some of them previous followers of dos Santos. Rumour is already doing the rounds that dos Santos was hanged by the Germans. I believe de Mello now realizes that an investigation is underway that may have a profound effect on his future. Maybe he knows that the only option open to him is to either fight to the death or surrender. But remember, he is a proud man."

That evening Werner drafted a long note to Louis, informing him of all that Don Pereira had said, despatching Pedro to deliver it. He noted his concerns regarding the size of de Mello's entourage and requested that Louis bring his force nearer to the hacienda.

Two days later Werner walked into the dining room for breakfast. He was immediately aware of a change in the usual morning atmosphere, of an air of anticipation. A look at Don Pereira at the head of the table left Werner in no doubt that today was to be different.

"Morning, Senhor de Almeida. De Mello will arrive today sometime. Be sure, he will be armed. I suggest you do something to ensure your own safety."

"A last favour, Don Pereira," Werner asked. "Please do not fly the flag today."

Pereira stared at Werner with his piercing grey eyes, saying nothing. Then he nodded his head.

After breakfast, Werner returned to his room. From his window, he could see the flagpole—no flag flew.

He put a small derringer, a two barrel pistol little bigger than his hand, into a pocket of his light summer jacket. Into a scabbard sewn to the inside of his riding boot, he slid a flat dagger. Around his waist he strapped a belt with a 9mm Parabellum revolver in a closed holster. This would not be considered untoward, as most riders wore weapons. He chose to spend the morning on the veranda, as this afforded him a view of the approach to hacienda. Similarly, Don Pereira never rode off, but confined himself to the ranch house.

"Riders approach," a servant called.

Werner rose from his chair, walking forward to the edge of the veranda, watching as a group of eleven riders appeared round the last bend of the track and cantered up to the hacienda. They dismounted, tying their horses' reins to the hitching pole. De Mello led them.

Don Pereira and his son Roberto stood next to Werner at the top of the stairs.

"*Buena Diaz*, your lordship, I'd rather you sent your men to the back of the house where my servants will attend to their needs. Please join us on the veranda," Don Pereira called out, waving a hand in greeting.

De Mello did not return the greeting; he hesitated for a moment staring at the rancher and Werner, unable to disguise his malice. He then nodded to his men, who walked round to the kitchen at the rear. De Mello and his assistant climbed the stairs.

De Mello pointed at Werner angrily. "What's this *porco* doing here? I should have my men kill right now."

"If it would've served any purpose, I would have already done so. However, I don't believe this would be a good idea," Don Pereira replied. "He is here at the request of the military and the new commander of the Benguela province. Things have changed dramatically, as I am sure you already know. Things are no longer what they used to be. I don't want my family stripped of its title and possessions and myself charged with treason."

"That's absurd—it won't happen," de Mello spat.

"Gentlemen, I suggest we sit and discuss this," Werner said.

"Who are you to discuss things with me or tell me what to do? You are powerless. I understand you are a German – what authority do you have? I'm the *juiz* for this *comarcas*, I could have you arrested!"

"Senhor de Mello, I doubt you would find anybody prepared to carry out that instruction. Listen, let's sit down and discuss this," Werner retorted.

De Mello stalked to the bench and sat down, his colleague joining him. Werner and the others sat down directly opposite. Don Pereira called for refreshments.

"Well?" de Mello said.

"I want you to surrender your rights to the mineral claim you have on this ranch. Although the claim is registered in Don Pereira's name, there are certain obligations registered in your favour. I need you to renounce these," Werner said straight-faced.

"Huh! That's presumptuous. And what do you propose to do with these rights?"

"I don't propose to do anything with them. They will be sold by the government of Portugal to a mining consortium, and Don Pereira here will have forty percent registered in his name."

"And if I don't agree?" de Mello sneered.

"You don't have a choice. No matter what, the military will relentlessly pursue you – you no longer have the backing of your brother-law; he is powerless, as you no doubt you already know."

"And you, Don Pereira, what do you say to all this?"

"I am fortunate: at the end of this, I will retain forty percent. Currently, the claim is registered in my name, but as Senhor de Almeida says, this is meaningless. I've never had any say. Now the government will cancel the claim and re-issue it. At least, this way I will have something enforceable by law, and I will also be exonerated from prosecution. Don't forget, we have been mining for a while without disclosure to the government, paying no taxes and smuggling diamonds: these are serious offences. I also now hear that diamonds from this mine were to be used to source illegal weapons by dos Santos, indirectly making us all, you, me and Batista, parties to this crime." He looked at de Mello sternly, every inch the aggrieved aristocrat.

De Mello gave a dismissive wave of his hand. "Don't believe everything you hear." He rose from his chair, followed by his right-hand man. "I'm on my way to the mine, Don Pereira, and I expect you to follow. If this man, this impostor, whatever," de Mello pointed at Werner, "makes any move against me, my men will forcibly retaliate."

De Mello descended the stairs calling for his men and they appeared at a run from around the building. Don Pereira remained at the top of the stairs.

"Senhor de Mello, I've made my decision," Don Pereira said, "I'm staying. I'm not about to go against the king and government, and I want you and your men off my land. I will give you five minutes."

De Mello laughed and said something to his assistant, who pulled his revolver. Almost simultaneously, Don Pereira produced a gun which he must have had hidden on his person. De Mello's assistant fired, and the bullet hit Don Pereira in the side, the impact spinning him around to collapse to the floor. For a shocked moment, no one moved, then Roberto sprang forward drawing a weapon. Another shot followed, a warning shot. The assistant waved his revolver, motioning to the others to hold their fire.

"Don't do it," the assistant shouted, "we'll kill you all."

All froze.

Werner grabbed Roberto by his arm and held him.

De Mello's riders wheeled their horses and galloped off. They had got no more than a few hundred yards when a column of mounted cavalry broke from the surrounding bush and galloped towards the hacienda, Louis in the lead.

Donna Rosa and her son bent over the prone Don Pereira.

"How bad is he?" Werner asked, hearing Louis climbing the stairs.

"He's shot in the side," she said, shouting to the servants to bring bandages and hot water. Werner watched as they carried him into the house.

The two officers greeted each other. "What a mess this is turning out to be. We've got to go after them," Louis said. "We've got to go now! I saw you flew no flag today and had my men at the ready, but it all happened so quickly – I'm sorry."

"I thought your people wanted to remain in the background," Werner spoke with growing frustration.

"How can we, he's arrived here with a fuckin' army," Louis replied irritably, "but he knows he can't beat us. He knows it's over for him in this country. He's probably planning to disappear somewhere. They've probably moved no diamonds since they lost that last lot to Philippe and Paulo. Can you imagine how many they must have in the strongbox now? I'm sure that's what he's after at the mine."

"If we go after him with the army, we change the colour of this whole operation, precisely what General Diaz and his command wanted to avoid," Werner shouted. "Otherwise they could have done everything without me. Diaz wanted de Mello to be his own worst enemy, to wreak his own destruction – that's what he wants!"

"Ok, let's follow, but do nothing. Let's see what they do. Just remember, I'm here to back you up, okay?" Louis said resignedly.

De Mello swore. The sudden intervention of the army changed everything; the cavalry emerging from the bushes had stunned him. The army would now be there on the periphery, always ready to intervene. They had just shot Don Pereira in front of a whole host of witnesses and this also lent a different colour to this fiasco. Damn, he thought. He should have stayed in Benguela. If he retaliated in any way, this definitely would become a criminal matter that implicated him.

He had to leave the colony, go somewhere else, Goa or Macau or even Brazil, but he needed the diamonds. He knew the strongbox on the mine contained a fortune; the contents would enable him to establish himself elsewhere and live a life of luxury.

"Don de Mello," his assistant said, unable to hide his concern, "the men are worried, we are now about to fight the army and they don't want to do that. Even if we were to beat them, there will only be more – we can never beat the whole army! We'll be imprisoned or die. What must I do?"

"Let them go," de Mello said resignedly. He knew his assistant was right. Let them all run and disappear. He would take the diamonds and flee. ""Let them go," he repeated, "but you stay with me. I'll see to it that you are looked after. I will leave Angola, but you can come with me. You know, we will have more than enough to go anywhere and start anew."

The men broke away, splitting up into groups and melting into the bush. De Mello and his assistant continued onto the mine.

When Louis realised that most of de Mello's men had fled, he reined his men in.

"Paulo! Bring my clothes," he shouted.

What the hell are you doing?" Werner asked.

"I'm becoming a civilian. I'm coming with you and so I will be witness to everything that happens without involving the military. The rest of the men will wait here."

Werner tried to argue with him, but he was emphatic.

Philippe interrupted them.

"*Mestre*, a horseman comes," he said.

A single horseman appeared, and as he came closer, Werner recognized Roberto Pereira.

"What are you doing here? You should be with your father."

"My father is okay, the bullet missed his lungs. My mother says he'll be fine. My father ordered me to join you and help you against de Mello who my father believes will try to help himself to all the diamonds and disappear."

"I know – he's probably right. Ok, let's go."

Louis had changed into his civilian clothes. He swung into the saddle, as did Paulo, now clad only in his loincloth, holding his rifle and short spear.

"This is now your operation, we'll do as you say," Louis said.

The six men rode off in pursuit of de Mello.

De Mello and his assistant rode into the mine, passing the workers excavating the side of the hill. The kimberlite pipe was now fully exposed, the yield incredibly rich. They dismounted alongside the sorting hut, looking across at the long tables strewn with washed gravel, the sorters—three men to a side—scrutinizing the wet gravel with trained eyes for the faint glint of a diamond.

"Tell them to take a break," De Mello told the supervisors. "You remain."

At his instruction, they opened the strongbox, and de Mello's eyes gleamed to see that it contained nearly a dozen pouches, the accumulation of the last few weeks of production. He gave two pouches to the supervisors.

"Pay off the workers from the cash in the strongbox," he said. "Whatever is left, pay as bonuses to whoever you want. You stay here at the mine, but send the workers home until further notice."

De Mello gave the confused supervisors no reasons for these instructions, but merely said that matters would be sorted out in a few days. He really no longer cared, knowing that he was never going to return.

"The two pouches are for you to split. Provided you continue to support me against the group backed by Don Pereira who are endeavouring to take over the mine." he continued fiercely. Elated at their windfall, the supervisors assured him of their support.

"Get out of here," he snarled. When alone, he pulled his money-belt from around his waist and stuffed the remaining pouches into its pockets, buckling it tightly under his clothes once again.

He returned to the sorting hut table, where he stood watching the perimeter of the mine. His assistant tapped him on the shoulder. "Behind us," he said. De Mello turned. On the edge of the clearing, six riders stood lined up abreast. He recognized all of them.

"Get the workers off the mine, all of them – now!" he barked at the supervisors.

The steam whistle blew, at first bewildering the workers still the middle of a shift. The six riders waited patiently, watching for well over an hour until the last of the workers had left. The communal huts were now empty, as the workers had left nothing but the makeshift straw pallets they slept on. Neither de Mello or his small group attempted to leave, but remained in the sorting hut. Werner could see weapons being distributed, rifles, shotguns and revolvers. Then they upended tables and other equipment, clearly intending to use these as shields and barricades to ward off any attack.

"They're not going to make a run for it. They're going to stand and fight. Being higher than us, they have an advantage. We'll be cut down before we can cross this open space. And don't forget, we dare not initiate an attack, we're supposed to be the good guys. The General said they must be the wrongdoers. We are merely to defend ourselves. How do you propose to get them to start the fight?" Louis said.

Werner had no idea whatsoever what would force de Mello and his band to attack.

"What if I let him know we've got his diamonds?" he said to Louis.

"Christus! That would be dangerous. If we lose this fight, we could go to prison or could even face a murder charge," Louis replied, clearly appalled by the idea.

"What about them shooting Don Pereira?"

"De Mello didn't do the shooting, so what do you think will happen? His lieutenant takes the heat and he goes free."

"There were too many witnesses. Don Pereira's family, the three servants on the porch and I'm sure that were we to win and any of his men were to survive, they would turn witness to save themselves from the noose. Don't forget, we are now pursuing them for the cold-blooded shooting of Don Pereira."

"Yes, I see what you mean. That should be more than enough proof."

It was now mid-afternoon. Werner looked up at the sky. A few clouds were visible.

"We'll wait for nightfall, that should level the playing fields. Maybe it will rain. What do you think?" Werner said.

They all agreed.

As Werner had predicted, the cloud mass continued to expand and by early evening, a black thunderstorm threatened. The first jagged flashes of lightning stabbed across the sky, followed by loud crashes of thunder. The first drops soon increased in intensity, until a typical summer deluge blanketed the mine.

"Let's go," Werner said.

The heavy rain gave them some cover, but still, crossing the open area in front of the sorting huts would be difficult. The defenders would see them once they were within fifty yards of the huts. No lamps were lit and the huts were in darkness.

Werner ordered Pedro and Roberto to flank the huts from one side, while Philippe and Paulo were to do the same from the opposite side. Louis and Werner would approach from the front. The back of the huts was impossible terrain; steeply sloped with loose gravel. They could see only two small buildings behind the hut, which Louis said looked like privies. Once those on the flank were in position, they were to open fire, hopefully drawing the defenders' fire.

The two officers waited, the rain slowly easing until it was just a steady downpour, the area before them occasionally lit by a lightning flash. Suddenly two gunshots rang out, followed immediately by a flurry of return fire from the huts, the muzzle flashes clearly visible.

"Let's go," Werner said.

The two men sank to the ground and leopard crawled forward cradling their rifles in their arms. The storm had drifted off, the lightning and thunder more distant. Werner prayed that a rogue flash would not illuminate them at a crucial moment as they lay on their bellies. From both flanks now, they heard the sound of gunfire being exchanged.

"I'm going to try and shoot at one of those next flashes from the hut," Louis said.

The two men were about three yards apart and had seen every muzzle flash that emanated from the huts.

"Ok, but once you've fired, let's roll a few more yards apart. They'll return fire for sure."

Lying on his stomach, his elbows propped on the ground, Louis looked down the barrel watching for the right moment. He soon pin-pointed the source of a flash, and took careful aim at where he thought it to be. He waited, the rifle rock steady. From the same spot in the hut, there was another flash. He pulled the trigger and the rifle slammed into his shoulder. He immediately rolled away from Werner as a sharp piercing cry split the night. Bullets threw up spurts of mud around where they had been, and the air reverberated to the deep boom of a shotgun, the heavy pellets impacting the ground near Werner.

"Fuck! That's buckshot!" Werner said to Louis. "Did you hear that cry, I think you hit somebody."

To their left were long tubes with about a three foot inner diameter, made of metal mesh, each end resting on a stand. The miners used these to sift the gravel, separating the smaller stones into various sizes. The tubes were rotated as the gravel was shovelled into one end and it would slowly travel to the lower end where the mesh separated the gravel by size.

The two men slowly crawled to these. They fired no further shots, not wanting to give their position away. Still ten yards from the sifters, the night sky was lit by a large lightning flash, immediately followed by both rifle and shotgun fire, all directed at the two men prone on the ground. Both wildly returned fire.

"Run!" Louis shouted, simultaneously rising to his feet and running the last few yards to the row of sifters, where he threw himself to the ground behind the heaped mounds of stone and sand. Werner was right on his heels.

"Louis! Are you ok?" Werner hissed.

"Yes, what is it?"

"We've got ourselves in a stalemate here. We've got to charge that hut."

"We can't do that, they'll just pick us off, they've got shotguns remember?" Werner retorted, his disbelief at Werner's suggestion evident in his voice.

"But if Paulo and Philippe give us continuous covering fire, maybe we can skirt round the hut and get to that steep slope behind it. There's a small rock-built building behind it, we could hide behind that."

Werner shouted instructions in German to Philippe, hoping none of the defendants could speak the language.

Again the two black men opened fire, soon followed by the other pair, laying down a barrage of withering crossfire, keeping the men in the hut pinned down behind whatever shelter they had.

The two officers sprinted for the brick building, expecting to be picked off at any moment. The building was not much bigger than an outhouse, but at least it afforded good cover. The defendants had seen the two run, but could only get off a few wild and off the mark shots.

Louis looked at the stout door of the building; this was bolted and locked with a big padlock.

"Werner," Louis panted, "this isn't a shithouse, it's the dynamite store – I'm sure of it. Look, that's why the big lock."

"Shoot it off."

"Are you mad? We'll blow ourselves and everybody else to kingdom come."

"Better than being stuck behind this building and shot at by de Mello. Here, let me do it, I'll be careful."

Werner took his automatic from its holster and proceeded to shoot at the wood that secured the hasp and staple, wood fragments flying in all directions. He made sure he was shooting upwards and not into the store. This drew fire from the hut as they realized what the two men were doing. Forced to hunker down for cover, lying on his back, Louis started to kick at the door with both feet simultaneously. With a loud crack, the wood gave, the hasp and stable torn from the door and dangling from the frame. The room was small, only about twelve feet by six feet. In the dark, they could just make out the wooden boxes packed against the walls.

Louis felt with his hands along the top of the boxes, finding one that had been opened, its lid just resting loose on the top. He stuck his hand in and withdrew a handful of sticks.

"Dynamite!" he said triumphantly.

"Yeah, but where are the fuse and detonator caps?"

"Give me a chance. I'll find them."

Outside the gunfire continued as Philippe and the others kept those in the hut pinned down even as they continued to pepper the brick building. Shots ricocheted into the night.

It took Louis five minutes to find fuses and caps and then another five to assemble a few sticks ready for use. He made these with very short fuses, Werner noticed.

Louis held a stick out to Werner, the fuse end pointed at him.

"Light it," he said.

"Don't you think those fuses could be a little longer?" Werner asked apprehensively.

"Stop worrying, they're fine, the idea is not to hang on to it once it's lit!"

"I take it that's the opinion of a dynamite expert." Werner dubiously pulled a box of matches from his trousers and struck a match, the sulphurous light briefly illuminating their near surroundings. The fuse took with a hiss and splutter, a small yellow flame spurting from its end.

Louis never hesitated. He threw it as hard as he could in the direction of the hut. It landed a few yards short, and both men dropped to the ground.

There was an enormous flash and deafening boom. The pressure wave washed over them, small stones rattling down on the hut.

"I couldn't throw the damn thing far enough, it wasn't heavy enough. Tie two sticks together, let's try that," Louis hurriedly said.

Werner tore off a piece of his shirt, using this to tie two sticks of dynamite together.

In panic, de Mello's men concentrated their fire on the brick building, and bullets bounced off the walls.

Again a match flared, and as the men in the hut realized what was about to happen, they concentrated even more fire on the building.

Louis threw the make-shift dynamite bomb, and this time he was rewarded with a clatter as the stick hit the wooden floor of the hut and skittered forward towards the centre.

The explosion was so intense they felt the shock through the ground and the rock-built store was bombarded by rocks, large ones this time. Werner looked up, his ears ringing; a fire had started in the partially demolished sorting hut, the interior chaotic with broken sorting tables and collapsed roof rafters. The fallen roof thatch rapidly fed the blaze and within seconds it had developed into a raging fire, the flames crackling and roaring as more kindling took hold. Out of the corner of his eye, he saw Paulo and Philippe charging the hut, their spears in their hands drawn back for a killing thrust.

"Don't kill them!" Werner shouted.

They either did not hear him or did not want to, caught up with the excitement and their adrenalin rush. In the firelight, he saw one of the defenders stagger to his feet, his shotgun in his hand. Too late; Philippe was upon him. The man had no chance, the assegai took him in the chest and his back arched as he threw his head back and his death wail pierced the night.

"Stop! Stop!" Werner shouted, rushing forward.

He tried to enter the hut. The fire was now out of control, one end of the hut burning fiercely.

"Where are the others?" Louis asked, his revolver in his hand.

"Major, they're dead," Paulo said, pointing at two bodies on the floor.

"God, they took the brunt of the explosion," Werner said. He saw that the one man's leg was blown off. There was another body lying a little further away, his eyes staring unblinking at the dark sky: a bullet had entered his neck and he had bled profusely.

"Philippe, make for the corral. They'll be after their horses to escape. Hurry!"

There was no sign of de Mello or his assistant. He realized that there had to have been five men and not four as he had previously thought. He could only imagine that another of the sorters had joined de Mello.

Philippe, Paulo and Pedro ran off in the direction of the corral; Don Pereira's son joined Louis and Werner; all stood in the open and watched the raging inferno devouring the hut. The fire was out of control, it would have to burn itself out. The fire illuminated the whole area around them.

"How many are still missing?" Werner asked.

"Just two – de Mello and Jorge, his assistant. The rest are dead."

"Louis, you stay here, I'm going to find Philippe and Paulo."

Werner walked quickly to the corral where he found the two men.

There was no sign of any horses or de Mello and his partner.

"They've gone?" Werner asked.

"Yes, they went north, maybe towards Huambo," Philippe said.

CHAPTER NINETEEN

The rain had stopped, and the spoor left by de Mello was well defined in the mud, easy to follow. Werner had to wait as it was still too dark to follow the man's trail: sunrise was two hours away. The sky, however, had cleared and the last of the clouds disappeared.

Some of the mine workers had returned. As they were no more than employees, not responsible for the actions of de Mello, they were sent home to let all know that the mine was temporary closed. Senhor Roberto Pereira, now standing in for his father, assured the men that once the mine started up again, they would be considered for re-employment.

Werner was only after de Mello, and if his assistant Jorge were to disappear he would not pursue him. The shooting of Don Pereira was really a police matter – they could go after Jorge and arrest him for attempted murder. However, if the man continued to fight, he would be pursued. It was decided that only he and Philippe would ride after the two men, while Louis and his men would stay and be ready to assist the Pereira family should the need arise.

Philippe saw to it that he picked the best horses and scrounged provisions from the others to last a few days. Werner wanted to be ready to leave at the first signs of dawn.

Dawn was still no more than a grey streak on the horizon. Philippe had already saddled the animals and as Werner stuck his foot in the stirrup to mount, Louis approached with Roberto Pereira and another man.

"Werner, you need to take Roberto with you: he insists and as it was his father they shot, he has a right. This is Michael Duarte, he is attached to the local policia, and in fact, he is in the man in charge of this area. The Pereiras reported the shooting to the policia who now wish to arrest de Mello and that deputy of his. If you refuse to allow them to accompany you, they'll set off on their own," Louis said.

"They'll slow me down."

"No, we won't," Pereira interjected. "We'll do as you say; you can lead." The young man looked at the police officer, who nodded his head in agreement.

"Werner, that's not a bad idea. If de Mello resists and you are caught up in a gun battle and he is killed, at least you will have a witness. The police will say they were resisting arrest. Nobody can then come after you," Louis said.

"Ok, you're right, I just may need a witness. Let's ride."

The dawn rapidly lit the surrounding bush as the four men followed de Mello's trail. It was leading north towards Huambo, or so it seemed. The kept the horses at a steady canter. He doubted whether de Mello, sure that Werner would pursue him, would have stopped to rest.

Werner was right. De Mello had not stopped but headed into the highlands. Once in the highlands, he would try to lose his pursuers in the rugged and twisted rocky ravines. He would not rest until he thought they had managed to throw their followers. Now in the foothills of the highlands, they forced the horses into a stream and followed its course for a mile or two. It was hard going but they urged the horses on, leaving the stream every now and then for twenty to thirty yards and then backtracking to the spot where they had emerged from the water. Hopefully this would mislead their followers, if only for a short while.

Werner's group made good time, keeping up with de Mello until he entered the stream. This delayed them; at first they did not know whether he had gone upstream or downstream. It took some intense and careful examination before Philippe could indicate downstream with a wave of his hand. De Mello's horses were shod, and Philippe had seen the scratches on the rocks from the steel shoes. The diversions delayed them but eventually, they found where de Mello had left the river and turned north further into the highlands. Already the sun hung low over the horizon.

"Philippe, find the highest spot you can for us to spend the night. Maybe de Mello will be fool enough to light a fire and we will see it," Werner said.

"*Mestre*, de Mello grew up in this country – he knows the bush, he'll not make any stupid mistakes," the black man replied.

They stopped in the shelter of an overhanging bluff near the summit of a large hill. Werner immediately climbed to the top with Philippe. It was already dark, a full moon rising on the eastern horizon. Slowly they looked around, Werner using his binoculars. There were no fires to be seen.

"*Mestre*, it is a full moon and there are no clouds. We will be able to follow the trail, although it will be slow, but we will cover a good few miles. In these hills there are only certain ways you can travel; it makes it easy to follow somebody once you've found his spoor."

"Ok, let everybody eat something and then we'll be on our way again."

It was close to two o clock in the morning when they came over a rise and saw a few fires in the valley below them. A wide river could be seen in the bottom of the valley, the moonlight reflecting from the flowing water.

"Careful, *Mestre*, that's a Kunehama village," Philippe cautioned. He dismounted and indicated to the others that they should do the same. He then took all the reins and asked Duarte to lead the horses back so that they would not give their position away.

The village was quiet, the fires allowed to burn low. Werner could see only two sentries: they were not looking out for attackers but rather watching for wild animals after their cattle.

"Do you think de Mello is here?" Werner asked.

"I don't know. He does not know the Kunehamas and they don't know him. I think it would be too dangerous for him to have stopped here. But I'm sure he is nearby, they need to rest."

"We also need to rest, at least until daybreak."

They skirted around the village and when they found a suitable spot a few miles away, they stopped to rest up.

The moment the sky began to lighten, de Mello awoke. The two men saddled up and mounted their horses. They were exhausted, having hardly slept knowing that they were probably being relentlessly pursued. During the night, they had nearly stumbled into the village. It was only at the last moment that they had become aware of the fires; they had immediately backtracked and then detoured around the site.

De Mello's horse was uneasy. He turned round and looked at Jorge; his horse was also jittery.

"The horses are scared of something," de Mello whispered, drawing his rifle from its saddle scabbard.

They reined the animals in. These were the foothills of the mountains, the ground rugged and hilly, not the type of terrain that appealed to lions as they preferred the plains.

"*Senhor*," the deputy whispered, "I'm sure it's a leopard."

The trail they were on was cut into the side of a hill. It was difficult to skirt away from it as the ground became almost impassable. De Mello carefully inspected the length of the slope and the buttresses that overlooked their trail.

"*Marde*, I see it, it is a leopard. We are too near, it will attack."

The horses were now extremely agitated, neighing frantically, and both men were fighting to keep them under control. De Mello took aim at the animal with the rifle, not wanting to pull the trigger as the shot would be heard for miles, but if it attacked, he would have no option.

"Senhor, don't shoot," Jorge hissed loudly.

It was too late, the leopard was already crouching, about to launch itself at them and the panicked horses. De Mello managed to draw a bead on the cat's body and pulled the trigger. The shot rang out, the bullet hitting the leopard just behind the shoulder blade—a heart shot, the slug exploded in the body cavity, the heart and lungs disintegrated. The leopard somersaulted backwards, falling to the ground and lying still.

The echo of the shot rolled through the hills.

All four men came to an abrupt halt, looking at Werner.

"It's him," he said, "Why did he shoot?"

"*Mestre*, it could be anything, lions, leopards, even Kunehamas. This is wild country, few people live or travel here," Philippe replied.

"Let's go!" Werner dug his spurs into his horse's flanks and lunged forward in the direction of the gunshot. He had a good idea of the direction, and knew it could be no more than a mile

213

or so away, perhaps a little higher in the mountains. He crested a hill and before him saw a little flat area amongst the hills. Two horses were running along a rough trail on the opposite mountainside.

"There they are," he shouted. A shot rang out, and then another. The two fugitives had opened fire the moment they saw their pursuers. Duarte immediately returned fire and the two men turned hastily, making their way along the mountainside trail looking for cover. Soon they disappeared behind the curve of the mountain.

"Come on," Werner shouted, "let's get them before they get away."

The four still had to cross the valley to get to the other side. Fortunately, the going was relatively easy through the small depression between the hills. Finally, they looked down into a large flat valley, and saw a small settlement with a few adobe-like buildings and quite an extensive corral with a number of holding pens.

"That must be Capira," the constable said. "There's a trading store there but I'm sure it's deserted. It belongs to a white Portuguese living with a black woman. He had a few men working for him and kept quite a few cattle. He used to trade with the local inhabitants. They all seem to have fled—you know, the war."

As he spoke, they saw the two horsemen enter the settlement, leading their two horses into a small corral that adjoined a partially derelict building, part of which was used as a stable.

"They're going to make a stand. They know they have no chance if they're caught in the open," Philippe said.

It was obvious that marauding rebels had already ransacked the settlement, probably at the beginning of the civil war. It had been burnt to the ground, but the main building still stood intact, although the hinges were torn off the main door and broken window shutters hung askew. Seconds later, a shot echoed off the hills, the bullet passing between the men looking down on the settlement. They had been seen. They immediately sought cover.

"Where are the locals?" Werner asked.

"They're probably in the bush hiding. They know the Portuguese soldiers will soon come. Maybe they've been and gone. Be sure, we're being watched, but they won't attack," Philippe said.

"Ok, off your horses. We're going to get nearer to the building they're in. Philippe and I will come in from the left side, Roberto, you and Duarte from the right."

The terrain was hilly, but the bush was not dense, and the occasional bare rock buttresses and patches of broken shale on the slopes did not provide good cover. Every time the people in the building saw a movement, they would fire, the shots close, their aim excellent.

"*Mestre*, we are going to have to give each other covering fire. We're too close now. If we all try and move they will definitely wound or kill one of us."

Werner agreed. He took up position behind a large rock and nodded to Philippe, firing off shot after shot at the two windows and door of the building as fast as he could until the rifle's magazine was empty. Philippe had scurried forward in a low crouch and was now about fifty yards ahead of him lying on his stomach peering around the trunk of a large tree. As Philippe laid down covering fire, Werner crouched over trying to present the smallest target and flung himself behind the tree. Fortunately it had a sizeable girth, being an old baobab. They were now about two hundred yards from the building. Whoever was shooting at them was a crack shot, with bullet after bullet hitting the tree at about knee height.

"Christus! This is dangerous. If we show ourselves, we'll definitely get shot. How are the others doing?" Werner asked.

"*Mestre*, they're in the same position as we are, only they're at least behind some rocks – far better cover."

A few more shots rung out, spitting chunks out of the tree.

"God, we've got to do something. We can't lie here all day!" Werner exclaimed.

"*Mestre*, I've got something here." Philippe had a satchel made of rawhide leather, which normally hung at waist height from a strap across his shoulder. He brought the satchel up so it lay between them. He opened the flap and withdrew four sticks of dynamite.

"Where the fuck did you get those?"

The black man grinned. "Paulo gave them to me, he got them from the Portuguese Major."

Werner was overjoyed. This was a windfall.

"Both you boys are going to get a medal for this, I'll make sure!" he laughed.

He looked at the sticks; they were complete with detonator and short fuse, ready for use. "There's a problem, we'll never get near enough to throw these. They'll pick us off."

He could hear shots being exchanged between the building and the other two. They were about two hundred yards away and as far away from the building, similarly pinned down.

"De Mello!" Werner shouted. There was no reply. Again, he shouted, but the only answer he got was an angry shot.

Werner did not doubt that they could overrun de Mello and his assistant but he knew they would take a casualty or two, and that he was not prepared to accept. Again, he carefully surveyed the area between him and the building. It was flat, all scrub removed, the ground covered with grass at knee height, still green from the recent rains. This was interspersed with a few trees, quite large, their trunks just thick enough to provide cover for one man.

"Philippe, it's not even midday yet, we can't lie here all day in the sun. What are we going to do?"

"Mestre, he won't leave, he has water and shelter. He's brought his horses into the building."

Werner lay on his stomach peering from behind the tree trunk, the Mauser K88 against his shoulder. He drew a bead on the open doorway and squeezed off a perfect shot. But what did he hit? Nothing.

"With this moon, as soon as it's dark, he'll be gone! We've got to do something!" Werner said assertively. Both knew that to throw the dynamite required one of them to reveal themselves. At this range, it was too dangerous.

"*Mestre*, do you see those broken corrals? Well, as soon as the sun sets, the cattle will return, even if there's nobody looking after them. These cattle have been doing this since they were born, every day they leave and every day as night falls they come back. It's habit. We must use them as cover."

Werner knew Philippe was right.

"Ok, let's fall back the same way we got here. Let Roberto and the policeman give us covering fire."

After much waving, the others understood. A half-hour later, all four had fallen back to where their horses were, well out of range.

Werner outlined Philippe's idea, the others agreeing. They did not know how many cattle were left although they had seen a few. Werner fretted, impatient to bring this to an end; it worked on his mind. He hoped de Mello would make a break for it, but he remained holed up in the building. The four of them took turns pumping shots at the door and windows. If de Mello had any sense, he too would attempt to make a break under cover of darkness.

"Let's move and find ourselves a cattle trail still in use that leads to and from the corrals," Werner said suddenly.

They skirted around the building keeping out of range and soon came across a trail worn nearly a foot deep into the ground. No more than a yard wide, the cattle trails circumvented any obstacle, never running straight, meandering around the smallest bush and stone, but invariably leading to the corrals. The hollow trails were filled with very fine talcum-like powder.

As the sun hung over the horizon casting long shadows, the first of the cattle appeared seemingly from nowhere, plodding along, the cows with their calves in tow, all raising clouds of enveloping dust.

The four men rode their horses amongst the cattle, hanging from their saddles, holding onto the saddle pommels, their bodies lower than the top of the horses. Those in the house would find it difficult to see them against the sun, particularly with the dust raised by the cattle. This would only work up to a point, certainly no nearer than a hundred yards or so, when the defenders would realize that there were horses amongst the cattle. They hung low alongside their horses, shielded from view, their animals keeping a leisurely pace with the cattle. No wind blew, the dust just hung in the air.

The powdered dust nearly suffocated Werner, even with the bandanna over his nose. The exertion of hanging onto the saddle pommel made him perspire and the dust stuck to his face. He waited for a shot; surely de Mello would realize what they were planning, but no shot rang out. He was surprised that he had managed to reach the corral, which was about a hundred yards on the other side of the building.

At the entrance to the corral, he dropped to the ground, pulling his rifle from its boot. Out of the corner of his eye, he saw the others do the same. Keeping the cattle between him and the building and crouched low, he ran for the cover of a long watering trough. He was incredulous; they still had not been seen. The trough was quite long, fed with water from a corrugated iron reservoir, a windmill pumping water to keep it filled. Little wind blew, the windmill's vanes forlornly stationary. Soon, all four men crouched behind the trough, the thirsty cattle avoiding them, drinking from the other side, their haunches facing the building, some bellowing at the men and their intrusion.

Around the building were odd items which could provide some cover if they were to advance. There was a derelict wagon, its one wheel collapsed; an outdoor brick oven close to the kitchen. The stout kitchen door was closed; it would take some serious effort to open that. Werner was sure this was barred. There were three windows at the rear of the building; all the shutters were open.

Werner turned to Roberto.

"We need covering fire. Philippe and I will make a dash for the building. We'll probably take cover behind that oven first. You make sure nobody steps out and tries to shoot us, okay?"

The young man looked at Duarte, who nodded his head.

"Okay."

"Start shooting," Werner said.

The two men opened fire, Werner and Philippe dashed across the open ground towards the house. Shots rang out, the bullets buzzing past their heads, but the shooters' aim was erratic as they were taking fire themselves. They ran past the brick oven, and made straight for the main building, where they flattened themselves against the wall, trying to regain their breath. Meanwhile, the other two maintained a steady fire on the windows.

Werner discarded his rifle and with his automatic in hand, flattened himself against the wall.

Only the tops of the hills were illuminated, the sun having slipped below the horizon. The two men were now about fifteen yards from the kitchen door. Werner pulled two sticks of dynamite from his pocket.

"Philippe, I want you to light one, and as soon as it explodes, immediately light another and hand it to me."

The black man looked at Werner, not quite happy at what Werner required him to do, but he nodded his understanding. Werner held out the first stick; Philippe struck a match, lit the fuse, which Werner immediately threw so that it came to rest on the sill of the kitchen door. The two threw themselves to the ground. The shock of the explosion was far worse than Werner had expected, and he was literally lifted off the ground by the pressure wave, his ears ringing as dust and dirt flew all over the place. The next thing he knew was a dynamite stick being thrust at him, the fuse spluttering through the dust. For a second he had forgotten his instructions to Philippe. In panic, he grabbed it and ran to what was left of the kitchen door, tossing the stick through the opening into the interior. He barely made it back to put the wall between himself and the building when the dynamite exploded. As the dust dissipated, any indications that there had once been doors and windows here was gone; only jagged holes remained. Anybody within the confines of the building had to be concussed!

All four men stormed in, spreading out, each firing off a shot or two. The room was a jumble of broken furniture – tables and chairs, a cast iron stove which lay toppled on its side, its chimney-pipe pulled from the roof. Racking had been blown off the walls, the contents now strewn across the floor, broken porcelain and glass jars. The top of the roof had been blown off, and parts of the cross-beams had collapsed onto the kitchen floor. Except for the bellowing of the cattle, there was no other sound. Slowly he moved forward, expecting a shot to ring out any moment. Roberto followed his example, approaching the doorway from the other side; they both flattened themselves against the wall, creeping forward, guns at the ready. At a nod from Werner, they stormed through the opening. There was no return fire. This room too was a shambles. There was no sign of de Mello. The next room revealed the same.

"They've somehow escaped," Werner shouted.

They rushed outside into the fading light. The horses were still in a small corral directly alongside the building, fortunately shielded from the explosions, although extremely agitated. If de Mello had escaped, he had to be on foot.

"Mestre, they've split up," Philippe said.

"How do you know that?"

"I just saw the other man; de Mello is not with him."

Werner marvelled at the man's eyesight. How could he see in this light?

"Which way is he heading?"

"He's heading for the high ground."

"And de Mello?"

"I don't know."

"*Merda!*" Werner disgustedly exclaimed.

"Wait! I see him." Philippe pointed towards the hills. It took a moment before Werner also saw him, scrabbling up the sides.

"Why didn't they take the horses?" Roberto asked.

"They didn't have time. After the first explosion, they realized we would be inside the building within minutes. The horses were corralled and probably going crazy because of the explosions – we would've been onto them before they could mount up." Werner paused for a moment.

"On foot, out here! That's crazy," Roberto gasped.

"Philippe, take some water; go after the deputy, don't worry about de Mello, I'll track him. Just keep the pressure on unless you are sure you can get him without getting hurt. Maybe it's better that you wait until morning before you make a move on him, but keep after him – make him run. You two wait here until we call for you."

Philippe and Werner refilled their water bottles from the trough outside. Philippe slunk off into the rapidly encompassing darkness, the moon and evening star already above the horizon.

Werner knew that the two fugitives would not be able to travel far, but would probably find a large tree to could spend the night in, jamming themselves into a comfortable position amongst the branches to keep out of reach of wild animals. He decided to follow at first light.

The sky was still grey, the ground covered by the slightest hint of dew. In the lowest parts of the valleys, a thin blanket of mist covered the ground. Werner made for the spot were de Mello had last been seen. He had learnt a good deal from Philippe about tracking, and sure enough, he soon found de Mello's tracks where he had scrambled up the slope slipping in places. By now, the first rays of the sun began to appear, and the face of the mountains was now bathed in yellow light.

Werner had a basic plan, but he was content to merely follow until it became evident what de Mello had in mind. Surely, the man realized that there was no point in returning to Benguela: that would be too dangerous.

He followed de Mello's spoor for an hour. The man was making no effort to hide his tracks. He was moving northeast; this could only mean that he was heading to Huambo, dos Santos' base. He wondered who was managing it now and on whose behalf. It must be generally known by now what had happened to dos Santos.

There was a mountain range ahead, its slopes steep, certainly not passable by anyone on horseback. De Mello was heading straight for a slight gap in the range, still a daunting trip.

By midday, pursued and pursuer had climbed high into the gap. Werner had to use his hands from time to time to scale the steep rock face. He had lost sight of de Mello, but if de Mello deviated from his route, Werner would see him soon enough against the rock faces on either side. The going was tough, the sun hot, and he took frequent sips from his water bottle.

He was negotiating a difficult piece, a deep flute cut into the rocks by the water course flowing down over eons, and he required both hands and feet to climb to the summit two hundred feet above.

Suddenly he heard the crash of rock on rock. As he looked up, a huge rock tumbled towards him, breaking loose other rocks as it fell and starting a small avalanche of rock and debris. He did the only thing he could; he flung himself into the vertical crevice of the flute, his body barely fitting therein, holding himself in position by spreading his legs and arms and wedging himself inside the pipe. The avalanche of rocks hurtled passed him with inches to spare, wayward chips and stones hitting him in the face. The further down the side it travelled, the more rock it tore loose from the mountain until it was a full-scale rockslide. Had he not squeezed himself into the flute, the slide would've taken him with it.

All was suddenly quiet again. Obviously, de Mello had started the rockslide, probably by dislodging a big rock. Did he know Werner had survived? He decided to wait his adversary out. Surely he would climb down to see if a body lay at the foot of the face.

Werner unslung his rifle strap from across his shoulder and placed the weapon on a small ledge that jutted out from the rock face. The crevice did not afford much shelter: still partially in the sun, he was soon hot and perspiring. For fifteen minutes, nothing happened. Suddenly a small rock tumbled past him, bouncing down the slope. He remained hidden, not knowing whether this was merely a remnant of the previous rockslide or had accidentally been dislodged. A minute or so later another stone rolled down. De Mello must be above him, slowly making his way down.

Before long he could hear the slight sound of movement as somebody slowly climbed down the rock face. He knew that de Mello would see the crevice and know that this was an excellent place to hide and that this would have protected him from the rockslide.

Werner took his automatic out of its holster, and released the safety catch. All movement above him ceased, the only sound was the faint whistle of the breeze. Had the man heard something? He waited; nothing stirred – no sounds.

Suddenly something flashed passed the opening in the crevice. Werner inched forward. It came into view again, swinging from the opposite side. De Mello was dangling from a rope, his feet clamped into a huge knot he had tied in the rope, and he hung on with one hand holding a revolver in the other. As he swung from left to right, he lined it up on Werner, pulling the trigger as he was directly opposite the flute. In that brief second as the man flashed past, Werner actually saw the revolver buck in his hand and smelled the slight trace of cordite as the weapon fired. The bullet struck him in the shoulder, the shock of the impact leaving him numb as he fought frantically to retain his position on the rocks, one arm and both feet spread against the inside of the pipe to stop himself from sliding down. His other arm was useless. He had dropped his automatic.

Again de Mello swung passed, and this time Werner was expecting both him and the shot. It ricocheted off the rocks, barely missing Werner. A rock shard struck him in the face, leaving a gash from which blood now trickled. His rifle! He jammed his feet firmly against the side and slowly reached over with his good arm. He grabbed it by the stock, crooked it under his arm and flicked off the safety catch. Thank God, he had loaded it when he had started to pursue de Mello. He managed to level it, and waited for de Mello. The man's shadow moved across the rock face before de Mello swung into view. In that split second Werner saw every detail clearly; the trimmed beard, the dirty dustcoat, the abraded and scratched black boots, the silver revolver in the man's hand. He saw de Mello's sudden shock at the sight of the rifle, just before he pulled the trigger. The rifle boomed in the confined space of the chimney, the recoil too much for Werner to absorb with the one hand and it fell from his fingers, clattering as it tumbled to the rocks below. The bullet hit de Mello in the stomach, the sheer force of the impact tearing the man's hands from the rope, and he fell, not making a sound as he bounced off an outcrop and then dropped thirty or forty feet to lie inert and broken at the bottom of the slope.

Werner's situation was precarious. He was at the limit of his endurance, no longer able to stop himself from sliding down the chimney. He inched himself down the chute painfully, rock by rock, his legs shaking from the exertion, expecting to slip any moment. The sweat poured from him, his face dripping perspiration, his underclothes sodden.

The moment his feet touched the bottom of the chute, he crumpled to the ground. Blood still poured from his shoulder wound. He couldn't move his arm. His automatic was lying nearby; he picked this up and stuck it into its holster. His water bottle was somehow still looped over his shoulder; he removed the cap and swallowed a few drops gratefully.

He tore a few strips off his shirt and tried to fashion these into plugs to stem the flow of blood from his shoulder. This was only partially successful, blood still oozed from the wound. Any movement just aggravated it.

He knew he had to stay where he was. If he moved away into the open and then collapsed, wild animals would get him. He drew himself as far back into the crevice as he could; if anything were to try and get to him, it would have to come in from the front. He drank the last of his water.

He came to with a start. Something had woken him; he heard nothing, but he smelt something, a mixture of unwashed fur and carrion, similar to the smell of a dirty dog. He stared through the slit in the rock. He could clearly see the sky beyond, illuminated by the full moon hanging in a cloudless sky. Whatever it was, it was very quiet; at first he heard no more sounds except the chirr of insects.

Then there was a low growl, a staccato sound, each syllable separate, each grr—grr clearly distinct, followed by a low cough. He caught a glance of movement against the light, fleeting, but it was enough for him to recognize the leopard. His hair rose on his neck. It is said that to be stalked by a leopard is to be stalked by the most dangerous animal in the world: it is certainly the most dangerous animal to encounter at night. Fear gripped him, this was a relentless and fearless killer. He knew that it was the smell of his blood that had attracted the animal. Why had it not gone for de Mello?

It suddenly appeared in the slit, swiping inward with its paw, the extended claws missing his face by only a few inches. The moment he saw the animal Werner pulled the trigger, the automatic's discharge deafening in the confined space. The animal disappeared and all he heard was a tumultuous growling and snapping. He had no idea whether he had hit it; everything had happened so quickly. His sudden movement had opened his wound, and the blood dripped slowly down his arm.

Within minutes it was just outside the crevice again, emitting a low growl with an occasional short cough as it paced up and down. It seemed to be contemplating its next move. One-handed as he was, Werner was no match against its speed and brute strength.

For a few minutes it prowled around outside the crevice. Then in a split second, it exploded through the narrow entrance, its stench overpowering, its claws extended, jaws open as it tried to reach him. He gagged at its foul breath, and fired wildly. The shot missed, and he desperately tried to bring the gun to bear again. Screaming at the top of his voice, he saw its silhouette clearly against the moonlight and pulled the trigger again. This time the bullet struck, driving the animal snarling and biting backwards. Again and again he fired, and the animal fell to the ground, trying to bite its side where the bullets had penetrated. Slowly, movement subsided and then what seemed like hours later, it dropped its head and lay still.

Werner's coat and shirt had been ripped to shreds and he had deep lacerations on his arm and chest which were now bleeding profusely. With difficulty, he tore additional strips from his tattered shirt and wound these round his arm. He was utterly exhausted and in shock, all resistance driven from him. Collapsing against the bare rock face behind him, he lay still.

Slowly he emerged from the fog of sleep, imagining that somebody was calling him.

"Mestre!" he heard.

"Mestre!" There it was again, now louder.

He knew he had to wake up, and clawing his way upwards from some deep abyss, he forced himself to open his eyes. The first signs of dawn filtered through the gap.

"Mestre!" he heard again.

"Here, here!" he croaked, and then tried to force himself to his feet. Eventually he stood, swaying, the good arm outstretched, supporting himself against the wall. He shuffled forward towards the opening and emerged into the light. A low-lying fog covered the valley below, the sun peeking over the distant horizon. Philippe was climbing the slope, still clad in his loincloth, the fur from some animal wrapped around his shoulders to ward off the early morning chill. When the black man saw Werner, his face split into a wide grin of relief, white teeth flashing.

"Thank God, oh you beautiful black bastard, am I glad to see you!" Werner quietly breathed, falling against his friend.

Philippe caught him, holding him upright as he assessed the extent of his master's injuries. Forcing him to lie down, he made him comfortable, giving him water and covering him with the piece of fur from his shoulders.

"Mestre, I found de Mello down below, so I knew you were here somewhere. The lions had got him, but there were still bones and his clothes."

From the bag hanging next to his side, the man extracted a blood-smeared money belt.

"This was de Mello's. The lions left it," he said. He opened the pockets and produced a few of the pouches. "There are seven of them."

Werner stared at his saviour in shock. A fortune of diamonds lay in their hands.

"What happened to you?" Werner finally asked Philippe.

The black man told him how he had relentlessly tracked de Mello's assistant through the night. The Portuguese man was no newcomer to Angola; it was soon evident that he knew the bush well, and he kept moving. Philippe sometimes lost his spoor but always managed to find it again. In the early hours of the morning, the white man finally stopped to rest alongside a small stream fed by a spring bubbling from a crevice in the mountainside, the water cold and clear. Philippe waited until the man slept then very quietly crept up to him. He sat down beside him and let him sleep. Jorge was so exhausted he was unaware of Philippe.

"When he woke and saw me sitting there, he was very frightened. I did not say anything, but sat there quite still, just watching him. Then he suddenly pulled a revolver from under the blanket. I grabbed his wrist and while he looked at me, I stuck my knife into his throat."

Philippe produced the knife; it was an evil weapon, a long grooved bayonet taken from one of the dead Portuguese soldiers.

"While he was dying, I told him this was the end, that he would never see his wife and children again and that you had killed de Mello, although I did not know that for sure at the time."

Philippe's voice was nonchalant. Werner could picture the ghastly scene: these people were not be trifled with. The law of the wild still prevailed, and they did not value life as the western world did. They could be insanely cruel, but that was just their way of life.

Philippe carefully inspected Werner's wound. Satisfied that he was not in immediate danger, he left his water bottle with Werner and handed him his revolver.

"*Mestre*, just stay here. Use that gun if you have to. I'll be back soon."

Philippe returned with Roberto and the constable, making a travois to move Werner and take him back to Don Pereira's hacienda. Here there were medical supplies and Donna Pereira, could help attend to his wounds. While not a doctor, she knew what she was doing and slowly she nursed both her husband and Werner back to health. The bone in his shoulder was broken, but fortunately not shattered. They bound it as tight as possible and kept him quiet to stop any movement.

For three days, Werner never saw Philippe. Eventually, he demanded from Louis to know where the man was. The Portuguese officer was reluctant to reply, avoiding his friend's eyes, moving from foot to foot and looking around the room, truly uncomfortable.

Eventually, Werner could no longer take Louis' mumblings and evasion.

"Where the fuck is he?" he demanded.

Louis sighed; he knew what was about to happen.

"He's gone to the mission to fetch the lady doctor, Dorothea, your friend," he finally admitted, glad to have that off his chest.

"Are you insane? You can't bring her here!" Werner sat up in bed, his alarm evident. "You're bringing her through Kunehama territory. She's a woman, she will be in danger!"

"Whatever, it is her decision," Louis countered.

"At least I should have been consulted."

"I know, but Philippe insisted and I eventually agreed. I was concerned for you. Your shoulder is broken. It needs to be properly set."

"Christus, Louis! If anything happens to her . . ."

"She'll be fine with Philippe. He has Paulo with him. They've got to be the best there is."

"It's over a hundred miles from here!"

"Not quite, but near enough. Besides, I've sent some of my cavalry to escort them from the border to here. The civil uprising is nearly over; I don't believe we have anything to fear, except what may happen to you. Your health is still in danger, you need the best attention."

It was six days before Philippe returned with Dorethea and a nurse, both victims of a very uncomfortable ride, albeit in a small relatively well-sprung carriage. They had loaded the carriage with everything they thought they might require – a virtual small hospital on the move.

Dorothea's only concern was Werner, and she didn't bother with a meal or a wash on arrival, but made straight for to the room where he and Don Pereira lay. At first, she ignored the Don, concentrating on Werner. Only once she was convinced he was okay did she check on the other man.

Although uncomfortable and not able to move his upper body, Werner had only a trace of infection remaining which occasionally spiked his temperature. When she arrived, it was normal, but certainly raised the mercury somewhat as she held his hands, fussing like a mother hen around him. It was obvious to all that here was a woman deeply in love with her patient and she did not care who knew.

The two women proposed to open Werner's wound and inspect the damaged bone. They prepared a separate room, scrubbing it with carbolic soap from top to bottom. They scoured the table selected to be the operating table with soap and pumice stone until it looked like the deck of a king's yacht. Sheets were boiled.

"If there are any germs still around, they've long left!" Louis told a nervous Werner.

Finally, they were ready, and after Werner himself had been thoroughly scrubbed, he was brought into the prepared room and placed on the table. Dorothea administered an anaesthetic and then removed all bandages, tut-tutting behind her mask as she exposed the wound. The jagged edges of the wound were still angry red with infection and a clear liquid with a trace of blood seeped through. Only once the wound was stabilized and the infection under control would she be able to properly set his shoulder and cocoon his upper body in plaster of Paris, leaving holes for his skin and the entrance and exit wounds to breathe so that these could rapidly heal. He would need a couple of months to recuperate—he certainly was not going to be moved in the next month or two.

Dorothea also attended to Don Pereira and was happy to note that his good wife knew her way around wounds and medicines. There was little additional that she could do for him – his condition was improving rapidly, and he was already able to shuffle around the hacienda.

Louis returned to Benguela, taking his *cavelherico* and most of his troops with him, promising to send word of what had occurred during the period that they had been away.

Within a week, with Werner now on the mend, Dorothea had also left, again escorted by Philippe and a few troops Louis had left on the ranch. She bade him a tearful farewell, extracting a promise that he would call on the Finnish mission, even if he still had to be Senhor Joachim de Almeida, a member of the Portuguese bourgeois who spoke fluent German and English. General Diaz and Major Zietzmann in particular, had no wish that it become general knowledge that a German officer was masquerading as a Portuguese entrepreneur.

Werner could now move around, although his one elbow pointed upwards just above the horizontal, and his whole arm and upper body was encompassed in a shell of rigid plaster of paris. Every day he would go for a short walk, exploring the immediate surrounds of the hacienda, taking in its beauty and history. It had been in the Pereira family from the mid 18th century and they had bred thoroughbred Arab horses that were famous throughout the colony. Large tracts of land were given over to the cultivation of sisal, and where previously all raw rubber used to be obtained from wild rubber trees, they had now planted these in established plantations. They were ardently passionate about their heritage, and practiced a culture maintained by the Portuguese aristocrats for hundreds of years, truly a breed on their own, reluctant to afford newcomers entry.

A few weeks later, a military despatch rider arrived on horseback and delivered a sealed envelope addressed to Werner. He was ordered to wait for replies.

Werner sat himself down in a corner of the veranda and opened the letter from Louis. Werner laughed at the salutation, the sarcastic bastard! Truly, they were good friends.

My dear friend Senhor Joachim de Almeida,

Although you are a German officer and a very good one at that, to me you will always be Portuguese and probably one of the finest men I will ever know. The same goes for your cavelherico, not that I'm forgetting my batman. Always remember our friendship; my house, wherever it may be will always be open to you.

Matters developed rapidly in your absence. The Governor-General was recalled by the king, no reason given. It was implied that he was to take up another important position, which we know probably will never materialize. Already a new juiz has been appointed for the Benguela district, and this was made public knowledge together with the information that de Mello had associated with a bunch of renegados and that in a pursuit operation, had been killed, along with all the renegados. This information was released by the Chief of Police in Luanda, supported by the acting Governor General of the colony and with the country's Chief Justice in attendance. Initially it created quite a furore, many questions being asked, but the Chief Justice deemed it too sensitive to permit release of all information. However, this is now old hat, nobody even asks anymore.

Yours truly, I might add, has been promoted again, this time to Colonel, surely the fastest promotion in the course of Portuguese military history. To add to this, Colonel Louis Antonio de Sousa is now the Chief Commanding Officer for all Southern Angola.

I should also add that from remarks made by Colonel de Oliveira, you could be in for a few surprises yourself on your return to SudwestAfrika.

All dos Santos' assets have been forfeited to the state. It was released that he was captured by the Germans with irrefutable proof of his involvement in gunrunning, the weapons having been found in his possession on German territory. They further released that he had been executed by hanging by the German authorities.

The despatch rider who carried this letter to you has also delivered a letter to Don Pereira from the Minister of Land and Mineral Rights in Luanda. As promised, Don Pereira now legally holds 40% of the mine, the rest forfeited to the State. However, the government is currently negotiating with a few companies concerning the remaining 60%. He should be comfortable with the outcome; it is as we promised.

I received a cable from Jurgen (had a problem getting it translated, knowing what I thought it contained, not wanting just anybody to read it!). Belgium he said was fabulous, beautiful people and extremely accommodating. There is certain correspondence on its way to you, which will set

225

it all out. He says we should all be very happy people for a very long, long time! Does that tell you something?

My wife and I, after hearing from Jurgen, have decided that I should resign my commission and emigrate to SudwestAfrika. Jurgen has suggested we, that is all of us, take up ranching. While they may not be landowners, Paulo and Philippe should join us as cattle-owners, we looking after their interests. The idea is we all help one another as we've done in the past. I thought this a brilliant idea; you need to think about this.

Werner mulled this over in his mind for a few minutes and decided that it truly was an excellent idea. All of them in SudwestAfrika, where the past proceedings in Angola were of absolutely no concern to the German government, and their wealth not under any threat as it was not acquired in SudwestAfrika.

He continued to read:

Of course, Senhorita Maria Williams contacted me, immediately wanting to know your whereabouts—she got hold of me through General Diaz. I never said where you were, but merely that you were in hospital recuperating from a gunshot wound, and that you were in excellent hands. Believe me, she knew precisely whose hands those were! The new juiz also assured her that anything that was rightfully hers at Huambo would be returned to her. She did mention that she proposed to cross the border into SudwestAfrika as soon as the Portuguese government proclaimed southern Angola safe. I believe you ought give that piece of news some thought!

By the way, I did mention to Maria that Major Zietzmann had enquired about her and that should she go to SudwestAfrika, then looking up the brave Major may be a good idea. He's besotted with her. I think she could be very happy with the man. Besides, the Major does not give a damn about protocol – and he would have the most beautiful woman in Windhuk on his arm!

God! Werner thought, Maria and Zietzmann together – that could solve a few problems!

My family and I wish you a speedy recovery and we look forward to seeing you shortly in Benguela.

Your friend,
Colonel Louis Antonio de Sousa

Never mind ranching in SudwestAfrika, the best thing he could do was to return to Germany until everything had settled down! But before he could do that, there was still a war on. Now that the gun-running ring had been broken, he probably would be ordered back to Windhuk, hopefully reporting to Major Zietzmann – surely they would still have use for his linguistic abilities? He did not feel ready for a permanent relationship with any woman. Actually, he needed to get away from both Maria and Dorothea for a while! Too much had happened in a very short space of time. He needed to find his feet again He had no wish to settle down just yet.

He requested pen and paper from Donna Pereira and began to write one of the most difficult letters of his life. He addressed the letter to Maria, telling her that she should remember that war still waged in SudwestAfrika, and that he was an officer in the German army. He said he wished to devote himself to his career as an army officer, see the war through and only then make any further decisions.

I will always fondly remember you and the moments we had together, but that you must understand that I cannot make any commitments, he wrote.

He then wrote a short letter to Louis merely telling him that he agreed in principle, that he would see him in Benguela, and that he proposed to return to SudwestAfrika by ship.

Donna Pereira had promised to carry out Dorothea's instructions to the letter, and Werner had to endure the plaster cast for the full six weeks before she removed it. Even then, his shoulder was still stiff, even though the wound had healed completely. He remained on the hacienda for another three weeks thereafter, enjoying the break and regularly exercising his shoulder and arm.

It was nearly ten in the morning when, with a screeching of steel upon steel, the train came to halt next to the platform of the Windhuk Bahnhof. Werner had advised no-one of his arrival but had left Louis in Benguela with promises that they would get together once the da Sousa family arrive in SudwestAfrika. Followed by a black porter, Werner stepped off the train on to the platform and looked around casually.

He reeled back as a soft body careened into him and arms clasped around his neck. In shock he stared into sparkling eyes and the delighted smile of Dorothea seconds before her lips met his in a passionate kiss. Over her shoulder he saw the beaming face of Philippe and the scandalised faces of spectators on the platform. Her behaviour drew quite a few stares: such a display of such passion in public was just not done!

Werner's arms closed around her and he lost himself in the feel of her soft mouth. My God, feeling her body so close against him made him realise just how much he had missed her. And how much he did love her! His planned resolve to approach his future cautiously evaporated as he held her tightly.

Any future without her at his side would be no future at all.

THE END

AUTHOR BIO

Peter Borchard's books of high adventure and suspense are a natural reflection of their author. Borchard, the grandson of German colonists who settled in Namibia in 1890 had a Namibian German father and French mother. His parents studied in Germany where the bulk of his family still resides today. He has created in RELENTLESS PURSUIT a novel so moving and powerful that his many fans throughout the world will not be able to resist it.

After living and studying in Namibia, France and England, Peter returned to his native South Africa. He was directly involved in assisting the then Rhodesia when that country declared UDI and assisted in breaking the embargo set by the UN by supplying and flying in various supplies – some of military nature.

Born in 1941, Peter Borchard started writing his exciting stories and novels during the beginning of the Angolan Bush War, at which time he worked as a banker. He is fluent in German, English and Afrikaans.

Peter has family who own farms on the fringe of the Namib Desert and the Kakaoveld on which he would regularly hunt. He has, however, very definitely given up hunting.

Peter's novels take place in Southern Africa, the area with which he is the most familiar.

He currently resides in Johannesburg with his wife. He has three children and three grandchildren.